FINDING HER VOICE

SHANTANEL PAYNE

Copyright © 2023 by Shantanel Payne
All rights reserved. This book or any portion thereof may not be reproduced or used in any manner whatsoever without the express written permission of the publisher except for the use of brief quotations in a book review.

Printed in the United States of American
ISBN: 979-8-218-33615-8
First Printing, 2024
Shreveport, LA 71119

Author's Note

The Summer character represents the everyday person struggling to support a loved one battling inner demons. This journey often leads to self-blame and feelings of responsibility for the loved one's recovery. How much of oneself is it reasonable to give up in order to save someone who may not see the harm they are causing?

Individuals facing challenges with addiction, abuse, or mental health issues often rely on loved ones for support. However, this can lead to a cycle of self-sacrifice, guilt, and blame. To what extent are you willing to compromise your own well-being to help someone who may be unable to see the destruction they are causing?

The cycle of codependency can be detrimental to both parties involved. When does the responsibility of the individual become more important than the love and care for the person struggling? At what point do we prioritize our own well-being over the desire to save someone who may not be willing to save themselves?

Chapter 1: Death Became Her

New Beginnings

The frigid wind pierced through her skin like a sharp knife as her teeth chattered from the bitter, chilly winter weather that overcame her. Her feet are being buried in the blanket of snow with each step. Paige knew she couldn't stop running; her life depended on it.

With each exhale breath, she could see breath vapors that dissipated in the midnight air. She could no longer feel her feet as they were numb from the freezing winter weather. The tips of the icy tree branches were like blades as the frozen limbs ripped through her nightgown and pierced through her skin.

Her heart pounded with fear as she heard the squeaky, crunchy sound of his footsteps in the snow, getting closer and closer. Paige knows she is close to the river as she can hear the water running downstream.

Fighting her way through the thick levels of snow, it felt as if her heart stopped when she approached the ledge with a steep drop-off. She was frozen in fear, unable to see the ground beneath her. The river water was black with no clear site. If she jumped, she could very well be jumping to her own death.

Hearing a male voice calling out to her, nowhere to run, she stands frozen in terror. His deep, intense, masculine voice rolled through the midnight air like thunder. She could hear his voice clearer and clearer, knowing he was closing in on her with every second that passed.

Nowhere to run, she stands facing the ledge, afraid to turn around and face the horror that stood a few feet behind her. She could hear the sound of snow crunching beneath his feet when everything went silent.

All that could be heard was the harsh sound of his breathing as he stood silently behind her. Suddenly, he screamed out her name, "Summer!"

She turned to face him, her voice trembling with fear, and let out a piercing cry, "Christopher, no!" She found herself staring down the barrel of a gun and then, "Boom!" The sound of the gun firing echoed through the air, and she saw the muzzle flash as the gun discharged. Paige is struck in the chest with the bullet as she is knocked over the edge by the force of the impact of the bullet. She could hear the wind whispering in her ear as she is falling to her death. Just as she's about to hit the bottom of the rocky river, Summer jumps up from the nightmare, holding her chest drenched in sweat. She sees nothing when she jumps out of bed, flipping on the light, checking her chest for a gunshot wound and her extremities for cuts from the frozen branches. She is still in shock; her body aches, feeling like every injury that occurred in the dream was real. Summer stood in front of the mirror, repeating to herself.

"You are okay. You are no longer Summer Taylor! She is dead. Paige Green is who you are, and Christopher Diamond no longer exists in your new life."

Sitting on her hotel bed, afraid to fall back to sleep, Summer has had recurring nightmares since escaping the clutches of Christopher. She is in a new state with a new identity, but the fear of Christopher's wrath plagues her every second of the day.

Summer felt like nowhere was safe. She had fled from Illinois and traveled as far as she could, but the constant stress of living on the run had taken a toll on her both physically and mentally.

Finally settling in Monroe, Louisiana, she checked into an extended-stay hotel and paid for two months in advance. She rarely left the hotel except to buy food, feeling like a prisoner in her own mind.

She was convinced that Christopher could hunt her down at any second. Broken from grief, she battles with the idea of suicide daily. She would sit and stare at the envelope with her parent's information in it for hours. Unable to open it, she knew it would be unbearable to learn her mother's identity and not attempt to reach out to her. She threw the envelope in the trash several times and would only dig it out; she couldn't bring herself to discard everything that represented her past and future.

Summer paced around her hotel room daily, feeling suffocated by the walls around her; she had no one to lean on for support. She craved her friendship with Ebony, needing to hear her voice, wishing she could listen to her unwanted advice and jokes that lit her day up daily. It was too risky; Summer couldn't endanger anyone else's life because of her bad choices. Having her mother's contact information weighed heavily on her; she knew that she needed to let go of her past, but instead, she found herself sitting, rocking back and forth, holding the envelope pressed tightly to her chest.

Despite her determination to move on from Christopher, she couldn't comprehend why her heart still yearned for the man who had once swept her off her feet. How could someone who professed to love her so dearly could keep such a significant secret from her, especially when he knew how much it meant to her?

Summer knew she had to decide either to end her life from the overwhelming sadness she felt every second of the day or start fresh as Paige Green. Doing so would require her to overcome her fears and leave her hotel room without wearing a khimar garment covering her entire face.

Summer stood in front of the mirror, gazing at her 5'6" frail body, knowing she had dropped under a hundred pounds. She was unrecognizable; she needed a reason to live, something to care about, and something to love. At her lowest point, she considered returning to Christopher and enduring the abuse if it meant she could get to know her mother. Knowing her small-frame body couldn't endure more and nothing would stop the abuse, she was his outlet of frustration. Summer knew in some sick way Christopher got off on her pain and weakness. She knew that in most situations, she was helpless and unable to protect herself, and it seemed as though he took delight in that fact.

She thought to herself, 'Hell, I might as well off myself rather than live in the hands of Christopher to beat life out of me slowly.' But how could she even think that way? She was determined to survive and wouldn't let Christopher Diamond, aka Psycho, take away her voice. She made a deal with herself to at least attempt to get out of the hotel and walk around the corner to the park only a few blocks away.

After managing to escape from Christopher's home, she had taken only a small duffel bag containing clothes but no personal belongings that she desperately needed. The fear of going outside the hotel had made her a captive in it, having to wash her undergarments by hand every three days. She had left Christopher's home with just a few belongings when she escaped the prison that was once her home. Still convinced Christopher's father could give in and reveal her new identity to him, she lived in constant fear. It wasn't a secret who helped her escape; Summer was so in a rush to leave the home she once shared with Christopher that she had forgotten to stop the security cameras and erase the footage.

Knowing, Christopher is fully aware that her magical escape was orchestrated by his father. He would make every possible effort and use all available resources to find her whereabouts. The big question would be whether his father would keep her secret identity hidden from the monster he created.

Chapter 2: Every Little Inch Counts

As weeks passed, Summer knew the only way she could survive and ultimately avoid a mental breakdown was to adventure outside her hotel room and disengage from her reckless behavior. Promising herself she would walk to the park, and if the park adventure felt safe, she would muster up enough courage to use a ride share to shop at the nearest Walmart.

Exiting the hotel, she felt a sudden surge of panic wash over her: she was already planning her great escape in her mind if needed. Fearful memories triggered a fight or flight response, as all of her senses were heightened. Afraid to venture up the block, she couldn't deny that the beautiful fall weather felt good against her skin.

As she gazed up into the bright blue sky, a gust of wind blew, causing all the trees to tremble to the left, releasing a colorful array of autumn leaves that danced around in the sky, swirling in the invisible wind. Summer inhaled as the lovely breeze blew against her face; she took a deep breath, attempting to drown out her fears.

Summer could hear pulsatile throbbing in both ears as she was overcome with anxiety. Not knowing Christopher's whereabouts, she was convinced he could be in a car across the street watching her every move. Knowing her last great escape was an epic failure. The images of herself and Mr. Jeffery on Christopher's office desk kept replaying in her mind. She never understood why he watched her for weeks at Miss Dangerfield's house before finally confronting her. Thinking back to Mr. Diamond's remarks about Christopher having mental problems, she couldn't help but wonder, "What was he thinking? What exactly was going through his mind as he spied on her before confronting her?" It was all a sick game to him; he allowed her a moment of freedom before hunting her down like prey.

'No more procrastinating,' she thought to herself. 'It's time to live or die.' If he were out there watching, Summer knew that the 32-inch door at the Woodspring Suites wouldn't stop his wrath. Summer adventured down the block. She had spotted the park around the corner on one of her daring adventures for a quick food run.

Arriving at the park, she felt a brief sense of normalcy for a second as she admired the beautiful autumn colors and the sound of the children running through the leaves as they played on the playground equipment. However, this site was bittersweet.

'What if,' she thought. She was craving for the baby she lost. As she dropped her head with tears streaming down her face, she suddenly felt a slight nudge to her pants leg. Looking down, she saw a beautiful baby girl climbing up her leg. The toddler had wandered off from her mother, who was sitting one bench over. Summer looked up and smiled at the mother, who made no attempt to redirect the toddler back to her.

"Don't mind, Alli," the mother yelled out. "She's usually very friendly," she added, mentioning that her daughter makes new friends weekly at the park.

"However, I should warn you she's also a biter." The mother chuckled heartily, without making any effort to redirect the toddler back to her.

Summer reaches down and scoops the toddler up, sitting her on her lap. The fresh smell of baby lotion swelled her nostrils. Immediately, her heart was overwhelmed with sadness.

'This should be my reality,' she thought to herself while she secretly sniffed the toddler's hair, the smell of innocence and new beginnings.

Summer sat with the little girl on her lap while the child's mother pushed the toddler's big brother on the swing. She lost track of time, as a couple of hours had passed as she sat with the toddler asleep in her arms. Meanwhile, Alli's mom had turned the park bench into her office desk, with papers laid out across the bench as she typed on her laptop and made several calls. Alli had taken a liking to Summer, and she didn't mind one bit, as she would spend three hours sitting in the park attending to Alli and her big brother as if she were their paid nanny on duty.

Summer found herself low-key stalking the toddler and her mother. Desiring a reason to leave the hotel, she discovered that every Monday and Friday was the family play day at the park. The family home was also conveniently located within walking distance of the park.

However, Summer was not interested in making new friends and was not yet ready to socialize. She kept her conversations with Mary Sue brief.

Instead, Summer made it her goal to bond with the adorable Alli on Mondays and Fridays, as she was allowed to feed and soothe the toddler to sleep. Little Mikey also grew fond of her; she made it a mission to bring goodies to the park for the children.

As she sat and rocked Alli while the toddler fell asleep in her arms, she knew in her heart she wanted to feel this type of joy daily. In those moments with Alli, her guards were down. Christopher didn't consume her every thought. Instead, she sat and pondered on her next move.

Mr. Diamond set her up nicely, so money wasn't an issue at that moment, but she knew she needed to invest the money in a business so she could start making money and save to possibly start over again with a new identity. She was fully aware that she lacked the knowledge and resources to disappear completely, so she needed to devise a plan to secure her future. One thing is for sure: sooner than later, she needed that fulfillment she felt when interacting with Alli.

'Sperm bank it is,' she thought to herself as she took a big sniff of Alli's hair.

Summer found solace at the park. She spent every available moment she could at the park watching over Alli or reading a book, falling back into her old habits when she was a teenager and getting lost in her reading. The days no longer stretched endlessly, and her appetite had returned, a sign of her gradual return to her old self.

She constantly worried about Mr. Jeffery and Mimi's home. She longed for her friendship with Ebony, knowing she could never see them again. It just wasn't safe.

Christopher had lost it; looking into his eyes, she saw only a shell of the man she once knew. All she could recall was the darkness in his eyes. It was as if she was staring into the eyes of a stranger, the very same eyes that once were the window into her soulmate's soul.

'He took everything from me. Why Christopher, why,' she wondered.

Chapter 3: Someone From Her Past

The room is dark, with only a faint glimmer of light creeping in from beneath the bathroom door. Suddenly, the sound of a creaking door startles Summer awake. She catches a glimpse of a male silhouette from the corner of her eye, causing her body to freeze with fear as she feels paralyzed and unable to move.

As the shadowy figure approaches her, she closes her eyes tightly, unable to stare death in its face. He leaned in and softly kissed her on the lips, whispering, "Open your eyes and look at me, baby."

Summer repeats to herself, "Keep your eyes closed; it's just a dream. It's just a dream."

"I'm sorry," he whispered softly. "Just look at me, please."

He slowly pulled the covers away from her body, exposing her to the cool air of the room. Goosebumps appeared on her skin, causing a shiver to run down her spine. She was still too afraid to meet Christopher's gaze, so she turned her head away as tears streamed down her cheek. She can feel him running his fingers along her cheekbones as he runs his hand down her body, sculpting her curvy hips, groping her between her legs as he aggressively stimulates her with his finger as he runs his fingers along her slit.

She is trying not to moan as her breathing got sharper. Summer can feel her body giving in to him pleasuring her, as she can feel how moist she has become. Christopher knows she has never been able to resist his sex as he is turned on by her erect nipples that are piercing through the white beater she is wearing. Without removing her shirt, he takes a mouth full of her breast, never removing his finger from the folds of her vagina. Sitting up on his knees, he uses his left index and middle finger to stimulate her G-spot and the right thumb finger to rub on her throbbing clitoris. Her body is shivering uncontrollably as she tries to drown out her inner voice that is screaming, 'What the fuck are you doing, fool?'

Nothing mattered in that moment but how Christopher was pleasuring her. As he could feel his delicate touch had brought her to the brink of climax as her vaginal walls contracted and began to tighten around his fingers. He stops stimulating her inner arousal as he gently removes his fingers from her and starts to make gentle bites to her inner thighs, kissing all over her soft skin. As her body trembles with anticipation, he takes his fingers, sliding them in and out of her as he slurps her juices from his fingers while staring deep into her eyes.

She craved to feel his soft wet warm tongue licking her clit. He knew her desires as he continued to tease her lady parts. She tried to push his face into the junction of her thighs as he grabbed her hands and pinned them down against her hips. She attempted to thrust her pelvis in his face, but Christopher would only softly lick her clitoris to tease her more. Summer's stomach tightened as her clit throbbed at the expected explosive climax her vaginal muscles craved so deeply for.

She couldn't take any more of his teasing. She wanted to feel his big cock pushing up into all her muscles. Squirming herself from underneath him, forcing herself on top as Christopher giggled in his cocky, arrogant way, knowing he was driving her wild.

She climbs on top of him, shoving his enormous throbbing cock inside her as he grabs her by the hips and thrusts deeper into her inner core.

Summer moans and screams out his name as the intense pleasure overtakes her. Her legs and arms start to clench while she digs her nails into his chest.

Christopher leans in and starts sucking her breast as he knows it is pleasurable to her and will make her climax harder.

Just as she is screaming, 'I'm Cuming, I'm Cuming,' a loud bump outside her hotel room door awakens her. She jumps straight up in bed, confused, as it was all a dream. Her heart is racing, quivering from her impending orgasm as her body is craving Christopher.

She had never experienced a wet dream before. She lay, panting in bed, holding her stomach, feeling as if her vagina had its own heartbeat, as it was throbbing for some deep sexual attention. She closed her eyes and slowly rubbed between the fold of her moist, swollen mound of love as she began to stroke her clitoris until she was screaming Christopher's name as if he were inside her.

As all her muscles started to relax and the surge of sexual emotions had passed, reality sat in. She rolls over with tears in her eyes. She craved so badly to feel Christopher inside of her. Knowing her thoughts were sick, how could she even crave for him in this manner, knowing everything he had done to her?

Summer sat in the chair beside the bed, staring at the hotel phone. She was feeling overwhelmed by her emotions. At that moment, she yearned for Christopher's touch. She couldn't comprehend the overwhelming need to be in his presence, which had taken over her every thought. She actually contemplated calling him and asking if she could come home.

'Is this why he is so obsessed with me?' she pondered. 'It is sickening to desire someone so badly and can't have them.'

At that moment, Summer did what Summer does best, rationalizing Christopher's reckless behavior.

Startled by a commotion outside her window, she sneaks to the window, peeping outside. A young woman is being physically attacked by her boyfriend as he is trying to snatch her from their vehicle. When the young lady wouldn't exit the car, her boyfriend began to pound on her.

Watching the abuse as it occurred was a trigger. With each blow she witnessed, Summer felt as if she could feel the blows she endured from Christopher.

Summer immediately got ill, running to the bathroom and vomiting. It was even more sickening that she had a weak moment for a man who took life from her.

Summer would beat herself up for an entire week for having that weak moment, falling back into her destructive behavior.

She spent the next six days in bed, so disgusted with herself that she almost gave everything up for a momentary weak sexual desire.

She gathered her strength, pulling herself together as she forced herself out of bed. She wrestled with the thought that she still had feelings of love for Christopher, not understanding why she couldn't just hate him and never think of him again.

Needing her Alli fix, she hurried to the park to see her before her playday ended. However, arriving at the park, there were no kids in sight. The one thing she looked forward to was not there. Feeling low and disheartened, she only wanted to return to her hotel room and hide under the covers. She slowly walked back to the hotel room, feeling defeated. 'Christopher always wins; no matter what, he finds a way to snatch any happiness that comes my way. Now my dreams aren't safe,' she thought to herself.

As she was walking back to the hotel at a slow pace, she noticed a large group of men exiting a restaurant. The traffic was too heavy for her to cross over to the other side of the street, so she just lowered her head and decided to walk around the group of men.

Unfortunately, one of the men stepped backward and tripped over her foot, causing his food container to fall on the sidewalk.

Summer apologized profusely, but the gentleman took responsibility and brushed off the pasta from her arm sleeve while apologizing to her.

"Summer!" A familiar voice yelled from the crowd.

"Is that you, Summer?"

Her heart immediately skipped a beat as she began walking off at an extremely fast pace.

"Hold on, Summer, wait, let me talk to you!" the voice shouted out as she began to run off.

Afraid to turn around, she dashes through the alley, attempting to take a shortcut back to her hotel. She immediately feels ill as she realizes the usually busy alley is empty, and she is alone, when she suddenly feels a tug at her jacket.

"Dammit, Summer, it's me, Stevin; please stop running," he said as he grabbed her and forced her to turn around and face him. Stevin then unwrapped the scarf from Summer's face and made her look at him.

"No, Stevin," she cried out in fear, overwhelmed with emotions. "It's too dangerous. You're putting both our lives in danger."

"Summer, who are you running from? Is it your husband? Is he behind all of this Summer? Let me help you," Stevin pleaded.

"No, Stevin," she replied. "He could be following you, and if so, you or leading him directly to me."

"Summer, I've been in town for two weeks. Your husband stopped following me months ago. Believe me, I know. I had to file charges when I learned he had a private detective spying on me. Being he was hired to stalk me, his surveillance of me was illegal."

"No, Stevin, I can't take that chance."

"Dammit, Summer, stop it," he screams as he grips her chin, forcing eye contact. "I don't want to lose you again. I just want. Please let me help you," he pleaded, pulling her into his arms.

She felt defeated and craved any sense of normalcy and human interaction. So, she let go and fell into Stevin's embrace as he held her while she cried.

"Sweetheart," he said, looking into her eyes. His calm voice soothed her, "You don't have to face this alone."

Summer was too exhausted to put up a fight, so she just let Stevin hold her close.

"Listen, I don't want my coworkers looking for me. Where are you staying?"

She shook her head no, refusing to divulge the information to him.

"Please, Summer," he pleaded. She raised her hand and pointed towards her hotel.

"What is your room number?" Stevin asked.

"255," she whispered softly.

"Okay, I have another lunch meeting and will return later."

"Please, Stevin, I can't let Christopher find me."

Stevin looked her in her eyes as he squeezed her hand encouragingly, reassuring her that he had her.

Summer returned to the room, peeping out the window, looking for any signs that Stevin had led Christopher right to her. Just the idea that someone knew her whereabouts made her sick with illness. She could have just very well signed her and Stevin's death certificate.

She sat in the same spot, consumed by fear, for hours. Suddenly, there was a knock on the door. Startled, she cautiously approached the peephole and saw Stevin waiting outside. She eased the door open, and he assured her that he had taken two different ride shares to get there, making sure that he wasn't followed. He assured her that he still had contacts in Illinois and that Christopher had not left the state.

Stevin embraced Summer, hugging her tightly; as he wrapped his arms around her, all he could feel was how emaciated she had become. She welcomed the warmth and comfort of his embrace; being in Stevin's arms felt incredible as she trembled from fear.

"Can I stay with you tonight so you can get some rest?" he asked, noticing the large dark circles under her eyes.

As he scanned the hotel room, he noticed that Summer had been surviving on Roman noodles and Vienna sausages for meals. Concerned, he asked her when was the last time she had a real meal.

Hunching her shoulders, she softly replied, "I don't know."

"Summer, if I order you some food from the restaurant around the corner, will you eat it?"

"Yes," she replied in a soft tone.

Stevin placed an order over the phone, requesting her key card to the room for re-entry, and walked up the block to pick up their dinner.

Summer felt she finally had something to look forward to for the first time in months. She secretly welcomes Stevin's company. She didn't have to pretend to be someone else and forget to answer to the fake name when she is called Paige.

She would give anything to stand under the shower and wash her hair. She had been too afraid to stand under the water with her eyes closed for a lengthy period of time. Not knowing how long Stevin would be gone, she quickly made a dash for the shower.

Summer was lost in the moment; it felt nice to stand under the water with her eyes closed and not have to worry about opening her eyes to Christopher choking the life out of her. She couldn't deny Stevin's presence gave her a little ease. Christopher would surely need bodyguards this time; he wouldn't be facing off with a frail elderly man.

She stood under the shower, massaging her scalp with her fingers. It was like an orgasmic experience for her scalp. Small life things of normalcy she had forgotten.

Enjoying her much-needed long and steamy shower, she lost track of time. When she turned off the water, she listened for Stevin in the next room, but she had no idea if he was back yet. She stepped out of the shower and dried off, only to realize that she had left her undergarments and clothing on the bed. Knowing that the hotel room was designed in such a way that the living area and kitchenette were in full view of the bedroom, she hesitated to step out undressed. Not thinking, she had forgotten to close the bedroom door, which seemed like a desperate move on her part, and she most definitely didn't want to give Stevin the wrong idea.

She gently opened the bathroom door and took a quick peek around the corner, then quickly made a dash to the bed, snatching up her undergarments. As she turned around, she saw Stevin sitting at the table with a clear view of her hotel bed. Stevin stared at her intensely; she felt frozen, as if he could see through her soul. Summer tried to move, but her feet felt as heavy as cement blocks. Despite her efforts, she couldn't look away.

'Move, fool. Walk back into the bathroom,' she thought to herself.

However, she remained frozen as if Stevin had her in a trance. She waited for him to blink, hoping it would release her from his spell. Then it happened: he stood and started walking towards her. The mere fact she is standing feet away from him with nothing, but a towel wrapped around her, hair dripping wet. It was as if she was screaming come fuck me, Stevin.

He stood directly in front of her, running his hand through her damp hair, pulling her to him. The touch of her soft, smooth skin drove him wild. He slowly went in for the long-awaited kiss he had been dying to do since the first day he met her.

Gazing into her eyes, he strokes his hand down her back, sending tingling pleasure throughout her body as she enjoys his light caresses against her soft skin.

When she did not resist him, he pulled the towel away, exposing her nude body, as he forcefully started kissing her on her neck, trailing his lips down to her breast. Wetness pooled between her thighs as his soft, warm tongue brushed against her erect nipples. Tracing his tongue around her areola, he wrapped his lips around her nipple and started to suck. Her knees buckled; she didn't think it was possible to sexually desire someone else in this manner again.

"No, Stevin," she said as she pushed him away, wrapping the towel back around her exposed body. "I'm sorry, Stevin. I am just not ready," she added.

Cuffing her face cheek in the palm of his hand, he looked her in the eyes and said. "No rush, sweetheart. You were always supposed to be mine, and I let you slip through my fingers once; it won't happen twice."

As he held her close, he adoringly softly whispered, "I'm here to ease your burden, not become one. You don't have to do anything you're not comfortable with. Now get dressed and come eat a real meal."

He walked out of the bedroom, closing the bedroom door behind him. Summer fell back onto the bed, heaving a sigh of relief. Who was she fooling? She desired him. She wanted him with an intensity that shocked her.

Needing to reassure herself that her lust for him was not a moment of weakness and that she genuinely desired him wholeheartedly. She vowed not to mislead him if her heart wasn't ready. She wouldn't allow a moment of desperation to unlock a door that he didn't have access to.

Stevin slept on the pull-out sofa, as he had to return back to New York and would be leaving Louisiana first thing in the morning. Promising her he would return in two weeks.

Stevin was even more determined to correct his wrongs. He took full accountability for letting her slip through his fingers the first time. Finally, the opportunity has presented itself again, and there wasn't a chance in hell he would let this moment slip through his hands again.

When Stevin first met Summer, he was hesitant, fearing that his direct approach might overwhelm her. He chose to step back and take a slow approach, allowing Christopher to swoop in and shut him out. However, in this second chance, Stevin is unwavering in his determination to be Summer's all.

Chapter 4: Make Love To Me

Living On The Wild Side

Summer remained held up in her hotel room for the next two weeks, consumed by fear that Christopher might have had Stevin followed. She spent most of her time seated by the window, her eyes never leaving the street below as she watched for any suspicious activity. Summer hadn't heard from Stevin since their last face-to-face encounter, and she refused to get a cell phone, fearing it might jeopardize her safety. Summer couldn't trust herself not to reach out to anyone. She checked into the hotel anonymously, rejecting all incoming calls. Since she hadn't shared her alias with Stevin, he could not contact her even if he desired to, leaving her to wait in a state of heightened anticipation for his return to Monroe.

Besides, she spent most of the time daydreaming about her and Stevin's steamy, hot kiss. She wondered in her Ebony voice how it would feel to let Stevin blow her back out. She chuckled to herself, thinking about Ebony's reaction if she could tell her about her and Stevin's steamy encounter.

So quickly, her laughter turns into pain. The thought of not seeing Ebony again shatters her heart into a million pieces. Enough of this sadness, she thought to herself. She hadn't seen Alli in three weeks and desperately needed her Alli fix.

Arriving at the park, little Mikey spots Summer first as he runs into her arms excitedly, checking her bag for his goodies. Alli followed as she gracefully stumbled and fell, trying to run to her. Summer swiftly picks her up, laughing at the effort pulling leaves from her hair.

As always, Mary Sue remains in her own world, grinning and waving at Summer from a distance as she talks on the phone. Summer so desperately wanted to offer her assistance in caring for the kids. She was afraid she would make too many mistakes not answering to the name Paige, and besides, if Mary Sue wanted to do a background check with her fake identity, it would cause red flags and very well give out her location.

As the hours pass, Mary Sue sat on the bench, typing on her computer while little Mikey, overcome by exhaustion, collapses on Summer's leg. And Miss Alli in her favorite spot in her arms, being rocked to sleep. Summer didn't mind; she found contentment in being around the children.

Her guard is always up, and she notices everything moving. So her senses were immediately heightened when she saw a gentleman dressed in a trench coat and a black beanie walking towards her. As he passed her, he bent down as if he were picking something up.

"Excuse me, ma'am, you drop something," said the gentleman.

She began to speak to inform him that the paper wasn't hers. The gentleman made eye contact, and it was Stevin smiling as he walked off. She waited a few minutes and then read the note, looking around to make sure she saw no one else. As she read, she blushed with excitement.

"*Hey there, my dear. I saw you leaving the hotel while I was parking my car. I followed you in my company vehicle and watched you briefly, observing your surroundings to ensure everything was alright. I didn't notice anything that seemed suspicious or alarming. Enjoy your time at the park! I'm heading to the store to grab some items for a special dinner that I'm planning for you. I'll see you when I get back.*"

Best regards,

Stevin.

Summer smiled as she balled up the letter. She knew she needed to return to the room and tidy up, as her housekeeping hadn't been the best. While saying goodbye to the kids, Mary Sue informed her that she had taken a job upstate and that she and the kids would be moving. Immediately, Summer felt overwhelmed with sadness and devastation. She used Alli and her family as an outlet; knowing she would be alone again with no one to communicate with was suffocating.

Making her way back to the hotel, she had to admit Stevin showed up at the right time. She didn't trust herself anymore, blow after blow, disappointment after disappointment. She would rather lock herself up at Mimi's house and not go out; at least she would be home.

Summer sat in disappointment, awaiting Stevin's return. Suddenly, there is a tap on the door as she opens, and Stevin is loaded down with shopping bags. He could see the doleful look in her eyes as he dropped the bags, begging her to talk to him. He grabbed her small frame body, scooping her up and sitting on the bed with her as she wept in his arms.

"I can't, Stevin, I just can't take it anymore. I don't want to live anymore; I just want all this pain to stop."

Stevin knew he didn't have the correct words at that moment, so he just listened and embraced her with all the compassion he could give.

Summer exhausted herself crying; she wept until she fell asleep, drenching Stevin's shirt. He held her for an hour before he eased her to the bed as he quietly tiptoed out of the bedroom to go make dinner.

THE NIGHTMARES DIDN'T STOP

"Behind you, Summer! Behind you!" Stevin shouted as Summer turned and noticed Christopher's headlights bearing straight towards her.

"NO!" she screamed, realizing she doesn't have enough time to move.

"Wake up, Summer, Wake up," Stevin said, trying to awaken her from her nightmare.

"It's just a dream," he assured her.

"Ooh, Stevin," Please don't leave me, she cried out as she wrapped herself around him.

"I won't leave you, sweetheart. I promise I won't."

As he tried to console her, he could feel her rigid muscles responding to his pleasant caresses as her body started to relax. His desire for her overcomes him as he gently starts to kiss her soft lips. She didn't stop him as she got lost in the moment herself.

She could feel him pull away as she opened her eyes and locked eyes with him. She looked up into his eyes as she lay cradled in his arms. It's as if time stopped and nothing mattered as she sat with her head cradled in his arm as he stared, admiring his perfect view.

She reached up, placing her hand on his cheek as if she needed to touch him to make sure he was real. Leaning in, her lips softly brushed his.

They stared deep into each other's eyes, just long enough that she could inhale his breath as she passionately kissed him, enjoying the feeling of being desired.

As the passion between them heated up, Stevin laid her onto the bed as he lifted her skirt, making his way between her thighs as she spread them wider apart, welcoming his advances. He slightly nibbled her clit through her silk panties as he savored the smell of her arousal fluids.

When she made no attempt to stop him, he pulled her panties to the side as he manipulated his tongue through her folds and licked her clit, teasing it with his tongue, causing her to let out a loud moan. His erection grew bigger as it twitched and throbbed with excitement as he watched her lift her shirt and expose her breasts. He eagerly watched as she started fondling her perky breast, squeezing her nipples. This only turned him on more as he slid his tongue deeper inside her.

Staring her in the eyes, Summer's eyes widened in anticipation as he began to suck her clitoris harder and harder. She curled her body into him with two handfuls of his curly hair. Having him please her while staring right through her intensified the pleasure even more. She throws her head back and closes her eyes, so overcome with pleasure she screams out, "Right there, Christopher, right there."

Stevin abruptly stopped and sat up on the edge of the bed. Summer was so embarrassed she curled up in bed and started crying immediately. Stevin stood and exited the room. Summer didn't follow him right away, as she was too ashamed and afraid that she had pushed the one and only person she had left away.

Summer knew she had to fix it. No matter what, she needed to fix it. She entered the adjacent room and found Stevin sitting at the pedestal table. She faced him, squatting down to his level and taking him by the hand. She looked into his eyes, struggling to find the right words to ease the pain and disappointment in his eyes.

"Stevin," she said. "Please forgive me. I don't know how to make this right; I don't know what to say."

"Are you still in love with him?" Stevin asked, his voice trembling with a mix of fear and hope.

"No, Stevin, I'm not," she replied. "You have to understand that Christopher was my first and my only. If anything, his name was called out of habit, not because he was who I wanted or desired. Please, Stevin, you have to believe me. How do I make this right? Please tell me how I can make this right. I can't lose you; you're all I have."

Still very much in his feelings, Stevin stands and pulls her up off her knees, requesting she sit and eat dinner before the food gets cold. She could see how standoffish he was and immediately lost her appetite, dropping her fork on the plate and demanding Stevin to be honest with her.

"Have I lost you? Stevin, please, I need to know."

"No, Summer, you haven't. I don't want to address this anymore," he said.

Summer jumped up from the table and attempted to run to the bedroom, overwhelmed with grief and feeling as if she would never see him again.

But he quickly stood up, pulled her by the arm, and made her face him. "Summer, if I were that easily offended or could be pushed away that easily. I would have walked out of your life years ago. Now sit down and eat," he demanded.

Not wanting to offend him again, she forced herself to eat dinner.

Stevin walked out to the car, returning with his overnight bags and laptop, and headed straight to the shower. Feeling as if Stevin was avoiding eye contact with her, she kept busy tidying up while he showered.

Summer was exhausted and drained, so she entered the bedroom and sat on the bed just as Stevin opened the bathroom door to let out the steam and defog the mirror. As he stood in the bathroom, with his body still wet and a towel wrapped around his waist, she couldn't help but stare. His body was lean, tight, muscular, and fine as hell.

'How did I miss all of this finest,' she thought. Stevin was an attractive and well-built man.

Without a care, he dropped his towel and stepped into his pajama pants.

'Dang!' She thought as her eyes went wide at the sight of his enormous cock. He also was very well endowed; he had a substantially wide penis. Summer clenched her invisible pearls and took a hard swallow as her eyes zoomed in on his manhood.

He stepped out of the bathroom, informing her he was turning in and was headed to the sofa. She took hold of his hand and pleaded with him, "Please, Stevin, don't make me sleep alone. Can you please hold me tonight if it's not too much?"

Stevin kissed the back of her hand and laid across the bed, checking his emails on his laptop.

Stepping into the shower, she stood completely still as the water ran down her body, thinking of a master plan to win him over. She knew she had to let all her walls down, and tonight, Christopher no longer had claim to her.

She was ready to give all of herself to Stevin. For the first time, her mind and body desired another man. His presence calmed her; every fiber of her being craved his touch.

Stepping out of the shower, playing back her dreadful outburst during their intimate moment, she feared his rejection.

She stood silently in the bathroom, contemplating her next move, while she built up her nerves to prove to him he was who she desired.

Who was she kidding? She just called Stevin, another man's name. She was one hundred percent sure he would object to any of her advances towards him.

As she slowly opened the bathroom door, Stevin's gaze met hers. She watched his reaction at the door as she dropped the towel, revealing her nude body to him.

Stevin immediately sat straight up in bed. He is frozen in silence, as he is just gawking at her; he never utters a word.

All the confirmation she needed was that very noticeable boner that continued to rise through his pajama pants.

As she starts to walk toward him, he places his laptop on the nightstand, laying back and welcoming her.

With her back arch, she slowly crawls into bed. She uses her teeth to untie the strings on his pajama pants. He wasted no time pulling his pants down. She struggled to keep her focus as she giggled at his enthusiastic behavior. Trying to look confident in her attempt to seduce him. Who was she fooling, she was just as nervous as if it was her first time.

She began stroking his impressive boner taking her tongue licking from the base to the tip of his massive cock, as she engulfed his pulsating head in her mouth as her tongue guided her lips down the shaft of his throbbing cock. He moans as her soft lips wrap around the head of his sizeable throbbing erection.

Deliberately stiffing her tongue as she slowly licks around the tip, enjoying the moans that escaped him. She grips his giant cock using an up-and-down motion with her hand as she begins to kiss and suck the head of his penis, swirling her tongue around it in a circular motion.

Stevin, a little rougher than what she is used to, takes a hand full of her hair, causing her to flex her neck. He grabbed the body of his sizable manhood and motioned for her to open her mouth wider. He places his giant cock in her mouth and advances it to the back of her throat while holding her head as he thrushes back in forth until she starts gagging.

Okay, she thought to herself. My gag reflexes are still intact, and I would like to keep it that way. She turns her head, easing some of him out, attempting to gain control. Not wanting to lose a tonsil, she immediately takes charge, pushing him back onto the bed. She squats down on top of him, slowly rocking back and forth, savoring the sensation as she slides his large manhood into her entrance, unable to take all of him in her.

She leaned forward as she slides his thick cock in her inch by inch, as her eyes rolled to the back of her head. This pleasurable moment was long overdue as she started riding him throwing her head back and forth as if she were possessed.

Stevin thrashes around, biting his lip and punching the pillow as he moans her name. Immediately, she had built up an intense climax and was ready to explode. Just as she reaches climax, he pulls out. He flips her over and begins tasting her.

Holding her breath, she bared down, attempting to have a long overdue orgasm, but Stevin is licking all around her arousal.

'The hell with this,' she thought, trying to ride him again when he refused her, requesting she ride's his face.

Summer granted his wish, wrapping her legs around his head and squeezing his face into her vagina. He circled his tongue around her swollen clit, and with one aggressive lick, he ran his tongue from her opening to her clit as his lips latched onto her swollen jewel.

Stevin sucked harder, spreading her lips wider apart, as he sucked and licked until she released a wave of orgasms back-to-back as she rode his face attempting not to smother him, leaving a pool of her moisture on his face.

"Delicious," he murmured, wrapping his hand around her jaw as he pulled her to him, kissing her so she could taste herself on his tongue.

She craved to feel her legs pent up, with Stevin stimulating all her vaginal muscles as his big cock pushed deep in her as she begged for him not to stop. He flipped her over onto her back, grabbed her hips, and firmly pulled her body against his, tilting her bottom up, forcing all of himself into her tight opening. He plunges deep into her quivering muscles that grip tight on his shaft. Unable to control his strokes, he attempted to take long, slow, deep strokes, but her muscles contracted in waves, and the sensation made him thrust harder and faster. She screams out in pleasure as he goes deeper and deeper. "Don't stop!" she screams. "Don't stop!"

Summer wasn't sure about the grunting noises Stevin was making, but she could feel his cock growing larger and harder as if he were about to. Then it happened; he screamed, "I'm cumming, baby, I'm cumming."

Huh, she thought to herself as she began to count the strokes in her head.

"Sorry, sweetheart," he said as he began to make excuses for his shortcomings, "Literally, baby, I was so excited. I've been waiting for this for a long time. Just give me a second, sweetheart."

Summer, disappointed and damn well not trying to hide it, turned her head and made no attempt to reassure his confidence. As she lay in silence, it didn't help he was snoring five minutes later. She laid next to him, pouting. When her inner Ebony voice quickly reminded her.

"Bitch, you're pouting because Stevin isn't living up to Christopher. I guess you will be mad when he doesn't disrespect you and knock you around. You better teach that man how to make love to you to your liking and get over yourself."

Summer immediately smiled, knowing that would be precisely Ebony's words of advice. She quickly got her attitude in check, rolled over, and kissed him as he smiled in his sleep, pulling her into his arms.

Chapter 5: Afraid To Make A Move

IT'S NOW ARE NEVER

The bright white rays of sunlight poured through the window, shining on Summer's face. She opened her eyes, her cheek resting on Stevin's chest, realizing she had fallen asleep in his arms. She gazed up at him, thinking he was still fast asleep, but made eye contact with him as she softly smiled.

His smile was energetic, and she couldn't tell what shone the brightest, his smile or the sun.

"How long have you been watching me sleep?" she asked.

"For about two hours," he replied.

"Why didn't you awaken me?"

"I enjoyed watching you sleep so peacefully in my arms. I didn't think I could find more things to love about you, but you keep amazing me. You are so beautiful," he said as his hand slid down her face in a warm caress.

Summer smiled, realizing this was the first time in four months she slept through the night and didn't awaken terrified or feeling afraid of the loneliness suffocating her; she felt alive and was ready for a second round of passionate sex.

Not wanting to look too desperate, she presses her face against his chest as she delivers small kisses to his masculine pecs, taking her hands rubbing from his chest to his lower abdominal muscles. He suddenly grabs her hand and kisses the back of it.

"Let me wash up so I can prepare breakfast for you."

Summer, feeling disappointed, rolls her eyes in the back of her head, thinking to herself, "Really?"

Stevin gets out of bed, walks into the bathroom, and steps into the shower, leaving her very unsatisfied with his choice to leave her in bed alone instead of making up for last night.

Kicking and thrashing around in the bed, she was determined to have him satisfy all of her sexual desires. She could hear the shower turn off. Rubbing her hands through her hair, she attempts to perfect that disheveled hairstyle that screams sex appeal.

Positioning herself in bed, intentionally revealing her nudeness, she slightly pulls the sheet down, exposing her breast as she fakes sleep. Desiring for Stevin to return to bed and take all of her.

Hearing the bathroom door squeak open, Stevin stands over her, kissing her forehead.

"The shower is all yours," he said as he walked out of the bedroom.

She jumped out of bed pouting, annoyed with Stevin's lackluster behavior and thought. 'What the...?'

"Looks like it's going to be a cold shower for me," she mumbled, feeling clueless and unused to not being sexually satisfied or desired. She was even more determined to figure out why Stevin lacked so much in the bedroom.

As she walked into the kitchenette, trying to avoid her inner thoughts being displayed in her facial expressions, she took a deep breath and sat at the pedestal table.

"Pretty sure this is my job," she said.

"Oh..., please believe. I'm not trying to take your job," he replied with a smile, reassuring her that he just wanted to cater to her this morning. Everything goes silent when Stevin turns and looks at her with a brooding expression.

"It's a must I return to Memorial Medical," he said.

With a surprised look, Summer asks Stevin why he needs to return to Illinois.

"Hell, I got to return and let the unit know I hit."

In typical Summer fashion, Stevin's comment goes right over her head.

"What do you mean, Stevin? You hit what?"

Stevin is standing in front of her, twirling the spatula with a sneaky grin. Motioning his body in a circular stroking manner. "What do you mean, Ms. Taylor?" He said as he rocked his hips back and forth. "Surely Amber and the crew would want to know I finally succeeded in getting Summer Taylor in bed," he said as he burst into laughter.

Summer suddenly jumped up from the table and lunged onto Stevin's back, wrapping her legs around his waist as she gently chokes his neck. Stevin twirls her around and around, throwing her back onto the bed, jumping on top of her, tickling her.

Summer screams out mercy as she cries out in laughter. Staring her in the eyes, he leans in with a passionate kiss. He quickly notices the sudden change in her eyes as they go from a bright ray of sunshine to a gloomy look of hopelessness, and her facial expression screams sad and depressed.

"What is it, Summer? Why the long face?"

"Have you ever thought, what if?" She said, her voice low and hesitant.

"What if we were together from the beginning? How would my life be at this very moment?"

Stevin swooped her up in his arms, reassuring her he is here now, promising to make her smile daily. Summer was touched by his solicitude for her.

However, Stevin felt conflicted because he knew he had even heavier news for her, and she would have to decide here and now if they actually had a future together.

"Summer."

"Yes, Stevin."

“I'm sorry, sweetheart, but we need to have a serious conversation about our future.”

Summer stared anxiously, not knowing where the conversation was headed.

"Do you want a future with me?" Stevin asked, dropping his head and looking down at the floor. The silence from her was gut-wrenching as she gathered her thoughts.

"I don't know how to have a future with anyone without putting their lives in danger," she said.

This only angered him. He couldn't stand the thought of her thinking he wasn't man enough to take care of himself or her.

"Summer," he said in an authoritarian voice. "If it were up to me, I would move you back to Illinois and dare that spoiled daddy's boy to come within an inch of you. Truth be told, you are the only reason I haven't returned to Illinois and whooped his ass."

Summer giggled to herself; it was flattering, but she knew Stevin was clueless about Christopher's destruction. "Stevin, please just stay away from Christopher. If you genuinely care about my well-being, please just stay away from him."

"Summer," he said as his voice elevated. "I can't live like this. Hell, you can't continue like this. And besides, before running into you, I was offered a position in another state, which would mean less traveling for me. Summer, I said yes to the new position and will relocate in a week. Please come with me, Summer. I have it all worked out. I leased some property under my company name, which can't be traced back to me. This is a fresh start for you, Summer, a fresh start for us. You deserve to be happy."

Summer sat in silence, picking at her nails. "Stevin, I can't travel by air. I don't want to be traced."

"Summer, I have already taken that into consideration. We will drive. It's only five hundred miles from this location. Baby, please allow me to love you and be there for you. Let me be the man you never had."

Stevin words sounded great, but Summer knew that she would have to leave her safe haven and take a risk with him, a risk that very well could cost both of them more than what Stevin could possibly imagine.

Stevin was down on one knee, holding her hand, and patiently awaiting her response.

"Where, Stevin? Where are you asking me to relocate?"

He smiled and replied, "Madison, Georgia," with a big grin.

She quickly snatched her hand back as the expression on her face screamed danger.

"What is it, Summer?" he asked, as he could see how emotional she had become.

She stood up and pulled a large manila envelope from a bag out of the closet. Standing with the envelope pressed against her chest, she decided to tell Stevin everything.

He sat in shock when he learned that Christopher had hidden such a big secret, denying her the right to her true identity and parents.

Summer knew she was walking into danger if she took this opportunity and setting herself up for failure, being that close to her mom.

Stevin didn't pressure her; he just reassured her it was her decision, and he supported it either way.

Chapter 6: Falling In Love

Stevin planned a road trip to get Summer out of her hotel room and mingling back into society. He heard about a local college homecoming, including a parade and other events she could enjoy. Rushing her to get dressed, he didn't want to miss the parade, being they had a forty-five-minute drive.

Summer sat on the edge of the bed, feeling anxious about the fact she had nothing to wear. She most definitely did not want to put on the khimar garment.

Feeling excited, Stevin had brought joy back into her life; she knew she needed to step her game up. Her outside appearance was truly lacking.

She couldn't deny that she was falling deeply for Stevin. She knew his feelings towards her were genuine because there wasn't anything to love about her current situation or unappealing appearance. He had been glooming over her despite the fact she had been looking like a ragdoll.

Returning from his car with a large shopping bag, she was surprised when he informed her he had purchased her some clothing.

After getting dressed, she stood in front of the bathroom mirror, admiring her new outfit. Just then, he walked in holding a long plum-colored wig. She couldn't help but burst out into laughter.

"Stevin, what is this?" she asked.

"I knew you would want to be in disguise, so I picked you something up."

"You picked this out?" she asked, still amused.

"Yes, I did," he said with a grin. "I learned a little about wig density and lace fronts on my journey to find you the perfect wig. I told the store owner to give me the old-fashioned slap-on wig like my grandmother used to wear, with an up-to-date hairstyle."

Summer was tickled to death; he knew more than she did. As she places the wig on, she can see Stevin biting his bottom lip in her peripheral view, looking as if he wants to rip all her clothes off and have his way with her.

"Huh...," she thought. "I know exactly what I must wear tonight."

As she stepped out of the hotel, she was quickly reminded of her reality when she exited the hotel doors with nothing covering her face, feeling entirely exposed.

Looking around as Stevin walks her to the passenger side of the car and opens her door. She felt her heart racing and body trembling in the passenger seat with nervousness.

Stevin reaches over and holds her hand. Ten minutes into the drive, Stevin pulls the car over on the side of the road.

Summer looks confused, not knowing what is happening.

As he exited the vehicle, he walked over to the passenger side and pulled on the door handle, requesting for her to unlock the door. He opens her door, gently grabs her arm, and asks her to exit the car. Confused, she abides by his request and gets out of the vehicle.

"You have been shaking in fear since we left the hotel," Stevin says. "Look around, Summer; it's not a car in sight."

He grabs hold to her, looking her in the eyes. "You have to trust that I will protect you at all costs." He pulls her in closer, embracing her with a comforting hug.

Stevin then requested that she drive, feeling that it would put her mind at ease if she had directions to focus on. He sat back and admired the view, as she was stunning to him.

Thinking to himself, 'Yeah, I'm a bad man. I finally got my queen,' he smiled, slumping back in the seat and enjoying the moment.

Summer's eyes lit up as they pulled up to the campus, seeing all the students standing out, enjoying themselves. She immediately thought back to her college days, being too shy to enjoy life. She would watch the band and majorettes practice after school, going home and practicing the moves in her bedroom mirror, trying to imitate their movements.

Unable to contain her excitement, Summer pulled on Stevin's arm and exclaimed, "I always wanted to be a drum major!"

Stevin laughed and replied, "Come on, little shy Summer! Nope..., I can't see you as a drum major."

Summer, in a sarcastic tone, "It wasn't because of the lack of moves, mister. I'm very flexible," she said with a mischievous smile.

Stevin did his spill on how they would enjoy today and live in the moment as they exited the vehicle, stressing to her he wanted her to have fun and enjoy herself.

He walks to the trunk, asking her to pop it open. As she walked to the rear of the vehicle, she noted Stevin had his own mini liquor bar stock in a cooler in the trunk.

Stevin requested for her to visit one of the vendor's food booths and purchase two large cups of ice. With a large cup of liquid courage in her hand, she was ready to enjoy herself, and that she did.

Stevin followed behind as her face lit up with excitement as the band marched by. Little shy Summer marched alone, picking up on some of the choreography, marching and changing formations with timing, perfection, and precision. She was so into it she was pulled into the routine for fun as they marched to the beat.

Stevin was amazed as she lit up and actually looked damn good, swaying her body back in forward. Running into Stevin's arms, full of laughter as she had shocked herself that she built up enough nerves to dance in front of the entire school, probably the two cups of clear concoction Stevin had mixed for her gave her all the boost she needed.

Stevin's plan was clearly executed, and the liquor did just what he wanted it to do, as Summer had forgotten she was a woman on the run. Tipsy and ready to party, she didn't hold back, piggyback rides on Stevin's back, and twirling through the crowd, she was finally living.

In the excitement of everything, she impulsively grabs him by the face and kisses him as she says, "I Love You." He stands there in silence. Yes, it felt like a lifetime he waited to hear those words.

However, Summer was under the influence of alcohol and caught up in the moment, so the impact of her words was not as strong as it would have been in a private, intimate setting.

Stevin had to physically pull her to the car; she was lost in the excitement. They had an hour-long drive to the hotel he had reserved. She was fast asleep before the car pulled off the college campus. He allowed her to sleep off some of the liquor she consumed.

Stevin nudged her as they drove up to the hotel and pulled into valet parking.

She quickly jumps up, asking. "Are we in Vegas?" with a confused look on her face.

"Yes, Summer, we drove to Vegas," he replied sarcastically. However, Stevin had booked a hotel at a casino in Shreveport, LA.

Summer was in awe of the flashing lights. She had never been to a casino.

“Let me get us checked in Summer, and you can rest.”

"Who's resting,” she asked? “I'm headed to the casino.”

"Okay…, I thought I was a man down; you still got gas in the tank?”

As they stood at the front desk checking in, Summer's wheels were turning as she spotted a gift shop with apparel across the way.

“Baby, give me a room key; I want to pick up some items from the gift shop. I will meet you upstairs.” She gives him a peck on the lips as she walks away with newfound confidence.

Summer was determined to drive Stevin wild tonight as she picked up items that were sexy and revealing.

Arriving at the room, it was a very nice hotel suite, but she had been wined and dined at some of the most luxurious properties around the world; she had seen it all. Stevin added a special touch to the occasion by bringing champagne and roses.

"Are you ready?" he asked.

"Let me freshen up and change.”

"Hell, Summer, that's another hour. I'll be asleep waiting for you".

"Well, go ahead downstairs, and I'll meet you there," she suggested.

"Are you sure?"

"Yes, I'm a big girl," she said confidently. "What floor will you be on?"

"Just keep my personal cell phone, Summer, and I'll take my work phone. Call me when you're ready, and I'll come back up and meet you."

Summer had her own plans; she had purchased a deep sequin V-neck shirt, which was long enough to wear as a dress. She wanted to make a statement tonight.

Summer thought it was hilarious that she could actually take her hair off and hang it on the towel hook. Rushing out of the shower, she had purchased shimmer and perfume from the gift shop; not leaving one stone unturned, she was determined to look and smell good for him tonight.

As she attempted to put her wig back on, she noticed that the wig started curling up; the shower's steam made the wig puffy.

"No...!" She cried out. The wig was a significant part of her plot tonight. When Stevin brought her the wig, it was straight with a few curls. She had just learned some techniques for styling her own hair; she most definitely did not know how to style a wig.

Deciding to wash the wig and blow dry it out to attempt to get a straight look, Summer noticed the wetter the wig became, the more defined the curls got. She placed the wig on damp, and it was beautiful. The final results were a wet and wavy deep curl. The hair God has shown up again on her behalf.

Sliding her dress on, she was a little too sexy, too much was revealing. She didn't know what Stevin's response would be, but tonight, she was ready to walk on the wild side.

Intentionally waiting until she made it onto the casino to call him, she was even more nervous from the looks she had already received from other men she passed while walking to the casino dock. Her heart started to race; maybe this wasn't a wise choice. She was taking a significant risk; she could never have dressed like this with Christopher. So quickly did she forget the scene in California with the infamous red dress.

Calling Stevin from the dock, he informed her he was at the blackjack table to give him a second to return to the room. She informed him she was on the casino floor and needed to know his location. He replied that he was on the first floor playing blackjack. Stevin stepped away from the table as he stood while he played to keep an eye out for her.

It was a Saturday night, and the casino was packed. As Stevin placed his bet, one of the guys at the table said "DAMN!"

Stevin quickly looked up as Summer was walking towards him. In shock at her appearance, he dropped all his chips in his hand onto the floor. He could care less; she was drop-dead sexy. She waited for him to pick his chips up and gather himself to see if he would respond negatively towards her look. Grabbing her by the waist, he pulls her in for a kiss. Stevin wasn't intimidated at all by her sex appeal. He welcomed it; she was his. She wasn't a trophy on a shelf; she was a trophy on his arm that he was proudly displaying.

She sat in his seat as she attempted to learn blackjack. One too many busts, and she decided she wanted to play the slots. Suggesting to Stevin that he can stay and play the tables. He wasn't having it; he was glued to her.

Stevin couldn't keep his hands off her as she attempted to play the slots, begging her to return to the room with him. Summer, making him sweat it out, finally agreed to return to the room. He stops by the concierge desk requesting a glass of cognac and a bottle of cabernet sauvignon wine be delivered to the room.

They stepped into the elevator, and as the doors closed, he pinned her against the elevator wall, attempting to slide his hand in her panties. She laughed and tried to fight him off as she reminded him they were being watched as the camera was very visible. "I don't give a damn, let them watch," he replied. Summer knew it was the alcohol talking.

As they exit the elevators, she screams out in laughter, holding her wig in place as he throws her over his shoulder, carrying her from the elevator to the room. Whispering in her ear as she attempts to unlock the door with the key card.

"Let's just see how flexible you are, Ms. Taylor."

Summer tried to change as they entered the room, as she had another surprise for him. Stevin wasn't letting go, holding on to her wrist; he would undress her at the door. Pulling the dress over her head as she stood topless, only cloth in her lace panties.

Stevin aggressively grabs her breast, tracing his tongue from her neck to her breast as he licks and sucks on her nipples. He runs his tongue down her cleavage to her stomach, dropping to his knees, gently biting and licking her inner thigh. He places her leg over his shoulder, spreading her inner lips apart. Taking the tip of his nose, he circles her clit, as he takes a big sniff his eyes roll in the back of his head, and the smell of her natural lubricant turns him on, igniting all his sexual senses.

Manipulating his warm tongue, licking between her folds, slurping her juices, as he proclaims how good she tastes while lightly nibbling and sucking her clitoris. He leads her to the bed and directs her to lie on her back.

Stevin walked around, flicking all the lights on, as he needed the room to be well-lit. Walking over to her, he ripped off the tiny lace g-string she was wearing. Taking her by her ankles, he flips her onto her stomach as he squeezes and lightly bites her ass cheeks. Summer squeezes and bites the pillow as his sexual bites sent electrifying sensations up her spine.

A knock on the door brings everything to a halt as room service delivers the alcoholic beverages he requested. He returns to the bedside and slowly pours the wine into her mouth; as the wet liquid runs down her neck and breast, he passionately kisses her. He runs his tongue down her neck, slurping up the wine as it runs down her breast. Waves of pleasure washed over her as she was ready to explode sexually.

Stevin walked around the bed, sipping on his glass of cognac, studying her body with his eyes, demanding she touches herself. Taking ice from the ice bucket, he circles her nipples with the ice and lightly blows on them. He pulls her by the legs, pulling her bottom to the edge of the bed. Easing to his knees, he takes a piece of ice, pours cognac into his mouth, and begins to taste her. She immediately thought to herself, 'Is this man putting alcohol in my vagina? What the hell!'

Stevin suddenly starts to choke; she didn't know rather to run and wash the cognac out of her vagina or give him mouth-to-mouth.

He quickly gathered himself, and his tongue became a human vibrator as he stiffened his tongue, massaging small circles around her clit. Wrapping his lips around the mouth of her arousal, he sucked and licked as the pleasure started shooting up her spine and through every inch of her body. His face was buried in her pool of moisture, exploring every inch of her essence.

Standing and taking another sip of his cognac, he crawls on top of her, requesting she hold her legs as he places her hands behind her knees. He said, "Now let's see how flexible you really are," as he slid all of himself inside her inch-by-inch, stroking deeper and deeper.

He pulls her into a state of compliance as he would have his way with her body. Holding her legs in the air, he crosses them, grabbing her by her ankles as she screams don't stop as she has a wave of orgasms back-to-back.

Summer's muscles are flaccid, her legs tremble from the sexual stimulation, and she has lost all control. Stevin dominated her body, and she got everything she desired and more.

He flipped and tossed her around effortlessly. Standing and pulling her body to the edge of the bed, as he flipped her over to her knees, demanding she arches her back, he smacks her ass cheeks, as the sound echoes throughout the room; he watches her cheeks jiggle from the vibration from the force of his hand.

He spreads her lips apart from behind and bent down, sliding his tongue into her entrance. She could feel his hand gently sliding up her back to her neck; when he pushed her head down demanding, she spread her arms far apart as he pushed her knees further apart, spreading her cheeks and sliding in deep and stroking harder as he commands her to assume that position and not to run from him, as she couldn't take anymore.

He grabbed her hips and pulled her back as he drove inside her harder and faster. She collapsed onto her stomach as he came right alone; he never stopped stroking, pinning her hands above her head. She was pretty sure they would get a knock on the door for a noise complaint as she screamed out in pleasuring pain.

"Baby, you have to cum," she loudly moans as she attempts to tap out, "I can't take anymore."

"I already did twice," he said. Demanding if she wanted him to cum for the third time, she must scream out to whom she belongs too.

"You, Daddy, you," she moans out.

Asking again in a demanding voice. "Who does she belong to," referencing her warm, wet hole between her beautiful legs?

"You, Stevin, she is yours," she moans out loudly in pleasure.

"Keep saying it," he demanded as his strokes got harder and deeper, and his large cock felt as if he was tap dancing on her bladder.

"You, Daddy, I'm yours," she screams when Stevin does one hard stroke, his body jerking as he moans her name.

Summer had nothing to pout about tonight as she passed out from sexual exhaustion. Stevin had given her exactly what she had been desiring of him.

As she slept, he sat up in the chair, quaffing wine from the bottle and staring at her naked body passed out across the bed. Satisfied that he finally broke her in, as he had desired to. He wasn't taking no for an answer. He was determined she would be moving to Georgia and would become his wife.

Chapter 7: The Big Move

Stevin is awakened by his cell phone ringing; he rolls over, snatching the phone from the power card. It's his mom, and he would need to call her back due to his pounding headache from the hangover he was battling.

He feels for Summer when he realizes she is not in the bed or the hotel room. Jumping up checking his watch, and it's after 2:00 pm. He looks out into the hallway; no, Summer. He also noticed his car keys were missing.

Calling the front desk to check if he had any messages, he was baffled as to why Summer would leave without telling him.

Standing at the washbowl, he could hear the hotel room door open, rushing out of the bathroom when he locked eyes with Summer as she smiled.

"What the hell, Summer? Why would you leave without telling me something?"

Standing against the door, she looked at him with a mischievous grin. "Are you missing her already? We haven't been gone for an hour, sir."

"Enough with the games, Summer, that wasn't cool." She advanced towards him; walking gapped-legged as she attempted to soothe him.

"I'm sorry daddy. I didn't mean to worry you," she says as she walks over, kissing his chest.

"Summer don't patronize me. And why the hell are you walking like that?"

"Oh, because my uterus was damaged by a giant anaconda last night."

Stevin smiles as he shakes his head, wrapping his arms around her and hugging her, asking, "What am I going to do with you?"

Noticing a plastic bag that she had stuff in her back pocket, he questions her whereabouts.' "You could have ordered room service. Why did you need the car?" He asked as he noticed her trying to hide the bag.

Snatching the bag from her back pocket, her natural reaction was to grab the bag out of his hand when she unintentionally scratched his arm.

In an aggressive manner, Stevin snatches away from her, giving her an unsettling look. She immediately became timid as she began backing away. Realizing he had frightened her, he quickly changed his demeanor.

"Come here, sweetheart," he says as he hands her the bag back and kisses her, apologizing for violating her personal space and privacy.

Summer opens the bag and gives the box to Stevin.

"Plan B. What is this, Summer?"

"It's an emergency contraceptive, Stevin."

"I know what it is. Why did you feel the need to buy it?"

"I'm currently not on birth control, and I just don't want to complicate things right now," Summer explains.

He grabs her hand and leads her to the bed. "Let's talk," he says. "I haven't been 100% honest with you."

Summer looks at Stevin with a curious but concerned expression. She immediately felt a knot in her stomach, worried about what confession Stevin was about to make.

"What's wrong, Stevin?"

“I got engaged before I left Illinois, Summer.”

Summer's eyes widened as she asked, "To whom?"

"Lisa from Human Resources. She was the person who helped me get out of that messy situation Amber filed against me."

With a hard eye roll, Summer mumbled under her breath, "That floozy."

"Now, Summer, you don't even know that woman personally; why does she have to be a floozy?"

"Because," Summer said as she rolled her eyes.

"Anyway, Lisa's number one focus was to have kids, and after dating for a year without using any method of protection, she never could conceive. Long story short, I was the problem. I have a low sperm count. Lisa, who was fifteen years older than me, needed me to make lifestyle changes that doctors recommended. However, I had just started a new job, and one of the biggest requirements was to travel frequently. I couldn't commit to the changes required of me, and as a result, she gave me the ring back and ended the relationship."

Summer sat silently, fidgeting with her fingernails.

He gave her a sidelong glance and asked, "Is this a deal breaker for you?"

"No, it's not," she replied quickly. "How do you feel about using donor sperm?"

"That would be our last resort, Summer. Are you okay with that?"

"It works for me," she replied.

"As for another important matter," he starts off with a commanding look and declares with confidence. You are moving to Georgia with me, and I'm not taking no for an answer. I will be by your side every step of the way. If you decide to burn the envelope and never open it, or if you choose that, you are ready to meet your mom. I will be by your side no matter what your decision will be. But at this moment, we, us, our adventure together starts here and now, and Christopher Diamond will not dictate our future. I understand and respect your decision to keep a low profile to avoid him finding your location, but it's time to start living your life!"

"Okay," she replied without any hesitation.

"Are you serious?" he asked, picking her up and twirling her around. He fell back onto the bed, still holding her in his arms, taking the Plan B box, throwing it across the room, and aiming for the small trash can. "We don't need this. Now, let's start working on our family," he said as he attempted to undress her.

"No, Stevin, she needs a week off," referencing her lady parts, she says as she burst into laughter.

"No, sweetie, she just needs some tender loving care," he declared as he positioned himself to taste her.

Summer's eyes roll back into her head from the extreme pleasure Stevin was giving.

Rose enters the home, followed by Kimberley. "I must say they put your grandfather away very nicely. Your dad did an outstanding job, or that dizzy cow he's dating finally contributed and did something right."

"Mom, that's not nice; Sarah is genuinely nice and really loves Dad. Sounds like someone is bitter," Kimberley muttered.

"What did you say, young lady? You're not too old to get smacked."

"Mom, please stop. I just lost Papa. Losing Mema last year was the hardest thing I ever had to deal with. Now, with this, it's not fair. I have no family but you and Dad. And Dad's family is so scattered I would need a private jet to visit everyone. Could you please just tell me why I can't meet your parents? What is the secrecy surrounding my grandparents? Were you adopted and don't know your family?"

"KIMBERLEY...! Today is not the day; I don't have time for your shenanigans."

"But why, Mom? Dad doesn't even know why you are so secretive about your parents. You guys were married for fifteen years, and he mentioned that your family has always been off-limits. Why is that, Mom? Why won't you tell us anything about them?"

Rose looked at Kimberley with a stern expression, her silence speaking volumes. Kimberley dropped her head, knowing her mom meant business and that her line of questioning could get her in a lot of trouble.

"Mom, I need to tell you something," Kimberley said hesitantly.

"What is it now, Kimberley?" asked Rose, sounding frustrated.

"But why do you have to sound like that? This affects my future, too, and I'm not trying to do anything behind your back."

"And what is that supposed to mean, Kimberley Michelle White?"

"Well, I was talking to Emmanuel, and...."

"Eee-man..., you who?" Rose interrupted.

"Mom, stop it. I already told you about Emmanuel several times."

"Oh, the young man who doesn't feel the need to grace my presence?"

"Mother, I told you he is very old school. He would like us to get to know each other better before we involve our parents, and besides, I would rather wait until he relocates to Georgia."

"Kimberley, where did you meet 'Eee-man...,' you who?" Rose asks while rolling her eyes.

"I told you, Mom, it's like it was meant to be," Kimberley responds excitedly. "We kept bumping into each other for three weeks straight until he finally approached me. He said it must be destined for me to ask for your number, the way God keeps placing you in my path."

"Get to your point, Kimberley, and get your head out of the clouds. You have been dating this young fella for three months; what is he waiting for, judgment day before I'm important enough to grace his presence?"

"Anyway, mother. Emmanuel and his partner just invested in a new company specializing in DNA and finding biological family members, and I took the test."

Kimberley is immediately startled by the glass pitcher falling from Rose's hands, shattering on the floor. Rose clenches her chest as if she is having trouble breathing and falls onto the counter with tears in her eyes.

"What have you done, What have you done?" Rose screams.

"What, Mom, what?" Kimberley asks in confusion.

"Have I not given all of myself to you? You have never needed for anything. The only thing I asked of you, and your father has asked of you, is that you respect my privacy regarding my parents. We have given you the best life any child could ever ask for, and this is how you repay us?"

Rose strides over to Kimberley and slaps her across the face. "Get out of my sight," she shouts. "Call your dad and leave my home now!" she screams, breaking down and collapsing to her knees.

Kimberley ran upstairs, slamming her door, throwing herself on her bed in tears, waiting for her mom to follow her and apologize. Rose had never punished her for anything, let alone laid a hand on her. She knew at any moment her mom would burst into her bedroom, filled with remorse for her violent outburst. She calls her dad, screaming, "Come get me, come get me now! Mom has lost it."

Rose was in a state of shock and remained curled up on the kitchen floor. Memories of Summer kept flooding her mind like flashes of fireworks: her baby girl, her sweet smell, and her beautiful smile. As she clenched her stomach, she immediately felt ill. The memories of waking up in the hospital and losing James and Summer in one night were overwhelming and consumed her every thought.

After having several mental breakdowns and being hospitalized for a year, after learning her parents gave her child away. Rose believed that in order to move forward, she needed to bury the memories of her past, including her parents, and pretend as if they never existed. She was even burying the memories of her own child, Summer.

She had accepted she would never see Summer again; all she knew was that her baby girl had died also that night. She searched for Summer for years; it was as if Summer Teller had disappeared, and her parents were given a life sentence for the murder of her soul when they written her off for dead and took her baby girl away from her.

Kimberley could hear the sound of her father's truck as it sped up the driveway. He took no time to high-tail across town and come to her rescue.

She is standing at the bottom of the stairs when her dad barges in, demanding to know Rose's whereabouts. Kimberley pointed towards the kitchen as she followed with concern about her dad's reactions towards her mom due to the way he had burst into the home.

She was taken aback when they located her mom on the floor, rocking and mumbling, crying as if she had had a nervous breakdown.

Kimberley was at a loss for words when her dad laid beside her mom, rubbing her face, calling her baby. Rose jumped into his arms as he picked her up, carrying her upstairs as if he were her savior.

David placed her in the shower and removed her wet clothing, requesting that Kimberley clean up the water and broken glass from the kitchen floor. This only infuriated Kimberley more. Her parents had been separated for six years, with her dad getting engaged to someone else. Yet, here he was in the home he left years ago, bathing his ex-wife, catering to her emotional needs as if he didn't have a fiancé at home.

Storming into her room, she quickly grabbed the phone to call Emmanuel and inform him of the situation and her mom's reaction. She explains to him that her car is in the shop, and she demands to stay at his rental home alone while he is out of state.

However, he denied her access to his home but agreed to set up a rental car and a hotel room for her. She flew out of her room to pull her suitcase from the closet, as her mother's bedroom was across from hers. She saw her father in bed with her mother, holding and consoling her. Which only meant one thing: they both were lying to her and had been keeping secrets from her her entire life.

Throughout her entire childhood, she had been entitled and spoiled rotten. At that moment, she had no concern for what her mother was going through. The only thing that mattered to her at the moment was that she had been lied to. Knowing whatever it was, it involved her maternal grandparents. Whom she longed so badly to know, and Rose wasn't going to stop her from uncovering the truth.

"Emmanuel, when will my results be back? I can't take this anymore. I need to know what are they hiding from me?" Kimberley anxiously asked.

"Give me a couple of days, baby. I'll be back in town, and we can go over the results together."

Kimberley hears a horn slightly blow when she realizes her car services have arrived. David jumped up from the bed as he could hear her leaving. "Young lady, we need to talk!" he shouted as she exited the home.

"Go talk to your wife. Oops, ex-wife Dad!" She screamed, slamming the door.

David White indeed knew why Rose kept clear of her parents. He was Rose's therapist and fell in love with her during her hospitalization while helping her through one of the most challenging times in her life. He knew how damaging these memories and topics could be for Rose. They both made a pact to ensure that her past would never resurface again, along with the parents who had written her off. Her past would remain buried, even kept from their beloved Kimberley.

Chapter 8: A New Scenery

MONROE, LOUISIANA

Summer decided to stay back in Louisiana to give Stevin time to arrange everything for their big move. In the meantime, she had to pack up everything in her hotel room. However, she was struggling with the idea that she would be so close to her mom yet be unable to reach out to her.

She threw away the envelope containing her parents' information because she knew she would be tempted, placing the trash bag outside the door for housekeeping.

She lay in silence as she could hear the cleaning crew pushing their carts down the hallway. However, as the squeaking wheel of the housekeeper cart stops in front of her door, her anxiety overwhelms her; she feels as if her chest is constricting with each inhaled breath.

Suddenly, she jumped out of bed, flung open the door, and found that the trash bag with her parents' information was gone. She runs up the hallway, grabs the housekeeper's cart, and screams, "Where's my bag?"

“Calm down, ma'am. We can help you once you're calm," one of the housekeepers said as they emptied their carts.

"I had a bag; I had a bag right there," she screams.

"Is this your bag, ma'am?" The housekeeper asked as she handed Summer the trash bag. She collapses to the floor hysterically, crying, and pulls the envelope from the bag.

"Ma'am, can we call someone for you?" The housekeeper asked.

Summer glanced up and noticed she had caused a crowd to gather around her. Pulling herself together, she walked back to her room.

Summer returned to the room and called Stevin. "I cannot spend another night alone here. I want to be with you right now."

"What happened? Please tell me what is going on."

"Please, Stevin, just get here, I need you. I can't stay another night here. Please set up some type of transportation for me; I'd rather go back to the hotel at the casino and wait it out. I just caused a scene in the hallway, and everybody is staring like I'm a certified nut case."

"Summer, it's only two days away. Can you tough it out for two more days?"

"Oh, alright. But if I'm not here when you arrive, check the looney bin. I'm pretty sure they'll be coming to take me away in a straitjacket soon," she said as the ended the call.

ALANTA GEORGIA

Kimberley continued to ignore all texts and calls from her parents. Refusing to return home, Rose was devastated, pleading for her forgiveness. After much persuasion from Emmanuel, Kimberley decided to return to her mother's home. The unspoken topic remains forbidden, but Kimberley couldn't care less; she'd have all her answers in a day or two.

Rose invited David over, hoping to ease the tension between them. Kimberley felt her dad would also be remorseful and cater to her bruised ego. However, her father's reaction was unexpected.

"Young lady, I didn't raise you to disrespect me or your mother," he said sternly. "You are nineteen years old now. If you're mature enough to mouth off and leave without a word, you're mature enough to face the consequences of your actions. Maybe it's time for some responsibilities such as paying rent and your own car note."

"Dad..., that's not fair. You two are the ones keeping secrets."

Slamming his fist on the table, David yelled, "Dammit, young lady, not another word! Apologize to your mother right now!"

Kimberley stood, walking in the opposite direction to reach Rose, avoiding walking past her father. She grabbed Rose around the neck and pulled her towards her. "Old lady, you know I love you," she said as she kissed her on the cheek.

They all burst into laughter as Rose was willing to accept any form of affection from her baby girl.

"Ms. White," Kimberley said. "Tell your sugar daddy to calm down, cause if he hollas at me again, I'll be forced to inform Sarah, his current fiancé, that he was over here bathing your lady liberty the other night."

David snatches his belt off, chasing Kimberley upstairs. As the house filled with laughter, Rose couldn't shake the feeling of impending doom. It was as if the rug could be pulled from underneath her at any moment, rocking her world. She silently prayed that Kimberley would drop the subject.

THE BIG MOVE

Summer welcomed a new scenery as she was packed and waiting outside on the curb with her bags when she received a call from Stevin informing her that he was fifteen minutes from the hotel. As he pulled up, he saw her standing there with her bags in her hands. Stevin was tickled to death. A far cry from the woman who had been so guarded and fearful of going outside just a few weeks ago was now standing there, fully exposed.

He embraced her, wrapping his arms around her, squeezing tight, and planting a sweet kiss on her lips. At that moment, he knew that she had chosen him, and their journey was just beginning. He vowed to love and protect her. He was on a mission to show her the meaning of true love.

"Sweetie, are you willing to share now what had you so upset the other day?"

Summer drops her head, mumbling in a low tone as she fumbles her words. Stevin refuses to pull off until he knows she is mentally okay and is ready for this big step. Reaching over, rubbing her face, 'give me a kiss,' he demands. She looks up with a big smirk and leans over to give him a passionate kiss, sending tingles down his spine.

"Did you turn in the key cards, or did you leave them in the room?"

"I turned them in, why?"

"I need an hour with you before we take this trip," he said.

She burst out laughing, amused by his desire for her, but she was eager to leave Monroe, Louisiana, in her rearview mirror. Promising to make it worth his wild if he would hold off until they arrived at their new home.

"Alright, my dear," said Stevin, turning to her with a curious look. "Are you prepared for this 8-hour long drive?" Summer smiled, placed her shades on, and shifted the passenger seat back.

As Stevin pulled away from the hotel, Summer looked out the window, reminiscing about happy moments spent with Alli at the park. This was just another sad chapter to add to her book of disappointments. She hoped this next adventure would be her best one yet. Clearly, she needed to distinguish reality from fantasy, and that's what Christopher was: an illusion that she perceived to be real. Now, knowing everything that glitters isn't gold.

Chapter 9: Let's Play House

MADISON GEORGIA

Stevin and Summer's eight-hour road trip turned into a twelve-hour journey due to multiple unplanned stops. Stevin insisted on stopping at various landmarks to take photos of him and Summer as they passed through different states.

Despite feeling exhausted, Summer was incredibly relieved to know that Stevin had arranged for the house to be furnished and that there would be nothing she needed to do but relax in the tub.

However, she felt excited but also a bit hesitant at the same time. Yet again, she was moving into another man's home to which she had no claim to. Especially considering she's now twenty-eight, and everything she owns could fit in the trunk of a car.

Stevin was like her worry whisperer; he could sense her change in mood. Her emotions were always evident on her face. Sensing her worry, he reached over, took her hand, and kissed it tenderly.

"Summer, I'm not here to hurt or disappoint you. If I didn't genuinely intend to make you the happiest woman on this earth, I wouldn't have walked back into your life."

Summer's face relaxed; in her heart, she knew this time felt different. As they pulled into the driveway, Summer's heart was filled with excitement as they approached the elegant, traditional family home. A fence surrounded the front yard, and it was gorgeous, with a beautiful farmer's porch that screamed, "Welcome Home."

Stevin instructed her to leave everything in the car and that he would gather all the bags after they had explored the inside of the home.

Summer is unaware that Stevin has already visited the house and has prepared some surprises for her. Stevin requested to pick her up and carry her over the threshold, symbolizing new beginnings.

As he opens the door, Summer jumps out of his arms, completely speechless. Stevin had everything perfectly arranged, including photos of them together hanging on the wall, giving the impression that they were already a family.

Stevin had taken pictures that he and Summer had taken on business trips and work events and edited them, cropping out other coworkers. She had never noticed that every opportunity he was given, he made sure he was position right next to her. Summer giggled to herself, thinking the gesture was sweet. Stevin took her by the hand.

" Come on, let's go to the bedroom, baby."

She hesitated, giving him a look. He burst into laughter.

"No, sweetie, that part will come later," as he led her through the house giggling.

Gesturing for her to open up the bedroom closet. He had taken it upon himself to shop for some clothing for her. As she flipped through the wardrobe, she noticed how much attention to detail he had paid to the type of clothing style she liked to wear, and her heart was overwhelmed with emotions.

"I'm sorry," she said as tears rolled down her face.

He wiped the tears from her eyes and said, "I'm okay with these tears; joyful tears are all you are allowed to shed." He then picked her up and laid her back on the bed, passionately kissing her.

"Stevin, no. I need to take a bath first. Let me freshen up."

"That's fine, sweetie. But I have yet to smell every scent she has."

"Now, that is just gross," Summer said, sticking out her tongue at him before running into the bathroom.

She was more concerned about Stevin's wellbeing. For weeks, he had been catering to her, and after a twelve-hour road trip, she wanted him to relax and be pampered.

She still had her go-get-him bag packed away in her duffle bag, items she had purchased from the gift shop to seduce him. Stevin dominated the night in the hotel; she never had a chance to use any of the items she acquired to please him.

Summer pulled some candles from her bag she had purchased from the gift shop, placing the candles around the soaking tub, she poured an organic, sensual bubble bath in the water. Then she dimmed the lights and slipped into her silk robe.

Summer located Stevin in the kitchen and took his hand, gesturing for him to follow her.

"You're out of the tub already?"

She grabbed his hand, urging him to join her, but he declined, saying, "Hold on, Summer. Let me unpack these bags." He looked up and noticed her wardrobe choice.

"Say, ma'am, what do you have on under that robe?" Summer walked off, turned around, and faced him as she got to the kitchen entrance. She drops her robe, revealing her nude body to him, and walks off, enticing him to follow.

Stevin knocked over the items on the counter, reacting as if it was his first time seeing her naked. He attempted to pick up the items off the floor; 'the hell with this,' he thought as he took off to the bedroom.

Locating her in the bathroom, his eyes lit up when he noticed the romantic gesture with the candles and soft jazz music he loves playing in the background. Stevin, excited and turned on, immediately goes for it, grabbing for her, ready to relieve his built-up excitement. She bats his hands down, "I'm in charge tonight," she declared.

He steps back, letting her have her way. She unbuttons his shirt, kissing his chest as she undresses him, leading him to the tub. As she turned to walk out of the bathroom, he called out to her, "Hey, where are you going? I thought you were joining me."

"I am, sweetie. Let me do me," she said.

She returns to the bathroom, bringing him a glass of wine, noticing that he has already stocked his personal liquor bar. She made sure to stay away from the cognac that was visibly noted well stock. She knew all too well what type of sexual energy it brings. She would prefer to keep her uterus intact tonight.

Stevin down the wine, pulling for her to join him in the tub. "Relax, Stevin, I'm all yours in a few," she said, running her hands through his curly hair while taking the sponge and washing his chest as she made her way down.

With built-up anticipation, he grabs her arm, pulling her into the tub.

"No, Stevin," she screams out in laughter. "I want to give you a massage first."

"Okay," he replied, as he ignored her request.

"Come on and slide back so I can wash her and get her ready to be tasted."

Pulling her back against him, she complied, lying back and melting into his chest as she enjoyed the firm, swift strokes of his finger massaging her clit until she screamed out in pleasure. She turns and faces him, kissing and biting his bottom lip.

"I want to please you in every way possible; let me finish my surprise."

Stepping out of the tub, she leads him to the bed and lays down a towel, instructing him to lie on his stomach. She stepped back to admire her man's fine, sensuous body, with buns of steel that looked like a perfectly sculptured masterpiece. She placed her oils within arm's reach before slowly squatting over him.

"Now, Summer, how long do you think you can squat on top of me and keep rubbing your bare-naked body on me, and I don't turn over and slide in you?"

"Relax, man! I'm all yours after your massage."

She begins with a small amount of oil, rubbing her hands together to warm the oil in the palms of her hands. Taking the bottle of oil, she drips it onto her breast and abdomen, oiling her body so she can easily slide against his.

Summer starts with his shoulder's, applying firm strokes, then using long strokes to his back. She leans in, kissing the back of his neck as she cresses her breast on his back as she slides up and down, tracing her erect nipples down his back. She raises up, attempting to make her way to his thighs when he flips over.

"No, Stevin, turn back over and allow me to finish."

"Oh, I am...," he said enthusiastically, as he requested she now massages his front.

His large manhood stands to attention as she directs her attention to his very noticeable boner. She instructs him to place his hands behind his head and leave them there.

She angles her body to the side so he can have the perfect view of her nude body. Arching her back and leaning in, she runs her tongue along the length of his manhood, delivering small sensual kisses to the head of his pulsating throbbing cock as she strokes up and down his shaft with her warm oily hands.

As the pleasure consumed him, he began squirming around in the bed, punching his hands together, attempting not to give in to his strong sexual urges. Summer notices the curling of his toes as he moans her name; this only makes her suck and stroke harder, knowing she is pleasing him in every way.

After moaning her name out loud one too many times, he attempts to gain control as he pulls her, gesturing for her to sit on his face.

"No, I'm not done with your massage yet. Lay back and enjoy," she demanded.

Climbing on top of him, dripping massage oil on his chest, he watches her pour oil on her breast as she slides her fingers in a slow-motion movement, oiling her breasts as she caresses them. Stevin reaches down, sliding his fingers between her folds, swirling his fingers over her clit. He thrusts his fingers deeper in her, penetrating her warm flesh as he could feel the tight grip to his fingers. Unable to contain himself, he grabs her by the waist, forcing all of himself into her.

"Sit all the way on him," he demands.

As she attempts to lean over, he forces her to sit straight up, demanding eye contact.

"Finish my massage, and don't stop" he requested.

Summer tries to rub his chest as her eyes roll in the back of her head as he strokes deeper inside her.

"Sit up and give me eye contact," he demands, pulling down on her waist as he inches deeper in her.

Collapsing on top of him as the pleasure has overtaken her, he gently grabs her by the neck and kisses her, forcing her to sit up and give him eye contact as he pushes deeper inside of her, driving his rock-hard erection deeper into her muscles.

Screaming his name as she climaxes. Her grip became tighter as her vaginal muscle contracted, gripping his rock-hard cock, tighter and tighter.

Unable to fight the urge to cum, he flipped her over, stroking harder and deeper until the intensity of the buildup of pleasure caused his entire body to collapse on top of her as everything went numb, except for the amazing sensation in his penis. He fell onto the bed, questioning her.

"What are you doing to me?" Summer, he asks.

"Loving you like you deserve," she assured.

He quickly popped his head up, looking her in the eyes, waiting to see if it was just a fly-in-the-moment comment like before. She notices the desperate look in his eyes for clarity.

Rolling over, she gently kisses his chest, softly kissing up his neck as she grips his face, kissing him on the lips.

"I love you, Mr. Stevin Bash."

She could feel his heart racing as the room went silent. He cupped her face and stared deeply into her eyes, urging her to repeat it.

"I love you, Stevin," she repeated, her voice filled with a depth of emotions that could not be mistaken for anything but pure, sincere love.

He passionately kisses her, saying, "I just needed to make sure you meant what you said."

Pecking him on the lips, she said, "I meant it the first time I said it." Then, she exited the bed, requesting that he join her in the shower.

"I can't walk! You screwed the feelings out of my legs!" he shouted. "Please bring a towel and come wash me up."

Stevin was on cloud nine, and it meant the world to him to hear those three words from her, knowing that her first "I love you" came from her heart and not from the liquor.

Chapter 10: I'm In Love

4:00am Madison Georgia

Summer was abruptly jolted awake by the blaring alarm clock. Stevin had turned the volume to the maximum to ensure that he would wake up on time for his first day at his new job. Summer groaned as she rolled over, resting her head on his chest.

"Do you have to go to work today?"

"Yes, yesterday was supposed to be my first day, but I had to take a detour and pick you up."

"Please call in and tell them that your flight was delayed. I want to spend the entire day sleeping in your arms," she begged.

"I'm sorry, but I can't skip work, Summer. I have to go in today."

"Oh, really?" she said, placing her head under the covers, pleasuring him until he was moaning her name.

With two handfuls of her hair, he wasted no time enjoying a morning splash. As she rolled over, just knowing he would fall back to sleep. Stevin jumped out of the bed and rushed into the bathroom.

"Where are you going?' she asked.

"To work, honey, but first I have to go wash my dick and wash away your hot bacteria you so lovely bless me with this morning."

He quickly closes the bathroom door to avoid being hit by the pillow she threw at him.

Summer races out of bed, determined to surprise Stevin with a delicious breakfast. She opened the refrigerator and found nothing, but stale fast food left from the previous night. She rushes into the bathroom and question Stevin.

"How can I fix your breakfast if we have no food?"

"I'm sorry, sweetie," he said while kissing her forehead. "Just order some takeout. I have an hour's commute, so I need to get going anyway. I will stop by the store after I get off."

She playfully rolls her eyes and jumps back into bed. Since she planned on sleeping in, it was the perfect time to catch up on some much-needed rest.

As Stevin left the house, she could hear the deadbolt lock and the alarm being set to stay mode. She then laid in bed, staring at the ceiling. For the first time, she felt happy without fearing the unknown. With no worries on her mind, she stretched her body, rolling back and forth in the bed, smiling. "I am in love, and it feels so damn good," she whispered to herself. Summer stayed in bed until she eventually fell back to sleep.

As she hears the loud beep of the garbage truck, she opens one eye and realizes that she has been abruptly interrupted from her sleep.

She is fully aware of how exhausted she is, knowing it would take a lot of effort to pull herself out of bed. However, she is determined to put her personal touch on the home by unpacking all of Stevin's bags and organizing the closet before he returns home. She texted him that she would like to cook him dinner and requested that she join him on the trip to the supermarket.

Stevin replies with a text. "Okay, sweetheart, I plan on leaving work early. I will bring you the car and allow you to go when I get off."

However, Summer didn't reply to Stevin's text. She had her own ideas, which included Stevin going shopping with her. She was determined to have her perfect family and do all the things she could never do with Christopher.

Summer spent half the day unpacking boxes, rearranging furniture, cleaning and polishing the countertops, and making sure all the windows and mirrors were sparkling clean. She also took the time to rearrange the photoshop photos on the wall, adding her and Miss Dangerfield's picture alongside Stevin's family photos.

Stevin left work early, tired from the twelve-hour drive, and he and Summer spicy sexual activity throughout the night. All he wanted to do was kick his feet up and watch the playoffs.

He enters the home with a surprised look on his face. The house was spotless before leaving for work, but he returned to a home that his woman had spit shine and put her touch into. He stood in the kitchen, rubbing his hand across the countertop, trying to figure out what she had done to make the countertop shine so nicely.

The curtains were pulled open, and it was very noticeable from the sparkle of the sunlight hitting the glass frame that the windows had been polished as well.

The only experience Stevin had living with her was in the hotel, which she did not keep tidy. Not knowing she was a neat freak who had a daily ritual of cleaning.

Summer notices Stevin's surprised expression as she enters the kitchen and wonders why.

"Hey, you," she says, greeting him with a hug. "Let's go shopping," she suggests with a smile.

"Go ahead, Summer. I'm going to relax and watch the ball game."

"Please, baby, come with me. I'll drive," she begged. She played on his emotions, telling a small white lie about being afraid to go alone when all she really wanted was the normalcy of going grocery shopping together.

"Dammit, Summer. Come on. Just know that I plan on being back home before 7 pm."

Walking out of the house, he wondered why Summer was marching out the door with a book that resembled a photo album. Too busy attempting to rush out the door, he did not question her. It was a quarter past five, and he was determined to make the trip to the store as short as possible.

As he sat in the passenger seat, he watched her sway her head back and forth to the music on the radio, lost in her own world. He smiled, happy she was finally content and secure in their relationship.

They pulled into the parking lot, and Summer exited the car with her book in hand. She grabbed a cart and directed him to grab one, too.

"Why do I need a shopping cart? We are not doing that much shopping that we both need carts."

"Yes, baby, I must keep up with my sale items," she said as she opened the book full of coupons, pushing past him and walking into the store.

"Hell No, Summer...!" He shouted when he noticed the book was full of coupons. "There is no way in hell I am shopping with coupons. We are financially stable. What are you doing? I am pretty sure you did not drag daddy boy to no damn grocery store with coupons, so why would you insult me in this manner."

She stood in the middle of the aisle with her head hung low.

"This was something me and Mimi did together, and I always found it exciting couponing with her. I just wanted us to shop together."

He pushed past her with an angry expression and shouted, "Hurry up, shit!" He then swiftly turned around to face her, asking.

"By the way, where in the hell did all of these coupons come from? When in the heck did you have time to cut all this crap out?"

"When I was in Monroe," she replied, shrugging her shoulders.

Stevin walks off, leaving Summer and her book of coupons. She smiles, following up behind him with her sale paper and coupons in hand.

An hour and a half later, they finally reached the register. Stevin was furious because he was missing the ball game, and they still had a 20-minute drive back home. When the cashier hit the total button informing Summer that her purchase was $308, Stevin immediately tried to swipe his credit card.

"No... wait... Stevin," Summer said. "She must do my coupons."

The cashier mutters under her breath, with irritation, when she notices Summer is holding a handful of coupons, and the cashier line of customers is growing longer and longer. Summer watched as the cashier swiped her coupons; half of her coupons buzzed invalid. Throwing a handful of coupons back to Summer, the cashier says.

"You cannot use these coupons; they don't match the purchased items."

Stevin again attempts to swipe his card. Summer, feeling frustrated, swiftly turns the credit card machine, blocking his card as she slowly picks up the coupons off the conveyor belt, throwing them back at the cashier and requesting that she scan them again.

"Ma'am..." the cashier states, displaying an unpleasant attitude. "I will not rescan these coupons; I have a long line."

Stevin stood with a look of embarrassment as Summer demanded the cashier manually input the coupons. He again attempted to pay when Summer, in an aggressive tone, demands to see a manager. She advises the cashier to shut off her light because she is not moving until she scans her coupons.

"SUMMER..." Stevin shouted.

She glared at him angrily as he walked away and sat on the bench with a look of disgust.

As the manager approached the checkout line, the cashier screamed.

"She is holding up my line and refusing to pay because her coupons are invalid."

The manager speaks to Summer, introducing himself as he shakes her hand.

"Christy, does the customer have the items for which she has coupons for?"

"I do not know Mr. Smith. I tried scanning them after her total, and it said invalid."

Mr. Smith called for another line to be open, directing the growing line of customers to shift to the following line.

The cashier grew more annoyed with Summer as Mr. Smith went through every package grocery bag confirming the items, making the cashier manually input the coupons.

Summer indeed had every item, and all her coupons were valid. Summer had drawn a crowd of onlookers who were determined to see who would win the battle: the cashier or Summer. As the cashier scanned the last coupon, Summer final total was $108.58. She was so satisfied with her victory that she never paid attention to Stevin, who had smoke coming from his ears.

"You can pay now, baby," she said softly.

Stevin quickly jumped up from the bench, swiped his card, snatched the cart, and stormed out of the store. She quietly followed as she was approached by older customers who praised her.

"You showed her, baby! You straightened her out!"

However, her smile quickly turns into a frown when she looks up at Stevin, who stares directly at her with a cold and unpleasant look.

After loading the groceries into the trunk, he snatched the keys from her hands and jumped into the driver's seat without addressing her. Although she felt Stevin was nothing like Christopher, there was still a fear of the unknown lingering in the back of her mind.

As she sat quietly, staring out the window, she tried to devise a plan to win him over before they made it home, as the silence was unbearable, and she most definitely didn't want to bring negative energy into the house that brought her so much peace. She thought back to her trip to the airport when Stevin himself had jeopardized her life and her quick thinking during the car ride home with Christopher.

"Baby," she said as she attempted to rub his leg, and he pushed her hand away.

"Please don't be mad," she says as she takes her seat belt off, attempting to kiss his neck.

"Move Summer," he said, pushing her hand away.

As her wheels start to turn, knowing Stevin has a high sex drive, why not use it to her advantage? She thinks back to Stevin's sexual public display he attempted on the elevators at the casino. At this point, she was willing to try anything to smooth the tension before they arrived home. She starts to unbutton her blouse, removing her bra, attempting to place his hand on her breast.

He shouts, "Summer, what the hell are you doing? Put your clothes back on."

She knew at that moment from the tone of his voice as his voice began to tremble, she had captured his attention.

She was more than determined to have his forgiveness before they arrived home. She places his hand back on her breast when she felt a slight squeeze. She knew she had him just where she wanted him.

Rubbing his crotch, she nibbles on his ears as she kisses her way down to his chest. She whispers in his ear; the moment I feel this car swerve, I stop, she declares as she starts to unzip his pants.

"Summer, move hell before you make us wreck," he said in a low tone as if he was attempting to fight her off with her head mysteriously being pushed down into his crotch.

Summer purposely turns down the music so Stevin can hear her sloppily slurp on his enormous cock. With a loud, sloppy sucking noise, she attempts to tea bag him while he is driving.

Overcome with pleasure, Stevin quickly swerved the car onto the shoulder of the busy freeway.

"Wait, Summer, wait, people can see in the vehicle.

"So what. Let them watch," she said as she adjusts his seat backward.

Stevin was more turned on seeing this slutty side of her as he took control, grabbing her by the head and turning her into a bobblehead; as he tapped dance on her tonsils.

The sexual public display turned him on as she could feel the tight grip of her hair; as he became more and more excited, the more aggressive he became, forcefully pushing his sizeable throbbing cock in her mouth. With two handful of her hair, he was holding her head down in place, forcing her to consume all of him as he roared like a grizzly bear. Finally releasing her from his grip, he sat for a couple of minutes needing to gather himself.

Summer, feeling empowered and less connected to Christopher as she explores more sexual pleasures with Stevin. She had a wave of confidence to wash over her; it wasn't enough to sleep with another man to break the hold Christopher had on her mentally. But in that moment, she allowed another man's seed in her mouth.

"Not as pure and innocent anymore," she thought to herself smiling.

Ironically, the car ride home remains quiet. Summer was still unsure what was going through Stevin's head. Arriving home, he made no attempts to stop her from bringing the grocery bags in.

Stevin has never allowed her to carry anything. Swooping up a handful of grocery bags, she would make two trips to the car before she said, "Forget this; he can get the rest."

Knowing there were only a couple of bags left, she waited for him to enter the home with the last few bags. When he never came in, she peeped out the kitchen window and noted him leaning against the car with his hand propped under his chin as if he were deep in thought. Summer thought to herself, 'Dang, I might have screwed up.'

She didn't know what occurrence to be more concerned about, her old lady behavior with the coupons or her sloppy slutty behavior in the car.

As she noticed Stevin grabbing the last bags from the car, she moved away from the kitchen window. He walked into the house, placed the bags on the kitchen counter, and approached her. She was startled as he swept her up around the waist with one arm, effortlessly lifting her as if she weighed nothing. She laughed and asked.

"What are you doing?" as he carried her into the bedroom.

Stevin never verbally replied, only slapping her on her backside as if he were disciplining her. He threw her onto the bed and forcefully kissed her as he ripped off her clothes, making hot, passionate love to her.

Stevin let out a loud groan as she could feel his throbbing cock pulsating his seed deep into her. He collapsed on top of her and immediately began to snore. Summer laid still underneath him, thinking to herself. 'I guess the game wasn't so important after all.'

Chapter 11: Opening Up Old Wounds

The warmth of Summer's embrace awakened Stevin as she kissed his lips and rubbed her nose against his.

"Good morning, sunshine," he whispered to Summer.

However, Summer quickly placed her hands over his mouth and said. "Don't speak, baby. Someone is in need of some serious mouth care this morning!" She laughed, adding, "I'm so happy that today is Saturday, and you can finally relax. I plan to pamper you the entire day."

"You better," he replied with a smile. "After that shit you pulled at the grocery store earlier this week, you owe me big time," he said jokingly.

"How do I owe you?" she asked. "I was just trying to look out for the both of us. Well, I guess since I'm the only one who benefits from the groceries and the cheap grocery bill, I'll just fix myself breakfast this morning."

"Yeah, right," he laughed. "Daddy doesn't play those games," Stevin teased. He then slapped her on her backside and asked, "Since you mentioned it, don't you think you need to be in the kitchen at this very moment?"

"I'm going, I'm going," she replied. "First, I need you to answer a question that's been bothering me all week."

"Yes, sweetheart, what's on your mind?"

"The other night, after we arrived home, I noticed you standing outside, lost in thought. Would you like to share what was going through your mind?"

"Summer, my thoughts, or just that; my personal thoughts, nosy woman."

"Well, if you're having second thoughts about us, then it is my business."

"Now, what gave you that idea?" Summer.

"Well, Stevin, you were pretty pissed with me the other night."

"Yes, you are right. I was very pissed with you. I am a man first, and I value respect. I feel that you completely disrespected me in that store."

"How Stevin? My intentions were never to disrespect you."

"Well, you have on several occasions, Summer!"

Summer remained silent, staring at the wall.

"So now you are in your feelings when I tell you how I feel?"

In a soft, squeaky voice, she said, "I'm not in my feelings. Is that all that was on your mind?"

"Well, if we are being honest, sometimes I feel like I honestly don't know you."

Summer suddenly sat upright in bed and faced Stevin.

"Now, what in the heck is that supposed to mean, Stevin?"

"I'm not saying it in a bad way, Summer. Hey, know I'm taking a risk just like you. Sometimes, I feel like I have more to lose."

"So, is all this because I took you shopping with me and used coupons? Really, Stevin!"

"No, this has nothing to do with coupons, I swear, Summer. Do I not have the right to fear the unknown?"

"What is the unknown, Stevin? Please tell me. What is the unknown?" Summer asked with a furrowed brow.

"I just don't want to end up like Christopher, running around searching for you in the daylight with a flashlight."

"Wow! So freaking unfair, Stevin," she yelled, rolling her eyes.

"Hey, young lady, watch your tone when you're speaking to me. Anyway, don't take that statement out of context, Summer."

"How else am I supposed to take it?"

"From the first moment you walked into my office, Summer, I was under your spell. I was captivated by your presence."

"Whose fault is that? I never did anything to you or towards you in a sexual manner to warrant such an attraction from you."

"And you are correct; that proves my point. There's something about you, the quietness, the innocence, that drew me in. But on the other hand, you have this wild side about you that I would never expect from you. You are an undercover freak in the sheets."

Summer snatches her arm from under Stevin's head and attempts to exit the bed. Stevin, full of laughter, held onto her, wrapping his legs around her as she struggled to break free. Laughing until he is in tears, he tries to explain that he is not saying it in a negative way.

Tired of struggling, Summer gives in, laying back on the bed with a disheartened expression. Stevin felt terrible realizing his remarks were enough to establish his woeful ignorance about their love life. Instantly trying to rectify his mistakes, he tries to find the correct words to fix the situation, knowing he had put his size thirteen foot in his mouth.

"Summer, I love you for who you are. All I meant to say is that you have a unique way about you that drives a man crazy, and yes, it can be scary at times. Because I honest to God, love everything about you. When I said that you were a 'freak in the sheets,' it wasn't meant to be negative."

"Out of all the things you could have said to me, Stevin, you compare yourself with Christopher, making excuses for his wrongdoing towards me."

"No! Summer, not at all. I was only saying that I can understand why your husband is obsessed with you. You are indeed one of a kind."

Summer pushed Stevin away. "Stop calling that maniac my dang husband. He is nothing to me. He is not my husband."

"Well, you married him, Summer."

"I never married Christopher. I am not his wife," Summer said firmly.

Stevin jumped up, grabbing her by the arm. "Wait a minute, Summer. You never married Christopher?"

"No. Where in the heck did you get that incorrect information?"

"Amber said!" Stevin exclaimed. But before he could finish his statement, Summer stormed out of the bedroom. Happy to hear the news, Stevin fell back onto the bed with joy in his heart. For weeks, he had been wrestling with the thought of not being able to marry her, worrying how he would convince her to file divorce papers. He was so excited about the news he received; it never dawned on him how upset she was.

Stevin headed into the bathroom to freshen up. He knew he had some making up to do as he could hear Summer banging dishes around in the kitchen.

As he entered the kitchen, Summer dropped her head and turned her face away from him, trying to conceal the fact that her feelings were truly hurt, and she had been crying. In her past, showing vulnerability had only led to more abuse.

Summer stood at the stove with her back towards him, he walked up behind her and wrapped his arm around her waist while whispering in her ear.

"I'm sorry, sweetheart." He reaches around her, turning the fire off and removing the skillet from the burner. "Look at me, Summer," he demands.

Turning her around, he felt deep sorrow looking into her eyes as a tear rolled down her face. He picks her up and places her on the countertop to have direct eye contact with her as he gently wipes away the tears from the corner of her eyes. When she starts to speak, he places his finger on her lips, gesturing for her to remain silent.

"First thing, my love, I've been in love with you long before you ever gave me any attention. I have grown to love you more and more with each passing day. Secondly, you are an amazing, strong woman. Yes, it is scary of the unknown. The moment you stop living for yourself and start living for someone else, and their heartbeat becomes your heartbeat, it's scary as fuck."

"The thought of losing you is an insufferable thought, and as far as our sex life, keep surprising me. I love every freaky moment I have had with you. Everything about you turns me on."

"If you really want to know why I was so deep in thought the other night. As mad as I was, my only thought was finishing what you started in the car. I thought to myself, I have indeed hit the jackpot when you walked back into my life."

Stevin leaned in, lingering his lips close to hers, looking deeply into her eyes as he lightly grazed her legs with his fingernails and began rubbing her thighs.

Slowly delivering soft kisses to her neck, he whispers, "Now we know what our first fight feels like in our new home. So, now let's see what makeup sex for the first time feels like."

Lifting her up from the counter, he cuffs his hand under her thighs as he carries her to the bedroom.

"Wait, Stevin, what about breakfast?"

"I have my entire meal in my hands, he says, as he walks to the bedroom, passionately kissing her."

ATLANTA, GEORGIA

The delightful aroma of freshly baked buttermilk biscuits filled the kitchen as Rose took them out of the oven and placed them on the rack to cool.

Kimberley had spent the entire week with Emmanuel, and Rose had been trying to reach her by phone without any luck.

Finally, she received a text from Kimberley saying that she was on her way home. Rose had missed her so much during the week she decided to surprise her with her favorite breakfast. However, she was suddenly startled by the sound of the front door slamming.

She heard the sound of glass shattering as the pictures on her wall fell down due to the force of the door being slammed. She ran into the living room to investigate the crashing noise. Kimberley is standing at the door, face flushed, with swollen eyes, as if she had been crying all night. She was holding an envelope, huffing and puffing, looking like a deranged sociopath.

"You are a fucking liar," she screams as she locks eyes with her mother."

"Kimberley, what is wrong?" Rose asked as she stood in shock.

"You are what's wrong, you. I hate you. Everything about this fake ass life you have built for yourself is a lie. Because of you... you... you... mother," she screams as she charges towards Rose, slapping her across the face with the large manila envelope, causing all the content in the envelope to scatter across the floor.

The first noticeable picture that caught Rose's eye was a picture of her parents. Rose slid to the floor as Kimberely stood over her, screaming insults at her.

"Because of you, my grandmother is dead, and I will never get to know her because you chose to gap your legs open at the age of thirteen and have a baby. Yes, Mother dearest, I know about your secret child, Summer. You ruined my life for an orphan brat you gave up. I dare you!" she yelled.

"I hate you; as of today, I have no mother. Just the mere fact that you were seventeen when you met Dad and screwed him shows how much of a whore you are. That explains why Dad does whatever you ask of him; you were his patient, and he could go to jail for statutory rape."

"You started sleeping with him as a minor," she screamed as she stormed upstairs to pack her bags, destroying the home as she ran through it like a tornado.

As Kimberely dramatically stormed out of the house with her belongings, slamming the door. Rose sat on the floor in disbelief.

The sudden gust of wind caused the papers to scatter and float in the air, landing at Rose's feet. As she picked up the scattered papers, she came across a photo that had landed upside down.

Rose flipped the photo over, she was surprised when she discovered it was a picture of her beloved daughter, Summer, when she was twenty-two years of age. There wasn't a question in her mind about who the young lady was. Summer had her dad's eyes.

Rose frantically started gathering all the papers. However, she couldn't find any additional information about Summer. She races over to the envelope, emptying out the rest of the content.

Picture after picture, document after document, all pertaining to Summer Taylor and not Teller.

Overwhelmed with emotions and unable to take in any more information, Rose bawled up on the floor, holding Summer's picture press tightly to her chest as she wept in sorrow and joy.

Chapter 12: The Truth Is Out

Summer started her day early by running errands. Stevin insisted that she go grocery shopping for some specific ingredients he needed for dinner. He had invited his boss and his spouse over for dinner tonight, and they would host the dinner at their home.

Summer wasn't thrilled about the idea of hosting a dinner; she wasn't even allowed to cook for, only shop for as Stevin demanded.

In her feelings, she wondered whether Stevin liked her cooking or not. Despite her feelings, she decided to suck it up and be a team player.

Two hours into the shopping trip, Stevin has called and detoured her twice with items he left off the list. Finally, on her way home, her phone is buzzing; it's Stevin requesting she turn around and pick up some celery.

"Stevin, I need to get ready for tonight. It will be your fault when I smell like onions and look unkempt around your boss."

"Relax, Summer. You have plenty of time to get dressed. Just text me when you are almost home."

Feeling very annoyed with him, Summer complied with Stevin's request and returned to the store. She wasn't willing to ruin his night to impress his boss.

Refusing to call when she was minutes away, afraid he would have more errands for her to do, she headed straight home.

Pulling into the driveway, she texted Stevin, requesting that he comes out to assist with the grocery bags. However, she has yet to receive a reply from him.

Frustrated, she huffed and puffed as she started to unload the car of the grocery bags. Placing the bags at the front door, she attempted to unlock the deadbolt, but she was stopped by the door guard that Stevin had latched.

She became angered and suspicious about his motives as she beat on the door when she couldn't get him to answer the phone. She attempted to walk around the side of the home to enter the house through the garage when Stevin opened the front door smiling.

"It's not funny, Stevin. Who's in here?" she shouted.

He burst into laughter at her adorable jealous rage.

"Awe... come here, sweetie," he said as he attempted to appease her.

"No, dang it, move; I am annoyed," she said, trying to push past him.

"Wait, honey, I have a surprise for you."

"Stevin, I'm not in the mood for your games; I'm tired."

"Now, dammit, Summer, I have been working on this all day; stand and wait right here until I come back," he pleaded. Summer's side-eyeing, Stevin gave in to his commands.

Snatching the grocery bags from the front door, he left her standing at the door as she could hear the clicking of the deadbolt and the door latch snapping into place.

Stevin then returned to the front door holding a blindfold, stepping on the outside, requesting she allow him to blindfold her. Though she was very irritated with him, she complied.

As she entered the home, several pleasant aromas hit her nostrils: fresh flowers, candles, and a savory smell. Stevin kissed her lips as he untied the blindfold.

“Surprise,” he shouts when she opens her eyes.

Beautiful, mixed, colorful bouquets of flowers were noted throughout the home. An excellent gourmet dinner for two was set up at the dining table, along with a beautiful birthday cake.

"You didn't think I would miss your birthday, did you?" She smiles as she gives him a big kiss and hug. Stevin feeling disappointed that he didn’t get the reaction he had played out in his head all day.

"Okay, Summer, what's wrong? Why the long face?"

"Nothing is wrong, baby; I'm very appreciative of all you have done.”

"Well, hell, you could have fooled me with your reaction.”

"I guess it's just new to me; I have never celebrated my birthday."

"Never...?" he asked in surprise.

"My mother, well, Mimi, was a Jehovah's Witness; it was certain holidays we didn't celebrate, and my birthday was one of them."

"Well, we promised each other new beginnings, which also means new traditions."

Summer looks up at Stevin with a half-smile as she is startled by the loud popping sound from the bottle of champagne he opened to celebrate her day. Pouring her a glass of champagne, he pulls out a chair at the table, gesturing for her to sit.

"What can I do to make this day memorable?" He asked.

"Pull up a chair and sit next to me so I can feed you," she replied.

"No, Summer, this is your day."

"I know, and this is what I want."

"Well, how about we feed each other?" Stevin said as he obliged her request. She stood, taking a seat in his lap, and she became extremely flirty as she sucked the food from his fingers.

"It's time to blow out your candles and make a wish. I have plans for the whipped icing in the bedroom later."

"Why do I have to blow out the candles?"

"So you can make a wish."

"I have my wish, and it's you," she said sweetly.

"Awe... how sweet, but we both know that's not true. If that were the case, why the long face?" He asked with a hint of concern.

"Stevin, to be honest, I really never cared to celebrate this day because, truth be told, I don't know if it's actually the day I was born on."

"Okay, enough of this, Summer, you have all the answers in that envelope. Stop torching yourself and find out who you really are." Stevin stands up and attempts to pull the envelope from the closet when Summer jumps on his back, begging him not to open the envelope.

Turning around, picking her up, he placed her on the sofa and commanded her not to move.

"Stevin, please don't, please!"

"I'm looking for my own sanity. I want tell you anything you don't want to know."

Summer pleaded with him not to invade her privacy. She knew once he opened Pandora's box, there was no turning back. She sat on the sofa, trembling with nervousness.

"Stevin, I don't want to know."

"I know, Summer, I want force this information on you."

He tore open the large envelope, and she dropped her head, overcome with anxiety.

"Okay, that's enough, Stevin. I will just throw the envelope in the trash."

In a stern voice, he replied, "Go into the bedroom if you're too nervous to watch, but I will get to the bottom of some of your answers today." Stevin pulled out some of the documents, making sure to leave all the photos in the envelope so she wouldn't be able to see them.

"Summer, can I tell you two things about yourself, and I won't force anything else on you?"

"No, Stevin, please don't."

"Baby, I swear, this is only pertaining to you and would clear up two things. You truly need to know. Take a deep breath, and trust that I have your best interest at heart. First thing first. Your date of birth is incorrect. Yes, you were born in October 1990, but your birthday was three days ago, not today." Summer looked up at Stevin with teary, gloomy eyes. Finally, she knew something truthful about herself, but it was a bittersweet moment knowing she had only scratched the surface of the truth.

"Summer, I know it's a lot to take in, but there's something you really need to know."

She dropped her head, bracing herself for more information. When Stevin stood up and walked towards her, Summer began to scream.

"No... Stevin! Don't bring that envelope anywhere near me!"

However, he dropped the papers on the end table, embraced her with a hug, and comforted her as she wept in his arms. Stevin attempted eye contact as he slightly lifted her chin, but Summer only buried her face into his side, refusing to make eye contact.

"Summer, stop trying to face this alone; you have me. What's wrong with me reaching out to your mom, explaining your situation, and setting up a secret meeting if that's what you and she would like to do?"

"Stevin, you don't get it; Christopher is dangerous. Do you understand this man took life from me? I told him I was pregnant, and he walked up to me, kissed me on the lips, and punched me in the stomach. I laid on the cold bathroom floor and bled until I picked myself up and drove myself to the hospital. Oh, guess what, I left. I packed up and went back home. He had me spied on for weeks until he decided to kick down the door and hold a seventy-one-year-old man at gunpoint. I was dragged away from the only home I have ever known, with Mr. Jeffrey being held against his will, while I was taken down the street to a deserted dirt road where he raped and beat me half to death. When will you get it? It's too dangerous."

Stevin pushed Summer slightly to the side as he leaned up, placing his head in his hands. He attempted to press his thumbs against his tear ducts as his eyes swelled with tears. Summer, noticing how upset he became, and tried to soothe him. He jumped up from the sofa, pulling his suitcase out of the hall closet.

"What are you doing, Stevin? Where are you going?'

"I am going to kill that son of a bitch."

Summer grabs hold of Stevin's arms' pleading for him to stop as he unintentionally drags her behind him as she wrestles with him, attempting to keep him out of the gun safe.

"Stevin, please, if you truly love me, please stop and talk to me." She wrapped herself around his waist, refusing to let go.

"Summer, he is a pussy; he knew he didn't deserve you, he used fear to keep you."

"Please hold me, baby," she begged. "If you act on your emotions, you will be doing the one thing you promised you would never do, and that's leave me."

Wrapping his arms around her, he just held her, trying to focus on their future and bury the anger of beating life out of Christopher. As they sat in silence, Summer, in her goofy way, looked up at Stevin and asked.

"So I can assume there isn't a dinner for your boss?"

Stevin burst into laughter. "Are you really asking me that, Summer?" he asked, shaking his head.

"Come on, baby, light my candles so I can blow them out and make a birthday wish. This was your idea, so come on, Stevin, she said, tugging his arm and pulling him towards the dining table.

"Okay, Summer, so this means you have to follow all my traditions."

"Okay, Stevin, anything to get you in a better mood."

As he lit the candles, he picked up the cake and instructed her to stand as he held the cake in his hand.

"Why do I need to stand?"

"Ma'am, did you not just agree to follow my instructions?"

"Yes, sir," she replied. "I did; I am ready to blow out my candles now."

As Summer blew out the candles on her birthday cake, she secretly made a wish. "I just want to be happy and bless with a baby," she wished, taking a deep breath and smiling. However, her joy was short-lived, as she was startled when Stevin smashed the cake in her face.

"What did you do that for?" she asked, confused.

Stevin laughing uncontrollably. "You said you agree to my tradition; cake smashing is one of my traditions." Summer stood frozen and speechless, with her face covered in cake icing. Stevin walked over to her, laughing. 'Come here,' he says as he licks the icing off her face. Summer is still frozen in place, arm stretched wide like a scarecrow. Stevin still unable to control his laughter as he walked her to the kitchen sink to help her clean up.

"It's all in my hair!" she cried out.

"I will wash your hair, Summer," he said, still giggling behind her back. He assisted her in removing the icing from her hair. As she turned to face him, he gently patted her face and hair dry.

"On another note, I will need to inform you of something else, Summer, as it's not a subject we need to put off."

"No, Stevin, let's not."

"No, Summer, really. I just learned why you were unable to find any information about yourself and your adoption. As you know, you were taken from your mother because she was underage. When your grandparents signed the papers, it was done as a closed adoption, meaning your mother lost all rights to you, and your file was sealed. When your documents was signed, the information, such as your date of birth and your last name, was incorrect."

Summer's eyes bucked as she was waiting for Stevin to clarify. "Summer, your last name is Teller, not Taylor. Your dad's name was James Ray Teller. Either someone really screwed up, or this was intentionally done."

Summer was overcome with sadness. "Why would they force us apart? Why was I not enough that my grandparents just threw me away, Stevin?"

As Summer cried hysterically in Stevin's arms, he started second-guessing, looking at the documents. His heart was overwhelmed with sadness seeing her so emotionally devastated. Stevin decided to keep the information to himself that Summer had a younger sister.

Chapter 13: His True Love

ATLANTA GEORGIA

David sat at his desk in his home office, sipping a glass of Hennessey and Coke while staring out the window. Rubbing the glass back and forth across his forehead, he is astounded by Kimberley's behavior. Images of Rose lying on the floor with blood on her face from the action of Kimberley haunted his thoughts.

"How could she: why would she disrespect her mother in that manner?"

David arrived to find Rose on the floor, her home destroyed by Kimberley. She had invited him over to enjoy breakfast with them. Rose was unaware that Kimberley had other motives, and the reason she denied them access to her all week was due to anger from the information Emmanuel provided her with. Kimberley hurried to her father's house after confronting Rose, although she refused to speak with him.

Unable to bring himself to look at her, David spent most of the day locked up in his office. Emmanuel had ghosted Kimberley, providing her with a missile to drop on her parents, and it appears he has vanished out of town, cutting off all communication without any explanation.

Kimberley was heartbroken from the information she had received about her mom's past and even more devastated about Emmanuel's sudden disappearance without a word. She only went to her father's home because she had nowhere else to go.

Resting her head in Sarah's lap as she wept, she couldn't care less about Rose's feelings or state of mind. Her crocodile tears were due to her aching heart for Emmanuel. She expected to storm out of Rose's home with her belongings, and Emmanuel would be waiting with open arms. Only to arrive back at his home with his car gone and her calls being forwarded straight to voicemail.

It was as if Kimberley had never received the information that she had a sibling. Getting to know Summer was the furthest thing from her mind. She had no interest in finding or meeting Summer, who she blamed for ruining the life she imagined she could have had with Rose's parents.

David entered the family room and found Sarah cradling Kimberley. The influence of alcohol has taken presence over his emotions, and protecting his sweet baby girl's feelings was out the door. He staggers into the room, his eyes bloodshot and sweat pouring from his forehead. He was even more angered to find Sarah comforting Kimberley, who showed no remorse for her actions. Stumbling over his words, "Kimberley Michelle White," he said, "I'm so upset with you to the point that I cannot process my own emotions."

"But... Dad!" Kimberley protested.

"Don't you but Dad me, remove yourself off that sofa and call and apologize to your mother, Now!"

"No, Dad, I want do it," Kimberley said, defying her father.

Snatching his belt from his waist, Kimberley sat straight up in fear. She had never seen this kind of anger from her father.

"Now, dammit, David! You will not lay one hand on this child," Sarah proclaimed. "You and Rose have some explaining to do, and I will be damned if you make this child feel as if she has done something wrong in searching for the truth."

"Sarah, you stay out of this, you know nothing on the matter. I didn't raise my daughter to disrespect her parents, and I will be damn if she starts now. You physically harmed your mother. Who have you become? What is this young man doing to your mind?"

"Dad, I dare you to fault Emmanuel for you and mother's lies if it wasn't..." Unable to finish her statement, David rushes to the sofa, snatching her up by her shoulders as he shakes her, demanding she never mention Emmanuel's name again in his presence.

“I never want to hear that young man's name in this house again. He is to blame for all of this.”

"No, Dad, your whore of an ex-wife is to blame for all of this.”

David slowly watched his hand fly up, slapping Kimberley across her lips. Sarah gasped as she looked at him in astonishment. Kimberley slowly eased back onto the sofa next to Sarah. Both were horrified by David's reaction. This was the man who never told her no and always stood up for her through all her wrongdoings. She had nowhere else to go; her father bankrolled her entire livelihood. She most definitely wasn't about to bite off the hand that fed her and disrespect him.

"I dare you, young lady, to sit under my roof and disrespect your mother or me," he yelled. Sarah, getting increasingly furious, sat in silence.

"How would you handle your mother's situation?" he asked. If my mother had made the decision to snatch you away from me after raising you on my own for three years. Then, placing you up for adoption and sealing the records where I would be entirely shut out of your life. All done while I was hospitalized in a deep state of unconsciousness after watching your mother being murdered. ‘Oh, how about this young lady?’ Place yourself in Roses's shoes, Miss Kimberley. You are thirteen and think you know what love is, and let your boyfriend talk you into having sex and getting pregnant on your first time. Not only do you believe your life is over, but you hide your pregnancy until you are almost seven months.”

“And when your parents find out, we set an appointment to have life ripped from you, despite your boyfriend's willingness to step up and do what's right, even begging me for a job that I could very well have provided through my company. It's too much for you to bear to even think about someone murdering this life you have nurtured inside of you that you feel moving inside of you. So you run off and attempt to raise the baby on your own. Trying to ease the burden off your parents when it was truly their reputation that was at stake.”

"Living from house to house, sometimes on the streets with an infant. Until one day, someone decides to murder your child's father and leave your baby next to her lifeless father, sitting in his pool of blood. And when that sight is too much for your young mind to process and, you break. The two people who should have your back the most come to the hospital while you are sedated, look their own grandchild in the face, and use their influence to move heaven and earth to make your child disappear."

"Little girl, you have no clue. Your mom spent a year in the hospital fighting with those images attacking her mind. Hearing her lost baby girl's cries played in her head over and over until it broke her mentally. So you would be correct; I met your mom when she was seventeen, a week before her 18th birthday. I was twenty-three, completing my first year of residency."

"I helped your mother through one of the roughest moments in her life. Not one visit or call from her parents. When she was finally able to cope with the outside world, she returned to her hometown and did a news interview telling her story, attempting to find Summer, and her own parents disowned her. Nowhere to turn, my mom: your grandmother took her in. It was then, when she was eighteen and started healing, I fell in love with her. Our love was innocent and genuine. Not some sick, disgusting molestation you attempt to make it."

David stops talking as he can see Sarah's face turn from sadness to anger. In that moment, it was as if he was confessing his love for Rose as he describes their love in the present and not past tense.

Sarah jumps up from the sofa running into the bedroom, crying as she attempts to pack her bags to leave their home. He runs behind her, realizing he has finally let the truth part from his lips. He was indeed still in love with Rose; these past events only awakened everything he had attempted to bury.

Kimberley, confused and full of sorrow, sits in her own emotions as tears roll down her face. Realizing she didn't have all the information, she felt ill from how she treated her mother after hearing what Rose had been through.

Hearing Sarah and her dad fighting and knowing all this commotion is because she couldn't leave well enough alone and respect her mom's wishes. She called Emmanuel several times, only to be forwarded to his voicemail.

Doors slam as Sarah accuses David of being in love with Rose, questioning why he even went to the house that morning when he told her he was at work.

Not thinking clearly, letting the alcohol cloud his judgment, he declares his emotional support for Rose, stating she needs me as if he was still treating her as a patient. Sarah storms out of the room, attempting to leave, as David is begging her to stay, offering to get a hotel room for the night.

Kimberley and Sarah sat on the sofa, comforting each other as David stood over them with his suitcase, apologizing. Sarah turns her head in anger, refusing to address him. Dropping his head, knowing his family is falling apart, he exits the home feeling broken and confused.

***

A loud knock at the front door awakens Rose. As she hastily tied her robe, she opened the door to David, who stood with a disheartened expression. She opened her arms to embrace him; it was clear he and Sarah had been arguing; she wondered if it was over her.

Guiding him through the house by the hand, she locks up and leads him upstairs to the bedroom that they once shared. Rose knew he just needed to be comforted; it wasn't sexual, but mentally. David had given up a lot for her, and as she cradled him in her bosom, she just wanted him to find some peace. She feared for her family's ability to cope with this tragedy, vowing to move heaven and earth to find Summer. Despite Kimberley's outburst, she forgave her, knowing that she was still unaware of all the pain and secrets that had been kept and hidden. It was time to confront some old wounds, and she knew she needed to be strong enough to face the possible outcomes.

Chapter 14: Check Yourself

The days felt longer and longer for Stevin. His new position kept him in the office longer, and having only one vehicle did not help. He had an hour's commute to and from work, leaving Summer without transportation, having to use a ride share, or running errands after 6 p.m. He wasn't too keen on her out so late alone. He felt obligated to run errands with her, as he felt she wasn't safe out so late without his protection.

Before moving to Atlanta, Stevin sat with Summer, developing some financial strategies to stretch her money. After much procrastination, she finally agreed to invest the majority of the funds Mr. Diamond provided her with.

She was finally seeing a return on her investments and being able to contribute to the household. This made her feel equal in the relationship and not so much as a kept woman.

Stevin finally made it home after a long day at work and being stuck in rush hour traffic. He plopped down on the sofa next to Summer, feeling drained.

Without a proper greeting or a kiss, he said, "Summer, it's time for you to purchase a vehicle."

"Stevin, you know that's not possible," she replied with a confused expression. "I can't put a car in my name because I don't have a license under my alias."

"Summer, you are getting a car! I can't keep running like this."

As soon as the words left her mouth, her tone turned nasty, and she smarted off. "I haven't asked you to do that. You still choose to run like this."

The room went silent, and Stevin sat up on the couch, dropping his head into his hands as if he were lost in his thoughts.

He felt unappreciated, and her tone alone was disrespectful. She could sense he was disturbed by her statement and attempted to rectify the situation, quickly correcting her tone.

"I'm just saying, baby. I can't purchase a car in my name. The vehicle will be in your name, so pick out whatever you want. I'll pay for the car, Stevin. I am fine driving whatever."

"How this conversation has become about money and you not trusting me to have your car in my name is beyond me, Summer."

"Stevin, that's not at all the problem."

"Is my understanding incorrect? Is that not what you just said? Okay, so let me find out if I can make a cash purchase in my name and if we could have the title and bill of sale notarized without filing the paperwork. Along with a notarized statement documenting that the car belongs to you," he said as he walked away, heading into the bedroom.

Summer enters the bedroom and finds him lying across the bed on his stomach. Straddling herself on top of him, kissing the back of his neck, he demanded she move off of him. He rolls over, attempting to walk away, but she grabs his hand and pulls him back onto the bed. "Stevin, please don't go," she begs. He lays back down on the bed and stares at the ceiling, avoiding eye contact with her.

"I'm sorry, Stevin, my lack of enthusiasm has nothing to do with you. When your life has been taken from you, and you are not capable of doing the simple things in life, such as buying a car. It takes a toll on me. I have no issues with the car being in your name. I trust you with my life, and I hoped that you would know that by now."

He reached up, pulled her closer, and ran his fingers through her hair while she rested her head on his chest.

"Tell me, sweetheart, what type of car do you want?"

She whispered, "I would like a Kia." She sat in silence, waiting for his reaction to her choice of vehicle.

"Alright, my love, go online and start looking for what you like, such as style, interior color, and so on," he said. Feeling a bit confused when she suddenly jumped up in excitement, giving him small pecks on his lips as she thanked him for being the man of her dreams.

Stevin was unaware that Mimi had gifted her her first car. The Kia she arrived in town in. Only to be beaten by

Christopher and forced to give the car away. He asked what she liked and listened attentively for her response. Her needs mattered.

Needless to say, Stevin didn't get a wink of sleep. Summer was so excited that she immediately started searching for a car online, not realizing she had never asked herself or had the opportunity to say this is what I want.

Although the first car from Mimi will always be priceless in her eyes, she can now finally purchase the car of her choice with her own money. 'Well, Mr. Diamond's money,' she thought as she chuckled. "Heck, I did put in enough false imprisonment hours at the hand of his demon seed; hell, I earned every cent of Mr. Diamond's payoff."

Besides, Stevin's investments had flipped her original investment, and she felt empowered knowing her money was making profits. She, indeed, would purchase another Kia, jumping for joy when she lucked up and found a Kia Stinger, custom design to her liking.

"PUSHED OVER THE EDGE"

Stevin, exhausted headed home after a long day's work, called Summer in the hope of getting some TLC when he arrived home. He pleaded with her over the phone to give him some much-needed attention as he hinted at what he desired.

"Hello, sweetie," he said as she answered the phone. "I'm exhausted, and all I want is to shower, cuddle up with you, and have you rub me to sleep."

"What exactly am I rubbing, sir?" she jokingly asks.

"I just need to feel your touch. I don't care what you rub. This day has been long and stressful, and I just need you."

"Okay, baby," Summer responded, "But I need to pick up some items from the store."

"Don't say 'okay baby' and then add a ...but... You can order whatever you need online and have it delivered. Besides, your car will be ready for pickup at the end of the week. It's nothing that we cannot wait for." He ended the call feeling frustrated because he didn't feel heard by her.

Stevin dragged himself into the house, utterly exhausted from his day, hoping for a warm embrace and dinner in bed. Summer came flying around the corner, fully dressed, disregarding their entire conversation.

"Baby, don't be mad at me," she said as she pried the keys from his hand.

"What are you doing, Summer? Where are you going?" he asked in a frustrated tone.

"Stevin, I forgot to order your protein powder, and we're completely out of eggs. You have to have breakfast in the morning; you don't have time to stop."

"Summer, I'll do without tomorrow morning; please go turn on the shower for me."

"No, you need your shakes in the morning," she replied as she walked out the door, ignoring his request.

Stevin stood in the kitchen speechless with his mouth open. He felt disrespected as the man of the house, and it seemed as if she didn't care about his emotional well-being.

Stevin dragged himself to the shower, angry with each passing second that she had not returned home. He sat at the dining table alone before retiring to bed.

Three hours later, Summer returned and did exactly what she wanted, running errands she had been waiting to complete all day, disregarding Stevin's plea for her attention. Tip-toeing into the bedroom, she slid under the sheets to snuggle under him, attempting to spoon, but he rejected her and turned to face the opposite direction. Nevertheless, she closed her eyes and fell asleep.

The security alarm awakened her, as Stevin forgot to disarm it before exiting the door and heading to work. No morning kiss, no goodbye; assuming he didn't want to awaken her, she rolled over, falling back to sleep.

Stevin glanced up, responding to the tap on his office door as his boss poked his head in. "Hey, Stevin, I need you to pick up Jerimiah's accounts this week, as he'll be out of the office for the rest of the week."

Stevin reluctantly agreed to take on the extra workload, not realizing Jerimiah had three face-to-face meetings scheduled for the day. He had planned on leaving early because he and Summer were expected to pick up her new car today. However, digging himself into more of a hole, he pushes his assignments on the back burner to prioritize his coworker meetings in order to have enough time to pick Summer's car up.

Feeling frustrated, Summer has been trying to get in touch with Stevin all day but has yet to receive a callback. She's excited about picking up her new car and has made multiple calls demanding a callback.

Finally racing out of the office, he returned her call and rushed to make the commute to pick her up.

"Hello, sweetheart. I'm so sorry, my day has been long and busy."

"Stevin, what the heck? I've been calling you all day."

"I know, Summer," I'm about to call to see if we can pick up the vehicle tomorrow.

"No, Stevin. I've been excited all day. Please don't take that away from me."

He agrees to hightail across town to pick her up. Summer awaited his arrival as she stood in the driveway, very annoyed at his late arrival. As he pulls into the driveway, his boss calls, requesting an update on Jeremiah's cases.

Exiting the vehicle, Stevin gestured for Summer to drive. She deliberately jumped into the passenger seat. He pulls his briefcase from the backseat, attempting to walk to the passenger side, when he notices she has refused his request. As he walked back to the driver's side, he placed a call to his assistant requesting she email him some information that was needed.

Summer sat in the passenger seat, huffing with a sour facial expression. As he ended his business call, she couldn't control her emotions.

"Stevin, why would you take on more assignments? You're already drowning in your workload alone," Summer said with concern.

"I know, Summer. It's not like I had a choice."

"This was supposed to be an exciting day, but your attention is all over the place," Summer pouted.

"It still is an exciting day, Summer. Me working shouldn't take away your joy," Stevin reassured her.

"Well, it does if you're not mentally present to share the moment. And get off the phone," Summer demanded in a loud tone.

"Okay, sweetie. Let me just send this last email to my boss," Stevin replied, attempting to text and drive. Suddenly, he hit the curb, and Summer shouted, "Stevin! You're going to kill us. Put your phone away!"

Summer's head jerked as Stevin swerved the car, coming to an abrupt halt.

"Who the hell are you talking to?" he shouted. "I am a man first, so you better check yourself before we have an issue," he said aggressively, leaning towards her. "Do we have a problem," he asked. She fumbled her words, surprised at his tone.

"I was just saying I didn't want you to wreck," she stammered.

"No! You were being disrespectful as always," he retorted.

"I wasn't trying to disrespect you," she said in a low tone, her voice squeaking, and her armpits starting to sting and sweat from the nervousness.

"I am a man, not a little boy toy. You will respect me. You need to show me some respect. Clearly, this relationship isn't for me, and I might just need to move on. No woman who claims to love me could be so disrespectful. Now, do you have a problem? Better yet, let me rephrase that. Do we have a problem?"

Summer, fighting back tears, shakes her head no, as she avoids speaking as her throat tightens.

"No, Summer. I need you to open your damn mouth and answer me. I asked do you have a problem?"

"No, Stevin, I do not. I'm not trying to be disrespectful towards you," she responded softly.

Putting the car into drive, Stevin looks at Summer as if her presence annoys him. Stevin knew immediately she was timid. He knew her little tics when she was nervous or scared. He was too angry to care.

She was biting the inside of her cheeks, trying to stop her lips from trembling with nervousness. He could see that she was visibly upset. Her lips trembled as her body jerked from anxiety. He noticed her turning her face as if she were looking out the window, patting tears from the corners of her eyes.

Her racing thoughts consumed her. The fear of the unknown made her ill, causing her palms to sweat. The car ride felt long and intense, and to add to her discomfort, Stevin didn't look at her and never uttered another word.

She felt lost and had no clear directions when they pulled into the dealership. Stevin threw the car in park and walked into the dealership without addressing her. Too afraid to move, she remained seated in the car.

"Hello, I'm Mr. Bash, and I'm here to pick up my vehicle," he said to the sales representative.

"Okay, Mr. Bash, I just need your signature on a couple of forms. Do you have someone to drive the vehicle, or are we delivering it?"

“No, my wife is right behind me. Let me call her to see what's taking her so long to come in.” Stevin called Summer's cell phone several times without an answer.

Summer notices Stevin and the sales representative exiting the dealership. As Stevin approached the car, walking quickly with an unpleasant look, he snatched open her door.

"So you're just going to be an ass, huh?"

"What did I do?" Summer asked. "I didn't know if you wanted me to come in or not. You didn't say anything."

"Answer your damn phone, Summer. I have called three times."

Summer started digging around in her purse, realizing she unintentionally left the phone on the charger at home. Stevin was furious and slammed the passenger door shut before storming away from the car.

He returned to the driver's side, throwing the car keys in the driver seat through the cracked window. Summer sat silently with her head down, without any clear direction as to which car she would be driving.

She still felt excitement as she saw her beautiful new car pulling up, knowing that she had custom-designed it. She noticed Stevin sitting in the driver's side of her new car, not knowing if he was about to test drive the vehicle around the block or driving it home. She sat and waited for him to give her directions. He drove off without saying a word when she suddenly noticed the brake lights as he started to back up.

He jumped out of the car with an unsettling look, charging back to the car at a fast pace.

Without any hesitation, Summer jumped out of the car and walked towards the car's rear, her voice shaking.

"I don't know what we're doing, Stevin. I assume you were test-driving the car."

"Come on, Summer." Stevin snapped. "Use your head. I need to drive your car home and ensure it's operating properly." He walked off and returned to the car, driving off before she could get in the driver's seat.

Summer programmed their home address in the GPS and decided to drive home slowly, hoping Stevin would have had the opportunity to calm down.

The ride home was gut-wrenching; her emotions had overtaken her as thoughts ran through her mind: would she be thrown out of the only house that had been a safe haven for her since leaving Mimi's home?

He had arrived home twenty minutes before her. As she drove into the driveway, he stood in the garage shirtless, holding a glass of brandy. He walked towards the car, sipping on his alcoholic beverage. He instructed her to park the car in the driveway as he was cleaning out the garage so he could make room for both vehicles. She got out of the car feeling uncertain, so nervous about her and Stevin's fight that she never stopped to look at her new car. He instructed her to enter the home through the garage because the front door was locked.

"Is this a trick?" she thought, as she could hear him walking behind her. She decided to stop at the deep freezer and pretended to grab a pack of frozen meat as she watched him from the corner of her eye.

He continued working in the garage, rearranging boxes. She walked into the house and sat cross-legged on the sofa, picking at her nails. It was very unsettling not knowing what was going through his mind. Less than an hour ago, he had questioned whether she was the woman for him.

She was startled when he walked into the living room and headed to the bar to refill his glass of brandy. Without making eye contact, she leaps from the sofa and heads to the kitchen to prepare dinner. He enters the kitchen, informing her he isn't hungry.

"I don't have much of an appetite. I don't want dinner. When I get hungry, I will fix myself a sandwich."

Summer placed the cube steak in the fridge and pulled out the condiments and vegetables to prepare him a nice sandwich.

"I just told you I wasn't hungry, Summer."

"I know you're not hungry, but I will prepare your sandwich for you," Summer replied as she sliced the tomatoes.

"No, Summer. I don't want my bread cold or soggy," he said as she continued to prepare the sandwich. "What did I just say," Stevin said, frustrated.

"I heard you, Stevin. I'm just slicing you some vegetables."

"Dammit, Summer! Do you not listen? I don't want shit from you!" Stevin shouted, slamming the glass of brandy on the counter and shattering the glass into pieces.

Summer threw both of her hands up in the air and backed away from the counter. He realized he had gone too far and reached out for her as she backed away with a look of terror in her eyes.

"Say, Summer, come here," he said, reaching for her as she pulled away. Cutting himself on the broken glass, he is unable to hold on to the grip of her arm when she snatches away from him.

Unable to attend to her bruised ego, he cleans up the shattered glass instead of addressing her. She quickly heads to the shower, trying to wash away the brandy that had splashed all over her. She attempts to wash her pain down the drain, backing up under the water and closing her eyes as she replays the last few months in her head.

"Where did I go wrong?" she thought as images of an exhausted Stevin flashed through her mind.

His workload had increased, and she had done nothing to lighten his load. He had been pleading for emotional support, and she knew she had been lacking. So it wasn't a surprise that he finally exploded; she had been taking him for granted while he had bent over backwards to accommodate all her needs. This blow-up was entirely her fault, and she had to own it. She needed to rectify it because, clearly, she missed the mark.

'Is love not meant for me,' she thought. She couldn't understand why she always ended up heartbroken. She had never imagined that Stevin could respond so hostilely towards her. All she knew was their relationship could very well have ended in the car.

Stevin entered the bathroom and leaned against the vanity, watching her as she stood under the shower with her eyes closed, holding herself and looking like a lost puppy. He had been fighting back his emotions, trying to drown out the inner voice that tugged so hard at his heart when it came to her.

Too stressed and angered in the moment to see how much he had hurt her earlier. He stood there, watching her. Stevin's heart melted as guilt consumed him. Looking at her breathing, he could tell that she was crying by the way her shoulders shook as she breathed while he watched her through the transparent glass shower door. As he gathered his thoughts, he watched the woman he was head over heels in love with upset, knowing very well that her emotional state had everything to do with the tone he had taken with her today. Knowing he would be just a shell of himself if he lost her.

Stevin knew he needed to be emotionally present with her during today's events, especially because she was thrilled about picking up her new car. She had expressed in detail what today meant and why. Summer had kept him awake all night with her indecisiveness about every decision related to the vehicle. Now, playing the day back in his mind, she never had the opportunity to enjoy the moment. Due to their disagreement earlier, she never even got to look at her car once.

She stood in the shower contemplating getting out, not wanting to exit the bathroom and face him until she could contain her emotions. She opened her eyes and turned to face the shower.

Summer was startled when she noticed him watching her as she showered. She gathered herself, stepping under the water, and washing the tears from her face, she reached to turn off the shower faucet. He stood facing her through the glass shower door when she noticed him placing the glass of brandy on the vanity and unzipping his pants as they dropped to his ankles. He advanced toward the shower.

As she assumes that he is ready to shower after a grueling day, she tries to step out of the shower to let him enter. However, as she opened the glass door to exit, Stevin stepped in front of her, blocking her way. It was clear from his body gesture he wanted her to remain in the shower.

Looking up in his eyes, she was quickly reminded of his masculinity as his energy was unmatched. His presence overtook her as he pushed her back under the shower head with his masculine chest as he stared deep into her eyes. Reaching around her and turning the shower faucet on, she jumps as the water hits her bare back.

Running his hand through her hair, he massages her scalp under the water as if he is attempting to wash today's events from her mind. He leans in and softly kisses her, gently pressing his lips to hers. Lifting her up under her arms' he brings her eye level with him, desiring for her to wrap her legs around his waist. When she didn't comply with his desires, he eased her down. With a quick scoop, he lifts her, cradling his hands under her thighs. She wrapped her legs around his waist and her arms around his neck.

The room is silent, hearing only the pitter-patter of the water as it runs down their body as they stare deep into each other eyes as if they are lost for words. She can feel his hands spreading her cheeks apart as he is trying to guide his large manhood in her with no hands. Breathing a sigh of relief, she relaxes her forehead against his as she welcomes every inch of his arousal.

"Can you forgive me," he pleaded as he drove deeper and deeper inside of her.

Unwilling to scream her forgiveness to him out of pleasure, she didn't answer, just moaning with each hard thrust. Besides, it wasn't her forgiveness he needed; it was his she so desired. With a tearful, wholehearted apology, "I'm sorry, Stevin. Please forgive me," she cried out as she confessed her love for him.

This only turns him on more, knowing her apology was genuine as she cries out her faults in neglect for him. Squeezing his broad masculine shoulders, she slightly bites them, enjoying every stroke. Her willingness to confess her faults and declare her love set all his senses on fire. All was forgiven.

Summer knew this was different as this wasn't manipulated sex or a sick game of mind control. But a partner who truly understood his wrongs and overreaction in a situation she created.

She felt heard and valued. Determined to take care of him in return, she made a vow to cater to all his needs and be there for him no matter what.

Her heart skipped a beat out of fear for the first time in their relationship. She always knew in the back of her mind that she could trust Stevin, and that he would never bring harm to her. However, today's event forced her into another reality, one she never wanted to occur again.

Summer felt like she had lost him, and this was a feeling she never wanted to experience again. Closing her eyes as he made passionate love to her, she slightly prayed that he could channel her love for him and her desire never to lose him.

Chapter 15: Let Me Cater To You

Summer felt like she was tiptoeing on eggshells around Stevin as his attitude hadn't improved. Afraid to rock the boat, she tried to avoid him on his long-hour workdays. Instead of reducing his workload, he kept adding more to it, causing him to be stretched too thin. He was determined to level up and take on a manager position in the new company; this would allow him to work outside the office and travel more. But at what cost?

Still feeling like she was missing the mark, Summer avoided him instead of embracing him. She couldn't help but wonder, 'What more does he want from me,' she thought. "I cook and clean; I'm home all day alone. What can I do to make this better?"

Determined to have a successful relationship, she headed to the store to purchase some items for movie night. She thought she would have Po boy sandwiches and finger food set up in the family room, and they would snuggle and watch a movie together.

Summer set the food up and ordered a movie she knew he would enjoy. Watching the clock, counting down the minutes until he would arrive home, all she desired was a big kiss and his masculine chest to rest her head on.

Stevin entered the home two hours past his usual time. She had fallen asleep as she waited for his arrival. She was awakened to the sound of his car keys falling to the floor as he entered the home, loaded down with his briefcase and papers. She attempted to embrace him with a kiss.

"Excuse me, baby," he said, turning his head and denying her. "I stopped and picked up a hamburger with extra onions. I need to go brush my teeth."

"Baby, I ordered us a movie, and I fixed some finger food we could eat while we snuggled and watched the movie."

"Summer, not tonight. I just want to turn in. I'm headed to the shower."

Feeling disappointed, she wrapped the food up and prepared for bed. The movie didn't happen; at least she could snuggle and fall asleep in his arms.

As she tidied up, she could hear Stevin exiting the bathroom. Stepping into the bedroom, she undresses, not bothering to put on a nightgown. She crawled into bed on his side, wearing only her panties, as she lay in his arms, embracing him with a hug as she kissed his chest.

"Goodnight, sweetheart," he said as he leaned in given her a peck on her lips. Gently sliding his arm from under her, he then rolled over and turned his back to her.

Feeling confused, she laid in silence in the dark before deciding to return to the sofa and watching the movie she had ordered. Lost deep in her thoughts, as the movie played, she couldn't help but feel as if she were losing him. She tried to rationalize in her head that he was only tired, and it was the job, and this didn't mean he was falling out of love with her.

As always, her past thoughts of feeling not wanted, afraid, and being alone started creeping in. Curling up on the sofa, she silently cried herself to sleep.

His voice later awakened her. "Hey, baby, what are you doing? Come to bed," Stevin said.

She popped her head up, rubbed her eyes, and looked around. Stevin grabbed her by the hand and asked why she had left him in bed alone. He motioned for her to come along and held her hand as they walked back into the bedroom.

They returned to bed, and Stevin pulled her in close to him, kissing her shoulders. He used his body language to reassure her that her presence was missed. That was all the confirmation she needed. She was determined to make him feel wanted and special.

***

Stevin hits the alarm clock, causing it to fall off the bedside table as he tries to hit the snooze button. He drags himself out of bed and makes his way to the bathroom to freshen up.

Jumping out of bed, Summer pulls a suit from the closet, laying it across the bed alone with a tie and pair of socks. She places his shoes at the bedside as she enters the kitchen to prepare him a cup of coffee. She returns to the bedroom, as he is already dressed in the clothing she picked out for him. Downing the cup of coffee, he enters the kitchen, admiring that she has a hot breakfast sandwich wrapped to go, along with his briefcase with his papers that she had organized for him.

She was excited about this morning; Stevin actually left out the door with a smile. Standing in the kitchen sipping hot tea, Summer was suddenly startled by the door opening. Stevin walked back through the garage door and embraced her with a hug. He lifted her off her feet and declared his love for her. Summer was more determined to have those types of embraces every morning.

Throughout the day, she sent "I love you" texts and emojis to him but didn't receive a reply. She called his office several times, only to be told he was in back-to-back meetings. He returned her call as he left his office and headed home. He spoke in a low, raspy voice as if he was drained and informed her he was headed home.

Standing at the door as he walks in, she takes his briefcase and places it on the counter as she leads him to the bathroom. He could smell the powerful, brisk scent of fresh cedar from the cedar and jojoba aromatherapy oil that awaited him as she had drawn him a bath.

Without speaking one word, they allowed their eyes to communicate as she stared deep into his exhausted hazel-brown eyes.

Unbuttoning his shirt, one button at a time, he stood patiently as she undressed him until he was bare. Directing him to the tub, she knelt beside him and massaged his legs and feet. Placing her feet in the water, she positions herself behind him, sitting on the edge of the tub.

She rubbed her hands in his soft, curly hair as she massaged his scalp until she felt his head drop as he had fallen asleep.

Summer helped him out of the tub and dried every inch of his body as he stood willingly, enjoying her pampering him. She tenderly applied moisturizer to his entire body. She instructed him to turn in, and she would serve him dinner in bed.

Stevin followed every command as he welcomed her, being more attentive to his needs. She returns to the bedside with his dinner prepared on the bedside tray; it was very noticeable that he was fighting his sleep, as his eyes screamed exhaustion.

With a gentle foot rub, she watched him slowly drift off as he could not muster up enough energy to finish dinner. What was very noticeable as she quietly snuggled under him was that he was restful. As she lay next to him, she realized that every relationship has to be approached differently.

Stevin desired to be pampered and appreciated. Words alone wouldn't be enough; he needed actions.

What a small gesture for a man who saved her from herself at a time when self-destruction was all she knew.

Vowing always to be his shoulder to lean on, she fell asleep planning for tomorrow; her goals were to keep him happy and constantly feeling appreciated.

Chapter 16: Reality Check

ATLANTA GEORGIA

Sarah is lying in bed, snuggling with David's pillow, feeling dismayed about the state of her relationship with him. She wonders how she got here, as being with David had made her the happiest she had ever been. David was the kind of man every woman dreams of. Sarah knew that Kimberley was part of the package. However, she didn't think he had packed all his emotions for Rose in his suitcase and brought them alone for the ride.

Burying her head in the pillow, Sarah decided she wasn't ready to give up on her relationship. Besides, Rose had her chance for true love when she was married to David. So, if she didn't seize her opportunity, it was no one's fault but hers.

Sarah decided it was time to establish some boundaries, and therefore, she needed to pay Rose a visit.

Sarah's stomach was twisted up in knots. She hadn't spoken to David and was unsure if he had checked into a hotel or gone to Roses.

The thought of his truck parked in Rose driveway made her anxious. She would be uncertain about what to do next. She breathed a sigh of relief when she pulled into Rose's driveway, and David's truck wasn't there. With an aggressive knock, she waited for Rose to answer.

As the door swung open, she could tell from the expression on Rose's face that she was the last person Rose expected to see standing at her door.

"Hello, Rose," Sarah said. "We need to talk."

"Hello Sarah, come in."

Although Sarah had been dating David for five years, she had never been to the home he had shared with Rose. As soon as she entered the house, she was taken aback; it felt like she had stepped into a shrine of David. The living room was filled with David's awards, trophies from his childhood, and several framed childhood photos. Even David's golf clubs were still in the corner of the kitchen as if he still lived there.

Overwhelmed with emotions, Sarah couldn't help but blurt out her thoughts. "Are you sleeping with my husband?" she blurted out abruptly.

With a slight pause, Rose hesitated for a moment before answering. She silently mumbled to herself, "Husband, my ass." Rose had always felt Sarah was interested in David since the moment she started working at the hospital years before their separation. Rose didn't feel she owed Sarah any explanation, as she didn't have David's last name yet. However, she felt that David deserved her gratitude as he had saved her life.

Finally, Rose replied to Sarah, "No, Sarah. David and I haven't been intimate since we separated. Furthermore, he has never disrespected you guys' relationship in regards to me."

"Well, I need you to cut him loose. What's noticeably clear is that your definition of disrespect can't be found in Webster's. This obligation he feels he needs to have when it comes to you is beyond me, but it ends today."

"Look, Sarah, whatever David wants is fine with me. If our friendship causes any strive in your relationship, I'll take a backseat so he can be happy." Before Sarah could respond, her cell phone rang, and it was David.

"Hello, David, let me call you back; I'm having a conversation with Kimberley's mother."

"You're having a conversation with who...?" David asked. "Where are you?"

"I'm here at Rose's home, and I will call you when I leave, Sarah said as she abruptly hung up."

Fixing her gaze back on Rose, Sarah winced before blurting out. "It's pretty hard to believe you're not still in love with my husband when your home still has his pictures from wall to wall. This is not healthy. Are you secretly wishing that he were still here? Is this why it looks as if he still lives here?"

"Sarah, as I've already said, there's nothing to tell, and this home still screams my family because it is my family and will forever be my family. This is David's home always; when and if I ever decide to remarry, I'll move out and start again. The house will eventually be passed down to Kimberley."

"Rose, that sounds ludicrous; you're saying that all of David's belongings, such as his photos and golf clubs, are still strategically placed around your home because it's a family home, and it has nothing to do with you being madly in love with him?"

"Sarah, I'm being very respectful, and now I'm asking you to leave my home. I have been truthful with you, but my responses aren't sufficient enough for you. It would be best if you talked to David instead."

Suddenly, the room falls silent as they both hear the sound of keys jingling. David has entered the home using his key to unlock the front door. Sarah was visibly surprised by what she was seeing and couldn't control her emotions. Her jaw dropped, and her eyebrows shot up in surprise. She asked David, "Why do you have a key to her house? Better yet, why are you here?"

David replied, "I was in this area when you informed me you were here. Why are you here, Sarah?"

"This is why I am here. What the hell is going on between you guys? This ends today."

Rose throws her hands up, trying to deflect the situation. "Look, this is between you guys. Let yourselves out; I have food on the stove."

But Sarah was determined to get to the bottom of things. "No, Rose, you don't get to stir the pot and hide your hands. This is a conversation between the three of us. You and David need to make me understand this hold you have on each other."

David attempts to downplay the situation, but Sarah isn't having it. She yelled out, "Dammit, David, you are about to lose me. Put our family first; you, me, and Kimberley are now living together. We should be your focus. I need you to cut all ties with Rose, as she's causing a lot of problems between us.

While standing in silence, Rose's only concern was David's happiness. Punching his fiancé in the eye wouldn't end well for his relationship.

"Rose is a part of my family and always will be," David said, frustrated that Sarah could think she could replace Rose as Kimberley's mom.

"Kimberley has a mother who can never be replaced. Sarah, you are very aware of the situation. I dare you to disrespect Rose in her own home."

Tears swelled in Sarah's eyes. She felt like Rose's feelings took priority before hers. "No, David, this is not okay. If you can't cut ties with her, our engagement ends Now!"

"David, take your fiancé home," Rose said. "You guys need to work this out among yourselves. I have stated one too many times we are not romantically involved."

"No, Rose, you might not be romantically involved, but you are damn sure mentally and emotionally involved. And that ends here and now!"

"Rose is my best friend, and I will prioritize my marriage over our friendship," David said. "But If you want our relationship to work, you have to trust me as your partner. However, abandoning Rose is not an option, as she has no other family."

Sarah's lips pursed as she clenched her fist. "I wont be home when you get there..." she shouted as she exited Rose's home.

"David, go after her," Rose pleads. "Don't allow her to leave like this."

"I can't, Rose," David replied when Rose demanded he stop her.

"And why not, David?"

"She's right. I'm in love with you," he proclaimed as he stood before her, and they stared deep into each other's eyes.

***

"Sarah, what's going on? Where is Dad, and why are you packing everything up?" Kimberley asked in confusion.

Too angry to shed a tear, Sarah stormed through the house, going from room to room, snatching photos off the wall, and pulling clothes from the hangers.

"Kimberley, out of respect for you, please let me be at the moment. I have too much anger in my heart for your parents to confide in you," she said before locking herself in the bathroom.

Kimberley lost for words, leaned against the bathroom door. She could hear Sarah sobbing uncontrollably. She didn't know what had transpired between Sarah and her parents. Feeling helpless, knowing there wasn't anything she could do to console her. Hearing the sound of keys rattling as David entered the home, Kimberley rushed downstairs with teary eyes and demanded answers.

"Dad, what is going on? Why is Sarah packing to leave?"

"Baby girl, you let me handle Sarah. I need you to go and correct things with your mom."

"Dad... I can't ... How can I face her after what I did to her?"

"Kimberley, your mom is more upset with herself for not being honest with you. She is hurting and needs you by her side. Yes, I'm still highly disappointed with your actions, but with that being said, your mother needs you more than ever. I also need some alone time with Sarah, so I'm asking you to give us some privacy."

Kimberley hesitated before speaking, "But... Dad!"

"Don't 'but dad' me Kimberley, I have enough on my plate. Please do as I am asking of you."

Unable to face her mom after being so disrespectful, she sat on her bed, contemplating getting a hotel room. She couldn't bring herself to face Rose. She didn't feel she deserved forgiveness.

Lost in thought, she was interrupted by her cell phone ringing. None other than the man who ghosted her, Emmanuel, has finally decided to reach out to her. She hesitated before answering in a soft, shaky tone.

"Hello?"

"Hello, baby!"

Kimberley, struggling to contain her emotions, remained silent.

"Kimberley?"

"Yes, Emmanuel, what exactly do we have to talk about?" Kimberley asked, her voice still shaky.

"I'm sorry, Kimmie," he said. "I had to disconnect. You were using me as a crutch. I felt the only way to push you in the right direction and mend things with your mom was to remove myself from the equation."

"So, let me get this straight. My partner, who should be by my side and supporting me, navigating through these emotionally challenging times, thought it would be best to deliver me some life-changing news that turned my world upside down. The one and only person I felt I could lean on decided to cut off all communication with me, causing me more pain. You are not blameless in this situation."

"Baby, I apologize for hurting you. That was never my intention. I couldn't be the barrier between you and your parents. If I had not removed myself, you would have planted yourself on my sofa, bawling your eyes out while continuing to ignore your parents' calls."

"So, Emmanuel, you purposely coached me into going and confronting my mom, knowing you were going to leave me?"

"No, baby. I purposely encouraged you to confront your mother so that the lies and hurt could be dealt with. My intention was only to help you start the healing process with your parents, not with me." Kimberley held the phone as the line went silent. "Baby, I understand if you need me to give you some space, but I only intended to help you, not hurt you."

She quickly responded, "No! I just need you. Please tell me you are back in Georgia?"

Emmanuel hesitated for a moment before answering, "Uh, uh," he said.

"Emmanuel, I need you. I really hurt my mom without learning all the facts. I'm currently living with my dad, but he just asked me to leave. He is demanding me to mend things with my mom."

"I agree with your dad. You must mend those fences with your mother and help her search for your sister."

"Wait a minute! What gave you the impression I wanted to meet her? That is not my desire."

"Kimmie, we will cross that bridge when it's time. Let's focus on getting you and your mother on the same page. You just admitted to me you feel you did wrong by her, and you know you need to apologize. So, let's start there."

"Please wait a minute, Emmanuel, you haven't answered my question. Are you back in town?"

"Yes, Kimmie, I am. But I have back-to-back meetings for the next two days. However, I will plan something special for you to make up for my absence only after you go and fix things with your mother."

"So my ticket to you is through my mom? Why are you so invested in my relationship with my parents anyway?"

In a furious tone, Emmanuel responds. "What do you mean?"

"Are you seriously asking me that? Are you questioning my intentions? And, by the way, are you a woman or a little girl? Why would I build a future with a woman who can't be woman enough to fix an issue with the one person she claims to love the most?"

Instantly feeling afraid that she could lose him, he had never taken that tone with her. She quickly became a yes woman and fell in line.

"No, baby, that's not at all what I meant. I am actually walking out of my dad's home now. I have every intention of making things right with my mom.

Now, I feel like I have pushed you away. Please tell me that's not the case."

"I need you to correct this issue with your mom, and we will take the next step in helping your mother and you heal by finding your sister. I love you and will check back in with you," Emmanuel said.

As Kimberley swiped the end button to end the call, she curled up in bed weeping. 'What just happened,' she thought to herself. 'Emmanuel had never taken a tone like this with me.' Not wanting to lose him, she pulled herself together and packed her bags to go mend things with Rose.

She was ready and willing to fix her issues with her parents, but he had another thing coming if he thought she gave two fucks about meeting Summer.

SAVING MY FAMILY

Rose sat on her back porch, taking everything in. In one breath, she loses Kimberley, and in another, she is just handed information she has been searching for half her life.

Despite everything, Rose couldn't help but chuckle softly as she thought back to the moment she had seen Summer's beautiful face for the first time since she was three years old. She reminisced on all of the good times that she shared with James and Summer before the fatal tragic night, which changed everything and still haunts her to this day.

Rose made sure to copy the photos of Summer, ensuring she would always have a photo of her sweet baby girl.

Then, on the other hand, David has just confessed his love for her. Deep down, she was jumping for joy; truth be told, she couldn't care less about Sarah's feelings. Not feeling any responsibility for the demise of their relationship, she secretly blamed Sarah for the demise of hers.

However, Rose feels a responsibility to be a great role model for Kimberley; she couldn't just jump headfirst back into a relationship with David. Not wanting to get her hopes up and still wanting to make David work for her attention, she had to play it cool.

Besides, David was the one who walked away from the marriage, not her. For the last six years, she has had to watch another woman live her life.

Hearing the alarm charm indicating the front door had been opened and closed, Rose called out, "David, is that you?"

"No, Mom, it's me," Kimberley said. Rose stood up, unsure of Kimberley's emotional state. She waited before embracing her.

Standing facing her mother, Kimberley wailed out an apology, "Mom, I am so sorry," she welp repeatedly.

Rose simply embraced her, holding her tight, reassuring her that an apology was not needed. "I don't need an apology. I only care that you are here and that you know that I love you."

Curling up on the porch swing with her mom. No words were needed, as Kimberley found comfort with her head lying in her mother's lap while Rose played with her hair. At that moment, they didn't need words to communicate their love and support for each other.

Chapter 17: Mending Fences

ATLANTA GEORGIA

Rose was an emotional wreck. She avoided discussing Summer in Kimberley's presence, fearing it would harm their relationship. She spent the majority of her day online searching for Summer Taylor. She had a starting point for her search since she knew Summer's last place of employment. However, Rose knew she would have to address this with Kimberley sooner rather than later, especially since she was planning a trip to Illinois.

David had disappeared, and his weekly visit had come to a complete halt without any explanation. Too afraid to learn the reasons why, Rose assumed he had chosen to work on his relationship with Sarah, so she decided to stay clear of him.

Kimberley has been the ideal daughter, helping Rose with cleaning, cooking, and singing her praises. Deep down, she knew that her actions towards her mother could be forgiven but never forgotten.

Emmanuel had returned, showering her with gifts and attention. She just wanted to live in the present moment and avoid any conversation related to her maternal grandparents and half-sister.

"Kimberley, have you spoken to your father?" Rose asked, hoping to gain information about David and Sarah's current relationship status.

"Yes, just briefly, Mom, he's having a tough time with the separation."

"What...?" Rose quickly replied. "Did he and Sarah separate?"

"Yes, they did," Kimberley confirmed. "I think it's really taking a toll on him. What happened between you guys?"

"I can't answer that, Kimberley. I'm still confused myself, Rose replied, while asking herself why David had chosen to stay away if Sarah was out of the picture.

"Kimberley, you should go and spend time with your father. I'm concerned because he hasn't been reaching out. That's not like him," Rose said, turning her back towards Kimberley, attempting to hide the sadness in her eyes.

Rose quickly turned to face Kimberley as her cell phone rang. Kimberley was sitting at the kitchen table eating a bowl of cereal and answered on speaker.

"Hello, baby girl," David said.

"Old man, come visit this lady before she has a heart attack. ...Ouch, Mom..." she screams as Rose smacks her with the wet dish towel.

"What's wrong, baby girl?"

"Mom is abusing me because I snitched on her. She's been pacing all week. Every time my phone rings, she's hovering over me, eavesdropping to see if it's you."

Rose buried her face in her hands, shoulders slumped, as she blushed with embarrassment.

"Tell my angel I'll be by later today."

"Hold on... Hold on... Your angel? I knew you were over here being slutty."

"Kimberley Michele White, watch your mouth," he said as he cleared the line.

She looked up at Rose, giving her a side-eye. "You little floozy," she says as she bursts into laughter. Rose was left speechless; her jaw dropped. She couldn't defend herself, and a huge grin appeared on her face.

"Honestly, Kimberley, your father and I are not involved," Rose declared.

Kimberley left the kitchen while singing, "Looks like somebody's stuck in the middle of a three-way love affair," as she stared at Rose with judging eyes.

Rose's eyes shone with excitement as if they were fireworks on the 4th of July. Finally, all the pieces of the missing puzzle were strategically being placed back in order, and it was time to complete the entire puzzle.

She dashed up the stairs and frantically threw clothes throughout the closet, searching for the perfect sundress to bedazzle David in. She hadn't gone shopping in years and wanted him to find her attractive.

Worried she might not have enough time to go to the store, she eased into Kimberley's room. She picked up a dress that was spread out on the bed and asked Kimberley if she was going on a date.

"Yes, mother, I am. Your future son-in-law wants to wine and dine me out on the town."

Rose stood at the foot of the bed, dangling a pair of Kimberley's heels from her finger, and asked, "How do you walk in these?"

"Easy; want you try a pair on, Mom."

"I don't have anything to wear with heels," Rose said. "I've never worn a pair of heels in my life."

"Never, Mom?" Kimberley asked, surprised.

"I just never had the opportunity to enjoy my teenage years and early twenties."

"Awe... Mom, that makes me sad. Let me give you a makeover. Please, Mom, let me do this for you, please!"

"I don't have anything to be made over in."

"No, Mom, seriously, I got the perfect maxi dress for you. Emmanuel purchased it for me, but it's a little too big. It will fit you perfectly. Try it on, please, mom, please!"

Rose hid her eagerness, knowing this was what she hoped for, so it did not take much persuading. Rose prances back in forward in the mirror, modeling the dress as it snugs her body perfectly.

"Mom!" Kimberley said with excitement. "You look beautiful, 'hot momma.' Okay!.. I got it from my mother, Kimberley said as she stood in the mirror next to Rose, comparing their looks. "Now, let me do your hair and makeup for you."

"I'm okay with the hair. I don't want my face done at all," Rose retorted.

"Sit in the chair, woman! You have entered Kimmie's beauty spa."

"Who is Kimmie?"

"My love name, darling," Kimberley replied with a smirk.

Rolling her eyes, Rose couldn't focus on anything but her makeover. The more makeup Kimberley applied, the more Rose started to second guess, putting Kimberley in charge of her makeover. After much fighting and wiping, Rose was finally satisfied with her look.

"Mom, it's time for you to step out of the house and enjoy your new look. Now, skedaddle, I must beautify myself and prepare for my date."

"I am, young lady. I'm headed to the back porch as we speak."

"That's not a back porch dress, lady!" Kimberley yell's as Rose exits her room.

Hearing David's truck door slam, Kimberley was eager for him to see Rose. She ran downstairs and flung open the front door. "Well, hello there, sir, how do you do?" she greeted him as he stepped inside the house.

"Hello darling, you look lovely. Where are you headed?"

"Mom and I have a double date. I'm introducing her to Emmanuel's business partner father. She is so excited that she even went out and purchased a new dress. Kimberley said with a smile. Fighting back, bursting out into laughter as all the blood seemed to have drained from David's face.

"Kimberley, where is your mother?" he asked sternly. "Oh, Mother!" she shouted as they walked through the dining room and headed to the back deck. David was instantly taken aback when Rose entered the home.

"Wow, you look beautiful," David said. "Can I talk to you?"

"Now, Dad, we don't have time today. You might need to come back tomorrow," Kimberley interjected. Rose looked bemused; she was unaware of the seed that Kimberley had just planted in David's head.

He pulls on Rose's hand. "Why are you doing this? Why now?"

"What am I doing, David?" Rose asked, still looking confused.

He was trying not to be led by his emotions, feeling as if his heart had sunk into his stomach. "I thought I made myself clear with our last conversation. Why are you doing this to me after I gave up my home for you?"

Rose, still looking confused, as Kimberley burst out, "I knew it!"

"Not now, Kimberley," he said.

"What is going on," Rose shouted.

Kimberley falls to the ground in laughter as she shouts, "GOTCHA!"

"This old lady not going on no date. Don't nobody want her but you. That should teach you both; I would think by now you guys should know keeping secrets from me only hurts our family."

"Kimberley, none of this was planned or thought out. Your mother doesn't even know what's in my heart. This is why I'm here, calling for a family meeting."

As everyone took a seat at the dining table, David took hold of both Kimberley's and Rose's hands. "Kimberley, it's vitally important for you to understand I have never cheated on Sarah with your mother or anyone else. Your mother did not ask me nor played any part in my decision to end my engagement with Sarah. However, recent events have opened my eyes and heart, and I realized that I could never fully love anyone because I could never detach from your mother. That is not fair to Sarah or me."

"Okay, this is when I exit left, Dad. I love Sarah, I do, but I'm team family, so with that being said, I pass no judgment either way."

"I will say," she says as she backs away from the table, clearing her path to run. "I think all those repressed feelings came flooding back when you were over here bathing her lady liberty, and I think you might have had a slip of the finger," Kimberley says as she runs upstairs.

"David, I told you she has your father's personality and his smutty choice of humor."

"I know, Rose. It's scary how much she acts and sounds like him. Now, let's shift our attention to ourselves." Rose falls silent and looks into David's eyes. "Talk to me, honey. Share your thoughts," he urges her.

"This isn't my conversation to lead; I didn't walk away from our marriage; you did," she responds.

"Rose, I walked away because you were living and breathing for Kimberley and me. I needed you to love yourself more."

Rose asked, "Why was it so wrong?"

"I can't be your everything. You must find happiness beyond me, Rose. You cannot live only for me and baby girl. Hell, she has nine toes out the door, then what? You need friends and a social life that doesn't involve us. I want to help you find Summer, but while we search for her, I also need you to find yourself."

David leaned in and gave her a soft, gentle kiss on the lips, but their brief moment of romance was abruptly interrupted by Kimberley marching down the stairs.

"Okay, old people, enough of the elderly porn; I'm out of here," she declared before turning to her parents.

"You know what, this is the perfect opportunity," she said, grabbing her phone and calling Emmanuel. "Baby, I'm here with my parents. This is the perfect time for you to meet them. How about you pick me up here instead of meeting me at the restaurant?"

David and Rose's expressions immediately fell flat at the mention of Emmanuel. Neither was enthusiastic about meeting him.

Kimberley's smile quickly morphed into a frown as her face tensed and contorted. "Okay, Emmanuel," she muttered in a low tone. She dropped her head as she ended the call. It was clear Emmanuel's reaction was negative.

Rose squeezed David's leg under the table, unable to bring herself to hurt Kimberley's feelings even more. David attempted to be delicate with his responses.

"Dad doesn't like this, baby girl."

"No, Dad, it's not what you think. He's upset with me for putting him on the spot. He just informed me that he had been working on getting his parents to Atlanta and setting up dinner for the six of us. He's annoyed that I'm making it look as if he doesn't want to meet you guys when it's the opposite. He wants his parents involved in our first meet and greet."

Rose's face was riddled with concern as Kimberley kneeled before her.

"Mom, please, I see it all over your face. It is fine; I promise you it's okay," Kimberley said as she stood up and left the house.

David hugged Rose, and they both agreed that there was something about Emmanuel that screamed danger, and their mission was to save their daughter from any possible heartbreak.

Chapter 18: Friends or Foes

On the surface, Summer's life couldn't be more perfect. Finally, it seemed that everything was falling into place in her life, and she and Stevin couldn't be happier. All the long hours and stressful workdays had paid off for Stevin. He received that promotion, although he was required to complete a certain number of hours at the office weekly. He could work his desired hours and make his own schedule.

Summer found herself always seeking out projects around the home to occupy her time. Anything that consumed her day, or she could give her undivided attention to, she did just that. The excessive stock of unnecessary food items in the kitchen pantry resulted from her extreme couponing hobby. Refusing to let herself be idle, she kept a journal of weekly tasks she commanded of herself, making sure to stay busy. She spent her entire upbringing keeping busy to avoid her reality, so burying her true feelings was all too familiar for her. So when the gardener wasn't able to show up due to illness, it was an added activity she could occupy her time with. So she cranked the lawnmower up and put her green thumb to work.

It was a hot, sultry day, but Summer didn't mind; she was use to gardening and doing yard work with Mimi. However, cutting the grass wasn't fulfilling enough. No, the shrubs needed to be outlined with more colorful flowers, and with a quick run to the local plant nursery, she could have the best-looking yard on the block. Three hours later, and a $1200 charge to Stevin's debit card, she was off to improve her garden.

While getting dressed for her adventure in the garden, she realizes she didn't purchase appropriate gardening attire. Dressed in Stevin's oversized button-down shirt, a pair of shorts that did not leave much to the imagination, along with her Koopa big-size gardening straw hat, it was time to garden.

Meanwhile, Stevin decides to surprise her with lunch and flowers after a short day at the office. Zone out to syncopated rhythms of his jazz music as he taps his fingers on the steering wheel; he was quickly taken aback, lowering his Ray-Ban shades in shock as he pulled into the driveway.

The first obvious issue was Summer, bent over in the yard with her cheeks hanging out, along with several holes she had dug up in the front yard. Before he could exit his vehicle, the stares from the neighbors caught his attention. Summer, in her own world, hard at work listening to music with her earbuds in, she never heard Stevin pulling into the driveway. She was startled, almost jumping out of her skin from the stinging she felt on her right butt cheek. Stevin open-handedly smacked her on her backside. Snatching out her earbuds, she quickly stood and faced him with a surprised look.

"Don't you think you need to put all that up?" Stevin asked.

"What Stevin?" Summer replied, clueless as to why he stared at her with annoyance.

"Summer, all your ass is hanging out those damn shorts. And what the hell are you doing?"

"Juan is sick and couldn't do the yard, so I decided to cut it," she said innocently.

"Summer, go inside". Stevin requested.

"Why, Stevin?"

"Go now, Summer," he demanded.

Summer looked around as she headed inside, noticing that several neighbors had gathered outside. She figured she had done something wrong, being she had never seen any of her neighbors hanging outside their homes.

Stepping into the laundry room, she quickly slid on a pair of joggers while waiting for Stevin to enter the house. When he never entered the house behind her, she walked into the kitchen and peeped out the window.

There was Stevin shirtless in his work pants, carrying the tray of flowers. He never bothered to come inside the house to change. Pulling a pair of tennis shoes from the garage, he immediately went to work.

Summer decided to prepare a pitcher of Mimi's old-fashioned lemonade and join him in the front yard.

As she approached him with the tray of beverages, he glanced up at her but never uttered a word. He continued working, not hiding his discontent with her. It was very evident that he was displeased with her. In an attempt to gain favor with him, she took a piece of ice from the glass and walked up behind him, kissing his back as she rubbed the ice across his bare chest.

Stevin interrupted her. "Move, Summer, I am sweaty."

"That's what I call good sweat, sweetie," she said as she turned his face towards hers and kissed him on the lips.

"Okay, Summer, please move and let me clean up this mess you made."

"I didn't make a mess," Summer replied in a high-pitched tone. "I know exactly where everything goes. Let me show you."

"You better not move your lil ass from that chair. What type of man do you take me for?"

"Oh my, sir, I will be a good girl and sit myself right here. Would you like a glass of lemonade, mister," she says as she mocks him.

"Yeah, woman, bring daddy something to drink and sit your little self back in that chair."

"Well, I must admit I have a pleasant view from here. But I'm just wondering if you can take a break, if you know what I mean," Summer said playfully, winking at him. "I'm going to need you to cover yourself up, mister. We have too many wondering eyes on the block staring today."

"No, darling, they are staring because I'm pretty sure you needed to get HOA approval before digging up the shrubs. And I'm pretty sure 'Mrs. Parker,' those little, short shorts, added to the stares."

"What is HOA? And who is Mrs. Parker?" Summer asked.

Stevin burst into laughter. "Homeowners Association, Summer. Baby Juan is the neighborhood gardener for a reason. Do you see anyone else outside digging up their plants because he is ill?"

"Stevin, I enjoy doing this. Mimi and I always garden together. Now, move over, and let me show you my vision."

"Well, I'm pretty sure Miss. Mimi taught you about the proper gardening attire, and those daisy dukes don't seem very appropriate, so I doubt she would approve."

"It's hot, Stevin, and I didn't have any gardening trousers. My legs break out in hives when I sweat. I forgot to purchase some breathable garden trousers.

Their brief disagreement was interrupted by their neighbor from next door. "Excuse me, good people," their neighbor said.

Stevin greeted the neighbor and asked him how he was doing. The neighbor quickly replied. "I'm going to need both of you guys to cut it out before you start a war in my household. Any second now, my wife will be looking for me to start digging and replanting flowers, and I don't need any additional stress and conflict," the neighbor said in laughter.

Stevin laughed and jokingly blamed Summer for the situation. "Just blame this little woman right here. This was forced on me."

"Hey now, I'm sitting right here," Summer said.

"It's great I have you both here at the same time. I know our wives have been chatting on and off in passing, but I wanted to officially invite you guys to our BBQ next weekend," the neighbor said.

"Yes, that's right. Your wife did mention this to me yesterday at the grocery store. Stevin, it slipped my mind, and I just remembered that I had to ask you."

"Sounds like fun," Stevin replied. "What can we bring?"

"Any side dish would be fine."

Stevin looked up at Summer with concern as the neighbor entered his home. "Are you okay with socializing in a secluded setting?"

"Yes, baby," she said. "I think it will be fun. Besides, his wife seems friendly and down to earth." On a side note, Summer added, "Stand back and look at what we accomplish; you can't tell me the yard doesn't look nice.

"Yes, Summer, it does. I just hope you are ready to pay the gardener."

"Now, why would I pay Juan for the work we did?"

"Oh no, honey, you are paying this gardener, and I'm not looking for monetary value for my service."

"Ha Ha Ha, I think I'm turning in early," Summer said as she let out a big yarn.

"Like hell you are," Stevin said, chasing her into the house.

TIME TO PARTY

"Summer, the man said to bring a side dish, not to prepare a feast for the entire party. How many side dishes have you prepared?"

"I know, Stevin, but I have overstocked the pantry, and I really need to get rid of some of this food."

"Why get rid of what you have, Summer, when you will only cut a million more coupons and replace it the next day?"

"Let me be, sir, I have cooking to do."

"We are not taking all of this food to the BBQ," Stevin said as he started to pull back the foil from the prepared dishes. "A couple of these dishes I'm personally keeping for myself."

"Please start taking some of the food over while I get dressed, and stop eating out of the food!" she shouted.

"Sure, let me load the car up," he says.

"Stop it, Stevin, with the madness. You're just going right next door. Have Carl stand by the fence and pass everything over. I'm headed to get dressed."

Summer can hear the men laughing and joking about the feast she had prepared through the bedroom window.

She gets dressed and is ready to socialize with a group of adults, something she hasn't done since leaving Illinois.

As she took a deep breath and stepped out of her front door to walk next door, she realized that Stevin was nowhere in sight. He had been thrilled to have someone to smoke cigars and drink cognac with, that he had apparently forgotten all about her.

Her hands were sweating, and she felt very anxious as she walked into the neighbor's backyard, unsure of what to expect from the evening.

Stevin noticed her nervous expression and embraced her with a hug, apologizing for not accompanying her over. He quickly returned to the men's table once she was seated and feeling more comfortable. There were only three couples attending, so the pressure had eased.

Jessica introduced her to her friends and thanked her profusely for all the side dishes she had prepared. However, looking over at the men's table, she soon realizes she probably did not prepare enough. Her food dishes were almost gone, being her food was the only dish that the men were attacking.

"Paige: Carl will be at your dinner table nightly. If you have yet to notice, he has been fixing several to-go plates as if he doesn't live here.

Jessica turns and yells over at the men's table. "Carl, stop eating all the food from our guests, and why are you fixing to-go plates as if you don't live here?" Carl, caught off guard, jumped and looked like a child caught with his hand in the cookie jar, responding with a mouth full of meatballs.

"Baby, I'm claiming our to-go plates now because Stevin has already eyed what he is taking back home with him as if he doesn't eat like this daily." Carl turned to Stevin and whispered, "Jessica will burn a pot of water. I need this food, man!"

The evening had been enjoyable for Summer. She had been sipping on a fruity cocktail that she had refilled twice. Even though she didn't engage much with the other guests, she felt content being around them in a typical social setting.

"Paige... Paige, Paige," Jessica repeated, bursting into laughter.

Maybe you need to stop drinking, young lady. You seem to have forgotten your own name!"

"Yes, I'm a lightweight, so you are right," Summer replied.

Feeling a little uneasy after making the big mistake and not answering to her alias, she was ready to end the night. Besides, Jessica had one guest that she couldn't stomach anymore. Nail had spent the last hour complaining about how stupid her best friend was for staying with her abusive husband. Summer, being a little tipsy and fed up with the lack of respect and privacy Nail showed for her best friend's relationship, had begun to sour on her stomach.

Nail carried on the entire evening, "I mean, I can't do it anymore. She is so stupid. All he does is beat her, and she attempts to hide the bruises. The foolish bitch thought she was coming to my house with that shit. I told her hell no. She can go cry a river on someone else's shoulder," Nail said as she continued to belittle her friends' character behind her back. "Stupid, she's just dumb, she... she... she." Summer had had enough.

"I'm just asking," Summer said. "Have you ever considered that perhaps she's in a predicament that she can't leave?"

"Excuse me?" Nail replied, her face contorted as if she dared Summer to address her.

"Not every person who is a victim of abuse is choosing to stay in a dangerous situation," Summer continued. "Maybe there are circumstances that you are unaware of that are preventing her from leaving. It's important to consider all possibilities and not jump to conclusions."

"Or maybe she is stupid as fuck," Nail said as she rolled her eyes at Summer.

"Okay, ladies. Let's change the subject," Jessica requested, attempting to defuse the conversation.

"No, Jessica, I don't have to change the subject because Patty, Patsy, Paige, or whatever her name is, feel the need to be in my conversation."

"I wasn't interrupting a private discussion," Summer said, defending herself. "You have spent the entire evening criticizing your supposed-to-be best friend. Who needs enemies with friends like you?"

"Bitch! I wasn't talking to you," Nail screamed.

"It takes a bitch to know a bitch," Summer replied.

She wasn't willing to be the mute mouse anymore, and she damn sure wasn't about to let Amber Jr walk all over her.

The conversation got so heated that the men had to intervene. When Stevin learned the subject of the discussion and what the women were arguing about, he quickly scooped

Summer up and thanked the host for the beautiful evening. Summer could tell Stevin was pissed as he walked ahead of her without addressing her. He asked in an unsettling tone, "Where are the keys?" Summer held her hand out, handing him the door keys. He aggressively snatched the keys unintentionally, squeezing her hand.

"Ouch, Stevin!" she screamed out. "Why would you squeeze my fingers together like that?"

"Please don't talk to me. I dare you to say anything to me right now!" Stevin responded.

Throwing the keys across the table, he paces back and forth, getting angrier and more annoyed by the minute.

"One night, can I have just one moment with you that is not dictated by your ex? Were you actually arguing with a stranger about Christopher?"

"No, Stevin! It had nothing to do with Christopher," she shouted.

"Like hell, it didn't. Everything you do revolves around that 'Son of a Bitch.' No matter how I try to pull you out of that dark place, you crawl right back into that dark hole".

"It's not your place to pull me out of anything. It's my sunken place to deal with. My argument had nothing to do with Christopher. That lady was an obnoxious piece of shit. She spent the entire night ragging about her friend and her abusive relationship to strangers."

"So the hell, What?" Stevin shouted. "What in the hell did that have to do with you? You are being extremely disrespectful towards me."

"How so, Stevin?"

"Because you continue to allow this individual to control your life."

"What life, Stevin? I don't have a freaking life. I mean, I'm grateful for you, and I love every minute I spend with you. But when you exit those doors, my happiness leaves with you. You have a life outside the walls of our home. You can pick up the phone and talk to your parents."

"Meanwhile, I'm in the same state my mom is in, and I can't even get to know her. You can leave home and travel using your real identity, not an alias. Heck, it's only so many times I can rearrange the canned goods in the pantry."

"That's your choice, Summer. You choose to live like this."

Summer's eyes swelled with tears as she stood speechless that Stevin let those words part from his lips.

"I'm not only fighting for myself but for the people I love. It's not just my life at risk but the lives of everyone who means something to me. Your safety and well-being are more important to me than my own life. I would never forgive myself if anything happened to you because of me. And no, this statement has nothing to do with your manhood or your ability to take care of us. You have no idea what Christopher is capable of. This is the same individual who beat me and left me barefoot without money or any identification, standing at a convenience store parking lot in California at midnight.

"Oh, you asked why?

"Because I involved the police in our fight. The same police officer who put me in the patrol car for protection would be the same officer who left me in the hands of my abuser.

"And all it took was a phone call from Christopher. This would be the same individual who attacked a 70-year-old man for defending me and dragged me out of the house while having his security hold Mr. Jeffery at gunpoint while he threatened to burn the only real home I have ever known down with Mr. Jeffery in it. So you have no idea, no idea," she said, trembling.

Stevin knew about her past before committing 100% of himself to the relationship, so even though he wanted to be angry. He had to swallow his pride and be the man he promised her to be.

He embraced her with a hug and apologized for taking that tone with her. Stevin knew her life with Christopher was a grim time for her; he empathized with her situation. But never could he imagine the abuse she endured at the hands of Christopher.

"Stevin, my stance had nothing to do with Christopher but the judgment itself. I'm tired of being judged. I have been judged my entire life. People on the outside have no idea what an abused victim faces day in and day out. You are stripped of your dignity and broken down inside out. You are being attacked physically and mentally behind closed doors on the inside by the person who promised to love you the most, and on the other hand, you are being judged and humiliated on the outside by individuals who should have your back.

"How can any broken individual pick up the pieces and begin to put themselves back together when the world makes you feel like you deserve to be beaten and stripped of your sense of pride because you didn't walk away fast enough?

"Hell, I placed my entire well-being in this man's hands. It kills me to think Ebony felt like Nail towards me. She was the only person I had to run to. So, no! I'm sorry I made you feel like my disagreement with that troll was about Christopher. Baby, it wasn't. It was me using my voice for the first time, and I'm sorry it had to happen at tonight's event."

He gazed deep into her eyes, looking beyond the shattered woman who felt stripped of her identity and self-worth. He stood up and continued to stare deep into her eyes, determined to make her his wife.

"I'm taking you to meet my parents," he said.

"How, Stevin? You have already stated it's a four-day drive, and I can't fly."

"You let me worry about the details. I'm so sorry, Summer. I only want to be your peace. I'm sorry for ever questioning your motives. He'll never hurt you again," Stevin declared as he held her tightly.

Wrapped in Stevin's embrace, Summer knew he was still clueless about the destruction Christopher causes. On the other hand, she was fully aware of Christopher's potential to turn her world upside down. He was her invisible hurricane, that destructive wind that she couldn't see but is very well aware of the potential destruction and chaos he causes.

Chapter 19: Let's Go Home

Summer sits nervously in the window seat of the bay window, staring out at the sky. Two days ago, Stevin woke her up to inform her that he had to take an urgent business trip out of state and had to leave immediately. No time to discuss his abrupt departure, he kept her mind at ease with multiple calls and texts throughout the day. She barricaded herself inside the house and refused to leave until Stevin returned from his trip.

Seeing a shadow appearing from her peripheral vision, she was startled at first glance. The neighbor, Jessica, surprised her with an unannounced visit. Wavering if she should open the door, her anxiety heightened her fears, as she trusted no one.

After the tenth knock, and it was clear Jessica hadn't given up, she crept to the door, removed the chair from behind it, unlocked the locks one by one, and pulled open the door.

"Paige, why did it sound like you were unlocking a vault? Honey, how many locks do you and Stevin have on this front door? Better yet, who are you trying to keep out, the mob?" She said as she burst into laughter.

"No, we're not running from the mob," Summer replied, laughing. "Our previous place of residency was broken into when I was home alone. So, I get anxious when Stevin has out-of-town business trips, leaving me alone."

"Well, no worries, that's why I'm here. I was very hesitant when Carl asked me to stop in and check on you after the debacle at the barbecue."

Summer quickly dropped her head, feeling embarrassed by her actions at Jessica's home on their last encounter together. "Yeah, about that, I want to apologize for my actions. Just know Stevin wasn't pleased with my behavior. I have been too embarrassed to come over and apologize."

Jessica burst out laughing. "I owe you the apology. I was afraid of your opinion after Nail's antics. You and Stevin appeared so upset when you left, and I was too chicken shit to come over the next day."

"Well, I am here because Stevin has assigned Carl to watch over you and the house. I don't know why Carl didn't inform him; we sleep with all our doors unlocked. This is a safe neighborhood, and besides, Barney Pfeiffer, AKA my husband, might be trying to make himself feel important. If you have noticed Carl sleeping in the hammock in the backyard, we are not on the outs. He has made himself your personal bodyguard. I had to wrestle him off the sidewalk last night. The fool purchased a tactical flashlight and proceeded to walk up and down the sidewalk in front of our homes."

"What did Stevin tell him that he felt the need to go to that extreme?" Summer asked with a concerned look.

"Nothing to my knowledge, but he would be out of town and asked if we could keep an eye out on the house. Paige, my husband, is trying to relive his high school days. He has gained some muscle and confidence. However, I want to make it clear that back in the day, I was the one who was kicking ass and taking names. I was his protector."

Laughter filled the room as Summer invited Jessica into the home.

"I would like you to join me at the salon today, and we can both get our hair and nails done," Jessica requested.

"That sounds like fun. Give me about thirty minutes, and I will be ready."

"No rush. Take your time, Paige. Come over when you're ready, and you can ride with me."

Summer felt a hint of familiarity, but she knew no one could ever replace Ebony. She picked up the phone and called Stevin.

"Hi, Summer. Is everything okay?"

"Maybe next time, you might want to inform me if you are going to have Mr. Otis, the security guard, monitoring me."

"What happened? Why are you calling Carl, Mr. Otis?"

Summer is unable to complete the story in its entirety due to Stevin gasping for breath due to uncontrollable laughter, causing him to choke.

"Baby, all I said to Carl was I would be out of town for a couple of days, and would he keep a watch out for you, if you needed any help around the home that required manpower. I promise you, that's all. However, I need to hang up because I'm boarding the plane."

"Wait, are you saying you are boarding the plane? Where are you going? Better yet, when will you be back?"

"Big Daddy is on his way home to you now. I was planning to surprise you."

Summer squealed with excitement on the other end of the phone as she jumped for joy.

"Okay, let me let you go. I'm running off briefly with Jessica to the salon."

"Okay, love. Tell Mr. Otis to stand down, that your true protector is in the sky, and on his way home. He states as he hangs up, still tickled at Carl's behavior."

Locking up and walking next door, Jessica is in her car, waiting in the driveway. As Summer entered the vehicle from the passenger side, no other than Carl, with his flashlight in hand, dashes out the front door.

"Wait a minute, wait one darn minute. No one informed me you guys were leaving." Carl shouts.

"Move out of the way, Barney Pfeiffer," Jessica says, as she speeds out the driveway.

"You have to return home, woman!" He shouted as he pulled a pair of handcuffs from his back pocket, dangling them in the air. "She's going to give me the respect I deserve," Carl mumbles as he enters their home.

***

Jessica's beautician was able to fit Summer right in as a walk-in.

"Have you thought about what style you want, the beautician asked as she flipped through Summer's hair."

"No, just my regular straight bob, I guess."

"You would look great with a pixie cut; you have the face for it. Remember Jessica, the style I wanted to do on you," she shouts across the room.

Summer, in her timid fashion, agrees to let the beautician have total ranks on the decision of the hairstyle, 'heck,' she thought to herself. "Ebony's beautician was pretty good, she knew how to style it and leave it just the right length." Summer was confident that she would love whatever style the stylist decided to do.

Feeling the beautician pulling all her hair back into a ponytail, she sat quietly, clueless as to what was about to happen. With one snip of the scissors, off went her ponytail.

Summer sat with tears in her eyes as the beautician twirled around with her cut-off ponytail in her hand as she dropped it into her lap. She sat speechless, feeling the swift blade of the scissors cutting through her hair. She could feel her hair falling down her face, feeling as if the beautician would never stop cutting.

Sitting in the chair, she felt like she was back in the group home. Her inner voice screamed to get up and stop her from cutting your hair. However, she sat in silence, fighting back tears, as strands of hair continued to fall onto her lap.

While the beautician worked on her hair, Jessica strolled around and suggested nail colors that she should try. Jessica's voice sounded muffled as if she was underwater. Summer felt like she was going into shock as she became light-headed.

"Don't worry about paying for anything today, Paige. It's on me," Jessica said.

With the spend of the chair, the beautician, with eager anticipation, waited for Summer to be mesmerized by her new haircut. Instead, Summer dashes from the chair, clinging to the detached ponytail as she runs out of the salon in tears. Leaving the beautician confused and lost for words.

Jessica followed Summer, trying to console her.

"Paige darling, did you not know what a pixie cut was?" she asked.

"No, I didn't think she would cut all my hair off and leave me bald," Summer squealed. "Why would anyone cut someone else's hair without their request? Stevin is going to be so disappointed. What if he's not attracted to me now?"

"Don't worry, let me pay and get the keys, and I'll drive you home," Jessica offered.

The ride home was tense and quiet, as you could hear crickets.

"Paige, just pull down the visor and look in the mirror; the cut is stunning on you," Jessica said, trying to lift Summer's spirits.

Summer hesitantly pulls down the visor to see her new hairdo for the first time. Upon seeing herself, she lets out a loud cry and exclaims, "I look like an ugly boy!" she screams as she bursts into tears and throws herself a pity party. However, her emotional moment is soon interrupted by Jessica's sudden shriek.

"It's all my fault. I'm so sorry," Jessica cried as she apologized hysterically for suggesting her stylist.

As the car rolled down the interstate, they whined the entire ride home like sick puppies. Jessica's phone rings, and it's Carl. He tries to comfort her as she blames herself for Summer's haircut.

"Tell Paige: Stevin is home now, so let him decide whether he likes her new hairstyle or not. This isn't your fault either way, honey," Carl said, attempting to soothe his wife.

Jessica gathered herself and said to Summer, "Paige, take a deep breath. Stevin is back."

Summer panicked at the news and pleaded, "Oh no! What am I going to do? I can't let him see me like this. Please ask Carl to bring me a hat out to the car."

Meeting them in the driveway with the hat in his hand, in typical Carl fashion, he had already rushed over to inform Stevin of Summer's hair disaster. "Paige, go home and let Stevin be the judge of your new hairstyle. He is waiting to see it," Carl said.

“How does he know?” Jessica yelled as she side-eyed Carl.

“Well, I went ahead and broke the ice for her,” Carl said. He stood with his chest out, looking confident in his executive decision to meddle in her business.

Throwing the baseball cap on, Summer stepped out of the car. She took her time as she eased in the front door. Stevin greets her with open arms, “Come here, baby. I heard you’re upset about your hair.”

Standing in the corner, she raises her arm, revealing the cut-off ponytail she clinched tight to.

"Damn, you cut off all your hair?" Stevin says as his eyes widen.

His reaction only triggered Summer, and the waterworks began as she burst into tears. Stevin tried to comfort her. "Stop crying, baby. Take off the cap and let me see your new look." However, Summer was reluctant at first.

"No, you're going to leave me. I look like a boy."

"Take off the cap, Summer."

"No," she says, shrugging her shoulders. Stevin quickly knocks the cap to the floor, picks her up, and walks into the bathroom. He places her in front of the mirror, forcing eye contact. She gazed up at Stevin, her eyes full of tears. She was too afraid to see his reaction, but she had to know how he really felt.

He smiles as he runs his hands through her hair. "Baby, I love it,” he said. “It makes you look younger, but at the same time, it's attractive as hell. ‘Wow, Summer,’ it screams confidence; it's edgy. Summer, it's sexy as hell on you.”

He turns her towards the mirror and runs his hands through the chunky crop layers that are framed by the feathered look. No matter what direction he runs his fingers, the hair bounces back perfectly into place.

"Summer, you have a red strapless dress I picked out personally in your wardrobe. Please put it on and get dolled up for me. I'm taking you out. I'm going to the guest bedroom to get dressed. I don't want to see you until you are completely dressed."

Racing to the closet, she pulled out the red dress. Determined to blow Stevin's mind, feeling she would need more than the red dress to feel confident, she pulled out her makeup bag. She hadn't forgotten all of Ebony's makeup tutorials. She was determined to look confident and sexy tonight, although it was far from how she truly felt.

Stevin stood across the hall, dressed in a pair of well-fitted black denim jeans, a stylish button-down black shirt, and a pair of Dolce & Gabbana loafers. He admired himself in the mirror while placing his presidential red-faced Rolex on his wrist to match her red dress. Stevin completed his look with a spritz of her favorite cologne. He strolled across the hall with confidence as he tapped on the bathroom door, informing her he was ready, laying back across the bed awaiting his surprise, which would be his sexy armpiece for tonight.

Summer completed her look with a coat of Vendetta-dark red lipstick. She stood in front of the mirror as she couldn't deny the new haircut screamed sex appeal. Running her hands through her hair, she had to admit it was much easier to manage than she initially thought.

Summer was now dressed and ready to be wined and dined; this would be her and Stevin's first official date. As she eased the bathroom door open, she immediately noted Stevin's striking appearance, looking like a perfected sculptural masterpiece. She thought 'Dang, I am truly a lucky woman.'

"How did I get so lucky?"

Stevin jumped up from the bed as he advanced towards her. He never uttered one word, just staring as if he were in a daze. He approaches her, running his hands through her hair as she leans in, grazing her face up his chest to his neck, admiring his fragrance.

With a handful of her hair, he passionately kisses her, attempting to remove her dress.

"No, Stevin," she said. "You are messing up my makeup."

"Screw this Summer we're staying in. You will be my entrée and my dessert," he said as he attempted to drop to his knees.

"No, Stevin, please don't take this away from me. I need to get out of this house."

"Summer, you are going to have to do something to assist me. My manhood is about to burst out of these jeans, and he is standing at full attention."

Seeing the disappointment in her eyes, he backed away and composed himself as they proceeded out the door.

Summer finally felt a sense of normalcy as they pulled into the restaurant parking lot. She was happy to be on a normal date with her man and ready to relax and enjoy the evening. However, she can't help but notice that Stevin's gaze is fixed on her as if he were a predator ready to pounce on his prey. She wishes he would stop staring and focus on their conversation instead of thinking about ripping her clothes off.

He slid an envelope towards her as she sat across the table from him. "What's this, baby?" she asked curiously. He urged her to open it and see for herself. Tearing open the envelope, she discovered two round-trip tickets to King County, Washington. Confused, she looked up at Stevin for an explanation.

"I'm going home, Summer, and I'm taking you with me."

With a disappointed look, she said, "Stevin, you know I can't fly, and who is Addison Brooks?"

"Sweetheart, I've mentioned my best friend Orlando to you before, but I haven't had the courage to confess that I've been confiding in him since I was nine. He knows everything about you, Summer," he said, pausing to gauge her reaction. Summer looked up at him, sensing his apprehension as he avoided making eye contact.

"On your first day, when you walked into my office, Orlando and my father were the first two people I called. My exact words to them were, 'I have met my wife.' They are aware of the struggles I faced, and Orlando knows our current situation."

"He is in charge of the New York office. He helped me secure our home, which is still registered under my company, without raising any suspicion."

"We both have contacts at various airports, and I wanted to arrange for a fake ID and have my people ready for you when you go through TSA. But as always, Orlando came through and delivered. While looking at your photo, Orlando mentioned that it's ironic how much you and his wife, Addison, resemble each other. She just has short hair," Stevin said with a smile as he slid Addison's ID across the table. Summer picked up the identification card and couldn't deny that she could easily pass off as Addison.

"Don't worry," reassured Stevin. "I have reliable people in place on the days of our travel who won't ask any questions as long as you follow my instructions." Her hands started to sweat, and she felt consumed by nervousness. Not only was she running away from Christopher, but now she had to add a felony to her record if this identity switch failed.

Stevin got up from the table and softly said, "Come on, baby, let's dance and live in the moment." He led her to the small dance floor in front of the stage, where a live band was serenading the crowd with soft jazz tunes. She laid her head on his chest and focused on the present moment, smiling and taking it all in. She felt weightless, allowing him to lead her steps without any distractions from her inner voice telling her that she shouldn't dance in front of the crowd or her fear of tripping in the heels she had worn to dinner. All she could focus on was the sound of his heartbeat as he caressed her close to him and gently stroked her back. It was time for a change, and it would start now!

Chapter 20: The Friendly Blue Skies

MADISON MUNICIPAL AIRPORT

Summer's hands were drenched in sweat as she clung to Stevin's arm for dear life. The loud thumping of her heart drowned out the surrounding noise as they approached TSA check-in. "Stevin, is that you?" the TSA officer asked as he and Stevin exchanged a firm handshake and conversed briefly. Summer breathed a sigh of relief as the TSA officer quickly scanned her fake ID and returned it without asking for any further inquiry. It was a home run. They had passed through security successfully, but she still felt nervous.

"Summer, can I have my arm back now? I'm starting to lose feeling," Stevin said, as she had a lethal grip on his arm, still afraid security could come charging at her at any moment. "I made a promise to you that I wouldn't put you in harm's way. If I didn't think we could successfully pull this off, I would not have put you in jeopardy. So, please relax, Summer," Stevin said reassuringly.

"It's easy for you to say, Stevin. You're not the one facing a 5 to 10-year sentence for identity fraud. As if I don't have enough on my plate already."

Stevin chuckled while assuring her that he would never let that happen. However, Summer couldn't help but think to herself, "Laugh now, cry later." Knowing her luck, she would end up in jail and be tracked down by Christopher, who would bribe a judge to sentence her to five years of house arrest under Christopher Diamonds' supervision.

Stevin placed his hand on her trembling legs. "Come on, baby, relax."

"I'm trying, Stevin. I really need to use the restroom. All this stress is about to make me lose control of my bladder."

Stevin pointed her towards the ladies' room and went back to typing on his computer. Summer sat with a hard stare to the side of his head, waiting for him to acknowledge her firm gaze. When he finally lifted his head, he realized that she was still there, refusing to go without him.

"Summer, No! I'm not dragging these bags through the airport, so you're okay. I can see the restroom from here, so you can go by yourself," he added.

"But what if something happens?" Summer asked anxiously.

"No, Summer. 'Don't but what me about anything else on this trip.' Relax and go to the restroom."

"Just take a deep breath," Stevin said calmly. Summer quickly walked to the restroom with her head down, silently praying that this trip wouldn't cost her her life.

After using the restroom, she quickly washed her hands as she needed to return to Stevin's side before she hyperventilated due to anxiety.

"Summer," a gentle voice whispered. She slowly lifted her head, feeling her heart beating rapidly. Sophia stood before her, causing Summer to gasp and cover her mouth in surprise. Her eyes instantly filled with tears. Sophia took Summer's hand and led her into an accessible stall, where they embraced tightly and wept together.

"Let me look at you," Sophia said as she admired Summer's new look, running her hand through her hair. "You look wonderful! Ebony will be overjoyed to know you're safe."

"No, Sophia, you can't tell her anything; it's too risky."

"Summer, at the very least, let me tell her that you're still alive and well. Summer, she cries herself to sleep every night, thinking that you're no longer with us. But you're standing here, alive and well,' Sophia says as she touches Summer's face, still in shock.

"I knew it was you. I was standing behind you and your guy friend, and I recognized you immediately. When I heard the TSA officer address you as Ms. Brooks. You looked so timid, and I didn't want to startle you. Ebony has filled me in on everything, and I know your situation. I also know the hell Christopher put Ebony and Thomas through after you disappeared."

"That's why it's crucial, Sophia, we don't involve her anymore. It's too dangerous for her and me. Sophia, please!"

"For my cousin's sake, can I at least let her know you are alive and well?"

"Sofia, Christopher can't be trusted, and I'm pretty sure he has or had Ebony's phone tapped. Therefore, you can only give her this information face to face, in a public setting, where you are sure nothing can be bugged, or the conversation could be monitored."

Summer looks up at Sofia with a smile and glassy eyes. "I'm happy, and I'm in love," she says. "He treats me like a piece of fragile glass, handling me with much delicacy. Please tell her I love her and think about her every second of the day. She is greatly missed, appreciated, and loved. She was and is my first and only sister and best friend. One day in the future, I pray to see her again, but for now, it's too dangerous. Just let her know I am okay."

Sophia embraces Summer, holding back tears, and assures her that she is loved and missed also. However, their brief reunion is interrupted by Summer's phone buzzing.

"I have to go, Sophia," Summer says. "I don't want Ste-" she stops short of saying his name. "My friend guy is calling, and I must get back before he starts to worry." Sophia allowed Summer to exit the restroom first, and she hung back to gather herself.

"Hey, did you suddenly feel sick?" Stevin asked. "Did you get the bubble guts?"

"No, Stevin," she replied. "I bumped into an old acquaintance." He sat up abruptly, grabbed her arm, and scanned their surroundings anxiously.

"It's okay," she assured him, wiping tears from her eyes. "It was Ebony's cousin Sophia from California. Now, Ebony will know I'm safe and happy with someone who loves me deeply. It saddens me that Mr. Jeffery doesn't know it."

"Did you tell the cousin who I was?"

"No, darling, it's too risky for all parties involved."

Stevin pulled Summer close and wrapped his arm around her, holding her tight in the busy airport as if they were the only two people there. Unbeknownst to them, Sophia was in the distance, secretly taking photos. She was determined not only to share the great news with Ebony but also to show her that her little caterpillar had transformed into a beautiful, confident butterfly and that she was safe and in love.

Stevin had claimed the window seat, leaving Summer's sandwich between him and a sweet elderly lady who wouldn't stop staring and smiling.

Summer looked out of the airplane window as the airplane reached a stable altitude. She felt grateful to be flying again. This time, the beautiful blue skies didn't seem so bleak anymore.

The overwhelming feelings of grief and sadness that had once suffocated her were no longer present. She looked up and locked eyes with Stevin.

He took her hand, interlocked their fingers, kissed the back of her hand, and she leaned over to rest her head on his shoulder. The elderly woman with snow-white hair sat up and smiled at the two of them. "Please, don't mind me," she said. "I simply adore love. I can see how he protects you. Just look at the way he looks at you, my dear. It reminds me of my late husband, Charles. It's important to appreciate true love when you find it, my dear. Not everyone is fortunate enough to experience true love in its purest form."

As she glanced down at their hands, she noticed that there was no ring on either of their fingers. "Uh-Oh," she said, staring at Stevin. "Why is there no ring, son?" She said, gazing up at him in disbelief. However, Stevin smiled and winked at her. With a huge grin, she said, "Okay, my darlings, I will let you be. You two make sure always to put each other first," she said as she sat back in her seat, eating her complimentary peanuts. Summer smiled, enjoying her view as she watched Stevin dose off.

Chapter 21: It's A Family Affair

KING COUNTY, WASHINGTON

"Are you ready for this adventure with me?" Stevin asked with a warm smile, glancing over at Summer in the passenger seat of their rental car.

"Not really; I'm terrified, honestly." Summer admitted, her voice trembling with anxiety.

"Now... now... young one," he said sarcastically, "The big bad werewolves won't gobble you up until the full moon sets in the west," he joked as he giggled. His voice filled with gentle humor.

Summer snatched her hand away with a sour expression. "Not funny, Stevin," dropping her head.

"Come on, baby, I promise this will be fun," he urged her, his eyes sparking with excitement.

As she stared out the car window with a sense of apprehension, she muttered to herself, "I thought California was going to be fun too and look how that turned out." Then she turned to Stevin and asked, "Could you please tell me a little more about your family background? It would help me know what to expect."

"As I have already informed you, I am an army brat. My father retired as a General from the Army, and my mother has always been a stay-at-home mom. My grandfather is African American, and my grandmother is of Italian descent.

My grandmother was particular about my father marrying someone from her own culture, so my mother is a full-blown Italian with a lot of fire in her personality. She is very passionate, sometimes too much for her own good."

"Well, does your mom want you to marry an Italian woman?"

"No, she has never expressed such a desire. She has always valued our autonomy and happiness above all else. Besides, my father's family is very involved in my life. Oh, by the way, you will be meeting them on this trip at some point."

She took a hard, long, deep breath as her anxiety level went from five to ten.

“We have about a 45-minute drive, Summer. Try to relax and nap before you break out into hives or hyperventilate. You're already looking pale in the face.”

"Yes, Stevin, I'm incredibly nervous.”

Exhausted from the long travel, it didn't take long for her to doze off, which was very short-lived. It seemed as if she had been only asleep for five minutes before she could hear Stevin calling out to her, informing her they had arrived.

Pulling up to the farm, she was immediately taken aback. The large wrap-around farm porch was packed with Stevin's family members. It looked like a family reunion, something she had only experienced watching on television.

"Oh... no, Stevin," she said worriedly, "I can't meet all these people simultaneously; this is too overwhelming."

"I know, baby," he said. "I asked my family not to do this when you arrived. Just take a deep breath and relax. I won't leave your side."

Stevin shifted the car into park and instructed Summer to wait in the car until he opened the door for her. She saw an older gentleman stepping off the porch and proceeded to walk to the car. Stevin ran up to him and hugged him as they bumped shoulders. From their striking resemblance, it was clear that the gentleman was Stevin's dad. As she watched them embrace with excitement, she thought, "Well, at least I know Stevin will age well." Stevin's father is a very striking and well-kept man.

"Come on, Dad," Stevin said. “Why does the whole family have to be here? I told you Summer isn't used to this type of environment. Meeting you and Mom alone is about to give her a heart attack."

"I understand, son," his Dad replied. “Understandingly. You know Irene had her hand in this. I asked your mom not to invite everyone over today. They've all been asked not to overwhelm her all at once."

As Stevin opened the passenger door, Summer stepped out and was immediately greeted by his father with a big, gentle bear hug. "I have been waiting for years to meet you, young lady. I'm just grateful you walked back into my son's life."

Summer heard the screen door slam and a voice from a distance shouting, "My baby is home!" Summer saw Stevin's mother running towards him with her oversized cooking apron flapping in the wind. As she stretched out her arms, she ran into Stevin's embrace, and he lifted her slightly and spun her around.

That embrace from his mom started a stampede as the entire crowd shifted from the porch and surrounded the car. Getting lost in the shuffle, she felt a nudge to the hand as Stevin returned to her side, pulling her away from the crowd.

Summer had given out hugs after hugs, but she had no idea who she was being embraced by. Stevin pulled her by the hand, and they walked towards his mother. He pulled Summer closer to him and introduced her, "Mother, meet Summer."

She warmly responded, "Ciao, Ciao. Piacere di conoscerti," and hugged Summer. Suddenly, a voice from the crowd interrupted their brief introduction.

"Stop the shenanigans, Aunt Irene. She is clearly black and doesn't understand a word you're saying." Irene quickly turned her head and saw Ciara, Stevin's first cousin from his father's side. Irene chased Ciara onto the porch and attempted to pinch her arm, feeling that Ciara had embarrassed her in front of Summer.

Irene shouted to the crowd, "Everyone, come inside!" She then added, "Except you, Ciara. You can go home," as the screen door slammed shut behind her.

Stevin hugged Ciara and laughed, "My dear cousin, now you know Mom won't let that go."

Mr. Bash, senior, had requested that the family remain outdoors to give Stevin and Summer some time to settle in. While most of the family complied with the request, the older aunts were not going to miss a moment of the meet and greet.

Mr. Bash Senior called out to Irene, "Did you set the kids up in Stevin's old room?"

As Irene exited the kitchen, you could hear the old wooden floors squeaking. "Yes... yes, I got Summer set up in the guest room upstairs and Stevin in his old room," Irene replied. Summer immediately agrees, following behind Stevin's mother as she attempts to lead her upstairs.

"Mom, we're not doing this. I guess I'll drive back into the city and get a hotel room," Stevin says.

"Nonsense, my boy, you know your mother is just joking," Mr. Bash Senior stated as he gave his wife an unsettling look.

Stevin's aunts whispered to Summer behind Irene's back, "No, she wasn't," shaking their heads.

Irene complimented Summer on her good manners. "I must say, Summer, your mom has taught you well. I love how you were willing to respect my home," she said, cutting her eyes at Stevin as she gave him a disapproving look.

His dad intervened, "Come on, Irene, give them a moment to settle in."

Grabbing their suitcase, Stevin led Summer to the back of the house, to his old room. He closed the door, hugged her, and asked if she was okay. As he rubbed her shoulders, he assured her that he knew she would do fine. Summer rested her head on his chest, relieved that the meet and greet with his family was nothing like the one with Christopher's family.

"Just be ready to gather in the kitchen," he said. "During every family gathering, my mother and aunts compete in a cook-off. You'll have the chance to taste my aunt's soulful collard greens and my mother's special meatballs. My mouth is watering just thinking about it. We always manage to bait them into cooking all our favorite dishes by the end of their disagreement. Just make sure to avoid getting pulled into their food war."

As they made their way back to the front of the house, they joined the older ladies in the kitchen. Their bickering could be heard throughout the home as they debated who has the best recipes.

Summer lifts her head and catches Irene's eye. "Come on, sweetheart," says Irene. "I need some help in the kitchen. Maybe you can drown out these old bats."

Stevin chuckles, as Summer is immediately timid about the thought of preparing food next to his mother. "Mother, you better watch out," he teases. "You might not want Summer in your kitchen. She has won me over with her cooking, and she's very skillful in the kitchen."

With the back of her hand, Summer swiftly smacks Stevin on his arm, gazing at him with wide eyes as if she could choke him at that very moment.

"Come on, Summer, let me see how you are feeding my baby boy," Irene jokingly demanded.

"No, ma'am," Summer replied respectfully, "Mimi has always taught me to know my place in another woman's kitchen. So I will just help cut up some vegetables if you don't mind," she replied firmly.

"Son, you have done well; this young lady has been raised correctly," Irene said, impressed again with Summer's manners. "Well, darling, your mother was very wise," she said as she nudged Summer. "It's so obvious your aunts are missing some home training," Irene tells Stevin while cutting her eyes at Mr. Bash's sisters.

The kitchen was filled with laughter as Stevin cut the rope, leaving Summer alone in the kitchen with his mom. Irene had convinced Summer to prepare the desserts, which garnered curious glances over her shoulder from Irene and company, as they observed the delicious apple pie that Summer had baked from scratch.

As the ladies placed the last dish onto the dinner table, Irene stepped out onto the porch and rang the dinner bell, signaling the family that it was time for dinner. Everyone rushed into the house, making space for the large crowd. Summer noticed that she was the only young lady who had been stuck in the kitchen with the older women while the cousins and girlfriends gathered outside to enjoy drinks and the outdoors with the guys.

Stevin watched from across the table as Summer and Irene prepared the table, grinning widely.

Summer was wearing an oversized apron and seemed quite comfortable around his mom.

"Okay, Mom," Stevin said. "Can I have my woman back now?"

"Stevin, leave her alone. She is helping set the table."

Suddenly, the screen door slammed, and a voice shouted, "Steve Bo, you're home! Come over here and let me size you up!" It was Stevin's oldest brother, Junior, who had arrived. Summer saw Stevin in a different role for the first time. He had lost all his swag. He was like a little kid being surprised by his big brother's presence.

Junior followed in his father's footsteps and joined the military. Stevin grabbed at Summer, removing the apron from around her waist. He introduced her to his brother with a sense of pride, as if he had presented a delicate dish. Stevin stood with nervous anticipation and waited on his big brother's response, more like his approval of her.

Junior's verbal approval was more than Summer expected as she shook his hand.

"My, my, my! Little brother, you have done well for yourself, quite well indeed."

Summer felt uneasy as if she was being examined like an object. She was over the meet and greet and eased herself down into the chair.

The family had a good time as laughter filled the home, as everyone stuffed their face and swapped childhood stories. Summer was exhausted and relieved when the night finally came to an end.

After showering and preparing for bed, Summer walked out of the bathroom and found Irene in the bedroom. Irene was putting fresh linen on the daybed for Stevin to sleep in. She clearly didn't want Stevin and her to share a bed.

Stevin walked in and rolled his eyes as he gestured for his mother to leave the room. Irene made sure to leave the door slightly open as she exited. Stevin jumped up, pushing the door shut, attempting to return to bed and fondle Summer. However, she quickly redirected him to the daybed, partially reopened the door, and returned to bed, leaving Stevin liquored up and unsatisfied as she directed him to remain on his side of the room.

Chapter 22: Life On The Farm

The sound of the squeaky hardwood floors squeak as Irene softly tiptoed to Stevin's bedroom door. Summer slowly opens her eyes as she can see Irene's shadow as she lurks at the door. Satisfied that the bedroom door remained open, she turned around and headed back towards the kitchen to prepare breakfast. Feeling excited, her family was back under one roof; Irene was determined to fix everyone's favorite breakfast dish.

Summer sat on the edge of the bed, rubbing her feet back and forth on the cold wooden floor. She peeped over her shoulder at Stevin, who was sound asleep. He looked extremely uncomfortable as the daybed was too small for him. Hearing the clanging of pots, she decided to assist Irene in the kitchen. After freshening up and putting on her clothes, she entered the kitchen. Her eyes widen as it looks as if Irene had pulled everything out of the cupboards as if she were preparing a feast that could feed a village.

"Can I assist you with making breakfast?" Summer asked.

"Of course, I would be offended if you didn't," she said as she smiled at Summer. Irene didn't see Summer as a threat to her title as the best cook in the kitchen. She felt Summer understood her place in her kitchen as the cook's helper. Surprisingly, she gave Summer free reign to prepare what she desired.

As the smell of sizzling bacon drifted through the air, the savory aroma traveled through their nostrils, awakening Stevin and his brother.

After working on the farm since dawn, Mr. Bash entered his home, washed up, and kissed his wife to thank her and Summer for preparing breakfast.

Meanwhile, Stevin and Junior, acting like carefree little boys, rushed into the kitchen to fill their plates with food. Although Summer felt invisible at the moment, she didn't take it personally and understood what it meant for Stevin to be home around his family.

Sitting on the bed, she swung her feet back and forth, wondering what the day held. Stevin had a large family, and although she enjoyed the laughs, a quiet and peaceful day would do her just fine.

Stevin bursts into the room, jumps onto the bed, and straddles her. He kisses her all over while proclaiming his love for her and how impressed his family is with her. She enjoys his embrace and lays in silence, running her fingers through his curly hair, taking in the moment. Suddenly, they are interrupted by Junior, as he abruptly barges into the room, pulling Stevin off the bed by the leg. "Come on, youngster!" he yelled. "Those mudcats aren't going to catch themselves."

Stevin turned to Summer and said, "I'm sorry, baby. We're going fishing." And with that, he swiftly left the room.

Summer heard some commotion coming from the front of the house. But before she could exit the bedroom, Camile appeared at the door and informed her that the elders had summoned her. Camile burst out laughing as she said it.

When Summer entered the living room, she soon accepted that the bickering between the two families was their norm and that they genuinely enjoyed each other's company.

The day felt long, as she had been left in the hands of the older women again, and Stevin himself was nowhere in sight.

Although Camile graced the family with her presence, she wouldn't lift a finger. She spent most of the day antagonizing her aunts and making sure she stirred the pot to keep the older ladies bickering. Cooking and sharing recipes were the main topics of the day. They prepared so much food that it could have fed the homeless.

Stevin's best friend Orlando had arrived at the farm; he had flown in from New York. Summer was caught off guard by this unexpected visit, 'Well, heck.' Summer thought. 'I will be alone on this trip and stuck entertaining Mrs. Irene and company.'

From the clear view of the kitchen window, Summer saw Junior walking alone up the hill with his fishing tackle in hand. Stevin was nowhere in sight. Summer began to feel a little abandoned, but she waited patiently for Junior to enter the house and inform her of Stevin's whereabouts.

Son, Irene asked, "Where is your father and Stevin? The sun will be setting soon."

"Well, Mother, Stevin is taking a walk with Dad," Junior winked and said.

"The walk," Irene shouted, and the other family members' faces filled with excitement. Summer was clueless as to what just happened. Little did she know, the walk in the Bash family was very important when someone was about to make a life-changing decision.

The atmosphere suddenly shifted as if everyone was anticipating something significant. Summer didn't know what was happening, but she was eager to be back in Stevin's presence.

Junior's phone rang, and he answered asking, "Are you ready?"

He suddenly ended the call and announced to the family that everyone needed to be on the west side of the farm.

The entire family gathered on the wraparound porch, standing shoulder to shoulder. Summer was mesmerized by the beautiful sunset as it was captivating. It was an endless journey of green pastures and trees being bathed in the burnt orange sunset. As Stevin and his dad approached the house, Junior nodded at his mom. Irene then called out to Summer, requesting that she go and meet Stevin out in the field.

Passing Mr. Bash, he stopped and gave her a big hug, telling her she was the daughter he never had. Reaching Stevin, she noticed that his eyes looked glassy, as if he had been teary-eyed while speaking with his father. Clueless about what was happening, she asked Stevin what was wrong as he took her by the hand.

"Summer, do you remember the day you asked me what I was thinking when I appeared lost in thought? That day, I couldn't find the right words to express how my heart skips a beat when I'm in your presence. How can someone walk into your life, and the second you look her in the eyes, you know you just met your soulmate? A feeling rushed through me like I had never felt, and I was afraid of it, so I took my time getting to know you."

Summer's body started to tremble with nervousness. Her emotions had gotten the best of her, and she was overwhelmed with anticipation. It was obvious where this conversation was headed.

"Summer, initially, I was disappointed about having missed the chance to be a part of your first experiences. However, I now understand that if I hadn't taken a backseat, I wouldn't have been able to demonstrate to you true love in its finest form, and all of your past would have remained hidden."

Dropping down on one knee, he takes her trembling hand and slides the ring on it, and before he can ask the question, she screams, "Yes, yes, yes!" and jumps for joy.

The screams of celebration filled the air as the family rushed to the field. Stevin and Summer shared a kiss while he twirled her around in excitement. Camile captured the entire proposal on camera, taking photos of the moment. However, Mr. Bash senior asked Camile to print the images only for their personal memories and forbade her not to post them on social media. Camile was a bit taken aback and confused but didn't question her uncle's request and agreed not to disobey it.

As everyone gathered at the dinner tables, Summer was too excited to eat. This time, the ring wasn't the only prize, but Stevin was.

As their fingers interlocked, she couldn't stop staring and smiling at him. Nothing would come between them and their love. As dinner winded down, the men planned a trip into town to a local bar. Everyone, except the aunts and Irene, would be going.

Stevin searched the house for Summer and found her in the bedroom, sitting on the bed.

"What's wrong, baby? I can see it all over your face," he asked.

"How mad would you be if I stayed in?"

"No, sweetheart! The real question is, how mad would you be if I went out with everyone to the bar and left you here alone?"

She quickly assured him, "Not mad at all! I want you to go out and enjoy yourself. You deserve all the happiness your family has given you."

"Can I persuade you to come out with us?"

"No, Stevin, the nightclub scene doesn't interest me at all."

As he dressed and prepared to leave, she walked him to the car, and they all loaded up and headed into town. Summer remained outdoors, taking a seat on the porch swing; she curled up and swung back and forth with a heavy heart.

"Well, my dear," Mr. Bash stated as he joined her on the swing. "Do you want to talk about it?"

She shrugged her shoulders and said, "I'm okay."

"Well, we both know that is long from the truth."

"You had an opportunity to join all the youngsters and have a good ole time in town, and here you are soaking. Let's be honest with each other, Summer."

As she rubbed her sweaty hands against her pants leg, she knew that what she was about to confess to Mr. Bash could potentially ruin her relationship with Stevin.

"Mr. Bash, I need to tell you something. I want you to know that I am incredibly happy, happier than I have ever been before. So, please don't take my downward demeanor as if your son didn't just make me the happiest woman on earth. However, I don't want to start this new journey with your family based on a foundation of lies," she said nervously.

Mr. Bash listened attentively, "I'm listening," he replied.

She continued, "I don't want you to think that your son hasn't made me the happiest woman on earth, she repeated, but I must be honest with you."

As she mumbles her words, she finally blurts out. "Being with me puts your son's livelihood in jeopardy."

Mr. Bash noticed that Summer was becoming emotional and stopped her. He said firmly, "Summer, there isn't anything I don't know about your situation." Summer's face dropped as she stared at Mr. Bash with a surprised look.

"My son and I don't keep secrets from each other. I knew about you the first day he walked back into your life. I was the first call he made when he located you in Monroe. I supported Stevin's decision to pursue the relationship then, and I approve of the marriage now. It's vital you stop fighting with Stevin and let him be the man he is, and that's your protector. Stevin has a father with some influence also, and I was able to help him with the issue he had with the private detective who was hired to investigate him. To clarify, Stevin doesn't require my protection; he only seeks my advice. Therefore, my advice to you is to let go of the past and embrace a new beginning."

"Although I acknowledge and sympathize with what you've been through, dwelling on it won't take you where you want to go. You will never reach your desired destination if you keep detouring and looking back in your review mirror."

"Do you love my son?"

"Yes, sir!" she quickly replied. "With all my heart."

"Well, start trusting him and allowing him to be a man."

"Does Mrs. Irene know about my situation?" she asked.

"No, and I have made the executive decision that this will be the last time we discuss it in this family. Are you a part of this family?"

"Yes, sir, I am."

"Well, consider your past buried and wiped clean. I will say this, and I haven't shared this with anyone else on this earth. This is the only secret I was willing to take to my grave because I didn't want the boys to feel like they were mistakes. I know what it feels like to lose your one true love."

"Don't get me wrong, I love Irene and my boys more than life itself, but I was deeply in love with my high school sweetheart. So, in love, I was willing to walk away from my entire family because my mom was gun-set on me marrying into the culture."

"Sandra refused to marry into a family that didn't accept her. She left town the night we were supposed to elope, and I never heard from her again. Even to this day, my heart still yearns for her. When my son described how you made him feel, I was reminded of that love. Your presence in his life brings him joy, and that's all that matters. His happiness overshadows any mishaps in your past. Now you know my secret, and I know yours. Dad is going to bed. Are you coming?"

"No, sir, I've fallen in love with this farm. It's so peaceful here that I could sit here all night."

"Well, goodnight, dear," he said as he patted her on the leg and entered the house.

While sitting on the swing, enjoying the moonlit night, she noticed car headlights approaching the house. It was her knight in shining armor. He exited the car, swaying with a big smile on his face.

"Why did you drive in your condition, Stevin? Summer asked, concerned.

He bopped down next to her on the swing. "Well, my dear, I got a call from Pops. I suspected you weren't being truthful about your reason for not joining us tonight."

"Stevin, I didn't want to deceive your parents, so I decided to tell your father the truth."

"So, do you feel better knowing that my father is aware of the situation? Do you feel relieved that he knows?"

"Yes, Hun, I do."

Stevin gazed at her with a flirtatious expression. "So, you know I've been drinking all night, don't you? And you are aware of the effect that brown liquor has on me... right?"

"Oh... heck no," I'm not having sex in your parents' home."

"Like hell, you aren't," he said, picking her up and throwing her over his shoulder as she screamed out in laughter. "Come on, ma'am, would you like me to show you around the farm and take you to some of the hidden spots where my brother and I used to bring the fast-tail cheerleaders?" Summer's laughter filled the night air, and she couldn't deny that sneaking around the farm was indeed a thrilling experience.

Chapter 23: A New Chapter

Waking up in Stevin's arms felt incredible, unfazed that she had broken his mother's first house rule. Irene was the furthest from her mind; nothing could ruin this moment. Glancing at her ring, it was beautiful, she had to admit, but the proposal under the gorgeous sunset alone with his family and friends was the topping on the cake.

Stevin embraced her tightly, pulling her closer as he peppered kisses down her shoulders. "Good morning, Mrs. Bash," he greeted her, his hands gently stroking her body.

"Baby," she said softly, "I wish we could live here on the farm. This is where I want to marry you. Just imagine it, Stevin. Right under the same beautiful sunset where you proposed to me."

He rolled over, pulling the covers over his head. "Summer, I spent my entire childhood striving to escape Resmond, and here you are, trying to pull me back in.

She pleaded with him, "Please, baby, look at the bigger picture. We'll be around your family. Just imagine our kids playing in that open field, little Stevin Jr. going to the lake and fishing with you. Please, baby, just think about it."

"You're trying your best to turn me back into a farm boy. Besides, let's plan this wedding first. We have to consider all of our options."

"Stevin, I just told you we can get married right out there in that field under that gorgeous sunset."

"So, what are you saying, Summer? You don't want a church wedding?"

"Stevin, we can get married at the justice of the peace for all I care," Summer replied, sitting up in bed and looking into his eyes as she declared, "All I want is You!"

He pulled her into his arms, and she rested her head on his chest. "I want whatever you want, Summer."

She popped her head up, "So, we can move here?"

"Now, darling. I didn't agree to that. Besides, you're just caught up in the moment."

She asked him, "What do I need to do to show you I'm serious?" as she kissed his chest.

"Well, for starters, you're kissing the wrong part of my body. You need to really convince me you are serious."

"What can I do to show you?" She asked for the second time. He throws the covers over her head as he pushes her head down to his crotch.

"Keep kissing, he requested."

"Like this," she replies.

"Like that," he moans as his eyes roll to the back of his head.

Interrupted by a slight knock on the door, it's Orlando requesting Stevin's presence. Stevin quickly jumped out of bed and started hopping around, trying to get his foot in his briefs. He unlocked the door and greeted him with a smile and wide eyes.

"My boy... bad timing," he said, talking through his teeth as he greeted Orlando with a sneaky grin.

"Stop defiling your mom's home and come see me off to the airport."

"Hey, Summer," Orlando said, peering over Stevin's shoulder. Summer burst into laughter and pulled the covers over her head.

"Good morning, Orlando. Are you not staying for breakfast?" she asked.

"We're all having breakfast now; we are just waiting on you two late birds." Ushering Orlando out the bedroom door, Stevin locks the door, turns around, and kisses Summer.

"Head to the shower and leave the door unlocked," he requested.

"No, Stevin. What if someone walks in?"

"No one will be using this back bathroom. Do what I said, little woman," he said, rushing out of the bedroom to join his family.

"Well, good morning, son," Irene said. "When did we start rising after 9 a.m.?"

"Mother dearest, your son had one of the best days of his life yesterday, and I overdid it with the booze."

"You weren't behind the wheel driving last night, correct?" And why is Summer late for breakfast? I was looking for her assistance this morning.

"Well, Mom, 'My Woman' was ordered by me to remain in the room with me until I awakened this morning. Besides the entire trip, she has been under you, and I want her back."

"So where is she now?" Irene asked.

"Summer is modest, and she's not coming out of that room until she is fully dressed. You guys start, let me go get her." Stevin hurriedly raced down the hallway, knowing they would miss breakfast. He quietly slipped into the bathroom, gently shut the door, and locked it behind him. He quickly got undressed and joined her in the shower, startling her as he swiftly pulled back the shower curtain. He quickly lifts her up, pressing her against the cold shower tiles as she tries to push him away.

"Come on, Summer. We only have five minutes before someone comes looking for us."

"Just wait, Stevin, are you trying to make your mom hate me?"

"That's fine, you can wait until tonight, but I'm going for mine," he proclaims as he takes all of her in the shower.

Upon entering the kitchen, it was evident that they had missed breakfast. Mrs. Irene was visibly upset and rolled her eyes at Stevin. "Summer," Irene said, "I suppose I can blame my son for your tardiness. I prepared a plate for you, but my son can wait until lunch to eat," she said, cutting her eyes at Stevin.

"Oh, Rene," Mr. Bash interjected, "let the young couple have their moment. They just got engaged and deserve some alone time."

"I have to run off anyway, Dad," Stevin said as he snatched a piece of bacon from Summer's plate, running out the door as his mom chased him with the broomstick.

Summer sat down to enjoy her breakfast full of laughter while admiring the joyful and family-oriented atmosphere she was about to become a part of.

She anticipated a relaxed day ahead as Stevin was heading to the airport to see Orlando off. Junior's wife and kids were scheduled to arrive soon, and Mr. Bash intended to keep the gathering confined solely to his immediate family. Mr. Bash had requested that his side of the family not visit the farm today so he could spend quality time with his sons and grandkids.

As the family sat around sharing funny family moments, Stevin recounted the tale of Summer's hysterical crying when she mistakenly cut all her hair off. Junior's teenage daughter instantly bonded with Summer.

The teenage girls stuck close to Summer, playing with her hair and attempting to teach her how to style her short new haircut. Summer relished in these family-oriented moments and cherished each one of them. The evening was perfect. Irene allowed Summer to prepare several of the dishes for dinner, and for a brief moment, it was like being back in the kitchen with Mimi. Irene even showed Summer how to fix her famous meatballs. How could this visit get any better?

After supper, the family gathered in the living room, and they continued swapping childhood stories as they laughed until they cried.

Summer enjoyed every detailed story, although she would remain quiet, avoiding sharing any of her traumatic upbringings.

Harmonic complexity tones suddenly filled the air, and it seemed like everyone except Summer knew what was about to happen. As the melody swelled in her ears, she began to feel strong emotions as she listened to the meaningful lyrics.

The family erupted in cheers when Mr. Bash entered the room, swaying his hips and two-stepping towards his wife. The kids continue to cheer as they encourage Mrs. Bash to join him in a dance.

Reaching out his hand, she smiled and nodded; she took his hand, and he twirled her around in his arms. Letting the rhythm control their movements, it was as if their bodies were in sync. Stevin reached out his hand, gesturing for Summer, as all the couples joined in, allowing the meaningful lyrics to express their love as they stared deep into their partner's eyes.

Summer, overwhelmed by her emotions, excused herself as she rushed into the bathroom, splashing water on her face, attempting to drown out the surge of emotions that had overtaken her. Forgetting to lock the bathroom door, Stevin entered behind her. He hugged her from behind, turned her around, and forced her to make eye contact.

"Do you want to talk about it?" he asked, noticing she seemed upset. Summer lowered her head and shrugged her shoulders, trying to downplay her emotions.

Stevin gently lifted her head and spoke softly, "You are about to be my wife. I feel your pain as my own. When you are sad, I'm sad. Your sadness deeply affects me. I'm emotionally connected to you, Summer, and I want sweep your broken heart under a rug and pile furniture on top of it to hide the cracks. I am your protector. I'm here to mend your broken heart, not bandage it momentarily."

She looked into his eyes and, with a trembling voice, said, "I want this, Stevin; no, I need this." She burst into tears and cried out, "I want what you have. I want my mother."

Stevin stroked the back of Summer's head, embraced her, and asked, "Tell me, what do you want me to do, Summer?"

Summer looked into Stevin's eyes and replied, "I'm ready, baby. I'm ready to meet my mom."

"Well then, let's go meet your mother," Stevin said reassuringly. "I don't want you to stress, Summer, but I've been working on a plan to set up a meet and greet, and I've just been waiting for your approval."

Summer remains silent. Stevin didn't need words; he was moving forward with his plan regardless. They rejoined the family back in the family room, and Summer snuggled up under Stevin as they watched his parents slowly dance the night away.

As they prepared for bed, Summer had one final request. She wanted to see Mimi's home before returning home. She asked if they could take a detour on the way home, rent a car with tinted windows, and discreetly drive by

Mimi's home. She hoped to catch a glimpse of Mr. Jeffery working in the garden next to Mimi's memorial tree.

Chapter 24: The Return Home

Stevin places their luggage in the trunk and walks over to the car's passenger side, where Summer is standing. He embraced her with a hug, gently stroking and squeezing her shoulders.

"Are you ready for this journey?" he asked.

"I don't know, Stevin. It's already hard enough being back home, but it's even harder knowing that I won't be able to set foot in Mimi's home. I hope that we can get some great footage on the camera so I can have a video of my home. It would be even better if Mr. Jeffery was working in the garden and you could capture footage of him. I would love to see him."

"Summer, have you considered writing to him, so he knows you are safe and doing okay?"

"No, Stevin. The less he knows, the safer he is. I can't involve him any deeper than what I already have."

"Okay, Summer, let's hit the road. We have an hour's drive to Mimi's home and must stay on schedule to avoid missing our flight back home."

Summer was grateful to Stevin for cutting his visit with his parents short by a day so they could fly to New York, rent a car, and drive an hour to Mimi's home. Summer wanted to capture footage of the house she shared with Mimi, and though she knew she was asking a lot of Stevin, she was grateful for his help. She held Stevin's hand and looked into his eyes, "Thank you. I know I've asked a lot from you, and I promise to spend the rest of my life showing you how much I appreciate you."

He leaned over and kissed her forehead. "Let's go, sweetie. I've enjoyed this trip, but I'm missing our home and bed. Yes, our bed. And while I'm on the subject of the bedroom, you have some making up to do," he said, causing her to look at him, puzzled.

"Me?" she asked.

"Yes, you," Stevin said. "You went straight, Suzy homemaker, prim and proper on this trip. When we arrive home, I'm going to need you to search through them skeletons in your closet and find Suzy's slutty sister you've been seducing me with. You know that lady I'm referring to, the one that likes to tea bag her man on the busy freeway, he said as he burst out into laughter.

She reaches over and pinches his side, shaking her head, amused by Stevin's ability to make her smile even in the most stressful moments.

As the car pulled out of the parking lot, she leaned back in the passenger seat, her palms sweating. She had to admit she was excited to be home, but her fear overshadowed any feelings of excitement. She knows returning home is risky and vows to remain out of sight to avoid any mistakes. Summer knew that her flying to New York would increase the chances of Christopher locating her.

As the hour-long road trip nears its end, Summer begins to panic. They are less than five minutes away from Mimi's home.

"Is the camera ready?" she asks anxiously.

"Do you have it set to record?" she continued, her worry increasing. Stevin, "Make sure you angle the camera so you can record the entire yard. And please zoom in on Mimi's memorial tree."

"Summer, just sit up in the seat high enough so you can actually see the property."

"No, Stevin, we can't take any chances of me being seen in this car. Please get to a safe speed where you can drive and capture some good footage for me."

"Okay, Summer, I can see the house now."

"Is it still painted white? Do you see Mr. Jefferey in the yard?"

"Hold on, little woman. Let me start recording."

"Hey, Summer, isn't that your car? I'm pretty sure that's the Kia you drove when you first arrived in Illinois. How did your car end up here?"

"That's a story for another day," she answered, slumping further down in her seat and reclining it.

"What do you see? Is anyone outside?" she inquired.

"Wait, Summer. Give me a chance to focus the camera. No one is outside."

"Please zoom in on Mimi's memorial tree. I bet it's in full bloom."

"Which tree are we focusing on, Summer?"

"There's only one tree on the side of the house next to the garden."

"There are two trees, Summer."

"No, there's not. It's the only tree next to the house," she insisted."

"No, Summer. There are two trees. One is smaller with a yellow bow tied around it," Stevin said.

"WHAT...?" Summer shouted as she popped her head up from the passenger seat, eyeing her house. "No, no, what is this? No, this is not happening; it can't be. Please tell me this is not happening."

"What's wrong, baby? What's going on?"

Summer fell to the floorboard of the car, sobbing uncontrollably. "No, Mr. Jeffery can't be gone. This is all my fault."

"Get up, baby, and calm down," Stevin pleaded. "It could be something else. 'Summer, please, baby, calm down." Stevin attempts to comfort her and rationalize different scenarios to calm her down as she screams out in sorrow. "It could be another family member."

"No, there is no one else," Summer cried out. "It was only me and Mimi, and there's no one else but Mr. Jeffery. Stevin, it's all my fault. I killed Mr. Jeffery. What if Christopher did this to him? This is all my fault. I ruin everybody's life that loves me. How could I be so stupid," she cried out.

Stevin grabs his phone, urgently searching the local obituary and confirms that Mr. Jeffery had indeed passed away two months after Summer's disappearance. He realizes that he needs to stop the car and comfort her, as she is distraught and overwhelmed with grief.

Stevin is worried about breaking the news to her and confirming that it was indeed Mr. Jeffery who has passed away. He knows he needs to be truthful with her. He decided to leave the highway, turning onto a dirt road away from the main road, far enough so that their car was not visible. Stevin exited the vehicle and walked to the passenger side, scooping her up from the floorboard.

Looking at her as her eyes widen with sorrow, he is afraid to say anything, worried about how much more she could endure. They sat silently as Stevin held her in his arms, comforting her, before showing her the article. Summer's knees suddenly buckled.

He helped her back into the passenger seat as tears streamed down her face and her breathing became heavy. Her eyes filled with a look of brokenness. It was like looking into a broken mirror with no reflection of the woman he loved.

"Summer, the article says natural causes. If the authorities had found anything suspicious, they would have noted suspected foul play."

"He died from a broken heart, Stevin, and I killed him. He worried himself to death worrying about me. I worried him to death," she screamed out in sorrow.

Stevin understood that words alone could not mend her broken heart. Therefore, he went to the trunk, took out a pillow, put a blanket on the backseat, and gently helped her lie down to soothe her before their flight. It was crucial that everything went smoothly while passing through TSA.

The ride to the airport was miserable for Stevin. He could hear her weeping inconsolably and knew he couldn't do anything to fix it. As she lay with her face buried in the soak-drenched pillow, she couldn't deny this was all her fault. There was only one thing Mr. Jefferey was committed to, and that was keeping his promise to Mimi. That he would look after her, and she had brought danger to his front door.

Summer couldn't stop the images that rapidly flashed through her mind. Images of Mr. Jeffery's face when he picked her up from the airport when she arrived back home broken and beaten by the hands of Christopher. And if that wasn't bad enough. His last memory of her is her being dragged out of Mimi's home by Christopher while he is being held at gunpoint.

"His poor heart, his poor little fragile heart," she cried. 'He died from a broken heart. I thought I was doing the right thing by not calling. I should have just called to say I'm okay. Oh my god, his poor sons. I can't allow my mistakes to affect anyone else,' she cried as she stared at her engagement ring, knowing in her heart what needed to be done.

She pulled herself together as they checked in and made their way through the airport. All she wanted was to return home to safety and hide behind that safe, protective bubble Stevin had created for her. But she couldn't help but wonder how long that safety net would last. Her world has proven happiness for her equates to danger for others. She came to realization that her happiness often came at the expense of her loved one's safety, and the thought of losing Stevin terrified her. She would die, just die, if anything happened to him.

As they boarded the plane, Stevin gave up his window seat to comfort her. He allowed her to cry herself to sleep as he sat silently stroking her hand, worrying about her mental state. Afraid this would put a halt to her reunion with her mom. Despite his concerns, he planned to move forward without Summer's knowledge. His one true goal was reuniting her with her mother, knowing this was the true source of happiness her heart truly craved and needed.

It has been two weeks since their return home, and Summer has hardly spoken a word. Staring from a distance, all Stevin can do is comfort her when she allows him to. Although he tries not to take it personally, understanding that her sorrow and discontentment are due to the loss of Mr. Jeffery and the fact she blames herself for his death. He knows he can no longer stand by and allow her to disappear in her own dark thoughts and memories. Standing by not doing anything wasn't an option.

"Summer baby, I can't even begin to imagine what you're feeling or going through mentally right now. But I know how I'm feeling watching you suffering through this, and it's unbearable for me. I can't continue to watch you like this. Hell, you can't continue like this."

He kneels to her eye level, takes hold of her hand, and they gaze into each other's teary eyes, unable to find the right words amidst the overwhelming intensity of sadness that consumed her. He leaned in, resting his head on her lap as she could feel him trembling. She couldn't bear the look of hopelessness in his eyes.

Summer was shaken back to reality. The man she loved was kneeling in front of her, trembling on his knees, filled with anguish due to her. She realized she couldn't keep going like this, especially at the cost of Stevin's peace.

Summer gently lifted his chin, looked deep into his eyes, and softly kissed his hands, then his lips. She gently kissed his forehead as a sign of her affection and sincerity towards him. Without uttering a word, she embraced him by wrapping her arm around his neck, and he could sense the intensity of her touch. Wrapping himself around her waist, he pulled her closer to the edge of the sofa, holding her tight. No words were needed. He was just grateful Summer seemed to have snapped out of that dark, sunken place she had crawled in for the last two weeks. He knew what must be done; he was just afraid to rock the boat too early. Nothing could go wrong with Summer meeting her mom for the first time.

"Kimberley, answer the door!" Rose screamed from the patio. The doorbell rang for the third time while Rose fumbled, attempting to put her feet back in her thong shoe, as she rushed to the door. As she swung the door open, a mail carrier greeted her and asked for Rose White. "I am Rose White."

"Hello, Mrs. White. I have a restricted delivery for you today. This confidential document requires a photo ID and your signature, ma'am," said the mail carrier.

"Okay," Rose mumbled with a confused expression as she stepped away from the door to grab her wallet for her driver's license.

"Who is the sender?" she asked.

"I am sorry, ma'am, but I don't know that information," the mail carrier said. The envelope had only her name and address on it, but there was no return address. She hesitantly signed for it, wondering why she was receiving a confidential letter. 'That scatterbrained, Sarah, better not have had me served with anything,' she thought. Convinced that the documents were from Sarah, she quickly opened the envelope, revealing a large white envelope that read: "STOP." It is vital that you follow all written instructions in this letter.

Immediately, the hair follicles on her arms contracted, causing her tiny arm hairs to rise. Rose's mind races with questions about the mysterious content of the letter. She shook the envelope to make sure no substance was sealed inside and held it up to the light, attempting to get a glimpse of its content. However, the envelope was too thick. Slowly, she peeled open the envelope flap and found a letter inside. She grabbed a glass of tea and retreated to the patio to read the letter.

"Hello, Rose," the letter began. "My name is Stevin. I understand that this letter may seem a bit confusing, especially given its unconventional delivery. However, it is of vital importance that you keep the contents of this letter confidential. I am unsure if this is a door you even want to open, but I wanted to reach out and introduce myself. As

stated, my name is Stevin, and I am engaged to a wonderful young woman named Summer Taylor, who happens to be your daughter. Again, I'm not sure if this is something you're interested in or if it's an opportunity you desire, but Summer has dreamed of this day her entire life. Due to your parents' manipulations and a state screw-up, Summer has grown up believing her last name was Taylor instead of Teller, even having the wrong birthdate. The only knowledge she has ever had related to you was her parents abandoned her at birth. Just recently, she learned your name, and what really happened to her birth father, and how she was taken from you. 'Why the secrecy?' you asked. Well, Summer met a young man by the name of Christopher Diamond..."

In Stevin's letter, he explains why Summer has gone into hiding and why she's afraid to reach out on her own. He also provided some background information about how he and Summer reconnected and their plans to get married. Rose was instructed not to share the content of the letter with anyone.

The letter stated that Stevin would give Rose a day to process the information and decide whether she wanted to meet with Summer. Additionally, the letter conveyed that if Rose wanted to proceed, she would receive another confidential delivery the following day, and Stevin would have everything arranged for their meeting. She was advised that if she accepted it, she would receive a burner phone with only one number saved, which she would use to call and speak with him. If she wasn't interested in moving forward, she could decline the second package and never hear from Stevin again.

Rose felt her heart racing and skipping beats as if she was having palpitations. With trembling hands, she called David.

"Hello darling," David answered.

"David, I need you to come home now. Please, I really need you," Rose pleaded.

"What's wrong" David shouts as Kimberley is his first thought.

"No, David, please just come home. Nobody is hurt, no one is hurt. Please, I need you. Please, David," Rose begged.

"Okay, I understand. Rose, please give me an hour as I am currently on a home visit with a client. I will head to the office afterward to reschedule my other appointments for a different day."

After ending the call, Rose felt extremely anxious, and her entire body shook with nervousness. She kept repeating to herself, 'Why make me wait? Why wasn't the phone sent with the letter?' There was no way she would get a wink of sleep until that phone was in her hands. Finally, her wish had come true, and she would be reunited with her daughter.

David burst into the house two hours later, frantically searching for Rose. He found her standing in the kitchen, tears of joy in her eyes as she held the letter in her hand. As she trembles with excitement, he walks up to her and attempts to take the letter out of her hand. She was unable to speak and lightly pounded on his chest as she pressed the letter in his hand.

"My baby, I'm about to be reunited with my baby," she said, gasping her breath excitedly.

David stood in shock as he read the letter. He embraced Rose with a hug as they held each other and wept. David was invested just as much as Rose. He had stood by Rose's side throughout these years and always felt as if he had also lost a child.

"Okay, Rose, we will follow his instructions precisely. Where is Kimberley?"

"I don't know. She stepped out and didn't inform me she was leaving."

"Well, let's not involve her until we know what kind of trouble Summer is in."

"I don't care, David! I don't want to lose my child again."

"I know, Rose, I know," he said as he stroked her back.

Chapter 25: Opening The Door To Her Past

Rose was unable to sleep and spent the entire night pacing back and forth. Making sure Kimberley didn't get wind of what was happening, she planted herself in the formal living room in the chair next to the front door, awaiting the delivery guy.

When Kimberley came down the stairs, she noticed Rose sitting in the formal living room. "Old woman, what are you doing? You never sit in the front of the house. Is that early dementia kicking in?"

"Yep," Rose replied sarcastically. "Just remember to tell the cops I have senile dementia when they're called out for me choking that scrawny neck of yours."

Kimberley mocked, "Hehe, he. You're not funny at all. Now get yourself in that kitchen and make my breakfast, old lady."

Rose thought to herself, "Maybe this is a good idea. It might help me focus on something else."

Rose was feeling a bit frazzled in the kitchen, banging the dishes around. She just couldn't get it together. She was a ball of nerves. She made such a ruckus Kimberley entered the kitchen to check on her.

"Mom, are you okay? All jokes aside, you seem as if something is bothering you. I'm starting to worry."

Rose walked over, attempting to hug Kimberley, as it warmed her heart that Kimberley was showing some affection towards her dear old mom. Rose was immediately met with resistance.

"Please back it up, lady. Save the mushy crap for dad. I'm too old for hugs and kisses."

Kimberley was always a tough cookie, even at the age of four. She demanded to be treated like a big girl, which meant no more hugs and kisses from her mother, and she stood by that request. If only she knew, all Rose desired from her was to be allowed to be mom and embrace her with as much love as possible.

Never mind about breakfast Mother; your son-in-law will be in town soon. I need to go get pampered. Rose rolled her eyes, mumbling to herself, 'Son-in-law, my ass.'

"Where's Dad?" Kimberley asked. "He never leaves this early for work."

"Your dad had to leave for work a little earlier than usual. He had an unforeseen event that occurred yesterday that required him to cancel several of his scheduled home visits. So, he needed to get his day started early this morning.

David had left home at the break of dawn attempting to catch up on the three canceled appointments yesterday, so he had to return to work, leaving Rose alone with her racing thoughts.

Rose sat alone, lost in an endless stream of thoughts. She imagined how it would feel to see Summer for the first time, to be able to touch her finally. She was relieved that Kimberley had left the house before the carrier arrived. Rose knew if the package arrived while she was there, she would have to fight her off to keep her from opening it. She plopped down in the chair, feeling her eyes grow heavy as she started to doze off.

When suddenly, the doorbell rang, and sure enough, it was the package she had been eagerly awaiting. She promised David she would wait until he got home to make the call, but she couldn't resist opening the box. Rose quickly tore open the box, reassuring the phone worked and a contact number was saved in the phone before retreating to the bedroom to try to take a nap until David returned home.

STOCKBRIDGE, GEORGIA

Stevin was sitting at his office desk when he received a notification from his burner phone informing him that Summer's mom had accepted the package. He smiled big, spinning around in his chair cheering. Without a doubt, it assured him Rose also wanted this meet and greet to happen. Stevin contemplated how he could break the news to Summer. He decided to coordinate with Rose and arrange everything, and only inform Summer on the day of the meet and greet so that she couldn't change her mind. He felt both excitement and fear, hoping his plan wouldn't backfire.

Stevin had been waiting all day for a call from Summer's mother, but hours had passed, and he had heard nothing. As he started to pack up his things at the end of the day, his burner phone finally rang. With excitement in his voice, Stevin answered the phone, "Hello?"

On the other end of the line, Rose replied, "Hello," in a low, squeaky voice, filled with excitement as she held David's hand.

"Oh my God!" Stevin exclaimed. "Give me a moment to gather myself. I can't believe I'm talking to you. You're about to change my life for the better."

Rose giggled with excitement, "You've already changed my life. You'll never know what this means to me."

"I understand," he responded, "I can only imagine. I have witnessed the pain in Summer's eyes daily. So, believe me, my heart is completely invested in helping you reunite with your daughter."

Rose leaped for joy on the other line as she silently screamed, "She wants me; she wants her mother."

Gathering herself, she says, "Stevin, please don't be upset with me, but my husband is here by my side. He is to me what you are to Summer. He has been my rock since my parents took her from me."

"Wait a minute," Stevin said, surprised with excitement in his voice. "Are you kidding me? Wow! That's amazing! It touches my heart to know that you didn't go through this challenging time alone."

"Hello Stevin, my name is David. Please believe me when I say I feel like Summer is my daughter. I met Rose right after her ordeal and have walked this journey with her. There's no way I would miss this."

"I hear you, good man. I wouldn't expect you to."

"Stevin, can you give us a brief background on this Christopher character and explain just how much danger Summer is in?"

"To be honest, David, I don't know. Yes, I know Christopher, and he comes from money. Summer was in an abusive relationship with him for years as he manipulated her because she had no one but him.

This is the same individual who actually found you, Rose, and kept it from her their entire relationship. If it were up to me, she wouldn't be in hiding, but the abuse she suffered from him has her terrified. So when his father helped her escape and assisted her with a new identity, he provided her with your information and everything Christopher had kept hidden from her.

However, one of his stipulations was for her to bury her past, and she could never reach out to you. Christopher has access to all your contact details, so they figured you would be the first place he would search for her. I do know he has some sick effectuation for her. She tried to escape him before, and he almost beat her to death. So, in her head, the threat is real."

Rose became extremely emotional over the phone. Hearing what Summer had been going through was too much to bear. Here, she thought she was mentally living in hell with the anguish of losing her child, but her baby girl was actually, physically and emotionally, going through hell.

"Stevin, could you tell me if she had a good childhood?" Rose asked with concern.

"Rose, I understand that you are already upset, and I don't want to add to it. I think it's better if Summer shares with you about her life. I want you to know that you walking into her life will be the best thing that ever happened to her. However, I have yet to inform her that I contacted you. She has dreamed of this day her whole life, but her fear for your safety overshadows any happiness she might feel."

"Stevin, please don't ask me to wait any longer. I need to talk to my daughter now," Rose said urgently.

"I understand, Rose. I have already looked into booking some hotel rooms in Rowell. Are you guys able to drive out tomorrow?"

"Yes!" Rose exclaimed excitedly before David had a chance to respond.

"Stevin, I don't think it's a good idea to set this up and leave Summer in the dark," David utter with great concern.

"David, I understand your concern. If I didn't believe wholeheartedly that this was the best course of action for Summer, I would not have suggested it. Let me handle this situation with Summer, and I will send you both the hotel information via text."

After ending the call, they all agreed to meet at the hotel. Rose and David would arrive an hour later, giving Stevin ample amount of time to inform Summer of what was occurring.

While checking his call log, Stevin noticed three missed calls from Summer. He texted her to apologize for missing the calls and informed her that his meeting had run a bit longer than expected, letting her know that he would be leaving the office soon. He was excited for her and didn't want to make any mistakes and ruin her reunion with her mom. He needed a moment to himself to devise a strategy to get Summer to Rowell without her figuring out his plans.

***

Summer greeted him at the door with a warm hug. "Bae, you're two hours late. I tried to reach you a few times."

"I know, sweetheart. I'm sorry I couldn't get back to you sooner. You won't believe the day I have had. But on a positive note, I'm taking tomorrow off and taking you on a nice drive. I've already booked us a room so we can get away for a day."

"What are we getting away from?"

"It's just going to be me and you, baby. You don't have to worry about anything," he reassured her.

"Who are we getting away from? Where exactly are we going?" Stevin, it's just you and me now," she whispered jokingly.

"Let me worry about that, little woman. Now, go to the bedroom so you can show me how much you missed me today," he said playfully, chasing after her.

Chapter 26: The Ultimate Reunion

Summer gazed out the car window, scanning from side to side, focusing her attention on the heavy traffic. To her knowledge, Stevin had decided to take her on a short road trip to spend some quality time with her outside of their home.

Silence filled the car as she could hear the cars whizzing by. Stevin remained silent the majority of the road trip as he tapped on the steering wheel as nervousness consumed him.

Excited about the surprise destination, Summer let him be. As the traffic came to a halt, she noticed Stevin checking his watch as if he were running late. Stevin knows time is crucial, with the traffic slowing down to a crawl. If this traffic jam doesn't start moving soon, he will have to reveal the true reason for their trip to Summer. Knowing she could very well freak out and force him to exit the freeway.

Looking out the window, she noticed the mile markers that signal they were fifty-three miles from Atlanta. Stevin could see the swift turn of her head, looking back at the highway sign marker.

"Baby, where exactly are we going?"

"We are about ten miles from our destination, Summer; if we can get out of this traffic, we will be arriving soon." He notices her rubbing her hands on her pants as she does when she gets nervous. Stevin knows time is crucial and not on his side. From the look of it, they will arrive at the hotel at the same time as Rose and David.

He needed to warn David but couldn't take out the burner phone without Summer noticing.

"Sweetheart," he said softly.

"Yes, Stevin? she answered.

"Do you trust me?"

"Of course, Stevin. That should be a given. Why are you asking me that?"

"So, if that is a given, you know my heart, and I only want the best for us."

"What's going on, Stevin? Why the secrecy?"

Just as he mustered up enough courage to confess what he had done; the traffic began to move. Stevin realized when they arrived and got checked in; he would have about twenty minutes to mentally prepare her for meeting her mother.

Meanwhile, Summer felt that Stevin was hiding something and wasn't being honest with her. But surely, he wouldn't force meeting her mom on her in this way, so that thought came and went without hesitation.

He drove into the hotel's valet parking with barely any time to spare. Fidgeting with his wallet, he impatiently waited for the hotel receptionist to check them in as she typed with no sense of urgency. As he hurriedly walked to the room, she found herself skipping to keep up with him. He wasted no time as he ushered her to the couch and closed the hotel door behind them.

"Look, sweetheart, this isn't how the day was planned out, but due to traffic, time is not on my side. Please don't be mad at me," he pleaded.

Her eyes widened as she pulled away, questioning him, "What have you done, Stevin?"

"Summer, please let me explain," Stevin said urgently. "We don't have much time. Your mother will be knocking on that door any second now."

Summer leaped off the couch and charged towards the door, shouting, "No, Stevin! How could you? How could you?" She cried out. "You've knowingly put my mom's life in danger. I can't bear to lose anyone else because of my selfish desires."

Stevin swiftly takes a hold of her, bear-hugging her from the back as he gently wrestles her to the floor as she attempts to run out of their hotel room. "No, let me go! Let me go!" She shouted as she struggled to break free from his grip.

"Dammit, Summer, stop and let me explain," Stevin pleaded.

Unable to break from Stevin's tight grip, her body goes limp as she lay and weeps in his arms. He could feel her intense anxiety as the vibration of her racing heart pounded from fear.

"How could you do this, Stevin? Look what happened to Mr. Jeffery."

He turned her around and forced eye contact. "Summer, I understand how crucial your mother's safety is. You have no idea what measures I took to ensure that a confidential letter was delivered to her and that only she could sign for it. The letter included everything, Summer, and it's nothing related to Christopher and your fear for her safety she isn't aware of. She has a wonderful, supportive husband who has been by her side throughout this entire ordeal. He actually called you his daughter. They have been given strict instructions on what to do. Summer, your mother wants this reunion just as badly as you do. She begged me not to prolong this reunion."

Looking up at Stevin with her sad, teary eyes, she smiled slightly. "What did she say?"

"Hell, she practically threatened to whoop my ass if I didn't make this happen ASAP."

"No, she didn't," she said, knowing Stevin was trying to get her to calm down and not flee before Rose arrived.

Stevin burst into laughter. "No, seriously, she begged me not to make her wait any longer."

"Have you spoken to her today?" She asked curiously.

"Yes, Summer, I did, and don't worry, after sending a letter by restricted delivery, I also arranged for a burner phone to be delivered the same way. I requested that she inform no one. David, who was once her psychiatrist, became her husband. He started treating her right after you were taken away. He strongly believes he is a part of this journey and has asked that we don't take away this moment from him. Now, my dear, go freshen up. They will be here any moment.

She held his hand tightly and said, "No, Stevin, I can't. What if I'm not what she expects? What if she doesn't want me?"

Leaning in with a forehead kiss, "Baby, that's the furthest from the truth. Also, when I read your documents, I did not disclose some information to you." Her eyes widen with the expression, 'Now What.'

"You are a big sister," he said.

"I am," she said with excitement."

"Yes, you have a younger sister. However, you won't be meeting her today as I have asked your mom to keep it between herself and David until we can get everything sorted out."

Her hands were sweat-drenched as she sat and waited on that anticipated knock on the door. The minutes felt like hours. Her past hurts, and rejection immediately started to creep back in as she relived the rejection from potential adoptive parents. She had never been enough, always unwanted.

An unfamiliar ringtone snaps her out of her deep thoughts. Stevin answered the phone and greeted David, "Hello, David. Yes, we are ready and waiting. Summer is aware of the situation." As he hung up the phone, he walked over to Summer and began rubbing her shoulders. "They are here," he said. Stevin attempted to walk away, but she grabbed his arm. "It's okay, Summer," he said, attempting to reassure her.

Stevin opens the hotel door and walks back over to Summer. She stands up and drops her head, closing her eyes as she positions herself behind him. As much as she wants this, she's afraid her mom will reject her.

Summer sensed a presence approaching her side, as she knew it was her mother, as her lovely fragrance filled her nostrils. Feeling Stevin as he stepped away, Summer stood motionless, still afraid to open her eyes, until she felt a soft touch caress her cheek. When she opened her eyes and lifted her head, she immediately gasped for air as her heart was overwhelmed with emotions she couldn't explain.

Rose grabbed her into her arms, and she held her tightly as they stood and wept in each other's arms. After a moment, Rose pulled back and took Summer's face in her hands to look at her closely. She needed to scan every inch of her baby girl.

Rose felt like she was looking into James' eyes as she was struck by how much Summer resembled her father. Summer was lost in the realization that she finally could see and touch someone who shared her flesh and blood, someone she belonged to and resembled.

Rose gently wiped away Summer's tears as Summer ran her fingers through Rose's hair and pulled on her ears as if to confirm that this moment was real and truly happening.

"I'm real, baby girl. Your mother is real," Rose cried out as she embraced Summer in a long hug.

Stevin and David both looked up, trying to hide their tears as they turned away to protect their manhood.

Rose took Summer by the hand, guided her to the couch, and sat beside her. Summer remained silent, lost in the moment, while Rose was eager to talk, as she wanted to know everything about her.

It was the opposite for Summer; it was as if she was floating and needed to live in the present moment. Instead of sitting up next to Rose, she curled up on the couch next to her and rested her head on Rose's lap, closing her eyes and weeping softly.

Summer finally felt like she could take a deep breath and breathe. The first impact of her mother's smell, her touch, was like an out-of-body experience. It was as if she was suddenly snatched up in this whirlwind of emotions as if she were traveling back through time, but this time, it was a journey of solace and relief.

As forceful wind and pressure spun her around, erasing her past memories of rejection and a lack of belonging, and then spat her out.

It felt like she was on the top of a mountain, breathing in fresh, clean air, and all the weight of depression, fear, and unworthiness began to fall off her shoulders. And as she descended back down to reality, her mind and body were exhausted. She just needed to be cradled in her mother's arms, as she was drained and needed to sleep.

That was fine with Rose, as she also took in the moment, feeling a mix of joy and relief as she softly stroked

Summer's hair, her heart full of love for her long-lost daughter.

Summer needed nothing from her mother at that moment but her love and affection. Her mind and soul were exhausted. This was an unexplainable peace she couldn't describe. For the first time in her life, she closed her eyes and knew her mother wanted her, and she wasn't a mistake, just thrown away like trash.

Startling Rose, Summer swiftly popped her head up and kicked off her tennis shoes. "Stevin, look! I have my mother's feet," she cried out, her voice filled with a mix of excitement and disbelief, as she lined her feet up next to Rose's, which were visible through her sandals.

"Our toes are shaped alike," Summer cried out, pressing her hands against Rose as she examined the creases in her hands.

Rose felt immense joy as she could see how the smallest things excited Summer. The sight of their similar toes and hand creases filled her with a profound sense of connection. Rose vowed to herself she would never lose her again.

Summer leaned back and rested her head on Rose's shoulder, as she took a big sniff of her hair. There wasn't an inch of her mother she wouldn't have a memory of.

Rose sat up and rolled up her sleeve, revealing her birthmark to Summer showing her another part of her that connected them.

Summer shouts excitedly, "I have the same birthmark on my arm!"

"I know," Rose replied, embracing her with a big hug.

"Well, David, would you like to join me at the bar?" Stevin asked. Let's give these two a moment of privacy, and we all can do a proper greeting when we return.

Stevin didn't bother to inform Summer that they were leaving to give them a moment of privacy. Nothing at that moment could break her focus away from her mom as she examined her from head to toe, finding any familiarity that connected them. She had a million questions for Rose, but at that moment, all she wanted to do was convert back to that little girl who felt abandoned and lost as she needed to rewrite history.

She rested her head back in Rose's lap as Rose hummed a lullaby she used to sing to her as a toddler. Rose also took in the moment; as long as Summer was willing, she could rock and sing to her for hours. They both closed their eyes and basked in each other love as if they had not spent the last three decades apart. The mental connection alone spoke volumes. It was as if they both drew much-needed strength from each other presence.

Rose knew Summer's sad eyes told a story of brokenness, and she would have to face some sad truths her firstborn daughter endured from her absence. Knowing a conversation was long overdue, but they had the rest of their lives to play catch up. In the moment, they both found themselves rewriting the past, sharing a connection only a mother and daughter could.

Miss. Dangerfield held a place in Summer's heart that could never be erased or replaced. But for her entire life, she craved for the unwavering, unconditional, and enduring attachment of her biological mother. Today was her moment to do just that, as she soaked in every inch of motherly affection that Rose was willing to give.

Chapter 27: Uncovering Her Pass

As Stevin and David clinked their pint glasses together, they raised a toast to ending the misdeed and unjust act that has been haunting Rose and Summer for decades. They both could only imagine the unknown toll it must have taken on them over the years. So, to finally end this dark chapter of their lives, it was time to start building new memories.

Stevin is determined to wash away Summer's past with Christopher and treat him like the insignificant person he is.

"Okay, Stevin, I need you to fill me in. Surely you wouldn't have gone through these great links to set this up if you didn't perceive this Christopher character as a threat."

Stevin chugged down his cold draft beer, and his eyes flashed with anger for a brief moment. "He's a pussy, and please forgive my language. He tortured her mentally and physically. To this day, I will never understand. He could have made this day happen for her the first day he met her. Yet, he was determined to isolate her from everyone. I believe that he never had any good intentions towards her. If he had, you guys could have been a big, happy family, given that he knew her desires and what this meant to her.

"So, no matter how much I don't want him to be a factor in her life or our life, he is. However, I want downplay the situation. Christopher is a psycho daddy's boy with money and connections. David, to be honest, I am uncertain about who poses a more significant threat, Christopher or his father. Christopher is a danger to Summer, but his father holds all the power and connections."

"Wait a minute, son," David interrupted. "I'm confused. You mentioned earlier that Christopher's father helped Summer escape, so why would he be a threat?"

"I fault myself every day for this, David. I was part of Summers' recruitment and was the first person to meet her in Illinois. As soon as I saw her, I knew she was meant to be my wife; it was like she was heaven-sent. She was this wholesome, quiet, very simple young lady who lit up any room she entered with her presence. Her innocence and not wanting to be seen actually made her shine brighter. When she arrived, she seemed so lost and unsure of herself.

"Hell, she wasn't sure of me either, being she never caught on to any of my advancements. Even though I was interested in her, I was not trying to scare her off by coming on to strong, so I thought I had time to work my magic.

"However, It took one night of her hanging out at a night club, and I lost her; just like that, I lost her," he said as he clings his pint glass on the bar, signaling the bartender for another cold draft beer. Stevin looked down at his empty pint glass, feeling regretful.

"I intentionally helped Summer receive a new position, which involved us traveling for the job, and Christopher didn't like it, he didn't like it at all. He didn't make her quit her job; he just convinced a coworker who was jealous of Summer to file a sexual harassment charge against me." David's eyes instantly widen with surprise.

"He did what?" David asked. "Wait, wait one minute, are you serious right now? Surely, you're pulling my leg. Are you telling me that this individual is so insecure and reckless that he would file a false claim or even manipulate someone else to file trumped-up charges that could have ruined your career and livelihood?"

"Yes, my good man, my life was turned upside down for a year. Thankfully, I had a good woman in my corner who fought tooth and nail to clear my name. Long story short, I never returned to Memorial, and I had a slight change in my career path.

"So when Summer disappeared, I was Christopher's first target, which I had no idea she had escaped him. I started noticing strange cars following me and weird beeping noises coming from my work and personal phone. At that time, I had already moved to another state and thought the Summer drama was behind me. I had no idea what was going on with Summer.

"However, as time went by, it became more evident that I was being followed. So, I reached out to my father, who is a retired general with some major connections. His close friend, Jim, used to work for the FBI and is now a private investigator who had a lucrative PI business. 'Notice I said had!' Jim indeed links the PI that was tailing me back to Christopher's father's company.

"I strongly suspect Christopher hired them to follow me, but everything he does apparently links back to his father's connections. To get to the bottom of this, Jim took it upon himself to thoroughly dig into Mr. Diamond's background.

"This is where it got sticky; this man is better protected than the actual president himself. People in high positions whom Jim had relied on for years stopped responding to his calls. Jim informed my father that he had received a call from a former FBI agent, warning him to back away from his investigations and leave Mr. Diamond and his family alone or else he would lose everything.

"The warning came a day too late. The following day, Jim's office burned down. Not only did he lose everything, but two weeks later, he was charged with arson for setting fire to his own business. His trial was a sham. Needless to say, he didn't go to jail, but he lost everything in the process.

"This tragedy to Jim wasn't a coincidence; without a doubt, Christopher's father has some major connections and will protect his son at all costs. In my opinion, I don't believe relocating Summer had anything to do with her personal safety, but protecting his son from his own destructive behavior, even if it meant breaking his heart to save him from his own self-destruction.

"So, no, I don't believe that Christopher poses a threat, but he is definitely reckless. I am aware that his father is a powerful man with connections that one would not want to cross."

"Well, does he still have you followed?"

"No, I was in another state and engaged to another woman at that time. I only learnt about Summer's situation a year later after running into her in Louisiana. She was in a fragile and vulnerable state, hiding away in a hotel and surviving on canned food. She happens to be walking from the park around the corner from her hotel dressed in Muslim attire. My coworker stepped back in her path, losing his balance, and our fate was sealed at that moment. I spoke to my dad and told him that my wife just walked back into my life, and I wasn't losing her again. Despite everything that had happened to Jim, he still gave me his blessing."

David asked, "Does Summer know how dangerous his family is?"

"No, David, I never shared that information with her. She has already been through a lot, and I don't want to traumatize her any further. She has been living in fear for a long time and only recently began to experience a bit of freedom.

"In fact, she just started venturing out of our home. I was able to convince her to travel with me to visit my family. I'm considering moving back home and giving the farm life a second chance to ensure her peace and happiness. One thing I am certain of is that Mr. Diamond wants Summer out of Christopher's life just as badly as I do, and as long as we stay clear of him, and any investigations related to him and his family. I truly believe he will protect Summer's whereabouts from Christopher."

David patted Stevin on the back and said, "Good man, you're truly a good man. Now, let's go check on our women." He checked his watch and noticed that they had been at the bar for two hours.

They softly stepped back into the hotel room, peeking their heads in to see how the reunion was going. They were greeted with a bright smile from Rose as Summer slept soundly with her head resting on Rose's lap. Rose carefully wiggles herself loose from Summer's embrace without awakening her. She embraces Stevin with a big hug and thanks him for bringing her daughter home.

"Stevin, we hadn't talked much; all she wanted to do was lay across my lap and hold my hand."

Stevin smiled as he reassured Rose that she had brought peace into Summer's world. She no longer has to fight this war of the unknown and feeling unwanted, as if she doesn't belong to anyone.

Rose turns to David with tears in her eyes and lays her head on his chest while looking up into his eyes.

"I can't leave her, David. I just can't," Rose said. "I didn't get a chance to talk to her, and there are so many unanswered questions. We have to stay; I must be here when she wakes up in the morning."

David wraps his arms around Rose and squeezes her tight.

"Well, you can thank Stevin; he has already planned ahead. We have adjoining rooms."

Rose tiptoes back to the sofa and softly pecks Summer on the cheek. She turns to Stevin and asks him to promise to knock if Summer awakens and needs her.

Stevin locked the door, ensuring they had enough time to enter the adjacent room before waking Summer up. He carefully slid his arms under her, trying to lift her without disturbing her sleep. As he began to carry her towards the bed, she suddenly popped her head up and looked around, realizing that Rose was nowhere to be seen.

"Where's my mom? Where is she? Was I dreaming this?"

"Don't worry, my dear. Your mom is right next door in the adjoining room. She didn't want to disturb your sleep. Let's rest now, and we'll have breakfast together in the morning. Your body is responding to all the stress you're under, so it's important that you take this time to rest. We need you to be okay, and your well-being is our priority. I have never seen you sleep so peacefully. Just rest, baby. Just rest," he says as he pulls her into his arms, running his fingers through her hair.

Summer cuffs her hands to her face as she can still smell the scent of Rose's perfume. Summer smiles as she snuggles up against Stevin, but a sickening feeling overtakes her as she realizes that in order to have a relationship with Rose, it will come with strict boundaries. Summer knows she can't lose her mom again.

Chapter 28: The Harsh Truth

Stevin slowly opens his eyes, greeted by the morning sunshine peeking through the hotel drapes. He smiles, feeling a boost of self-gratification and overwhelmed with joy, knowing that he has gifted Summer her dream and reunited her with her mom.

As he takes a long stretch, he reaches behind him, feeling for Summer, but her side of the bed is empty, and the sheets are cold. Confused, he sits up and blinks as his eyes adjust to the light. Scanning the room, he tries to locate her. He gets out of bed and calls out for her, entering the other room only to find David lying on the hotel sofa.

"Good morning, David. You look uncomfortable."

David nods yes as he slowly rises from the sofa, holding his back as if he were in pain.

"I guess it's clear my little lady has found her way to her mom this morning," Stevin says with a chuckle.

"Yes, your little woman came scratching on the door like a little kitten at 5 am. I just opened the door and exchanged rooms with her, so excuse my lack of attire. I know she was eager to be under her mom."

"Well, let me get dressed, and we can get started on breakfast for the ladies," Stevin suggested.

"Now, that's where you're wrong," David countered. "The kitchen is Rose's domain, and I don't mind it at all." Stevin laughed out loud as the look on David's face suggested he had definitely misspoken by offering for him to cook.

"We can order breakfast and have it delivered," David suggested.

"It would be safer to go and pick some items up and pay cash. I purposely booked these suites under my company account. It would be best for neither of us to use our credit cards on this trip. Better safe than sorry. Besides, I purposely booked a suite with a kitchen so Summer could cook. Since she loves cooking, I thought it would be a wonderful experience she could share with her mom."

"Good thinking, Stevin; that's a great idea. Rose is also passionate about cooking and catering to the family. Let's ask the ladies for a shopping list. Besides, I need to get back into my room to get appropriately dressed, and I know Rose could use some personal items, too. We packed light."

With a slight tap on the door, Summer opened, smiling from ear to ear as she greeted them. Summer and Rose had spent the past four hours catching up and getting to know each other better. Rose shared her childhood memories and upbringing with Summer, and Summer learned more about her dad and how much he loved her, as Rose shared stories about the two of them and how much James was indeed a girl dad.

"Okay, Mr. David, I guess I'll let you borrow my mom," Summer said as she burst into laughter.

"Yes, Summer. Let's allow David to get dressed. We also need you ladies to put together a grocery list so that you can cook us hardworking men some breakfast," Stevin said with a smile.

"I would be delighted," Rose echoed.

As the door to the adjoining room closed, Summer jumped into Stevin's arms and kissed him, thanking him for giving her the opportunity to reconnect with her mother.

"Bae, I learned so much about my dad," she said, bouncing around like a ball of energy. "My mom told me that I was a daddy's girl, always demanding his attention. I wouldn't let her sit on his lap or show any affection towards her in my presence. She said I was glued to his hip."

"Summer, did you guys talk about your upbringing?"

"We spoke briefly about it, but there isn't much to discuss. I prefer positive vibes only. The only thing she needed to know was about my sweet Mimi."

Meanwhile, David watched Rose as she washed her face at the washbowl, humming a sweet melody with a smile. He Inches up behind her and gently kisses her on her neck.

"By the way, did you mention to Summer how Kimberley feels about the situation?"

"No, David. I don't want to cause her any more disappointment and pain. I will sit Kimberley down and smooth their relationship over first," Rose said firmly.

"No, Rose, there have been too many secrets in this family. I refuse to start this relationship off with lies. Either you be honest with her, or I will," David replied with equal determination.

"David, please. Not today. Don't do this," Rose pleaded.

The conversation ended with a knock on the door from Stevin, informing David that he was ready for the trip to the store.

"Stevin, where is Summer?" Rose asked, her expression full of concern.

"She's just freshening up; just know as soon as she is done, you better believe she'll be back on your heels," Stevin replied as the men walked away, laughing.

The day started perfectly. The gentlemen had returned with groceries for dinner, and since the morning had flown by, Rose and Summer had decided to start preparing dinner early so the four of them could finally sit together and get to know each other better. The conversation was honest and open, covering the good, the bad, and the ugly. The subject of Christopher remains off-limits; however, it was a topic they all agreed needed no discussion.

"So, Summer, how are you feeling?" David asked.

"Incredible! Somebody pinch me; I feel like I'm dreaming," she exclaimed.

"Ouch!" she screamed. "Why did you pinch me, Stevin?"

"Heck, baby, you just said pinch you," Stevin said, as the table bursts into laughter.

"Summer, your mother and I talked about being transparent and not starting this relationship off with secrets," David explained.

"No, David," Rose shouted in a demanding voice.

"I'm sorry, Rose. I must be honest with her," David said.

Summer's face immediately became glum with worry.

"What is it, David?" Summer asked.

"My sweet Summer, you are my daughter in every way that matters. I have fought this fight with Rose from the first day I met her. I felt every inch of the love, sadness, and brokenness she endured. So I know her heart is pure at this moment, and she wants to protect you. However, you have a sister. Kimberley Michelle White. He states as he shakes his head. We raised that knucklehead with no boundaries."

"She is a spoiled, entitled brat that I love to death. But my daughter lacks compassion. She grew up with no siblings; hell, she was too mean and bossy to keep friends." Rose giggled and dropped her head in her hands.

"Summer, my father, recently passed away, and he and Kimberley were very close. She felt my family was gone, and Rose's family had always been off-limits. She also craved for family connections. So, she did some research behind our backs and learned about you. The information she received about Rose parent's and their relationship was incorrect, and she believed her mom got pregnant and shunned her parents for you. So, in Kimberley's world, you are the catalyst that kept her from knowing her extended family."

As Summer's head dropped, Stevin felt his anger growing as he pondered, "Why now, and why in this moment?"

"That's ridiculous," Stevin exclaimed in a deep voice. "It seems like she should have sympathy for her mom and sister. Why wouldn't she be happy to gain a sister, especially if her true craving was family connections?"

Summer asked concern, "So, she doesn't want to get to know me?"

Rose stood up and hugged Summer. "Baby, she just hasn't had the opportunity to hear my story. Someone gave her incorrect information, and she came to her own conclusions. It caused a great deal of damage to our relationship and trust. When we reunited, we avoided discussing the subject. But I promise you, Summer, when she learns the truth, she will be excited. Mommy will fix this."

"Summer, we honored Stevin's wishes and informed no one of this meeting, even Kimberley. So, to Rose's defense, she has yet to be given the opportunity to correct her wrongs in not being honest with Kimberley, and to Kimberley's defense. Put yourself in her shoes. This secret was hidden from her her entire life. There was no opportunity to understand. When she learned of her grandparents, she also learned her maternal grandmother had expired, and there would never be an opportunity to meet her. I said all that to say you and your sister's personality is like oil and water. She might surprise us all when we sit down and speak with her. But I wanted you to know the absolute truth of the situation."

"Your sister is sweet," Rose stated. She just has the emotions of a rock. She will love you and accept you. I know she will. We all have things to work through. We have to take her feelings into account. I have kept this secret from her her entire life. She is within her own right to be upset."

"Yes, Mom, you are correct. I feel much better now that I've heard your perspective. She has every right to feel slighted, as she craves family and understanding. I'll give her the space and understanding she needs; I'm confident she will come around."

"Mom, I'm sorry to hear about your mother's passing and the missed opportunity to mend your relationship."

Rose was taken aback as David shouted, "Damn, Rose! Why couldn't you have passed on Summer's compassion to your other daughter? That non-compassion receptor has your mother's name written all over it. I won't take responsibility for that genetic factor she lacks; she takes after your side of the family."

The room was filled with laughter as David tried to lighten the moment.

Chapter 29: Learning To Love Again

As the months passed, Summer spent every moment she could with Rose. They had both returned home, and life as they knew it would never be the same. The dire need for a sense of completeness no longer existed. That dark cloud had been replaced, and she felt whole for the first time in her life.

Rose had devised a plan for her and Summer, and they met throughout the week in different locations.

David and Rose had become regulars at their home. Summer had even taken on a selfish stance. The meet and greet with Kimberley kept being pushed back, and she didn't mind at all. She was soaking up all Rose's attention, and, at the moment, Kimberley's need for space didn't sound so bad.

The burner phone required minutes to be added weekly, sometimes twice a week, as Rose and Summer talked for hours throughout the day, consuming as much of each other time as possible. Kimberley also noticed the changes in Rose's behavior. Previously, she had to persuade her mom to leave the house, but now Rose can't seem to stay home.

Kimberley was thrilled that her mother was leading a more active lifestyle outside the four walls of their home. She attributed her positive change to her father's increased involvement, as Rose and David had begun taking weekly road trips, which she assumed would help to rekindle their romantic life.

On the other hand, she couldn't care less. Emmanuel had permanently moved into town and wanted to spend every moment with her, even pressing for a meet and greet with her parents.

THE TIME IS NOW

"Old people," Kimberley shouted as she demanded her parents' presence in the family room. "I have some news, and we need a family meeting."

"Well, Kimberley, I am happy you are calling this meeting," David echoed. "Your mom and I need to share some important information with you."

"Okay, pops, let me go first because I am sure my news is more important."

Rose rolls her eyes in the back of her head, as she shakes her head. "Yes, my child, nothing is more important than queen Kimberley," Rose stated in a sarcastic tone.

"Well old people I think your son-in-law might be ready to pop the question."

The room went silent, as tempers flared.

"I will be damn if you will sit in me and your mother presence to brag on a coward who hasn't felt the need to get to know us, and think I will give you, my blessing."

"Dad, this would normally be the time I exit left and ignore your calls, but this is important to me. If you will give me a moment to explain before rushing to judgment then you would know that, not only is our relationship getting serious, but he is ready to meet you guys and properly introduce himself, and give you guys an opportunity to get to know him. As I had told you before, the only hang-up was him not being present in town and him wanting both sets of parents to be involved before we officially started putting titles on the relationship."

"Now that the opportunity has presented itself, he would like to meet both of you. We are trying to get his parents to fly out sooner, but I have requested for him not to continue to disrespect my parents who are present in town and wishes are to meet him. He has respected my request, and I am asking you guys to respect my desire and feelings for him, because dad I am truly in love with him. And I know he is in love with me."

David and Rose knew they couldn't fight her on this. They had bigger fish to fry, like breaking the Summer news.

So a compromise for a compromise would be the best approach. They both could never respect Emmanuel actions, his absentee, and lack of respect for them had burn a hole in their trust for his true desires and respect for their child.

"Okay, baby girl, Mom would be delighted. No correction, we both would be delighted to meet him finally. I know your father also wants to see you happy."

Kimberley immediately lifted her head and jerked her upper body into an upright position, covering her mouth with her hands, looking with a surprise expression as her eyes watered. "Really you guys" she said in a squeaky tearful voice.

Rose's eyes immediately began to swell with tears. Seeing Kimberley being emotional was a shock to her.

"You really love him, my sweet girl," Rose said as Kimberley embraced her with a hug. David watched as he tried to fight back tears. This was a side of Kimberley that he had never encountered before. He prayed to himself that Emmanuel was all the glitz and glam that she had made him out to be.

Kimberley stood up and walked across the room to sit on the sofa beside her dad. They all exchanged hugs and wished her the best in her future and relationship with Emmanuel.

"Now, Kimberley, Dad needs you to have the same respect and open mind for the news we are about to share. This is difficult for your mother, so she needs you to listen carefully."

Rose began to speak as she held Kimberley's hands. "Baby girl, mom has two daughters who I equally love the same. The only difference between you and Summer is that you had me in your life, and the privilege of being your mother wasn't ripped from me. Summer was stolen from me," Rose said as she broke down in tears.

To her surprise, Kimberley squeezed her hand tightly, wiped her tears, and said, "Mom, I know. Dad told me everything. It wasn't fair what your parents did to you."

"No, it wasn't," David echoed. "So when I met your mom, I knew how important family was to her. Keeping information from you wasn't us trying to hide the truth, but rather protecting your mom and what she knew she could mentally handle and process to move forward. A prime example of why we left her family and, unfortunately,

Summer's existence a secret is because I have witnessed firsthand what this tragedy did to your mom. And you yourself also witnessed it."

"I know, Dad. No one wants to see their mom on the floor crying inconsolably. And let's not forget the infamous slap that broke my jaw."

"Girl, stop it," Rose said.

"Mom, you know you slapped me into kingdom come that day."

"Little girl, please," replied Rose. "But, on the other hand, baby girl, Mom has located your sister."

"What do you mean mom, located her where?"

"She has come back to me, Kimberley. Your sister is alive, beautiful, and doing well."

"How do you know this?" Kimberley asked, surprised.

"I have met with her baby."

Kimberley immediately becomes standoffish, pulling away from Rose as she snatches her hand away from her.

"Are you kidding me?" How disrespectful is this BS," she says as she stands up, attempting to storm off.

"Young lady, sit your ass down and show your mother some respect," David responds firmly. "I have had just about enough of your selfish behavior and disrespect. I dare she share with you something that is so dear to her heart, and you respond like this."

David looked at her with disgust and asked, "Who are you? Where did we go wrong with you? I can't even look at you. Yes, we have located our daughter, and I said our daughter. Because she is just as much a part of my life as she is in your mother's, and I accept her with open arms. Who wants nothing more but to meet you and be a big sister. No, correction, who is so excited to be a part of your life and our lives. And we have put your mother's ability to be happy and feel complete on hold because we continue to dance around your feelings."

"But... Dad, how is it fair to me?"

"Kimberley, you're absolutely right. I dare your mom to miss the opportunity to know her daughter because it's unfair to you. Can you remind me again why it's so unfair?

Humm, let me think; surely, there are a million reasons why this unjust act affects you. Let me think. Remind me one more time because I can't think of one damn reason," David shouts.

Rose interrupts, grabbing Kimberley by the hand. "Baby girl, just talk to me. What are you so afraid of? Why are you fighting this so hard?" Rose asks.

"I don't know, mom.".

"Kimberley, you set all this in motion. You expressed your desire for more family. You have a big sister who loves you and wants to be a part of your life. Why are you fighting this?"

"Mom, I'm not sure. Nothing feels natural about this."

"Kimberley, I didn't raise you to behave like this. How can you ask me to give Emmanuel a chance, and in the same breath, you deny your own flesh and blood?"

"Okay, Mom, okay. I will give her a chance," she said in a sarcastic tone. Rose pulls Kimberley closer to her, as she is pleased with the bit of cooperation she might be willing to offer. As David never utters a word. He could see the disappointment all over Kimberley's face. He knows she's seething inside and has no intention of playing nice. And he would be correct, as she stewed in her self-indulged entitlement.

Kimberley could care less about Rose's happiness and had no desire to play happy family with Summer. If Rose wants to treat her like the second-class daughter, she has no problem with moving on with Emmanuel and starting a new family.

She sat, absorbing all the information about Summer and her past. It was like a black hole, sucking up information in deep space, a black hole of emptiness. Kimberley was given all the details about everything, including the importance of Summer and her location, remaining a secret between the three of them. She was strictly forbidden from telling anyone, even Emmanuel.

Chapter 30: No Regrets

Summer learned the cat was out the bag and Kimberley knew of her reunion with Rose. The fact that Rose never mentioned Kimberley tagging along for a meet and greet, or the simple fact that Rose and David had visited twice since the news had been shared and her dear old sister made no effort to tag along was all the confirmation, she needed that her sisterly love wasn't wanted. Summer couldn't explain her emotional detachment from the situation, but she didn't care in the moment. She had Stevin and Rose. She also had gained an honorary dad, so Kimberley could join the caravan of love or continue to isolate herself; it would be her choice. She just reached a point that anything that didn't bring joy and happiness into her life didn't matter.

Stevin returned home after a long day at work to find that no dinner or warm embrace awaited him. He noticed several loads of unfolded clothing piled up on the sofa. Walking into the bedroom, he found Summer stretched out across the bed.

"Hey, Summer, did you have errands to run outside the home or was something else going on today?"

In a snappy tone, she replied, "No, why did you asked me that?

"Well, baby, there are several reasons. By the look of the large pile of clothing stacked on the sofa, you haven't had a chance to get much done, and what's for dinner?" he added.

She threw the covers back, stormed out of the room, and headed to the kitchen, banging pots around.

Walking into the kitchen, she never acknowledged he was standing in the kitchen doorway. Stevin just walked off and headed to the shower. After finishing up in the bathroom, he noticed that Summer had returned to bed and left a sub sandwich and chips on the dinette table for him. As he sat alone gulping down his meal, he sums up Summer behavior as being depressed from her sister's rejection, being five months had passed and no attempt on Kimbereley's behalf to meet.

Snuggling up in bed behind her attempting to rub underneath her shirt, only to be rejected.

"No, Stevin. I am just not in the mood."

"Dang, Summer, I can't rub on you now?"

“No, you are attempting to rub on my breasts, and they are sore.”

“Hell, Summer, I want to be understanding, but this behavior is very unattractive.”

“I can't reject you once, Stevin,” she asked. “I always give you sex when you ask. Is it a big deal because I stated I was not in the mood one night?”

"My point exactly! Summer, your behavior and attitude have been unusual this week. You've been snappy and having mood swings all week."

"Stevin, am I not allowed to have a bad day?"

"You are, baby, but you need to admit that this issue with your sister is bothering you more than you want to accept."

She mumbles something in response as she turns away, throwing the covers over her head.

***

Stevin repeatedly hit the snooze button but finally managed to drag himself out of bed. He had a restless night, tossing and turning, confused and not understanding Summer's behavior towards him.

Summer opened her eyes as the bathroom door closed, immediately feeling guilty and remorseful for her poor behavior towards him. She knew she owed Stevin an apology but couldn't shake off the overwhelming sense of gloom that was sucking the joy out of her. Finally, she got out of bed, determined to do what needed to be done.

Stevin looks up as he hears the bathroom door open. However, he fails to acknowledge her and continues to wash his face. She snuggles up behind him and kisses his back while apologizing for her behavior. Stevin turns around and embraces her, accepting her apology with open arms.

“I don't know what's wrong with me lately, Stevin. I hear women talk about PMSING all the time. And I am feeling all the symptoms. I am having mood swings, tender breasts, irritability, you name it, I am feeling it. I will be glad when my cycle starts and ends. I have never felt like this before.”

“Bae, please forgive my bleak behavior. I haven't felt like myself all week. You are the one constant source of joy in my life, and I am forever grateful for that. I can't imagine living without you, and the thought of losing you makes me feel like I would die if I ever lost you.”

“Listen here, little woman, I would like to think I know you like the back of my hand. So, I won't hold a bad day against you. However, Daddy is going to need dinner, a clean house, and some wifey duties performed at the end of the night," he said sternly.

"Sure thing, big daddy," she replied, mocking him. "I'm getting to it; I'm getting to it," she added quickly.

***

As the week came to an end, Summer's mood had not improved, and her energy levels had decreased. The trip to the grocery store was a drag as she sat in the parking lot, trying to talk herself into getting out of the car.

Summer felt as if the years of accumulated stress had finally taken a toll on her, and her body was finally responding. She walked into the grocery store, not bothering to use her coupons and only picking up the bare minimum to get through the week.

As she was browsing the hygiene aisle for sanitary napkins, her attention was caught by the pregnancy tests, causing her to quickly turn her head and zoom in on the box.

She is two weeks late and has multiple symptoms that point to pregnancy. She scrolls on by, "nah!" I am just late due to the stress.

With a swift cart turn, she returned to the aisle and stood before the pregnancy test, contemplating buying one. Not wanting to get excited about nothing and getting let down, she convinced herself it wasn't possible, but she would check just to be safe.

She and Stevin have never practiced safe sex, and she hasn't ended up pregnant yet. What would make this time any different?

She decided not to share this with him; she would take the test, and there wouldn't be any reason to get him excited if it were negative.

Summer sat on the toilet as she contemplated taking the test. Knowing her heart would be heavy if the results were negative. The irony was that the moment took her back to the worst moment in her life. Maybe it wasn't Stevin at all; perhaps the reason she hasn't gotten pregnant is due to the trauma she suffered at the hands of Christopher.

She gathered the courage to take the pregnancy test and waited silently as the minutes ticked by. Unable to bear the suspense, she watched as one line appeared. Ten minutes passed, and no second line appeared, indicating a negative result. It was evident that she would not be getting a second line, and she wasn't pregnant. She was so focused on the test that she didn't hear Stevin enter the bedroom and call out her name.

"Hey, bae, give me one moment!" she shouted as he attempted to enter the bathroom, slightly opening the door.

"It's not like I haven't seen you naked before," he jokingly said.

"Stevin, give me my privacy. I will be out in a moment."

Stevin closed the door and never responded, walking back into the living room and waiting for Summer to exit the bathroom.

Sitting on the sofa, flipping channels, he has had a long day and cannot cater to her mood swings, noticing again, no dinner on the stove.

Summer walks into the family room and sits on the opposite end of the sofa. Stevin immediately gets up and heads straight into the bathroom to prepare for bed. Upon entering the bathroom, he noticed there was no odor, and the tub was bone dry.

The question became, what exactly was she doing in the bathroom that required privacy? After searching the cabinets and finding nothing, he looks down and notices a plastic bag tied up in the trash. Ripping open the bag, he finds a pregnancy box with a negative pregnancy test.

Stevin becomes livid. 'How could she? Why would she hide this from me?' These thoughts consume him.

Removing the testing stick from the box, he exited the bathroom with the testing stick in hand. Stevin returned to the family room where Summer was seated. He sat across from her and asked, "Is there anything we need to talk about?"

Summer looked down and shook her head no. Stevin slammed the testing stick on the table and repeated his question, "So, is there something you need to tell me?"

"I didn't tell you anything because it was nothing to tell."

"Okay, let me make sure I understand this correctly. There's a chance that you're pregnant, and instead of allowing me to enjoy the moment with you, whether it's good news or bad, you chose to keep it from me."

Summer stood and walked over, sitting on Stevin's lap. She had obviously hurt his feelings by the disappointed look on his face.

"I wasn't hiding anything from you, Stevin. I never intended to go to the store to purchase a pregnancy test. It so happened while I was picking up some sanitary napkins; I happened to come across the pregnancy test. I was curious when I started thinking about my recent mood swings and fatigue, so I decided to check. That's all."

"So, why the secrecy when I came home?"

"It wasn't secrecy; it was disappointment, and there was no reason to share the disappointed news and disturb your peace."

"So you're saying you're hurt and disappointed?" Stevin asked.

"Yes, I am. I would have loved for a positive test."

It was evident from the gloomy look in her eyes as her face expressed disappointment. Stevin couldn't help but feel responsible. She obviously felt she couldn't express her true feelings from protecting his.

"Summer, I need you to talk to me; this is a sensitive topic, although we haven't taken any steps to prevent this. If having a child is a step you are ready for, we should take the necessary steps to aid in helping us have a child."

"Stevin, I really don't want to address this tonight. Can we revisit this in the morning, please?" Summer said with a mix of emotions. She didn't want to hurt Stevin's feelings but also needed time to process her disappointment. She knew that having a child wouldn't be easy and that additional help might be required, which was too much of a risk at the moment.

Stevin walked away to prepare for a shower, and Summer stayed on the sofa, needing a moment to herself to process the negative pregnancy test. Minutes later, she could hear Stevin exiting the bathroom. Exhausted from a long day at work and the mental exhaustion of having to face reality, he could be the very person that denied her a chance of having her own family. He also needed a moment alone. The look in her eyes said it all: could history be repeating itself?

Stevin had fallen asleep, stretched out across the bed, without having dinner. Three hours later, he woke up and realized that Summer had not come to bed. He found her snuggled up on the sofa and gestured for her to come to bed with him. However, she refused, saying she was watching TV and would remain on the sofa for a little while. Too tired to argue, Stevin went back to bed alone, knowing something had shifted tonight in their relationship.

Chapter 31: No Secret Is Safe

Stevin and Summer carried on as the weeks went by, as if the pregnancy scare never happened. Instead of addressing the elephant in the room, they continued with their daily routine and avoided any discussion about having a baby.

Stevin was too afraid of her resentment, and Summer was too fearful of her reactions toward him if the pregnancy didn't happen naturally. They both hid their true feelings and tip-toed around the conversation. Summer wasn't willing to risk it all; she knew it involved them seeing a fertility specialist, and that risk outweighed her desires.

"Stevin," she shouted from the kitchen, "Are you dressed? Mom and David will be arriving soon."

Entering the kitchen, he gave her a gentle shoulder rub and kissed her on the cheek.

"I'm dressed, Summer. And as always, you have prepared a feast. Go ahead and tidy up before they arrive. I will finish cooking."

He removed Summer's apron and placed it over his head. "I will finish this feast," he repeated as he twirled around the utensils in his hands. "Just call me Sir Master Chef."

Stevin heard the doorbell ring and went to greet their guests at the front door. "My good man," David said, "I see you have been preparing dinner. Come on, Rose, I think we should head out to a restaurant if Summer has allowed Stevin to prepare dinner. It might not be edible."

Rose giggled as she entered the home, given Stevin a peek on the cheek. The noticeable savory aroma, dancing throughout the air, led them into the kitchen.

Stevin gave them a tour of the food, making up fake names for the dishes in a horrible Italian accent as he attempted to take credit for the meal.

Rose quickly turned to Summer as she entered the kitchen. "My sweet girl, once again, you have outdone yourself. I can't wait till the day we can host you guys, and I can cook for you."

Without wasting any time, everyone gathered around the table to relish the lavish meal that Summer had prepared.

The room echoed with laughter as Stevin and David had grown quite charming with each other and were having a great time together. Their corny jokes were golden to them, making the moment even more delightful.

"I would love for you guys to join us and go out dancing, David requested. I have been trying to convince Rose to get out of the house and join me on the dance floor like we used to do in the good old days."

"Mom...you...dance?" Summer asked in a surprised tone. "Well, I know I didn't inherit that skill from you."

"Yes, she does," David echoed. "Your mom and I were part of a dance group, and we loved to line dance."

"Don't let Summer fool you guys," Stevin interjected. "Remember, I saw you cut loose in Monroe on the college campus."

"There's a difference between marching and actually having rhythm," Summer said. "And besides, anyone can dance when they're intoxicated."

"Hey, Stevin, you guys have to come out to the house. I recently got a Masterbuilt grill combo that is absolutely amazing," David said as his eyes lit up with excitement.

"David, you know it's not safe for them to come over," replied Rose.

"No, listen, Rose. The tenant in Dad's house lease is up, so the property is now empty. My dad's home is an hour and a half away from here, and it could be the perfect neutral spot for the girls to meet."

"We can keep it low-key, invite a few of my childhood friends from the neighborhood, and dance the night away. No one needs to know the background story or the story at all. My dad's home sits on acres, so we'll have plenty of space."

"David, that sounds like a great idea. It will give Summer an opportunity to meet her sister. If you guys can limit the number of guests and ensure Summer safety and she is comfortable with it, I'm also okay with it. It doesn't sound too risky."

"Baby girl, what do you think?" Rose asked.

"I'm okay with it, Mom, as long as you guys take the necessary precautions and keep it at bay."

As the conversation shifted to the gentlemen's employment, David was surprised to learn about Stevin's long commute.

"Why didn't you look for housing closer to your job to decrease your commute time?" David asked.

"I figured it would be safer for Summer to be further out," Stevin explained.

"So, are you guys buying this home?" David inquired.

"No, David," Stevin replied.

"I leased this property under my employer so it wouldn't be traced back to me."

David turned to Stevin with an amused expression. "It seems as if you have based your entire life and the way you operate around Summer's needs. I am just curious: what does Stevin want and need?"

"For this little lady to be safe and happy," Stevin replied as he squeezed Summer's hand.

Rose sat with a smile, as her heart was filled with appreciation and gratefulness that Summer had Stevin in her corner.

"Baby girl, it feels like everything has come full circle. David was, and still is, to me what Stevin is to you. He can attest to everything Stevin has done for you."

"Our circumstances were different, but I know what it feels like to breathe and feel like the world is sucking life from you. I only stand here before you today because he didn't give up on me and loved me unconditionally."

Summer sat, gazing at her plate of food, lost in thought. Although she was fully aware of all the things Stevin had done for her, hearing it out loud, felt different. It really put perspective in place on just how much he had sacrificed for her.

Summer lovingly expressed, "I love him, I know what I have and whom I have in a man, and he is truly one in a million. I will forever be indebted to him for his love and sacrifices."

"Tell me what you love about him, or in other words. How did you know he was the one?" David asked.

Summer wasted no time responding. "First thing, his love is pure; it is its own reward. This man loved me at my worst. He loved me when there wasn't anything to love about me. He loved me when I didn't know how to love myself. He has and continues to make sacrifices for my happiness and well-being. If he told me today that he was moving to space and all I could bring was a pair of socks, and it could only be just the two of us, I would follow without any questions."

As the room fell silent, David broke the somber atmosphere with a joke, "I don't know about the space part," he blurted out, and the room filled with laughter.

"David, you know what I mean," Summer said, shaking her head.

"I would follow him anywhere, even to the moon and back. And, if this is what my family unit looks like, consisting of just the four of us, then I am just fine with it."

"Now, on a serious note," David said as he attempted to reset the mood.

"Son, I know, and you know I know the sacrifices you have made for my daughter. But what I want you to take from this conversation is her response. She didn't waver, and there was no hesitation in her response. She didn't have to pause to think about what you meant to her. The way her eyes lit up and swelled with tears. The trembling of her voice as she spoke from the soul about what your love means to her. These are connections that are hard to find. So my good man, if you ever get weary from your well-doing, just know you have a good woman who truly loves you and parents that will be forever grateful for you and support you guys."

The serious conversation left the air thick in the room as everyone felt choked up with emotions.

Rose walked into the kitchen to find Kimberley stuffing her face with the leftovers that Summer prepared.

"You know, Kimberley, I find it hilarious you have put no effort forward in meeting your sister, but you are the first one in the kitchen searching for leftovers that she has prepared."

"Hey, is it my fault the girl can cook? Would you have me starve, mother dearest?"

"Kimberley, drop the attitude, as discussed yesterday. We will be meeting at your grandparents' home, and so help me, God. Little girl, you better not embarrass me."

The conversation was cut short by the ringing of Kimberley's cell phone.

"Oops, Mom, got to run. Someone that actually brings substance into my life is calling," she said as she rushed up to her room and fell back on the bed.

"Emmanuel, if I hear that girl's name one more time, I swear I will be ill for the rest of the year."

"Baby, why are you fighting this connection with your sister? You asked for this, Kimmie."

"I know, but why does it have to be forced on me? I didn't agree to attend this barbeque. I was told it was happening and that I had better show up with a smile."

"I will walk in on your arm," Emmanuel suggested.

"Wait, really? No I couldn't. I was sworn to secrecy. They would disown me if they knew I told you."

"Nobody said they have to know anything about that. You are also setting up a meet and greet between me and your parents. What's the difference?"

"You're right, but I don't want to taint their first impression of you."

"Let me worry about that. You know my charm is irresistible," he said confidently.

"Well, I need to get their permission first."

"No, you do not! I will be your surprise guest, and besides, when they see how well-behaved you are, they will contribute that to me. And, moving forward, we can finally start moving forward as a family unit. We might actually get an invite to tag along on one of their weekly family road trips together. Now, just leave it to me. I just need you to fix your attitude towards your sister before the barbeque."

Kimberley sat quietly on the other line. She had agreed to go along with Emmanuel's plans. Besides, what would be the big deal? There wasn't anything she hadn't shared with him related to her long-lost sister.

She thought to herself, 'Hell, they owe my man some gratitude. This little reunion between Mom and Summer wouldn't have occurred if it weren't for Emmanuel.'

However, something within her was telling her not to spring Emmanuel on her parents in this manner, as she would drown out that reasonable voice in her head that kept screaming to put Rose's feelings first.

Chapter 32: The Cat Is Out The Bag

Summer joins Stevin in the living room, snuggling up next to him on the sofa. Their silent cuddling moment was interrupted by the ringing of his cell phone. Summer could tell something was wrong by the disappointed look on his face as he ended the call.

Stevin Summer asked, "Why the long face?"

"That was the job calling, Summer. I might have to miss the barbecue. Looks like I might be traveling this weekend."

"Well, we might as well cancel it," she said. "I won't be attending it without you."

"Let's just wait, Summer; David has put so much effort into planning this party. So, if I can't get the dates moved around, I'm going to need you to put on your big girl panties and attend it alone. This weekend is not about me. I would love to be there, but this is about you and your family. If I have to work by chance, David and I will ensure you're set up comfortably."

"What kind of statement is that? You are my family. I want and need you by my side, and besides, it's not so much a need but a desire. All of this is happening because of you. It wouldn't feel right without having you there, Stevin."

"Okay, sweetie, let me make some phone calls, but just know things are not looking promising," said Stevin.

Stevin found himself overwhelmed as the week was winding down and the weekend barbecue was approaching. Juggling work and attending to Summer's needs had taken a toll on him. He had to pull some major strings to have another coworker replace him on an important work trip and to make matters worse; his assistant had resigned, leaving him with a new assistant he wasn't familiar with.

Unfortunately, the new assistant failed to attend any of this week mandatory meetings, and Stevin wasn't pleased and needed more time to replace her.

Stevin was working from his home office, attempting to prepare some notes so his coworker would be well briefed before the upcoming meeting. His stomach rumbled louder than his thoughts, but he had no time for a break. He called out to Summer, asking her to prepare him some lunch. He had been feeling irritable all week, and Summer's mood swings were not helping the situation.

As Summer entered the room with his lunch, they were both startled by the doorbell.

"Are you expecting someone, Summer?" Stevin asked with concern.

"No, Stevin," she replied, also looking worried.

Stevin quickly scrambled to bring up the video feed on his tablet to check the doorbell camera. "What the hell?" he exclaimed.

"What is it, Stevin? Who's at the door?" Asked Summer, concerned.

"It's my new assistant," he said, looking puzzled and worried. "I don't know how she found out where we live. Something is not right. Stay here."

Stevin walked out through the garage door and approached the front porch to confront the assistant while Summer watched from the tablet.

"How can I help you, Morgan?"

Stevin's aggressive tone startled her, and she jumped when he approached her from the side.

"Oh my, Mr. Bash, you startled me," she said nervously. With an aggressive tone, Stevin demanded to know how she got his address.

"Mr. Bash, please don't be upset. My sister works in HR, and my daughter has been sick. As you know, I have been absent from the last three staff meetings. I am expected to fly out with Josh this weekend, and I don't have the itinerary to make the necessary plans. The hotel rooms haven't been confirmed. Josh stated I needed to get with you and that he only filled in at the last minute. I have been calling you, and my calls have been forwarded to voicemail," she explained.

"What is your sister's name?"

"Mr. Bash, please," she pleaded.

"What is her name?" he demanded.

"Ashley Darks," she replied.

"Morgan, please leave my home. The itinerary is the least of you and your sister's worries," Stevin said firmly.

The assistant refused to leave. She approached him, grabbing his arm, begging for his understanding.

"There is never an excuse to violate anyone's privacy in this manner, Morgan!" he stated firmly, suspecting that Christopher might be involved.

As Morgan continued to plead for his forgiveness, Stevin tried to enter the house through the front door. Meanwhile, Summer sat at the desk, becoming anxious, as the audio on the tablet suddenly stopped working. She could only see the assistant grabbing Stevin's arm, and the conversation seemed personal.

Besides, she wondered why the assistant was dressed that way while showing up at her boss's house as Morgan was wearing a mini skirt with a halter tank top.

Summer was quickly led by her emotions that she quickly became jealous instead of being worried that her and Stevin's location might have been compromised.

Stevin continued verbally reprimanding his new assistant, but he was caught off guard when the front door opened. He immediately grabbed the doorknob, slamming the door closed. That only enticed Summer's curiosity more as she swung the door open wide.

Stevin quickly and forcefully pushed her back in the door, closing the door shut again. This startled Summer as she didn't attempt to exit out the door again. Morgan hurriedly left the porch and returned to her car.

Stevin memorized her car's license plate number as she drove off. He was angry with the situation but even more upset with Summer for being so careless and reckless.

Clearly, Summer was acting on her emotions, and her common sense had flown out of the window. Stevin quickly entered the home to write down the license plate number. Summer could be heard in the kitchen banging dishes around, clearly upset that another woman had shown up at their home and was physically pulling on Stevin as if emotional ties were attached to their conversation.

The fact that Stevin had pushed her angered her more. He was unconcerned with her attitude at that moment and had no intention of pandering to her ego. They were both potentially in danger, and he needed to find out what was going on. As he searched through the pile of papers on the desk for his work phone, he quickly turned to Summer, who entered the room.

"Have you lost your mind? Why on earth did you do that?" he asked. "If you're so eager to be reckless and throw everything away, why are we even doing this? Christopher could very well be behind this, and you just played right into his hands. Why did you reveal yourself?"

"Why was she here, and why was she pulling on you, Stevin?"

"That's a damn good question," Stevin shouted, turning his attention to the person on the phone.

"Orlando," he shouted as he filled him in on the situation. He put the phone on speaker as he tapped on his computer, researching Morgan and Ashley Darks.

Orlando confirmed that Ashley worked in HR.

"That still doesn't explain how they got the address, Orlando."

"That's a given, Stevin. When Ashley couldn't locate your personal address, she probably immediately started looking at our corporate leases," Orlando explained.

"But my name is not on the leases," Stevin said, puzzled.

"Yes, but Ashley manages those accounts; she probably gave Morgan the address of each property lease using the date you started. There's no telling how many doors she knocked on before reaching you."

"I don't like this, Orlando," said Stevin.

"I understand your concerns, Stevin. However, I want to assure you that the situation appears to involve two irresponsible sisters who are trying to cover their asses. As I review Morgan's resume, it's clear that her credentials do not qualify her for her job duties. It seems that Ashley pulled some strings to get her hired, and Morgan has not been fulfilling her job requirements. This was evident when she showed up at the office dressed in inappropriate street attire, demanding the Boston trip itinerary despite being absent from work for three consecutive days. Morgan has been the topic of conversation around the Georgia office all week. Apparently it's been a big buzz, big enough it got back to my office.

"I believe both of them should be fired," Stevin said."

"They are harmless, Stevin, but their actions are foolish. Besides, I think it would be best to handle this situation with caution," replied Orlando.

"I want them both gone," demanded Stevin.

As Stevin continued to speak with Orlando, Summer pretended to sweep the floor to eavesdrop on their conversation. She quickly became embarrassed, realizing the big mistake she had made and how she could have very well blown their cover. As Stevin informs Orlando about Morgan and Summer's interaction, she attempts to make light of the situation using the tip of the broomstick, poking Stevin in his thigh.

He swatted at the broomstick several times, demanding her to stop, as he was getting agitated as he attempted to carry on a phone conversation with Orlando.

She became increasingly playful with the broom, and she continued to poke the back of his thighs. In an angered tone, he requested to call Orlando back to address Summer's inappropriate meddling; as he swiftly turned to demand her to stop, he was met with the tip of the broom being hardly jabbed in his family jewels.

Summer could see the pain all over Stevin's face as she started to run. He rushed towards her, wanting only to grab the broom and break it across his knee.

He grabbed the broom and attempted to wrestle it from her, but Summer clinched on tighter. Anger took hold as he tried to wrestle the broom away, and he pulled with all his strength.

Summer's feet left the ground as she held on for dear life. Stevin forcefully let go, not realizing his own strength at that moment, sending Summer's body flying backward. She lost her balance and hit her head on the corner of the wall. Stevin's heart sank as he watched her small, petite body slam forcefully against the wall.

As he watched her body go limp, fear set in. He immediately ran to her side, calling her name with no response. "Summer, baby, please talk to me. I'm so sorry; I'm so sorry," he pleaded.

She could feel a sharp pain in the back of her head and ringing in her ears. Her vision was blurred, and she felt nauseous and confused.

As she tried to focus, she became combative, screaming in fear, "Christopher, no! Please don't hurt me. Please don't hit me. I'm sorry."

She tried to stand but fell back over. Stevin tried to hold her in a bear hug to calm her down and reorient her, but she shivered in his arms from fear, with the look of doom in her eyes. He stepped back to give her space and let her regain consciousness fully.

However, even as she began to come around, there was a look of gloom and doom in her eyes, as if he were the enemy. With every attempt to approach her, her cries grew louder.

"Summer, please! You have to know that was a mistake," he pleaded.

But she screamed, "Stay away from me!" As she regained her composure, she made a dash for the door.

"No, Summer!" he screamed, trying to console her, but it only made the situation worse. She grabbed her purse and the car keys. He threw himself against the door, pleading with her not to leave.

"Please baby, don't leave, not like this, please. Just calm down so we can talk," he begged.

"You promised me you wouldn't hurt me like he did," she cried out.

"It was a mistake, Summer. I never hit you, and I never desired to harm you. I just wanted to take the broom away," he explained.

"But you promised me, Stevin, you promised," she insisted. "I want to go; please just let me go," Summer pleaded.

"I understand, Summer, and I'm sorry. But please, let's talk about this," he said.

"I want to go; please just let me go," she demanded.

"No, Summer, I will go. You stay here. I will leave," he said, gently stepping back from her. He tried to hug her, but her body stiffened in fear. He realized he had to stop and give her space; he was only making a terrible situation even worse.

"Summer, look," he said as he slowly backed away. "I'm going to pack a bag and leave. You can trust me. I will give you time to think."

Stevin was still in shock, unable to process what had just happened, attempting to understand how it went so wrong so fast. It was heartbreaking to see the hurt and disappointment in Summer's eyes. He knew he had to leave and give her a moment.

As he entered the bathroom and began to pack, he heard the alarm chime, indicating that the garage door was open. He raced to the kitchen to prevent her from leaving the house, but it was too late. All he could see when he exited the door were Summer's taillights as she drove away. He wanted to chase her down in his car, but he knew he could very well cause her to crash if she perceived him as a threat.

He entered back into the home, his eyes swelled with tears, another knife to the heart as he picked up her diamond engagement ring off the kitchen table. He sat at the table, crying, wondering how everything could have gone so wrong. Suddenly, he jumped up and started throwing things around the house in anger. As a lamp shattered against the wall, he fell to his knees, devastated and broken. He tried calling Summer's cell multiple times, but she didn't answer.

Pulling into the hotel parking lot, she rummaged through her purse and realized she had left her wallet behind. After digging through her purse, she found enough cash to cover her stay for three nights.

When she checked into the hotel, her only form of identification was her Paige Green's ID. She had a bag of clothes in the trunk from a trip she previously took with Rose, as well as her laptop.

After settling into the room, she crawled into the bed without wanting to think about or process what had occurred. She had a pounding headache, and all she wanted to do was sleep and block out the last two hours.

ATLANTA GEORGIA

The ringing of her cell phone suddenly awoke Rose. She patted David to wake him up. "David, it's Stevin," she said.

"What time is it?" David asked, still groggy.

"It's 2 am," Rose replied.

"Hello, Stevin, what's wrong?" she asked worriedly. "Please calm down, son," she pleaded as Stevin cried out, "Mom, she left me."

David sat upright with concern, hearing Stevin's voice full of distress through the phone.

"What do you mean, Stevin?" Stevin remorsefully recounted the events that occurred earlier in the day. David and Rose made several attempts to reach out to Summer, but she did not answer.

As Stevin's night ended, he found himself lying on Summer's side of the bed with her robe, devastated at the thought that he had lost her. He could never imagine life without her. He replayed the fight over and over in his mind, asking himself, 'Why had he let the broom go with such force, and why hadn't he fought harder to make her stay.'

Nothing in that moment could soothe his broken heart. Without a shadow of a doubt, she was the air he needed to breathe, and his life would be suffocating without her in it.

Chapter 33: The Wrong Choice

Summer woke up with a splitting headache and reached for her phone. She had silenced it when she arrived at her room, so she hadn't heard it ringing throughout the night.

As she checked her phone, she saw that she had 102 missed calls between Rose and Stevin. It was clear that neither of them had slept much. She was still hurt and confused about Stevin's actions, so she wasn't ready to talk to him yet, and she couldn't face him at the moment.

However, she didn't want Rose to worry. So, she replied to her missed calls with a text message that said, "I am okay. Give me a moment to gather my thoughts, and I will call soon."

Summer phone ding seconds after sending Rose the text. Rose replied, "Baby girl, please hurry and call Mom; I need to hear your voice."

Summer didn't say much in her response, only replying with a heart emoji. She needed time to think. What would be her next move? How could she be sure this would be a one-time, isolated event?

If she welcomed this behavior by forgiving him, she could very well be opening Pandora's Box. Either way, the pain was too much to bear at that moment, and she needed a moment to clear her head.

Rose called Stevin to let him know that Summer was safe and sound, and that she had sent a text message to let her know.

Stevin was devastated that Summer didn't consider his feelings or trust him enough to know that he would never hurt her. He felt a mix of sadness and anger that made him increasingly frustrated and upset. He called David to vent his frustration and begged him to help him fix the situation.

"Son, give her a moment; from everything you guys shared with Rose, you may likely have unintentionally triggered her PTSD. Similar situations can trigger physical and emotional abuse. Her brain can't differentiate what happened then from what is happening around her now. As much as it hurts, you have to give her space."

"Okay, David, despite my reservations, I've decided to take the trip to Boston. At least she will know I'm out of town and can feel safe enough to return home. Please don't let her cancel her plans to visit you guys this weekend. She needs to be around family. I'm going to follow your advice and give her space to process her emotions."

Stevin ended the call and began to pack, calling his boss to inform him that he'll be taking the assignment back on.

LET'S TALK

"Hey, Mom," Summer spoke softly as Rose answered.

"Baby girl, you have scared me half to death. Where are you?"

"I am not far from home. I am at a hotel about 10 miles from the house."

"Who booked the room, Summer?"

"I did, mom. I used my alias."

"Summer, that's not safe. You need to leave that hotel. You don't know if that identity has been compromised."

"I will, Mom. I just needed some time; it just hurt so much."

As she began to tell Rose her side of the story, Rose listened with open ears, never interrupting, allowing her to express all her emotions.

As Summer paused, awaiting some motherly advice, Rose took a deep breath and said, "Baby girl, I support you wholeheartedly in any decision you make, but I have to be that voice of reason.

The one thing I haven't heard throughout this conversation is whether you feel or felt that Stevin is a threat to you." There was silence on the phone.

"Summer?" Rose asked.

"Yes, mom, I am here. No, I have never felt that way."

"Summer, when you guys were wrestling for the broom, do you recall Stevin's demeanor? Was it anger and threatening, or was it just irritation?"

"Mom, at that moment, it was both anger and irritation," Summer admitted.

"So, are you saying he purposely intended to cause you physical harm?" asked Rose.

"No, Mom, that's not what I meant. I made him mad, honestly, as I played it back in my head over and over again. He wasn't threatening me. He kept repeating give me the damn broom; I'm going to break it in half."

"I was just immediately scared, and I was afraid to let go," she giggled as she said, "Heck, Mom, we both had the broomstick refusing to let go. I just remember my feet leaving the floor, and I held on for dear life. He attempted to shake the broom loose, and when he couldn't, he let go."

"So, again, Summer, did he push you? Did he attempt to cause harm?"

"No, Mom, I don't think so; I think he was tired of wrestling for it and let it go, but he did push off with a lot of force. That's when I lost my balance. After that, everything was a bit hazy, but I do remember seeing Christopher coming towards me when I opened my eyes."

"Baby girl, I have been on the phone with Stevin since last night, and he is devastated by the physical and emotional anguish he has caused you."

"I want to make it clear that if I didn't genuinely believe that you mean the world to him, and without a shadow of a doubt, this man was put on this earth to protect you. I would not be advocating for him."

"Do I believe he attempted to cause you harm? No! Do I think he's at fault? Yes!"

"When he felt that his emotions were getting the best of him, he should have walked away; the same for you, young lady. However, I don't believe he would turn his world upside down just to become the same monster he has vowed to protect you from."

"Your father counseled him earlier, and right now, it's essential for you to also speak with him from a professional standpoint so you can start working through this. Now, the consensus between Stevin and your father was for him not to try to contact you at the moment and to give you some space to process what happened between you guys. I'm going to hang up now and have David call you."

As David counseled Summer over the phone, she began to open up and express thoughts and emotions that she had buried since childhood. She wept so that she needed some time to process her feelings and trauma before reaching out to Stevin and understanding his perspective.

As she lay in bed, thinking about her future with Stevin, she eventually fell asleep as time continued to pass.

Meanwhile, Stevin woke up to his 11 pm alarm, alerting him that it was time to get up, get dressed, and head to the airport. He immediately searched for his phone with great disappointment, only to realize that Summer hadn't made any attempts to contact him. He freshened up and left the house to catch his flight. Summer's silence made it clear that he had no reason to stay. Maybe this trip would provide her with some much-needed space.

***

Summer rolls over, jumping straight up in bed. She has slept the day away and is now ready to speak with Stevin. With great hesitancy, she begins to dial his number, nervous, not knowing how to start the conversation.

Stevin is at the airport checkpoint when he hears his phone ringing. It's after midnight, and he knows it must be Summer calling. Anxious to get through security to return her call, he watches as the security line moves at a painfully slow pace.

Meanwhile, Summer is on the other end of the line; her heart sinks as she slowly drops the phone from her ear. The pitting feeling of doom hits her stomach as her first thought is that Stevin might be finished with their relationship. He has never ignored her calls before, except when he's at work and unable to answer. She wonders if this incident was enough to push him to his breaking point.

The feeling of being hurt and confused was immediately replaced with that unknown feeling of worry and hopelessness. She wondered if she ended it all by running out on Stevin, despite knowing he truly loved and adored her.

Stevin was held up at the checkpoint along with other passengers, as he had no time to return her call; he needed to hightail straight to the gate to catch his flight. Before he could completely board the plane and be seated, his phone rang again as he fumbled with urgency to get his earpiece in his ear. "Hello, Summer, Summer," he repeated fearing the call had dropped.

"It's me, baby," she said softly.

"Please hold on, sweetheart. Let me get to my seat," he said, struggling to hear her over the noise.

She listen to the rumbling on the other line as she was confused by his statement.

"Hello, hello," he repeated when he finally managed to get his earpiece in.

"I'm here," she said.

"Oh, baby, it's so good to hear your voice. Please tell me you are physically okay. Did I hurt you?" he asked urgently.

"I'm okay, Stevin. I think we both hurt each other mentally, emotionally, and physically."

"Summer, baby, that wasn't my intention. I swear to you, it wasn't. I just wanted to take that damn broom and break it. That's all. I promise that's it. I just need to see you, Summer; I will never be able to forgive myself for causing harm to you."

"Where are you, Stevin? What did you mean by, get to your seat?"

"I decided to go to Boston."

The phone suddenly went silent. "But why Stevin? Why would you leave, and you know the barbeque is tomorrow? You promised me that you would attend with me, Stevin."

"Baby, for all I knew, I lost you; I had to do something to keep my mind busy. My thoughts were not safe. Besides, you needed to know I wasn't there so you could feel safe to return home."

"I feel safe to return home, Stevin; in that moment, I didn't know how to process what happened."

"I know, baby, and I know that is all my fault, and if you find it in your heart to come back to me, I will spend the rest of my life making it up to you."

"Come home, then, Stevin, I'll meet you there."

"I can't, Summer; I actually have to hang up now because my flight is about to take off; I have a three-hour layover. I'll reach out to you then. Just go home, Summer. Please be safe and go home."

They both ended the call with regrets. Summer had no reason to rush home to an empty house. Her last thought before rolling over and falling asleep was her inner voice, which continued to scream out, 'I made the wrong choice!'

Chapter 34: An Unwelcoming Presence

Summer was awoken by the ringing of her cell phone. David and Rose were urging her to hit the road, and they were not taking no for an answer. As she remained held up in her hotel room, trying to encourage herself to get out of bed, she dragged herself to the shower.

She wasn't due to check out until noon tomorrow, and besides, she wasn't in any rush to run back home to an empty house. She texted Stevin, requesting money to be transferred to her Tap Pay account so she could pick up some items for her road trip. He pleaded for her to return home and get everything she needed, but she couldn't bring herself to go back to an empty house with no warm embrace.

As she headed to the store to purchase an outfit for today's event, she received several texts from Rose telling her to hurry up. Rose and David had already started the party early, as they had begun the cookout with some of David's closest childhood friends from his old neighborhood.

Meanwhile, Kimberley sat in the driver's seat of her car, sweating profusely as she and Emmanuel had arrived at the barbeque. She pulled into the driveway and instructed him to park his vehicle on the street. She called her dad and asked David if Summer had arrived yet.

"No, Kimberley, why are you asking?"

"Please gather Mom and you guys come to the front of the house," she requested. 'I have someone I want you to meet."

She hung up quickly without giving David a chance to respond. She wasn't about to dare give him enough time to flip out over the phone. She felt that if she just pushed Emmanuel on them in person, they would have no choice but to accept him being there.

She eases out of the car knowing she had probably damaged her parents' trust, and she want be able to stop this trainwreck if it goes left.

She proceeded to walk towards Emmanuel as they stood at the end of the driveway holding hands.

"Rose, darling, come here," David said urgently. "Come walk with me to the front of the house. I'm pretty sure your child has brought a plus one."

"I'm going to beat the crap out of her, David, if she has," Rose declared.

As they both turned the corner and gripped onto each other tightly, there Kimberley stood with Emmanuel by her side, smiling from ear to ear. David held onto Rose tightly as he felt her pulling away to approach them.

"No, Rose," he mumbled. "This is not the time to address her. Let's just play nicely. We have a house full of guests."

It was clear Emmanuel arrived with a chip on his shoulder, and his arrogance was evident as he walked towards her parents, his head held high with a sense of self-importance and entitlement as if he belonged there.

His arrogance radiated as they approached Rose and David. Kimberley dropped her head as she began to speak, introducing him to her parents, saying, "Mom and Dad, I would like you guys to meet Emmanuel."

Rose could see how timid she looked, and she didn't want her baby girl not to feel the love and joy today would bring. Rose muffled up a smile, which immediately turned upside down as Emmanuel gripped Kimberley's chin, pushing her head up, demanding she hold her head up high. He states that this is a joyous occasion, not a funeral.

David swiftly pulls Kimberley to him, as he's seconds from punching Emmanuel lights out.

"Well, Rose, I must say that you are incredibly beautiful," Emmanuel said. "I always knew that the woman who gave birth to my soul mate had to be equally as pretty, if not more beautiful."

David squeezed Kimberley's shoulders as he attempted to gather himself and hold his patience.

On the other hand, Emmanuel seemed captivated by Rose as his focus was only on her, as he extended his hand out to shake her hand. He waited patiently until Rose's hand was positioned directly in the palm of his hand before shaking it.

"I'd like to formally introduce myself, My name is Christopher Diamond," said Emmanuel.

Rose immediately snatched away as she quickly backed away in disbelief.

"What are you saying, Emmanuel?" asked Kimberley with a confused expression.

"Well, my darling, Emmanuel is my grandfather's name, which is also my middle name," replied Christopher. "A few years ago, there was a shift in my life, and I knew God would protect and provide, so I started going by Emmanuel."

Kimberley was furious and attempted to scold Emmanuel for keeping her in the dark and then revealing something so significant in front of her parents without informing her beforehand. However, little did she realize that Christopher had been deceitful about his true identity and intentions.

Kimberley's banter was interrupted when Rose began to scream, "Leave, Leave my home now!" She shouted and ran to the back of the house.

David, however, remained calm while Kimberley panicked and demanded an explanation for Rose's behavior towards Emmanuel. But Christopher stood with his chest out, and his arrogance overtook the moment. He wanted to show Rose and David who he really was and how much power he had over both their daughters.

David caught up with Rose as she screamed, "He's been plotting this for years. He used her, David, he used her! How can you remain so calm?" asked Rose.

"Listen, Rose, this isn't the time to fall apart. Yes, I want to beat that smug grin right off his face, but we must prioritize Summer's safety first. I will hold him and Kimberley here. You call Summer and get her to turn around. Stevin is out of town, so we must get to her before that animal does."

"And what about Kimberley, David?" asked Rose.

"She's here in our presence; we can keep her safe, but Summer is about to walk right into a trap he has been devising for years."

Summer's phone rings, and she picks it up. Noticing it was Rose, she answered, "Hey, Mom, I'm 15 minutes away."

"Turn around, baby girl, turn around. Don't come here, it's not safe."

"What's going on, Mom?" Summer screams.

"He's here, Summer, Christopher is here."

"How? What do you mean he's there?"

"He manipulated your sister. He's been dating her for two years using a different name. Summer, he's just like you described. He walked up to me and shook my hand, introducing himself as Christopher Diamond. He wanted me to know who he was. Run, baby. Mom needs you to run and hide. Take your burner phone and go to a different hotel, Summer, not the same one," she stressed.

"Momma, everything is at home. I have another ID I can use to book a room. I just need to make it home. Mom, I need you guys to keep him there as long as possible, only if it's safe. Remember, he's very dangerous. I need to go back to the room. I left my laptop. I can't take that chance of leaving my computer there. I have all my financial information on that laptop."

"No, Summer, it's too dangerous. And why haven't you checked out of that hotel yet? It's too risky to go back there."

"Mom, it's even riskier for Stevin if Christopher gets hold of my laptop. I have to go back," replied Summer.

"Go, Summer, go, but please be careful," Rose pleaded.

Rose ended the call with Summer as she frantically searched for David. She peered around the corner and noticed Christopher's car still parked on the street. She eventually found David ransacking his dad's office, searching for the keys to his gun case.

"David, what are you doing?"

"I can't, Rose, I just can't. Forgive me for leaving you guys like this, but I'm about to put a bullet right between that son of a bitch eyes."

Rose was in a state of panic and started crying out, "No, David, no!" She ran out of the house, frantically searching for

David's best friend, Sam. She tried to explain the situation to him and asked him to make David stand down.

All hell broke loose when Sam learned of the situation and informed David's other friends. Sam then turned to Rose and apologized, saying, "I'm sorry, Rose. This coward and his destruction ends today. If he doesn't leave here in a body bag today, I guarantee he will leave here a vegetable."

"Come on, Sam," David shouted. "The arrogance of this son of a bitch."

Rose hurried towards the front of the home, frantically searching for Kimberley. She needed to protect her from both Christopher and the destruction that was unfolding before her very eyes. However, as she reached the front, she was shocked to find that Kimberley's car was gone while Christopher's car was still parked on the street.

The men surrounded Christopher's car, shouting, "Get that, Mother Fucker!" but Christopher was nowhere to be seen.

Rose panicked as she realized that Kimberley was with that sociopath. She had run off in a tizzy to protect Summer, leaving her baby girl in the hands of Christopher.

She began calling Kimberley's phone, but there was no answer. She then texted her, pleading for her to return to her grandparents' home and get away from Christopher. Suddenly, Kimberley appeared outside, with tears in her eyes, clutching onto her grandparent's portrait.

"What's going on, Mom? You guys ran Emmanuel off," Kimberley said.

"What do you mean, Kimberley?" Rose shouted. "Where is your car?" she asked. Kimberley, where is your car?

"Emmanuel asked to borrow it."

"No, Kimberley, what have you done?" Rose shouted.

"How long has Christopher been gone? Tell me, tell me now."

Rose raced to the end of the street to inform David that Christopher had left. The men quickly got into their cars to search for him, suggesting that David remain there to protect his family if Christopher returned. Meanwhile, with her voice choked with tears, Kimberley stood in the driveway, screaming and confessing their love for each other.

"Child, have you gone mad?" Rose exclaimed. "This is your sister's fiancé, a sociopath lunatic who deliberately sought you out to track down your sister."

"That's not true, Mom, that's not true," Kimberley protested. "He loves me and has never hit or threatened me."

"Why would he Kimberley? You were just the bait to catch what he wanted. You led him right to her."

"Everything is not always about Summer, Mom."

David interjected, trying to reason with her. "Kimberley, hunny, your life, your sister's life, is in danger. Open your eyes, baby girl."

Kimberley dismisses David's plea, turning her back to him.

"David, get her out of my sight before I knock some sense into her," Rose said. David also wanted to shake some sense into her, but all he could do was hold his baby girl, as she, too, was a victim of Christopher's madness. She, too, needed protection and comfort in that moment.

Rose was distraught as she frantically tried to reach Summer and Stevin, but there was no answer. The big question was, when did Christopher sneak off, and did he know where Summer was staying?

Chapter 35: No Where To Run

Summer taps her ink pen on the bank counter while nervously waiting for the bank teller to return with her withdrawal. She begins to notice that the waiting period is longer than usual and starts to feel anxious as she knows she has no time to spare.

Standing on her tippytoes, she stretched her neck to look for the teller who had been assisting her. As she noticed the teller walking back to her workstation, she also noted the gentleman who accompanied her.

"Ms. Green?" the gentleman said, addressing her.

"Yes, sir, I am Ms. Green."

"Hello there, I am Mr. Shagreen, the bank manager. Unfortunately, we are unable to process the withdrawal at this time," Mr. Shagreen explains. Summer looked confused and began to question the bank manager as to why she couldn't withdraw funds that belonged to her.

"I'm sorry, sir, Mr. Shagreen," she stated. "I am confused as to why I am being denied my own money that I entrusted this bank with. I make withdrawals weekly from this account. What seems to be the problem today?"

"I understand your frustration, Ms. Green. However, to withdraw the amount of funds you requested, we need two signatures, which means that Mr. Bash needs to be present. Unfortunately, without his presence, you can only withdraw your daily limit of $1200, which doesn't require the other party's signature."

Both parties must sign to access funds exceeding the limit set when this account was opened. Summer started to sweat profusely, and her lips began trembling.

"Are you okay, Ms. Green?" the bank manager asked with concern as he noticed her sweating and trembling lips. “Ms. Green is everything okay,” the bank manager repeated. "Is there something we can do for you," he asked in concern as it appeared all the blood had drained from her face. She quickly remembered the incident from California, which quickly reminded her to 'trust no one.'

"No, thank you. I will take the $1200. Mr. Bash is currently out of state, but I will have him call and resolve this when he returns." As she quickly exited the bank, she knew she had enough money to fly to Stevin's destination but needed to find his location.

Frantically, she returned to her car, dialing Stevin's number over and over again. She cried out for help on his answering service, "Please, baby, pick up. I need you. I'm scared, and I don't know what to do. I don't know what Christopher knows or if it's safe to return home. I just need you right now. Please, baby, pick up."

As she contemplated her next move, she realized that only one person could save her life in this dire situation. Even though she was dreading it, she knew that Mr. Diamond was the only one who had any influence over Christopher, and it was a matter of life and death.

She sat trembling in fear in the bank parking lot, desperately searching the internet for Mr. Diamond's contact information. Locating his office number, she dialed and silently prayed for his cooperation.

"Hello, Diamond Inc. and company; how may I assist you?"

"Yes, this is an urgent call for Mr. Nate Diamond Sr."

"One moment, please. I'll transfer you to his receptionist."

"Hello, this is Penny. How can I help you?"

"Yes, this is an urgent call for Mr. Diamond. I urgently need to speak with him."

"I'm sorry, unfortunately, Mr. Diamond is not available at the moment. May I have your name and number so he can return your call?" Penny asked politely.

"Penny, is that what you stated your name is?" Summer asked.

"Yes, my name is Penny."

"Hello, Penny. My name is Summer Taylor, and this is a call I personally know Mr. Diamond won't want to miss. Just inform him Summer Taylor is on the line and the call is regarding his son."

After a brief moment on hold, Mr. Diamond answered the call.

"Hello, this is Mr. Diamond. Who is this?"

"Hello, Mr. Diamond. This is Summer," she said softly.

"Why are you calling my office? Is this some kind of joke?"

"No, sir. He found me, and I need your help. Please, sir, I need you; I have no one else to turn to," she pleaded.

"What? "How did he find you, Summer?" he shouted in a deep voice. "Tell me how," he demanded.

"He started dating my sister and manipulated his way into her life just to get to me," she explained.

"And how would you know this, Summer? The only way this would affect you is if you did the exact opposite of what I asked you not to do when I betrayed my son for you," he said sternly. "So, you tell me again, young lady, how in the hell did my son find you?"

"Through my mom," she said in a low voice.

"You imbecile! How stupid are you? I risked my entire family for you, and this is how you repay me. How reckless are you, just blatantly disrespectful," he shouted. "I moved heaven and earth to ensure my son could never trace you, and this is how you repay me?" In an evil tone, he ended the call, stating, "You deserve everything that's coming your way. And trust and believe the only person I will be saving in this situation is my son. At any means necessary!"

Summer sat in silence as he abruptly ended their call.

She suddenly exploded with anger, as she started screaming and beating her hands against the steering wheel until her phone shattered. The screen cracked, and the back cover and battery scattered. Her only choice now was to return to the hotel, retrieve her laptop, and pray Stevin had emailed her his itinerary as he has done every out-of-state trip.

As she pulled into the hotel parking lot, she drove slowly while scanning the area, checking the license plates of other vehicles for any signs of danger. She needed to get in touch with Stevin urgently but struggled to locate the back of her phone and the battery, digging between the seats with no time to spare and unable to follow up with Rose to learn Christopher's whereabouts.

She gave herself a strict five-minute deadline to retrieve her personal belongings and laptop from her hotel room. Walking swiftly through the parking lot, her heart racing with anxiety. She took short, quick steps, looking around as if she were expecting Christopher to turn the corner at any moment.

As she reached her room, she quickly scanned her keycard. Her heart was pounding as she felt the adrenaline rush through her body. She hurriedly opened the door and shut it quickly, then leaned against it, taking long, deep breaths to calm herself and slow her heart rate.

She panted as her entire body quivered in fear. She could feel her heart racing and her blood pressure increasing. Her body and brain signaled the built-up anxiety, triggering a stress response as she knew she had to escape from danger. She quickly rushes into the room, passing the restroom and racing to the bed for her laptop. She cleared the wall that was blocking the view of the bed when, suddenly, she was startled by the flicker of the lamp light as she saw someone sitting in the chair next to the bed.

"Hello, Summer," Christopher said in his arrogant and confident tone. The coldness in his eyes made her heart quiver as he seemed to get off on seeing the fear in her eyes. As he stood up, her body froze in fear. She couldn't move; the fear consumed her entire body. Her inner voice screamed, "Run, just run," but her legs wouldn't move. He walked over to her slowly and gently grabbing her neck. He repeated her name as he circled her, sniffing her skin as he took a handful of her hair.

"Why would you cut off all my beautiful hair?" He asked, gripping a tight fist full of it. He spoke to her as if they hadn't spent the last few years apart. She was his, and there was no acknowledging that he had just hunted her down like prey and the life they shared was over. The fear consumed her as she lost control of her bladder, and her pants became visibly saturated as urine ran down her leg.

"Go and clean yourself up," he demanded. "You have five minutes, so help me God. If you try anything, I will break your fucken neck where you stand."

Still frozen in fear, she stood stiff and afraid. He shouted "move now, Summer" as he followed her to the bathroom and turned the shower on, ripping off what he could.

Taking his phone out of his pocket as he faced time with a guy he called KILL BILL. You know what I want to see, he told the individual on the phone as he stood in front of her, making her watch as Kill Bill was scoping out her parents' home. He ordered him to take out the targets if he didn't hear back from him in the next fifteen minutes.

Summer cried out, reaching for the phone as she screamed NO! He slams her against the shower tile, yelling "Don't touch me," as he raises his hand in the air as if he were about to strike her. Her entire body cringes as she has flashbacks of his abuse.

"Do what I say before I make you watch him bury your mom alive."

He released her, walking off, patting his sleeve dry as he demanded her to hurry up, but she couldn't move. Her legs felt as if they gave out as she collapsed to her knees on the shower floor and started sobbing. She couldn't believe what was happening and kept telling herself, 'This can't be real.'

Afraid to walk out of the bathroom, she knew she was on borrowed time. She slowly walked out of the bathroom as he snatched the towel from her nude body. He placed her undergarments in her hand, making her get dressed in front of him. His eyes scan every inch of her body. She felt so violated, feeling as if she was being made to get nude in front of an absolute stranger.

"Where is your phone?" he asked. She slowly pointed at the floor where she had dropped it. He picked up the shattered phone and screamed, "Where's the back?"

She replied, "I don't know, I couldn't find it. I dropped it in the parking lot while getting out of my car."

He then demanded that she finish getting dressed. She fumbled for her clothes on the bed as he had emptied out her bag, throwing everything onto the bed. Her hands hit her laptop, which was positioned under the pillow. She quickly pushed it further under the pillow, knowing that if Christopher found it, her life would end where she stood.

Her laptop contained a complete record of her financial records, personal emails, and a complete road map of her activities with Stevin.

Knowing at least ten minutes had passed since Christopher's phoned his goon, she was anxious for him to make the call. She was too scared to speak up but eventually softly pleaded, "Please, Christopher, make the call."

With a smug smirk, Christopher glanced down at his expensive watch and announced. "You have four minutes to get out of this room and into my car."

She scrambled to put on her clothes, as she was only half dressed, and rushed towards the door. Christopher took his time as she became increasingly anxious and started to panic loudly, begging him to make the call. Her behavior began to attract the attention of another guest.

"Calm the hell down, one more damn word. I will walk away and leave you standing here, and you can spend the rest of your life searching for your mother's body," he warned her. She promptly straightened up and quickly walked out of the lobby into the parking lot.

"Where's your car?" Christopher repeatedly asked her. She could not take him to her car, as Stevin's name was all over her paperwork. Needing a distraction. Knowing Christopher didn't want any attention brought to them, she began crying hysterically and begged Christopher to make the call despite his objections.

He attempted to guide her towards her car. However, she fell to the ground and continued to beg him to make the call. Christopher eventually took out his phone and made the call, resetting the next call time for thirty minutes. "Now get your ass up before I stump you where you lay."

With a lethal grip on her arm, he dragged her to the car; he threw her into the passenger seat, squeezing her hand with a firm grip as she cried out.

"You have one more time to disobey me, and everything, as you know it, ends tonight."

She slumped down in the seat as she watched the hotel disappear in the sideview mirror. Christopher was right about one thing: everything she knew, happiness, love, and the feeling of belonging and family ended the moment she entered her hotel room and closed the door.

Chapter 36: The Ultimate Betrayal

Summer knew the vehicle they were riding in belonged to Kimberley. She and Rose had the same taste in perfume; from the smell in the car, it seemed as if Kimberley bathed in it. And besides, Christopher wouldn't be caught dead driving a Camry. It didn't help that the inside of the car looked like someone had thrown up a bottle of Pepto-Bismol from all the pink décor in the vehicle.

It felt like they had been driving for an hour. She was certain at least thirty minutes had passed, being Christopher had placed a call to KILL BILL. This time, he instructed his goon to communicate with him only via text, leaving Summer in the dark.

As the car slowed down, they turned off onto a dirt road. She began hyperventilating, remembering the last dirt road he drove her down, she damn near lost her life. Her first thought is, "I am about to die."

"Calm the hell down," he shouted. Irritated by her rapid breathing.

She sat up in the seat; she needed to see her last surroundings, more like where she would take her last breath, when she noticed a small house in the distance. Christopher placed the car in park, leaning back in the seat and taking a deep breath as if he had accomplished the impossible. He then placed his head in his hands and rubbed his face before turning to her.

"Moving forward, Summer, you write your own destiny. You betray me. I will make you suffer by watching me burn down everything you love before I split your throat. I will only ask you once, and if you hesitate, I will burn the image of your family being tortured in your brain. You will beg me to kill you."

He exited the car, walked over to the passenger side, opened her door, and snatched her out of the vehicle. As she was being forcefully taken into the house, she glanced around.

‘The pretend house that he called home felt dark,’ just like his empty and dark soul, she thought to herself. Nothing about the house matched his personality.

She stood in the middle of the living room while he gathered papers and packed up any evidence of his presence in the home.

Suddenly, the sound of a car pulling up could be heard. He looked down at his phone as he started swearing, pacing back and forth.

"This stupid bitch" he shouted. "Sit your ass down, Summer" he demanded. Then he turned to her and smiled.

“Hey, you never met your little sister, huh?”

“Nah... you haven't because she hates your fucken guts. How fucken ironic! Your first meet and greet will end with me putting a bullet in her head, and you will have a front-row seat to witness it.”

Summer slowly eased down in the recliner, with her hands covering her mouth as tears streamed down her face. She was frozen in fear.

"I beg of you, Christopher. Please don't hurt her," she begged.

"What will you do for me in return?" he asked.

"Please, let's just go. I won't fight. I'll go wherever you want," she pleaded, trembling nervously.

As she covered her mouth in disbelief, her eyes and mouth widened, and she felt sick to her stomach. She prayed he wasn't the monster he claimed to be as he left the room. His threats seemed so far-fetched, and she didn't know if he was truly capable of carrying out these egregious acts he threatened to do or if he was just trying to scare her into submission.

Regardless, she wasn't willing to take any chances and risk her family's safety.

She could hear him and Kimberley talking as the front door was in her line of sight.

"Why haven't you answered my calls?" Kimberley asked.

"I'm taking care of business, Kimmie."

"Please tell me my parents aren't right; please tell me you love me," she pleaded.

He slightly grazed her face as he gently rubbed it and said, "Baby, I need you to put your big girl panties on. Some things are kept from you for your own good."

His answer wasn't satisfying to her. She turned as if she was leaving, only to turn around and push past him with force, making her way inside the house.

There, she was finally face to face with her sister. Her eyes bucked; the resemblance was uncanny. However, in that moment, her fight for Emmanuel meant more than a half-sister whom she absolutely wanted nothing to do with.

Summer is frozen in fear, staring at Kimberley like a deer caught in headlights. Her eyes are red and swollen, and she trembles in fear. She is too afraid to speak up because she believes Christopher will harm Kimberley if she gets in his way, and she would be forced to watch him harm her sister.

She watches helplessly as Kimberley becomes outraged and turns to him, shouting, "You're lying to me!"

"No, you're wrong," he stated. There's more to this situation of which you aren't aware. I'm sorry I couldn't be honest with you, but your sister stole from me. She packed up and left our home, stealing what was mine, and I need it back." He attempted to pull her out the doorway.

Kimberely's eyes remained fixated on Summer. She waited for her to dispute his claims, but Summer never uttered a word. Christopher managed to pull her back outside onto the front porch.

"Do you want to be my wife?" Because you sure are not acting like it," he asked.

"I do, Emmanuel, I do."

"It's just..." she trailed off, her voice choked up as she dropped her head with teary eyes.

"Your sister stole a large amount of money from me. Please return to your parents' home and tell no one you have seen Summer here with me. I need until the morning as she has agreed to transfer my money back into my account, which can't happen until the morning. I can't let her out of my sight tonight."

"Well, I can stay and help you," she suggested.

"Dammit, Kimmie, you're not listening." I don't want to do anything that might set her off and cause me to lose everything. All I'm asking is that you trust me," he pleaded.

"Can I trust you?" he asked, gently rubbing her arms as he stared deep into her eyes, pulling her away from the door, ensuring they were out of Summer's view. He lifted her slightly and kissed her, reassuring her of his love for her.

"Can I count on you, baby?"

She nodded slowly, ignoring her intuitions, as her gut feeling screamed this wasn't right and something was wrong.

"Now go home and wait for my call. Thanks for bringing me my car. Here are your keys," he placed the keys in her hands with a gentle squeeze as if he regretted asking her to leave.

"Emmanuel," she said as she refused to call him Christopher.

"Did we meet by fate, or was all this just to get to her?"

"Kimberley, I knew the moment I met you, that I was willing to walk away from the money and my search for Summer. If I had thought that my pursuit of Summer would come between us at any point, I would have kept my identity a secret. But I knew I could trust you and that you are my future."

With those words, Kimberley's loyalty was sold. She stood by the man she knew as Emmanuel, and as far as she was concerned, she had never met this unwanted sister and had no intention of sharing with anyone what she had witnessed at his home tonight, including the presence of an unwanted sister.

Christopher stood on the porch and watched Kimberley's car drive away from the house. He arrogantly enters the house and returns to the living room to inform Summer that she was never seen tonight.

"You see, unlike you, your sister is willing to risk it all for love."

"Now, we're heading to the airport," he says, placing two passports on the table before her.

Suddenly, he slams his fist on the table and yells, "No more distractions, do you hear me!"

He then sat on the table directly before her, pulling out her cell phone from his back pocket and examining it closely. He then took out his cell phone and made a call to one of his goons. "Where are you? I need to know your location," he demanded.

"Okay, okay," he repeated.

He raised her phone and read the back of it. "Hey, can you check if we can get a battery for an Android RAXX 12 tonight? And if not, I need someone who can transfer files from a cell to a computer."

After hanging up the phone, he gathered his belongings and left her phone on the table. "Christopher, I am thirsty," she pleaded as she begged for water. He never utters a word to her but slams a water bottle on the table.

A few seconds later, a car could be heard pulling into the home's driveway. He walked out to meet with the driver as their voices were mumbled, and their conversation was difficult to hear.

Summer snatched her cell phone from the table, poured water into the back, and then the tiny speakers. She patted the phone dry while applying pressure to the front screen, hoping to damage any working parts. She noticed some sale papers on the table. She pushed the phone slightly under the papers, hoping he would forget it. She was as good as dead if he managed to retrieve any of her personal information from the phone.

After watching Christopher and his goon load boxes into his car, he returned to the house and demanded that she get in the car.

She walked slowly, observing him as he snatched the passports and other documents from the table, leaving her cell phone behind. She decided to create a distraction. She quickly walked to the car in what seemed like a running motion, making him think she was trying to make a run for it.

She knew he would be watching her like a hawk and would follow behind her closely. She prayed he didn't remember he didn't grab the phone from the table.

Her distraction worked as he was so focused on her escaping that he came running out the door behind her, holding onto her arm.

He ordered his goon to drive them straight to the airport. Halfway through the drive, he opened his briefcase and started patting around his papers.

"Where the hell is your phone?" he shouted, raising up intimidating her with his body language as he demanded to know the whereabouts of her cell phone.

She threw her hands up to protect herself from any possible blows and replied, "I don't have it; I swear I don't have it. You had it Christopher." Frantically screaming at the driver to turn the car around, his driver reminded him that he had no time to return, and he really needed to make his flight.

He immediately made a call demanding the person on the phone to go to the house, pick up the cell phone, and meet him at the airport with the phone, stressing he needed that phone ASAP.

It was clear he wanted to know her whereabouts and who she had been with; she was just confused as to why he hadn't demanded those answers personally from her. Could he possibly already know?

He took a small glass and a bottle of water from his briefcase, mixing a powdery substance into the glass. He stirred the substance in the glass and handed it to her, telling her to drink.

"No Christopher, I don't want to drink this."

"You can drink it on your own, or I can have the car pulled over and pour it down your damn throat."

"Please, no." Why do I have to take these drugs? I promise I want make a scene. I will walk to the plane I promise."

"Drink, Summer," he demanded.

Her lips trembled as she took a swallow of the bitter substance. Drink it all now and stop playing with it, he said.

Suddenly, the driver hit a pothole, and the liquid substance spilled all over the seat. Snatching the glass from her hand, he scraped the residue of the powdery substance from the bottom of the glass, forcing his fingers into her mouth. He placed his hand over her mouth with such force she felt as if he was about to suffocate her. His sizeable muscular body overtook her. She immediately went limp as she had no desire to feel Christoper wrath. It didn't take long as she felt nauseous and couldn't keep her eyes open.

She thought to herself, 'She would rather die falling into a deep sleep and never waking up again rather than have Christopher slowly beat the life out of her. Or even worse, she has to remain in this loveless relationship for a duration.' She became even more nauseous at the thought of having intimate moments with him.

As their car approached the private runway, she suspected that he had bribed the officials as they had a private TSA screening. She felt weak and exhausted as if she were walking on clouds. She had no strength to resist him. All she wanted was to sit down and rest her eyes.

Suddenly, her surroundings started to spin, and she felt very sick. The last thing she could remember was Christopher standing over her and saying, "Sleep now," as her eyes became too heavy to remain open.

Christopher paced up and down the aisle of the plane, anxiously checking in with his henchman, who had been trapped in a five-car pileup on the interstate. The associate had been tasked with retrieving Summer's phone from his home but had yet to make it there. Christopher knew that if he left without her phone, he would have to rely solely on Summer's word regarding her whereabouts and who she had been with for the past three years.

Looking up, he noticed the captain gesturing for him to return to his seat as the plane was waiting to pull off. Sitting in his seat, he watched the runway disappear, along with any secrets that may have been stored on Summer's phone.

Chapter 37: From Paradise To Hell

"Summer, wake up! Wake up now," Christopher demanded. "Here, drink this water. I need you to walk through customs; I need you to be up and alert."

"I can't walk," Summer replied. "My head is spinning, and I don't feel good."

"Come on, baby, lean on me," he said as he comforted her. Too weak and confused to resist him, she accepted his embrace and held tight onto his arm, trying not to fall. Everything was hazy, and all she wanted was a bed.

"Here, Summer, put on these shades to help block the sunlight."

As they approached security clearance, she could feel Christopher's hands getting sweaty and his body slightly trembling.

"Ma'am, can I get your passport, and where might you be traveling to today?" the officer asked. “Ma'am, ma'am, can you hear me?" The CBP officer repeated as she tried to get Summer's attention.

"I'm sorry, ma'am. I mean Ms. King," Christopher says, as he reads her name badge. "My fiancé has terrible anxiety when it comes to flying," he explained. "I told her not to overdo it with her Xanax," he said, handing over a bottle of Xanax prescribed in Summer's name.

"I understand, sir, the officer said, "but I need her to answer."

Christopher turned to Summer, saying, "Baby, if flying is causing you to be this nervous, I could always have Bill fly your mother out to help with the anxiety."

Summer immediately perked up and replied, "I'm good, Christopher. The medication has made me loopy, but I am okay to fly."

The officer asked, "Ma'am, is the pink LV luggage yours?

"Yes, it is," Christopher replied quickly. "Her passport is actually in the side pocket," he added, pointing to the bag, which he had conveniently stored next to engagement photos of him and Summer.

"I'm sorry, sir, but I need you to remove her passport and ID from her luggage," said the officer.

Christopher intentionally scattered their engagement photos on the table, locating Summer's ID in the mix of the pictures.

"Sorry for the inconvenience, ma'am," he added.

Looking up at Summer, the officer said, "It looks like you are a lucky lady. Your photos are beautiful."

The conversation then shifted to how beautifully Christopher had planned out their engagement. The mere fact Summer was out of it and could barely stand on her own two feet was overlooked entirely by the officer. The CBP officer even assisted Christopher in placing her in a wheelchair, speeding up the process.

Too weak to fight, too scared to scream for help, the only thing Summer was sure of was she was taking him far away from her family and keeping them out of harm's way.

As she sank into her seat, she remained alert enough to realize that he had taken her through US customs, which only meant he was taking her out of the country. Her stomach twisted into knots, and tears swelled in her eyes. She knew that her life, as she had known it in the last few years, was over.

The thought of never seeing Stevin again was unbearable. She knew how much he loved her and knew that he would never be able to forgive himself as he would blame himself for this. If only she could talk to him, he would know he was the best part of her life. She had never experienced life and what it meant to be valued and loved until she met him.

As she drifted off to sleep, she found comfort in the thought that Christopher couldn't erase her memories; he couldn't steal the joy Stevin brought into her life. As she fell into a deep sleep, she dreamt of being carried towards a pair of white double doors that swung open. Standing at the altar was, Stevin dressed in all white, with his captivating smile and his hand extended to her. But her feet wouldn't move; it was as if something was holding her in place. As she turned to pull her long white lace train to set herself free. She pulled and pulled; when she started to gather the dress up, Christopher suddenly grabbed her hand.

She struggled to fight free and reached out her hand for Stevin, but suddenly, she noticed him stumbling back as he stared down at his pure white suit, now saturated in bright red blood. He clutched his bleeding chest as he dropped to his knees. She started to cry hysterically, fighting to get free, but Christopher's grip only became tighter.

“Stevin...no! No... No...No... Stevin... Stevin...Stevin!"

She suddenly jumped up, with her eyes snapping open. Covered in a cold sweat and shaking, her heart pounded as she locked eyes with Christopher. He stared suspiciously at her with his eyebrows scrunched together and a tense jaw. Summer shivered with terror, worried that she might have called out Stevin's name in her sleep.

Christopher continued to stare at her with cold eyes, which made her feel even more paranoid. Slumping back down in her seat, she stared out the window. The sky looked extremely dark, but the ground below was even darker. She knew she was staring down at the black, bottomless ocean. As the plane started to descend, she felt a lurch in her stomach. Still unable to see any light on the ground, she grabbed Christopher's hand with a look of terror.

"There's no ground, no ground," she exclaimed.

"Summer, sit the hell back," he mocked.

She tightly closed her eyes as the plane shifted and dropped. She had no idea where she was being forced to travel, but surely, everyone on the plane couldn't be on a suicide mission. She kept her eyes shut tightly until the plane's wheels hit the runway with a jolt. She took a deep breath, knowing that her hell had just begun.

She had been in his presence for over 24 hours, yet he had not questioned her even once. She knew this meant only one thing: he needed to be in an environment where he could express his anger physically.

As they exited the plane, the sun began to peak, revealing a remote island with a small airport. She is confused, as she sees no hotels, no roads, only a small boat that the ocean could swallow up. She stood in disbelief as the islanders started to load Christoper's bags onto the small boat. She wasn't allowed to ask questions as his demeanor had changed. It was as if he knew she was now at his mercy, and he was in control.

He dragged her to the boat without uttering a word, just grabbing her by the shirt and pulling her towards the water. They were accompanied by an older gentleman who spoke a little English and a young boy who spoke in his native language.

As the older islander spoke, he spoke with urgency, pointing up to the sky and warning Christopher about the rain, as the sky looked like it was about to open up. As she sat near the back of the small speedboat, she immediately became drenched while holding on for dear life. Ten minutes into the boat ride, the sky opened up, and rain poured down on them.

Large, hard raindrops bucketed down on them, as waves and harsh rain pounded the boat. Digging her nails into the seat, she closed her eyes tightly as she prayed for her life.

As the boat's speed slowed, she peeked to see her surroundings. All that could be seen were forests and tall trees on a remote island. As the back of the boat pivoted towards the sand, the young child jumped into the shallow water, and Christopher handed him his luggage. She watched as the young boy waved through the water back and forth, taking bags to the shore. He gestured for her to exit the boat as she, too, had to jump off in shallow water. Still confused as to where they were going, a little shack on the island became more apparent behind the trees. It looked as if it could be blown down with one hard wind.

Her feet sank into the sand as she approached the gloomy, tin-roofed shack. A small step led up to a porch that squeaked with every step. The hot, wooden two-bedroom shack felt like a prison. Upon entering the house from the porch, she found herself in a small living room that opened straight into the kitchen. The only furniture in the living room was a used bench sofa and a 13" TV VCR combo. The sole means of outside communication was a satellite phone, which Christopher kept locked up.

"Summer, please clean up and change. You'll find your clothes in the first bedroom straight ahead," he said.

Christopher could be heard making plans with the older gentleman to return the following day. She walked slowly and glanced around the small room with the metal-framed bed. He had given up everything to imprison her in a shack that was being run by a generator. She wondered how they would survive here, what they would eat, and how they would manage to live in such conditions.

There was a small Jack and Jill bathroom connecting the bedrooms. The cabinets were fully stocked, and she had clothing awaiting her. This kidnapping was planned and well-calculated. She eased down onto the toilet as she noted a spot of blood in the seat of her underwear. Too afraid to address him directly, she searched the cabinets for sanitary napkins, as the bathroom cabinets squealed when opened. Christopher burst into the bathroom door demanding to know what she was searching for, grabbing her arm.

“I needed a personal item, Christopher; I am looking for a pad.”

“Are you saying you are mysteriously on your cycle?” He shouted while snatching on her underwear, checking for blood. He reaches into the top cabinet, throwing a pack of pads at her as he walks off, slamming the bathroom door.

She steps into the shower as she chooses clothing that completely covered her body. Her heart pounded as she watched the door for him to enter at any moment. Stepping out of the bathroom, she walked into the bedroom with him sitting on the bed. She froze, standing against the wall.

"Summer, sit down," he demanded.

She eased onto the bed, almost jumping out of her skin, when he quickly turned to face her.

"Did you cheat on me?"

She stared at him with such a disgusted look as she sat in silence. He jumped up from the bed when she didn't answer, marching towards her.

"No, Christopher, no," she pleaded. She screamed, begging him not to harm her, but he reacted to her "No" as if she was stating, "No, she hasn't been with anyone."

He immediately dials the crazy down, sitting back on the bed. That was a clear sign that he knew nothing about her whereabouts or who she had been with.

"I need you to be honest with me, Summer. If I find out you are lying to me, you better tell me the damn truth. Are you still my pure white rose?" he asked sternly. "Tell me, you haven't destroyed your body with another man?"

Summer sat in silence, unsure if he was testing her or if he really didn't know anything.

"Your muteness is telling me you're not being truthful with me," he said.

She felt uncomfortable and wanted to shift the conversation away from herself by flipping the Q&A on him.

"My muteness is in disbelief that you are questioning me after you intentionally sought out my sister, slept with her, and even built an entire relationship with her. But you love me," she says sarcastically.

Her statement dialed the crazy backup as he jumped up from the bed and started destroying the room. Turning his rage toward her, nothing to hide behind, she balled up on the bed in a fetal position, attempting to block his blows. Snatching her by the foot, he pulled her to the end of the bed, straggling himself on top of her.

"This is all your fault," he screamed. "You made me defile myself. You corrupted the purity of our love when you decided to allow my father to turn you against me."

Puzzled, she thought to herself, 'His father turned me against him? He's completely rewriting our past.'

"You!" he screamed. "No one but you are at fault for me sleeping with that disgusting pig. I dare you to blame me for something you have caused."

Dry heaving as he was overcome with nausea at the mere thought of sleeping with Kimberley. Grabbing her by the wrists, pinning her back onto the bed as he attempts to kiss her. She turned her head, refusing him. He grabbed her by the face, turning her head and forcing eye contact as she tried to fight him off. She refused to have him touch her; she would rather die. It would be rape; he would have to force himself on her before she would let him touch her ever again. The feeling of his lips grazing hers was repulsive to her.

"Please, Summer, let's start over. I want what you want: marriage, kids, and our families to join together as one. You can have a relationship with your mom, Ebony, and even that old fart, Mr. Jeffrey."

"How dared you! How dare you!" She cried out. Mr. Jeffery is dead! I killed him, running from you. He died from a broken heart because it wasn't safe for me to pick up a phone to tell him I was okay. You have taken everything from me, Christopher, everything."

He loosen his grip and dropped his head. He had big plans for their day on tomorrow, and tonight's events wouldn't ruin them.

"I will sleep in the other room tonight and let you gather yourself. You only have one night to come to terms with your future, which will be with me forever. Please don't test me!"

He stood in silence, staring at her. His desire to have his way with her was strong, but what he had planned was even greater. She would become his wife tomorrow, and they would consummate their marriage as husband and wife.

Summer curled up in bed in disbelief; she felt completely helpless. She knew there was no way of escaping this prison Christopher created. Her heart bled tears of pain for Rose and Stevin. She knew by now they were aware of her disappearance and who was behind it. She couldn't imagine how difficult it must be for them, knowing this has to be torture for them both.

As she lay there, staring up at the ceiling, she couldn't help but reflect on the time she shared at the farm with Stevin. She refused to think about what would come next, knowing that Christopher's wrath had yet to be unleashed.

Chapter 38: Fighting A Losing Battle

Summer had a restless night; she tossed and turned all night. The thought of Stevin returning home to an empty house and not knowing her whereabouts was gut-wrenching.

The old tin roof made creaking noises all night long. She stayed up all night, listening for Christopher, fearing that he would walk in and force himself on her. She sat up in bed with her legs huddled up to her chest, anxiously watching the door. As her mental capacity evaporated, she could no longer reject her body's need to sleep. She slowly nodded off, feeling the mattress shifting, her eyes open wide to him staring at her.

"Please tell me you didn't sleep sitting up like this. Have you slept at all?" he asked.

She didn't know how to respond, as she refused just to play nice. However, on the other hand, she was too afraid of what he might do to her if her reactions didn't align with his.

"Christopher, what are we doing here? We can't live like this."

"We will damn well live exactly like this until I can trust you," he replied sternly.

"But Christopher..."

"That's enough, Summer. I have already placed your clothes and makeup in the bathroom. Get dressed. And Summer, if you do anything to fuck up today, any unwillingness on your part and my words will turn into actions. I will not say anything more, and that's a promise."

As he turned and gave her a menacing look, she felt a shiver run down her spine. She knew she couldn't risk disobeying him. There was no way she would tempt him.

As she entered the bathroom, she was shocked to see a white wedding dress hanging from the shower rod, causing her to drop to her knees in tears and clutch her chest.

Covering her mouth as she attempted to weep silently, but her pain and emotions had overtaken her. She was startled by the sudden knock at the door as he demanded that she be out on the porch in thirty minutes.

She gathered herself as she began to get dressed. She didn't bother with makeup, as her tears would only wash it away. She knew she was about to sign her life away, and there was nothing she could do to prevent it.

As she stepped out onto the porch, she was greeted by the young boy who spoke no English. He gestured for her hand and led her to the other side of the shack. There stood Christopher, the older islander, and another elderly man holding what appeared to be a bible, who were waiting for her.

What was clearly absent was the beautiful sunset, as it had been replaced by gloomy clouds. The musician had been replaced with the sounds of crashing waves that resembled loud thuds that were in sync with her throbbing heart. The Tiare Tahiti flowers had been replaced with dried seaweed.

She kept her eyes fixed on her feet, clutching her dress as she deliberately watched where she was stepping. Her head hung low as tears streamed down her face. She didn't want him to see her crying and risk him feeling embarrassed. But it was as if someone turned on a faucet and broke the knob to shut the water off.

He walked over to greet her and gently lifted her head by her chin.

"Why the fuck are you crying?" he mumbled.

"It's nothing like our vision board," she whispered.

"Summer, you can still have your dream wedding. You can have it all. No one is stopping it but you," he said as he pulled her towards the elder who was officiating the wedding.

The older islander handed the elder papers as he turned to them, motioning for them to verify their documents. As she looked down at her documentation, her birth certificate, proof of residency in the state of Illinois, and passport were all in her birth name, Summer Teller.

As they held hands and faced each other to repeat their vows, his grip on her hand was enough warning for her to repeat every word without hesitation.

This was it. Her life, as she knew it, ended with two words, "I do." The moment was sealed with a kiss as he held her tight and sucked breath from her. The sad part of it all was that the excitement he exuded seemed as if this moment was consensual.

As he hung back, signing paperwork, the young boy who comfortably squeezed her hand escorted her back to the shack. Although he couldn't speak English, it was evident from his gentle hand rub of comfort that he knew that she was being forced to be there against her will. She wondered to herself, 'Just how much does he really understand about the situation?'

She sat quietly, waiting for Christopher to come inside. He could be heard making calls out on the porch. As the sunset faded, she sat on the sofa in misery, wondering what was next. The front door squeaked open as he requested her presence outside. He had built a small bonfire on the beach. As he helped her to the ground, he took a squat in front of her.

"You are my wife now, Summer. Everything changed today. Our past has been rewritten. None of the hurt we cost each other matters anymore."

"The unforgettable has been forgiven, such as I slept with your sister or you running off shattering my world. All should be forgiven for both of us—no more holding on to the past that has haunted us both for the last four years. I am willing to move forward and forgive you. Let's start over, baby," he gestured as he grabbed her hand.

Unable to stomach him, she started swatting at the air as if flying insects were attacking her. I'm going back in Christopher; I don't have any bug repellent on.

She walked back in and headed to the shower. She sat on the toilet, looking down at her pad as it was dry. She only spotted a little, as she was hoping for a massive two-week flood. He burst into the bathroom without knocking, noticing also that she wasn't bleeding, and immediately started shouting, "You're lying to me already?"

"How did I lie, Christopher?" You yourself saw the blood.

"Get in the shower, Summer," he yelled.

Standing under the shower, her entire body trembled in fear. She was out of time. She knew he would force himself on her. Her heart and body belong to Stevin, and there was no way she could willingly have sex with him. He made her skin crawl.

No sooner than she exited the bathroom, she was greeted by Christopher lying across the bed.

“The boy has brought fresh food. You can pull out the hot plate and make us dinner. But first, I need to feel you. I've been waiting so long.” He reaches up, pulling her to him, as her entire body stiffens with rejection. He pulled up her gown, rubbing her breast, and he gently kisses her stomach.

"No, Christopher, it's too soon; I don't want to have sex on my period. You will only make me bleed worse."

“Dammit, Summer, I need you,” he said as he gestured for her to get on her knees. He wanted her to perform fellatio. She pulls back, shaking her head no. His body language quickly changed as he tensed up.

"I wasn't asking," he said with a firm grip on her lower jaw.”

She slowly kneeled as he placed his penis next to her lips. As she opens her mouth, she immediately gags, crying out, "No, I can't; I'm sorry. I just can't."

This only infuriated him as he struck her across her face. Falling to her back, she pushes back into a corner, holding her hands up as he charges directly for her.

"No, Christopher, no," she cried out.

He was so angered that he punched in the wall above her head. Storming out of the bedroom, he slammed the front door, making the walls feel as if they were caving in around her.

She knew that rejecting him would come with consequences. Her first thought was to start dinner and make herself busy quickly. She pulled herself off the floor, her face burning in pain. She rushed to the bins under the bed, searching for heavy clothing she could pile on.

After getting dressed, she noticed he remained outside, pacing on the porch. She entered the kitchen and started unwrapping the fresh fish, herbs, and vegetables. Searching for anything that would assist her in making dinner, he walked back in and sat on the sofa directly in front of her. His emotions screamed anger as he looked her up and down, noticing she had put on extra levels of clothing as if the first rejection didn't sting enough.

He stood, destroying her only means of entertainment as he ripped the power cord from the back of the TV. He slowly wrapped it around his hand and gestured for her to return to the bedroom. She backs up slowly; "Christopher, no, please, no," she pleaded.

"I'm about to start dinner, Christopher. You haven't eaten; let me fix you something to eat, please."

"Get in the fucking bedroom," he screamed.

Her feet were frozen, and she couldn't move. Christopher charged towards her, grabbing a handful of her hair as she kicked and screamed. He pulls her into the bedroom, throwing her across the bed onto her side. She turns over, facing him, pleading for mercy. He rushes out of the room and back into the kitchen, grabbing a large knife. The fear she felt when he entered the bedroom was unimaginable. She was about to be butchered to death. Her first thought was to grab his hand and fight for the knife. Using the butt of the knife, he strikes her in the head. The blow sent her falling backwards onto her back. The fight was over; she had no more fight as she lay limp and accepted her faith.

Taking the blade's tip, he starts cutting off the oversized thick clothing. He butchered every piece of fabric on her body. Leaning over as he reaches for the power cord, she grabs for the covers, causing him to flip out of the bed. He jumps up with the cord in his hand as he strikes her multiple times over her entire body. Her screams were so loud that he never noticed the loud crashing sound outside the living room window.

The young boy had decided to sneak back and check on Summer, only to be peeping in through the window when he witnessed the beating. He was so startled that he fell back, knocking over chairs on the porch as he ran away.

Taking the power cord, Christopher tied Summers hand to the iron headboard as he had his way with her. The forced loveless intercourse only angered him more. The fact that she didn't desire him made his orgasm less intense. Untying her hands, he snatched the cord and started back striking her.

Her torture felt as if it lasted all night. Her piercing screams filled the air, clashing with the ocean waves crashing into the rocks. She was at his mercy, with no one to help her.

For the next few weeks, he afflicted enough pain that she was in total submission. His desire for sex was unmatched. He forced himself on her daily, sometimes multiple times throughout a single day. She put a new meaning to the word Stafford Wife!

Chapter 39: Help Me Find My Daughter

Rose embraced Stevin with a big hug, squeezing him tightly as he welcomed her into his home.

"Come in, Mom. Excuse the house. Cleaning has not been a priority," he said.

"I Know, son. How are you holding up?" Rose asked, concerned.

"I don't know, Mom," Stevin says as he breaks down, collapsing to his knees and crying out. David enters the house and helps him to his feet. Rose was too distraught to offer any comfort to anyone, including herself. She stood silently, looking at all of Summers's belongings that Stevin had set up like a shrine.

"Son, I'm telling you, like I told Rose, I need you guys to remain strong. The one thing we can hold onto is that his obsession with her was to have her. So, no, I don't believe he has harmed her. We just need to find her," David said, trying to reassure Stevin.

Stevin couldn't control his emotions as he cried uncontrollably while walking towards the sofa. Rose stood up and went to sit beside him. She wrapped her arms around him and gently swayed him back and forth. She knew what he was feeling, as life had disappointed her yet again by snatching her baby girl from her grip.

David watched from a distance, concerned about Rose's mental state. She has been acting like a zombie since the day of the BBQ, when Summer went missing. "Mom, what did the Fulton County detective say?" Stevin asked.

"Absolutely nothing," Rose replied. "They made me wait two weeks before even meeting with me. As soon as I disclosed that she was going by Paige Green, they wanted to treat it like she was just on the run again."

"I wanted you to come with us to file the report in Morgan County since this is where she resides. We can file it under Paige Green or whatever. We just need to get the ball rolling."

"Hello, my name is Detective Shaw. I apologize for the delay. Since this case was initially filed in Fulton County, I needed to follow up with their department first. So, let's get started.

"Detective, my name is Rose. Can I ask you a question?" she inquired.

"Certainly," you stated your name was Rose, correct?"

"Yes, that's correct. My name is Rose White." Rose hesitated momentarily before continuing, "Do you have kids, Detective Shaw?"

"Yes," Detective Shaw replied, "I have three daughters and one son."

"Can you imagine one of your children going missing?"

"No, I cannot imagine that Mrs. White. It's a difficult thought to bear."

Detective, when I was a teenager, my daughter was taken away from me without my consent or knowledge. Twenty-eight years later, she walked back into my life and filled a deep, dark hole that was so dark and deep I didn't think it could ever be mended. So, all I am asking is that you hear us out with an open mind and heart.

"I promise to do everything in my power to assist you in finding your daughter if there is evidence supporting a missing person status," Detective Shaw said. "Now let's get started."

Three hours into their meeting, Stevin shared everything he knew starting from the first day Summer walked into his life. Rose also shared private messages that she had not discussed with David. Messages from Summer opening up about the abuse she suffered at the hands of Christopher.

At the end of the meeting, they were left in the detective's office for an hour before he returned.

"Sorry for the wait. I have started the missing person procedures for your daughter, Summer Teller," he says as he reaches out and takes Rose's hand. Overwhelmed with emotion, Rose collapsed onto his desk.

"This is what I have so far regarding Summer's case. It turns out that Summer never checked out of the room. However, her computer and clothing were turned over to Fulton County on the same day you attempted to file a missing person report. Stevin, since the car is in your name, it will be released to you from the Fulton County impound.

There was nothing suspicious found in the car or the room related to blood or a struggle. The back of her cell phone, along with the battery, was discovered inside her car. Stevin, as you mentioned earlier, all of her last calls were made to you, except for a call placed to Christopher's father's office in California. Furthermore, you were also cleared of any suspicions as they confirmed your whereabouts."

David became angry and interjected, "Hold on a second! Are you telling us they knew all this and failed to share it with us?"

"Yes, Mr. White. They did not have any cause to disclose this information to you," Detective Shaw replied. "Nevertheless, there were some questionable incidents that took place on the night when Summer returned to the hotel.

Now, things start to get suspicious," Detective Shaw added.

"There were some events that occurred on the night of Summer's return that raise concerns. According to the security camera footage, she entered the hotel, walked towards her room, and looked behind her several times. However, there is no footage of her leaving the room or hotel. Which we know is impossible. The hotel staff reported seeing a commotion in the parking lot between a gentleman and someone matching Summer's description not long after she was seen on the hotel footage. So, that lets me know that the video was tampered with.

Again, the last number she called was Diamond Inc. and company. However, we cannot confirm with whom she spoke. An attempt was made to speak with Christopher's father, Mr. Nate Diamond, but his attorneys immediately shut it down. The only statement his attorney would give on the matter was that his client only met Summer once at a party years ago; which he didn't have any interactions with her then as she was never introduced to him, nor his family.

Now, as far as Christopher, he hasn't been seen at home or in his clubs for several months. To be exact from the report from Illinois, when the officer went by to speak with Christopher, they met a talkative groundskeeper who revealed that Christopher is only home for two or three days out of a month, if that. He mentioned that he became a ghost after losing his fiancé a few years back.

However, the groundskeeper could not provide any details about what happened to the fiancé but spoke very highly of her. At the moment, I will avoid reaching out to Mr. Diamond. I most definitely don't want to set off any alarms that could hurt the case.

Therefore, I will begin my investigation by checking the airport records and running Summer's name through the database. Additionally, I need to obtain the address where Christopher was residing while using the alias Emmanuel."

Rose fell to her knees, wailing in gratitude and sorrow. David embraced her, allowing her to grieve and release her emotions, knowing this situation would finally break her mentally.

Chapter 40: New Life

Two months had passed, and Summer's life had turned into a nightmare; each day felt like a living hell for her. The beating would only stop because she conformed to his good girl; she moved and breathed Christopher's needs. She learned if she pleased his sexual needs by putting on a show of enjoyment, it bought her a day or two of not being fondled.

"Summer, Llay has brought dinner," Christopher said. "I need you to prepare the fish."

The smell of the fish wafted throughout the small shack, making Summer feel queasy.

"Christopher, I can't stand the smell of the fish. Maybe something is wrong with it," she said.

Slamming his hand on the wall, Christopher replied, "Dammit Summer! No excuses. Nothing is wrong with the fish. Get in the kitchen and start preparing dinner."

"Maybe I just can't eat it anymore, Christopher. It's making me sick."

As he turned and motioned towards her, she abruptly jumped out of bed. She quickly cut through the bathroom and emerged on the other side, sprinting into the kitchen. She would rather barf all over the floor than risk getting beat for not obeying him.

After a few seconds of unwrapping the fish, she suddenly held her mouth and ran out of the front door, vomiting. She could hear Christopher walking up behind her as she reached back, begging him not to strike her. To her surprise, he placed a towel in her hand and helped her clean herself up. He then assisted her to the shower. As she allowed his embrace, the motion sickness was intolerable.

"Christopher, please let's go home; I can't live like this anymore. I need to go to the doctor." She pleaded with him, but he sat up deep in thought.

He thought, 'I could have a yacht anchored and live in luxury, but he knew it was too risky.' His father would hunt him down in seconds if he started spending money to make her living arrangements comfortable. He remained silent for too long, causing her to plead with him again.

"Summer, what do you want me to do? This generator cannot handle anything else. And what about Issy and his family? They rely on those payments. They are working for us."

Looking away in disappointment, she began to wail even louder.

"Okay, Summer, in order for me to get you what you need, it's a two-hour-long boat ride to the other side of the island. That means you would be alone for at least four hours. What if a storm occurs and I can't make it back to you. What then?" Christoper asked. Summer stood up and walked outside to escape the smell of the fish.

"So now what? You're angry and going to remain outside in the heat?"

"I can't stomach the smell, Christopher. You have to get the fish out."

"So, what do I eat then, Summer? And what about you?"

Summer refused to respond. Christopher started to walk away when he quickly turned back on his heels and asked, "Summer, when was the last time you had your period?"

She sat with a puzzled look on her face. She had been under so much stress she hadn't realized she had only spotted a day, and her cycle never returned. She quickly grabbed her stomach with an expression of fear. He reached down to touch her stomach when she lost her balance, flipping the chair backward in an attempt to get away. He reaches and grabs her to break her fall.

The worst day of her life is when he took life from her. She could never forgive him for punching her in the stomach and stepping over her as she loudly pleaded for his help. She wanted no parts of his hand on her stomach if there was any chance she could be pregnant.

He grabbed her and could instantly feel the fear she had of him as her entire body trembled.

"Summer, please don't treat me like this," he said, dropping to his knees and placing his hand on her belly. "I told you at the beginning of this, I want what you want. If you are pregnant, outside of you walking back into my life, this would be the best thing to happen to me in years."

Thinking to herself, 'I didn't walk back in your life, you psycho.'

In a trembling voice she requested him not to touch her stomach. "Christopher, please don't."

"Summer, you really hate me," he said in a sad tone as he remained on his knees, clinging around her waist. He stood up to face her, and she was fearful to find him almost nose-to-nose with her. Despite her fear, her emotions were raw, and she had to express the hurt he had caused her.

"You took life from me."

'Screw that,' she thought, 'let's be real.' "Christopher, you hated me so much that you killed your own child. You punched me in the stomach and allowed me to miscarry alone on a cold floor for hours, begging for your help."

She pushed away from him as his grip got tighter. He looked her in the eyes as his eyes swelled with tears.

"Summer, I'm so sorry," he cries out. There's not a day that goes by that I don't replay that night back in my head and wish I could change everything.

As anger consumes her, she snatches away from him, and without fear, she starts to swing, landing punches in his back. He took the blows as long as he could before grabbing her and gently pushing her backward, laying her back on the porch, and pinning her hands down to her side.

"I am sorry, Summer," he cried out. "I fucked up! Can I fix what I broke? Damn, baby, please give me a chance to make it right."

The air was filled with silence as they lay on the porch, with him holding her tightly in his arms and refusing to let go. She stared at the night sky, wishing upon a twinkling star to rescue her from his madness.

"Come on Summer let's go in, please." He assisted her to stand, pulling her to her feet, but she pulled away. He pulled her into him with a tight grip as she rejected him, which quickly upset him.

"Next time you want to run off and leave me, you might as well take a gun and put a bullet in my fucken head. You have killed every living piece of me these last three years. If I had found you in love with someone else, I would have killed all three of us." He loosened her arm, walked away, and left her alone on the porch.

She eased her way into the bedroom as she could hear him rattling his lockbox when he suddenly started talking on his satellite phone. She overheard him making plans to purchase a bigger boat, dry ice, and at least three pregnancy tests. From his phone conversation, it was evident that he was making arrangements that would cater to their needs on the island, and she realized that she was stuck with him.

She sat up in bed, rubbing her stomach. "I can't believe it. Could it really be true? Am I pregnant?" She smiled, but tears started to roll down her cheeks.

Regardless of who the father was, this would be her child, and she wouldn't give it up, no matter if the father was Christopher.

Lost in thought, she didn't hear him hang up as he had made his way into the bathroom, standing against the wall, watching her smiling and rubbing her stomach. This only gave him confidence that they had a chance. If she were pregnant, it would be his way of slithering back into her life. Knowing from his reaction, if she wasn't pregnant, she knew he would make damn sure she became pregnant.

She looked up and was startled by his shadow looming in the darkness. He emerged from the bathroom with a smirk, as if everything between them were good. Standing at the foot of the bed, he starts crawling into bed towards her with a look of lust, gently kissing her as if the desire were mutual.

Feeling her hesitation, he strategically placed his hands around her neck, reminding her who was in charge as his grip got tighter when she hesitated to show affection. In his sick way, he wanted her to desire him.

He forced her to straddle him as he slowly unbuttoned her blouse. He stared deep through her as if he dared her to reject him. He gestured for her to finish unclothing herself, demanding she remove her clothes slowly.

He forced her to ride him, staring deep into her eyes. The electrical cord stayed at the bedside as she was reminded of what could happen if he felt she wasn't enjoying the sex as she should.

To be forced into sexual acts with the man she despise was unbearable for her. At that moment, she felt a shift within herself; it was as if she had become the monster she had been fighting so hard to escape. With every stroke, she stared deep back into his eyes; she could see herself splitting his throat.

Imagining his facial expression as she pretends to love him and make love to him, and as he closes his eyes, enjoying the moment, he is surprised when he is startled by a cold blade to his throat.

This was the woman she was becoming; she actually got off on the thought of harming him. Her head swayed back as she dug her nails into his chest, imagining him crawling at her feet, begging for her mercy as he bled out. She imagined laughing at his plea as she got off at the thought of the wicked monster being destroyed. Her strokes became faster and harder as she collapsed onto his chest and felt numb all over. He had broken her; she just climaxed to the idea of murder.

Who am I

The following morning, she sat on the porch, contemplating his murder. How would she escape? She knew she couldn't make it off the island, especially since Izzy and the kid worked for Christopher.

It was apparent Llay was growing fond of her; he hung out on the porch with her every chance he got. The boy didn't speak English, and she could not communicate with him verbally. Knowing he would be her only chance to escape the island.

Izzy came through as promised and showed up in a bigger boat. She thought, "There was never a reason for them to live in these conditions; this was truly a punishment from hell he inflicted on her."

She watched as Izzy and his brothers unloaded coolers of dry ice. They seemed to have dug a deep hole, mixing and pouring what looked like cement. She knew not to get too close, "Curiosity killed the cat."

Christopher walks onto the porch and approaches her. "Hey baby, I need to travel and pick up some supplies for you. I will leave Llay with you so that you won't be alone. But before I go, let's take care of this first." He pulls out three pregnancy tests.

They both waited in suspense while Christopher made her use all three tests. Her heart raced with excitement; she should feel guilty for wanting this so badly. As she started to count the days in her head from her last cycle, she was immediately frozen in thought. She hadn't had a regular cycle for months and had been spotting on and off for the previous four months.

It's possible that she could have been pregnant when she took the test at home, and the pregnancy might have been too early to be detected. The mood swings and the bad attitude towards Stevin all seemed to make sense now. Fear drowned out any excitement she had. Christopher would kill her and the baby if it weren't his. If he took her to the doctor and a sonogram showed anything different, she was as good as dead. She needed the test to be negative. She was startled out of deep thought when Christopher shouted for joy, spending her around as all three tests showed two faint lines in the test window indicating three positive pregnancy tests.

She stood in shock as he dropped to his knees, kissing her stomach and talking to the baby, making a promise to be its protector. He was only happy because he knew this would ensure his hold on her; they would be bonded for life. He left out the door excited as he skipped to the boat. She sat on the bed, feeling anxious as her stomach was in knots, replaying the days and months prior to her kidnapping. As she couldn't rely on her cycle to determine the date of conception, she felt in her heart there was a 95% chance that the baby was Christopher's

Chapter 41: The Truth Hurts

ATLANTA GEORGIA

Detective Shaw paid a visit to David and Rose at their home in Atlanta to provide them with an update on the investigation. He also needed to speak with Kimberley, who had refused to participate in an interview for months.

"Thanks for driving out, detective, and please understand I don't want to come across as being ungrateful. But it's been three months since our first meeting and now four months since my daughter went missing, yet we still know nothing."

"I completely understand your frustration, Mrs. White; please believe me, I do. But where's Stevin and your other daughter? Let's allow all parties to arrive before I start updating you on the progress of the investigation."

"I just hung up with Stevin. He should be pulling up any moment," David said as he called for Kimberely to join them. She entered the room with a pompous gait and appeared very withdrawn. She wanted no part of the meeting, and her body language expressed loudly and clearly how she felt.

The sound of the doorbell ringing eased the tension in the room as Kimberley's attitude was suffocating.

"Excuse me, that's Stevin at the door," David said as he left the room to greet Stevin. Kimberley had heard the name Stevin mentioned several times in passing these last few months. She had assumed he was someone her parents had hired to find Summer. So imagine her surprise when she learned her unwanted sister was engaged to him.

"Sorry for my tardiness. I am Stevin, Summers's fiancé, he says as he attempts to shake Kimberley's hand.

Upon hearing this, Kimberley's demeanor suddenly changed as she became livelier, smiling as she shook his hand, saying, "Oh, so you are soon to be my brother-in-law?"

However, this angered Rose, as she knew Kimberley's wicked smile was due to her feeling like she was no longer in competition for Christopher's love if Summer had a man.

Rose's eyes gazed across the room with a hard stare. She could never imagine she could have so much contempt towards her own child.

"Ms. Kimberley. I am Detective Shaw. I really needed to get some information related to Christopher's whereabouts. Do you think you can help your mom out in assisting us?"

"I haven't seen Emmanuel, and I don't know where he is," she said with an attitude and a stiff neck roll. "Do I need to scream this from a mountaintop?"

"Well, young lady, I'm not convinced you're being honest," Detective Shaw replied. "The night your sister went missing, what do you know about it?"

"Hmm," she murmured. "That's yet to be determined."

"Dammit, Kimberley!" David shouted. "You know something, and you're not telling us. Your sister's life could depend on it!"

"I don't know anything," Kimberley protested. "Just leave me out of it."

But Detective Shaw was unconvinced. "Yes, you know something," he said in an aggressive tone of voice, his annoyance showing." Christopher left in your vehicle, leaving his car parked at your grandparents' home. Hours later, his car goes missing, and you arrived back home in your vehicle. So, if anything unfortunate has happened to your sister, I will charge you with aiding and abetting."

Rose jumps up, running out of the room in disbelief. David runs behind her as Kimberley sits on the sofa next to Stevin with a mug expression.

"Come on, Rose, come on," David says, rubbing her shoulders. Keep it together for Summer; she needs you to remain strong."

David took Rose by the hand, and led her back into the room, and sat close to her, gently rubbing her hand. Rose apologized for running out.

"Detective, can you just update me on where you are in the case," Rose asked.

"Yes, Rose. We did locate Summer's phone at Christopher's residence. It didn't highlight anything new that her phone records didn't show already. But we did test prints from a bottle of water that was left on the table, and the DNA analysis confirmed that Summer was inside the home. However, there was no evidence of a struggle or blood in the home, and this was the most significant finding."

Kimberley mumbles with a hard eye roll, "Because he's not a murderer."

"That's to be determined; I dare you to defend this serial sociopath!" Rose shouted, turning her attention back to Detective Shaw.

"Go ahead, detective, and continue."

"I can confirm the day she went missing; she was spotted alive. It appears that they have left the country."

"Rose gasped, holding her mouth."

Detective Shaw continued. "Fulton ended their investigation due to surveillance showing her willingly going through customs arm-in-arm with Christopher."

They all echoed the same expression and blurted out, "She would never go willingly." It had to be forced; if she walked on her own accord, it had to be because he was threatening her.

Stevin interjected, "You best believe it was due to her being afraid and protecting Rose or attempting to protect each of us in this room," he said, mugging Kimberley.

"Stevin, you are correct. Summer used her birth name, Summer Teller, on the passport she presented to leave the country. I am currently searching through the databases to locate documentation indicating when and in which state the passport was filed. Being, Summer has never used the name Teller before.

I also dug a little further, interviewing the CBP officer who processed them. She did remember Summer on that day. She stated Summer could barely stand, so she had to get her a wheelchair. She also said Christopher pulled out a prescription of Xanax with Summers' name on it, stating she was afraid to fly and suffered from severe anxiety. That he thought she might have taken too many trying to relax for the long flight."

“He's a damn liar. She's not prescribed any medication. You can search our home from top to bottom. You will not find one prescribed medication in her name.”

"I believe you, Stevin. Here's the kicker: when Summer was unable or unwilling to answer the CBP officer's question, she revealed that Christopher asked her, 'Do I need to fly your mom out to assist you.' This statement prompted an immediate response from Summer. The officer stated she didn't think much of it because he had documentation and pictures of their engagement.”

"He's such a fucken con artist; those engagement photos are damn near five years old, if not longer." Stevin was livid, even more angered by Kimberley's facial expressions. He had never wanted to hit a woman before. But he could slap her into reality. He stood walking to the other side of the room; he could no longer stomach being in her presence.

Rose exclaimed, "How can one man cause so much destruction and be allowed to get away with it? How many laws must be broken before he and his father are held accountable?"

Detective Shaw explained, “We are investigating the crimes of kidnapping, false imprisonment, and forced displacement, however, as we continue to search for their whereabouts. We have encountered a setback in our search because the private plane and pilot involved are owned by Diamond Inc., and Christopher's father is tying up every legal avenue to release the flight information. My guess is that he is trying to locate his son and Summer before we do, and he could potentially pay her off again, which is alleged.”

"What about the money?" Rose said. "All the money Mr. Diamond gave Summer proves he's involved and knows more than what he is admitting."

"Rose, the only person that money is linked to is Stevin," Detective Shaw explained. "Stevin deposited a large amount of money with someone using fake credentials. I've been cautious in my investigation to protect everyone involved. Summer never reported any abuse related to Christopher, so we need to be smart about this."

"She stole from him," Kimberley interjected. "The only person who should be charged is Summer. Emmanuel told me that she had his money and promised to return it the next morning when the bank opened. She's the fraud, not Emmanuel."

"Hold on a minute," Detective Shaw said. "How do you know all of this? You just told me and your family you had no contact with Christopher."

"I don't," Kimberley stammered, realizing she had said too much. "The night of the barbeque, he and Summer were at his house when I picked my car up. He told me in front of her what she had done and that all he needed was until morning to get the transfer done."

Stevin was taken aback by her statement and promptly stood up, "Hold on a second. You saw Summer and didn't offer her any help? Knowing what you knew, you just left her with that monster?"

"She needed no help!" Kimberley blurted out.

Detective Shaw sat upright in his chair. "What do you mean? Did she try to signal for help? Tell us, Kimberley, what did you see?"

"She was sitting in the chair crying. She didn't say anything," Kimberley replied.

"So you mean to tell me you walked into the room with your sister clearly visibly upset, knowing she wasn't at his home willingly, and decided to sit on this information for four months?" The detective said with a puzzled and angry look. "If your parents weren't under the amount of stress they are under, I would lock you up now, and that is still to be determined."

Kimberley said, "I looked her in her eyes; she didn't even blink or give me any indication she needed my help."

Detective Shaw was fed up with Kimberley's nonchalant attitude as he sat up to face her.

"She could have very well saved your life on that night. Because rest for sure he threaten your life and your parent's life. Her stiff, cold eyes and disposition were pure fright from watching her baby sister possibly being harmed right in front of her. And Ms. Kimberley, if it was as he stated, you should find comfort in knowing their flight was in the air before your head hit the pillow, he says sarcastically."

Rose stood up slowly and walked towards Kimberley. With all her might, she backhanded Kimberley across the face and grabbed her by the shirt, attempting to drag her out of the house. "Get out... get out... get out!" Rose screamed loudly as her body trembled with anger. "How could you do this?" she continued to scream. "If my child's life is taken because of your stupidity, I will hate you for life."

Stevin grabbed hold of Rose, pleading with her to let loose of Kimberley as he eased her to the floor, cradling her as her emotional anguish was gut-wrenching.

David sat in disbelief; his anger at that moment couldn't allow him to bring himself to look at his own flesh and blood. 'Where did I go wrong? Who is this person?' He thought.

"Get her out of my house now, get her out. Before I forget she is my child, I need her out of my presence."

Kimberley glanced at her father, who hung his head in shame. She slowly made her way out the door and sat in her car, replaying her mother's words and the look in her eyes. Suddenly, Detective Shaw emerged from the house and walked straight towards her car, tapping on the window. She rolled the window down.

"Kimberley, if you still doubt Christopher Diamond's true character, let me read some statements from people who know him. They describe him as a manipulator, womanizer, abuser, and a spoiled daddy's boy."

"That person is not your knight in shining armor. There is no record of him ever using or going by the name Emmanuel."

"Let me also read some notes from witnesses who knew your sister personally; the innocent person in this situation, who you very well could have saved."

"Hmm, let me see, how about this one? 'Quiet, reserved, a sweetheart, a victim of abuse.' Oh, maybe this statement from her immediate supervisor can shine some light on her character. 'She states a darling. She was a dedicated hard worker and a great communicator and could have had an outstanding career with the company,' but her personal life was a distraction. She showed up to work on several occasions, unable to leave her office due to the visible bruises."

"Her HR reported before abruptly quitting, she walked into the office, face black and blue, requesting for family leave. Her best friend Ebony recalls the last time she saw Summer was the day she had to pick her up off the ground as she was distraught due to the loss of her baby. Her fiancé Christopher was so jealous of his own creation that she might give the baby too much attention that he punched her in the stomach and left her lying on the floor, bleeding."

"So get this through your head. This individual sought you out. Oh, you asked how. He investigated your sister before dating her, learning potent information about her, such as you and your mom."

"The information she had searched for her entire life. Not only did he withhold this information from her, but he also used it to get to you. Nothing about your relationship with him was or never will be real."

He walked away, leaving Kimberley to soak in her own stupidity. She sat quietly, replaying her conversations with Christopher in her mind. From the very beginning, he had shown a keen interest in knowing everything about her family. He had urged her to get to know her maternal grandparents and to find Summer.

She thought back on occasions when he damn near threaten to stop talking to her if she didn't accept Summer in her life. The worst image of them all was that of Summer shivering uncontrollably in fear. She knew something wasn't right on that night, and Christopher was not being honest with her. Her hatred for Summer had clouded her judgment and placed her sister in a life-and-death situation. Kimberley desperately needed to fix this; she just didn't know how.

Chapter 42: Scared To Run

Summer sat on the porch soaking up the sunlight; this was her reality. She was more convinced than ever that her child belonged to Christopher, judging by the size of her small round belly, and it was time for her to accept this life.

Llay had grown fond of her and the baby, and he had become her new admirer. When he wasn't working for his uncle or Christopher, he spent his free time carving baby rattles from wood for the baby. His eyes always had a story to tell, but his English was so poor all she could do was nod her head and smile in response.

However, on that particular afternoon, she was surprised Llay wasn't sitting at her feet carving. This was unusual since he had not missed a morning coming to visit her before.

The highlight of her day was feeling her little bundle of joy playing soccer in her belly and watching Llay carve. The baby had softened Christopher, the abuse was less frequent, and the meals improved with the makeshift freezer; he was able to create storage for food. He even surprised her with another portable battery-operated TV/DVD combo. Unable to watch live TV, she had memorized every movie that was available to watch.

"Summer, I'm heading out to pick up some items and get the boat serviced. I need to make sure the proper service is being rendered. I can't take any chances of something going wrong with our only means of transportation on and off this island. Llay should be around soon; his uncle hasn't seen him today."

"Could you please bring me some different snacks? I'm getting tired of eating fruit all the time."

"Summer, I can't just walk into a store and pick up cupcakes; they don't have American-type junk food. It's not available here."

"Well, why can't I just go with you and see for myself?"

Christopher walked away, ignoring her request. She watched the boat disappear into the horizon as the sun reflected off the ocean waves, creating a sparkling effect. Despite its beauty, the sight had become a daily nightmare for her.

She quickly fell asleep, only to be awakened by Llay, who gestured for her to follow him. Unable to understand his verbal request, she followed him.

She looks around, confused, as he is pulling her with urgency. She is led through the wooded area as she stumbles over branches and the flip-flops she is wearing keeps getting tangled in the weeds.

He pulled her through the woods until they reached an opening that led to the other side of the island. He handed her a paddle and showed her a makeshift boat he had made for her, giving her a means to escape. "Come, come," he repeated, urging her to get on the boat.

This was her great escape; she finally had her chance to freedom, but as she attempted to step onto the boat, it started to rock uncontrollably. The bottom of the boat filled with water, and she struggled to steady herself as she sat in the middle of the boat. She quickly jumped off, asking, "How far, Llay? How far is the boat ride?"

Unable to understand her question, Llay kept trying to get her on the boat. She continued, "I'm scared, Llay, I'm scared. The boat is taking on water," pointing at the water at the bottom of the boat. He jumped off the boat and started to search for twigs, weeds, and grass to fill the hole to keep the water out.

Meanwhile, Christopher had a change of heart; he had Izzy to turn the boat around, deciding to bring Summer along to give her a chance to see new scenery. However, he was surprised to find that she was nowhere to be found.

He searched throughout the small shack, shouting her name, when suddenly he took off running, yelling her name as he ran through the woods. Izzy followed behind him with urgency, knowing the only way Summer could leave was with the help of his nephew.

Summer could hear Christopher yelling her name from a distance, and her heart sank. She grabbed Llay by his arm and kicked sand over his manmade patch of twigs and grass.

Summer snatched Llay's fishing net from the boat and pulled him away, gesturing for him to throw the net in the water. She wanted to pretend as if they were fishing.

Christopher burst out of the woods like a wild hog. Izzy couldn't match his speed. He knew that if Christopher reached Llay before him, he would harm him. Summer noticed Christopher was charging full force towards them as she attempted to shield Llay while screaming, "We are just fishing; he's just trying to teach me to fish."

He snatched Summer, causing her to fall backward, as he smacked the boy across the face, knocking him to the ground. Just as he raised his hands in the air to hit him again, Izzy grabbed hold of his arm, forbidding him to strike the boy again.

Izzy helped Llay get up from the ground while scolding him for taking Summer away from the house and guiding her to the other side of the island. He assisted Llay back to the small boat, ordering him home. Summer shouted, "Izzy, he just wanted to teach me to fish," as she held his fishing net in the air.

Christopher suddenly turns his rage towards her, grabbing her by one arm and pulling her with force. Not giving her a chance to make it to her feet, he dragged her back through the woods, causing puncture wounds, along with scrapes and skin burns to her right side. Summer protected her stomach the best she could, as it was clear he didn't care if he harmed her or the baby.

"Christopher, please stop, please don't the baby, the baby Christopher. Let me walk, please."

Every time she attempted to stand, he purposely would drag her back to the ground. He dragged her all the way back to the shack as he threw her on the bed, leaving her only to make sure Izzy left the island.

Christopher stood on the porch, and he and Izzy avoided eye contact as Izzy walked straight to the boat.

Christopher watched from afar as the boat disappeared from his view. Summer laid in bed holding her stomach as her body was severely cut and bruised. Although she was in grave pain, her only concern was the baby as she lay still, praying for movement. She could hear him entering the small shack as the floors squeaked as if they were warning her.

"To think I turned around to take you with me, and this is how you repay me?" Christopher yelled.

"What did I do, Christopher?" Llay only... Before she could finish her sentence, she could taste his breath as he got eye to eye demanding, she shut her fuckin mouth with the lies?

"You want to leave? You want to leave?" He shouted.

"Yes, I do, take me fuckin home," she demanded.

He effortlessly snatched her up, throwing her over his shoulder as she attempted to fight him off. He picked her up, carrying her to the porch as she kicked herself loose, falling to the porch.

Grabbing a handful of her hair, he pulls her through the sand, down the beach on her back to the water. Standing her up, he places his hand around her throat as he marches her backwards into the water. He only felt rage and hatred for her. They had grown closer over the past few months, and he had given her the best of himself. He gave up everything he knew for her, living like a bum. But the first chance she got, she tried to run away. He was determined to make her pay in the worst possible way.

Slightly picking her up out of the water, he slammed her back with force, submerging her underwater. Her tiny arms were no match for his masculine power. Struggling to get out of his grip, she loses breath. Just as she couldn't hold her breath any longer, he brought her up, submerging her under again.

She threw her arms around his neck the third time he lifted her out of the water. Panicking, as she struggled to breathe, she screamed out, "The baby, Christopher, what about the baby."

He suddenly released her as he stood waist-deep in the ocean, holding his head, screaming like a madman.

Struggling to get away, she exerted all her strength to return to the shore, dragging her body through the water that seemed to pull her down. It felt like she was carrying a ton of weight as she struggled to pull herself forward. After reaching the shoreline, she collapsed onto the sand, unable to move, as all her muscles locked up, and she couldn't move. Feeling helpless and at his mercy, she did not know if he would drag her back in; she was too weak to run as she remained face down in the sand.

Panicking when she felt his presence standing over her as the water from his body dripped onto her. She was as good as dead. She had no fight left. She could see him walk off, leaving her lying in the sand. He was indeed the monster he claimed to be. The life they created meant nothing to him.

As night came upon her, she lay shivering in the cold sandy waters with open wounds. She attempted to stand, but her legs couldn't hold her weight as the sand was like weights around her ankles. She slowly crawled back to the shack as her knees were raw. She managed to pull herself up the stairs; as she opened the door, there he sat, eating and watching a movie in comfort after he had basically left her for dead.

She crawled into the bathtub; she needed to clean her wounds, knowing if any of them got infected, he wouldn't get the necessary medical attention she needed. Her entire body shivered uncontrollably. The well water wouldn't get warm enough to warm up her body temperature. She hasn't felt the baby move or kick since earlier.

She could barely walk, but she managed to pull herself up off the shower floor and dragged herself to the bed. She wrapped herself up in a robe and blankets to get warm, rubbing her stomach, attempting to stimulate the baby. When the baby failed to kick or move, she started crying and praying hysterically.

"Please move, please. Mommy is so sorry, so sorry," she cried out.

Summer was upset with herself and regretted she even made any attempts that could put her in this very position.

Christopher sat quietly in the other room as she cried out, "You promise you wouldn't hurt our child. How could you, how?"

Never uttering a word, he pulled the throw blanket over himself and settled in on the two-seater bench sofa. He knew it was time to end this. He had injured her to the point of no return, and there was no way he was taking her to anyone's hospital.

Mentally and physically exhausted and in severe pain, her body finally shut down, and she passed out from exhaustion.

At 3:00 am, Summer was awoken by a hard thump on the right side of her belly. The baby had become very active, causing her to jump up in surprise. She grabbed her belly tightly and silently rejoiced for the life of her unborn child.

Bright and early, they were startled out of their sleep by Izzy's banging on the door. She was curious about what was going on in the other room but in too much pain to get out of bed to see what was happening. It sounded as if Izzy was preparing breakfast. She was startled by Christopher entering the bedroom, avoiding eye contact, as he reached across the bed, grabbed her ankle, and chained her to the bed.

"Christopher, what are you doing?" she asked with concern.

"You have lost those privileges," he replied sternly.

"But how will I eat or use the bathroom?" Christopher, I am badly injured; please don't do this.

"Summer, the chain is long enough to reach the toilet. If you tamper with it, it will tighten around your ankle." He walked away, ignoring her plea.

"Christopher, God forbid if something happens to you, I would be left stranded alone, chained to this bed. Why do you think this is acceptable to leave me like this?"

He returns to the room and drops a plate of scrambled eggs, a slice of bread, and a bottle of water onto the bed. He then walks away again, refusing to acknowledge her pleas. Christopher and Izzy exited the shack, leaving her chained to the bed.

Three hours had passed, and no Christopher. He left her without extra food and water. She struggled to walk to the bathroom, and the chain only worsened her situation. She attempted to drink water from the faucet. Unable to tolerate the well water's taste, she felt like she was drinking thick mineral water.

She uses the water to moisten her lips and body, trying to stay hydrated and cool. He closed her in without a breeze; she could only assume to keep Llay out. The 6th hour had arrived, and he had clearly abandoned her on the island. Her idle mind ran wild as every horrible thought ran through her mind. Suddenly, the door swung open. In walks Christopher carrying boxes into the shack. As he entered the bedroom, she angrily threw a hardback book at his head. He picked the book back up, throwing it back at her, hitting her in the middle of the forehead. She burst out in tears.

"You left me here without food and water," you are truly a monster.

"Stop with the dramatics, Summer. You could get water out of the sink."

"I can't drink that; it has a weird taste. I'm pregnant, and you left me without food and water," Christopher!

"Hmm," he said. I thought the baby was dead, the way you carried on last night."

"Hopeful wishing on your part, huh?" She said.

He walked out of the bedroom, refusing to entertain that comment.

"I need a doctor, Christopher. I hurt all over, and these wounds are going to get infected if they are not already."

He returns to the room with a large zip-lock bag full of medical supplies and ointment.

"You're a nurse; figure it out."

"Christopher, I can't dress the wounds by myself."

"Well, tell me what the fuck to do and save the sarcasm."

With a confused expression, as he concentrated hard, it took him an hour to apply the antibiotic ointment and dress her wounds. He knew he was on borrowed time. She needed medical attention that he couldn't provide.

Chapter 43: To Death Do Us Part

Tensions were high between Christopher and Summer. He realized she would never look at him the same. He thought that if he could take her back to the States, back to their home in Illinois, the baby might change things. Christopher needed to know if Rose and David had made him a wanted man, and he knew exactly whom to call.

"Hello?" Kimberley answered.

"Hey baby," Christopher said.

"Are you serious right now, Emmanuel: Christopher, whoever the hell you call yourself?"

"Kimmie, don't be like that."

"You played me. You did all this to get to my sister."

"I see your parents have turned you against me."

"No, Christopher Diamond, you did that all by your damn self. I haven't heard from you in six months. I haven't spoken to my parents in months, and the reason for that is not because of any fault of theirs. It's because of you, Emmanuel, or should I say Christopher? Your actions have led to this situation. So, no, you can't fault my parents; it's all on you."

"Wait, why haven't you spoken with your parents in months?" he asked.

"My mom disowned me when she found out I saw Summer with you, and I never reported it," she replied.

"Why the fuck would you tell them that, Kimberley? His heart sank as she implicated him in Summer's disappearance. Kimmie, can you please tell me exactly what you told them and to whom you said it."

"Well, I told my parents, Summer's fiancé, and the detective."

"Summer's what? he asked in a loud tone.

"Yes, her fiancé," she replied. "You're out here risking it all clearly for someone who has been moved the hell on."

"What's his name, Kimmie?"

"Why?"

"What's his fucken name Kimmie?"

"Stevin, and why?"

"Stevin Bash," he asked angrily.

"I think so," I'm not for sure. "But why does any of this matters? Where is my sister, and have you harmed her?"

The call suddenly dropped. Kimberley realized she might have very well signed Summer's death certificate. She immediately called her dad hysterically crying, informing him of Christopher's call and the information she shared with him.

Summer nearly jumped out of her skin as she was startled by Christopher's entrance as he slammed the door, almost bringing the walls down. She sat up in bed, unable to run, and couldn't escape him. She immediately knew that he was aware of something from the intense look in his eyes.

"So, do you have something you want to tell me?" he asked. She slowly shook her head no.

"Where's your ring?" Summer

"In the drawer next to me," she replied.

"Not mine. Where's the ring your fiancé Stevin placed on your finger?"

'Oh shit,' she thought to herself. 'I am dead.' Refusing to answer, she just stared with a blank expression.

"So you not denying it?" Christopher asked.

"Christopher, I'm not about to play these games; I don't know what you are talking about.

"Bitch! I will kill you where you lay. Stop playing with me, Summer."

Her entire body tensed up as she realized there was nowhere to run and no way out of this situation. Her only chance of survival was to lie better than him. "I'm your wife, Christopher, and I'm pregnant with your child," she said, hoping he would calm down.

"Wait a minute," he said, pacing back and forth. "This baby might not even be mine. You haven't had an actual period since you've been here with me." The rage in his eyes blazed as his pupils clustered with burning fury, and she knew she needed to lie and lie convincingly enough to turn the tables. Her life depends on it.

"So, you forced me onto this remote island for months, created life with me, only to get scared of being a father and try to find a way out?" she said, trying to sound hurt and angry. "This is why I fought so hard to block out how much I really love you because I knew when I opened my heart to you and showed you I loved you, this is what you would do: crush me."

"Summer, you can drop the act and stop pretending now. Owoo: Bitch, you act so well. Great job, bravo! Bravo, but your sister has revealed the truth."

"My sister! Yeah, my little sister. "Hmm, let me see; oh, the one you have screwed for who knows how long. The one you gave your heart to and forced her into a competition with me. Would that be the sister you're referring to?"

"Priceless!" she said. "I knew you would build me up to break me. I gave you my heart, I gave you the best of me and you destroyed every inch of me. So go ahead and do what you do best, and that's showing me you never loved me. I am nothing but emotional collateral damage from your childhood."

Christopher stood in silence, listening intently as she revealed her feelings. She told him she loved him and was afraid to open up again, but if she had allowed another man inside of her, he could never love her again.

Christopher walked out of the room slowly, needing time to think before he reacted. He stood on the porch, listening to his racing thoughts. Every crashing wave felt like a blow to his heart as images of Stevin's hands all over her raced through his mind.

Kimberley would have no way of knowing who Stevin Bash was, and even if it was a different Stevin, it still meant Summer's innocence was gone. She wasn't pure anymore. She was defiled and worthless, like a filthy rag that needed to be discarded. He needed to know as he desperately called Kimberley back, but she refused to answer.

With one call that could risk it all, he called his father's PI to confirm Stevin's current location. The PI confirmed Stevin Bash was employed in the Macon, Georgia, area but had no listed place of residence.

It was too much of a coincidence. Christopher stood speechless, frozen in hurt and disbelief. He placed a call to Izzy requesting the boat ASAP.

Summer sat up in the bed; her body was stiff, and pain radiated all over. She needed to make a run for it and hide out in the woods. Anything but lying in the bed knowing Christopher would return and kill her if he confirmed what Kimberley told him was true. She knew he wasn't letting this go.

Suddenly, she was startled by the sound of the chair crashing through the living room window. She was out of time; his rage had begun, and she knew this was it.

He kicked down the front door and charged directly towards her. Summer's life flashed before her eyes. He launched at her, falling on the side of the bed. She leaped to the opposite side of the bed, falling backward onto her back.

Her feet were tangled in the cover, preventing her from running. She broke free and stood; it looked as if lightning struck, and all she could see was bright white. Both of her ears rang, and the pain in the back of her head was indescribable. She fought not to lose consciousness as she dropped to her knees.

Large pieces of glass surrounded her as the lamp shattered on the back of her head. Christopher reached down, grabbed her by the face, and rammed her head into the floor. Her entire body went limp; she became sensitive to the light, and his shouting voice was drowned out by the intensifying ringing in her ear that became louder.

Her broken body wasn't satisfying to him; it was the ultimate betrayal, and he needed to finish her. He climbs on top of her, places his hand around her throat, and starts to strangle her with all his might. Attempting to fight him off, but her weak blows to his chest weren't a match for his rage to end her life.

Reaching for anything to defend herself, as she battled to breathe, she felt around, picked up a large piece of glass from the shattered lamp, and stabbed him in the neck. He immediately let go and stared deep into her eyes, shocked, grabbing for his neck. If his eyes could talk, they cried out, "Why, how could you?"

Summer rolled over gasping for her breath, knowing she needed to get to him and apply pressure to the bleeding. She wasn't that monster; she couldn't kill anyone. And besides, if he died on the island, she would die also. She attempted to get up on all fours and crawl to him, but the pain and dizziness overtook her as she collapsed back to the floor. Still in shock, Christopher manages to push back to the wall, resting his back on the wall. He was scared to turn his head as he could feel the warm blood trickling down his neck and back. "Summer, please help me; I'm dying," he cried out.

"Get up Summer, help me."

Summer, filled with sorrow, she couldn't watch him die. She scooted towards him, ordering him not to pull the glass out and be still. She fumbled for the medical bag he brought her with the medical supplies; tearing open gauze packs, she had him hold a little pressure under the site where the blood trickled out. Knowing if she nicked an artery, he only had minutes, if that.

"Summer, please call Izzy now," Christopher requested with a shaky voice.

"How Christopher? Where is your phone?" Summer asked.

Christopher begged for her to locate the satellite phone and hit redial, which would automatically call Izzy. Summer scooted on her butt to the living room and found the phone at the front door on the porch. Izzy answered the phone on the first ring, but his thick accent and the howling wind made it difficult for her to understand him. The ringing in her ears didn't help either.

She cried out, "Izzy, we need help," Christopher is dying, and he needs help. Please, Izzy, call for a helicopter." Not knowing Christopher had already summoned for the boat and Izzy was close by.

The wait felt like a lifetime as Izzy ran into the shack, stepping on shattered glass and the living room door that Christopher had kicked off the hinges.

"Izzy, he was trying to kill me; he hit me with the lamp over my head and tried to strangle me. I didn't mean to stab him; I promise I wasn't trying to harm him."

Izzy helped Summer off the floor, sitting her on the bed as he looked at Christopher's injury.

"It doesn't look good, sir; the nearest hospital with air support will be an hour away from the mainland."

"Let's go, Izzy. Help me get to the boat before I die," Christopher demanded. "We will call for assistance once we get to the boat.

"Summer, can you make it to the boat on your own," Izzy asked.

"She's not going. Handcuff her to the bed," Christopher demanded.

"Sir, we can't leave her here. Her head is bleeding, and her body is black and blue. What about your baby, sir?"

"Izzy, do you want to go to jail? You knew I've been holding her against her will. You are just as much a part of this as me. Get me to help, and I will send someone back for her that will protect us both."

"No, no, you can't leave me here. I need help also, Christopher."

"Izzy, go get the small set of handcuffs from the safe, and cuff her to the rails."

"Izzy, please don't do this. I promise I won't say anything. I just want help for my baby. Izzy, please," she cried out.

Summer cried and pleaded with Izzy as he cuffed both of her arms above her head to the metal frame bed. She was left alone, broken, and scared as she screamed and pleaded for her life and the life of her unborn child.

The cold ocean breeze chilled her entire body as she shivered in pain. The broken door and window exposed her to the harsh outside elements. She had a terrible pounding headache, and her entire body ached in pain. Her hands were going numb due to the tight handcuffs that were affecting her circulation. She was extremely thirsty and desperately needed water. She remained in the same position all night, afraid to move with even the slightest movement because of the tightening of the cuffs.

The warmth from the morning sun shone on her, allowing her body to warm up as she finally dozed off from exhaustion. She felt no movement from the baby, but her mind couldn't let her think the worst. She couldn't mentally keep it together if she didn't have her baby to fight for.

The scorching heat and hungry pains soon woke her. She lay gazing at the ceiling as she traveled down memory lane, thinking of Rose and Stevin. If she died in that moment, she could finally say she knew what it meant to be truly loved and wanted.

As night came upon her, she knew her body was given out as she couldn't feel the ocean breeze; she couldn't feel anything anymore. She felt as though another day had gone by, but she was too weak and disoriented to be certain. Her surroundings appeared pitch black.

Suddenly, she felt a strong kick from her precious little bundle of joy. She sensed a hand on her stomach, and a warm sensation spread throughout her body. She opened her eyes slightly and called out, "Mimi." Miss Dangerfield was standing by her bedside, cradling a baby girl in one arm and comforting Summer with her other hand while rubbing her round belly. "Mimi," she whispered softly.

Summer's body shifted, and her arms dropped. She could see glimpses of Izzy and Mr. Diamond.

Meanwhile, she could hear Mr. Diamond ordering the group of men that stood over her, speaking in their native language as they searched for a vein to start an IV. She was too weak to speak and struggled to keep her eyes open, but she kept whispering, "Mimi... Mimi."

Chapter 44: Like Father Like Son

Summer awoke to the sounds of beeping monitors surrounding her. She felt a sharp pain in her head as she shifted her head from side to side, realizing she was in a hospital room. She immediately reached down, grabbed her stomach, and felt the straps of the baby monitor she was attached to. She glanced over at the monitor, and there it was, a strong heartbeat beating with purpose. She jiggled her stomach; she needed to feel her baby move. Summer was startled when the door opened, and a nurse walked in.

"Good morning, sleeping beauty, you're finally awake," said the nurse.

"Where am I?" Summer asked.

"You're at the Los Angeles Health Medical Center," replied the nurse.

"How did I get here?"

"Well, you have been with us for about a week. Do you have any remembrance of your and your husband's boat accident while on vacation?"

"Where is Christopher?" asked Summer.

"Well, if you are asking about your husband. I'm not sure about that information. In my report, I received that your husband was too ill to travel with you back into the country, so you had to return without him for proper medical care for you and your baby. But your bodyguard is waiting outside. Would you like me to call him in?"

"Bodyguard?" Summer asked, surprised.

"Yes, my dear. You have been under strict security measures since you were admitted to my floor. You would have thought you were a member of the president's immediate family, the level of protection you have been provided. If you wish, I can ask your bodyguard to come in and explain everything."

"No, thank you," Summer quickly replied. Please don't. "Where's my hospital phone?"

"Well, your father requested that your hospital phone be removed for your safety. If you need anything, your bodyguard will assist you."

"I need to make a call. Can I please use your phone?" Summer requested." She desperately wanted to call Stevin, but she was tarnished. It would crush him to know she was pregnant with Christopher's child. She couldn't bear to put him through that. She knew she had to let him go.

Summer quickly dialed Rose's number, but there was no answer.

"Mommy, it's me. I have been told I am in... What hospital am I in?" Summer asked.

The nurse took the phone, "she is in Los Angeles Health Medical Center." She is registered as a private patient, so you can call the nursing station and ask for room 405." The nurse stated, handing the phone back to Summer.

"Mom, I don't know how long I've been here," Summer said.

Suddenly, the door swung open, and Summer jumped quickly, hiding the phone under the covers. The bodyguard, Mr. Diamond hired, overheard the commotion from outside which prompted him to enter into the room.

"Hello, Mrs. Diamond," he said. "I will inform your father-in-law that you are awake."

"Are you done here? He asked the nurse."

"No, I need to take her vitals," she replied.

He stood closely watching every move the nurse made.

"Can you please stand outside the door? I need to check her foley catheter."

He turned his back towards them, facing the wall, as he refused to leave the room. Summer slowly slid the cell phone back to the nurse.

"Mrs. Diamond, are you okay with him remaining in the room while I perform my assessment?" The nurse asked.

"Yes," Summer replied.

Unaware of what was happening and what Christopher had planned for her, she was afraid to be defiant. She knew all too well the power Christopher and his dad had, and there was no way she wasn't playing by their rules.

The nurse completed her assessment, feeling very uneasy about the situation. She turned and looked at Summer with a concerned look.

"Do you need anything at this moment?" The nurse ask.

"Can I have a hamburger and fries?"

"Let me get the doctor so he can examine you and order you a diet."

After the nurse left, the guard stayed in the room with Summer, and she didn't ask any questions. An hour later, the door squealed open, and the sight of Mr. Diamond sent fear throughout her entire body. She didn't know Christopher's condition, and she feared for her own life.

"Hello, young lady," Mr. Diamond said.

"How is Christopher? Is he okay?" she asked.

"He's okay, no thanks to you."

"I wasn't trying..." she said when he abruptly interrupted her.

"Save it. I don't want to hear it, Summer. Let me tell you how it's going to be from now on. I have a grandchild involved now, so this family is stuck with you. There's no more disappearing on your part. Christopher is in the hospital getting the help he needs both mentally and medically. You are damn lucky you hit muscle and missed vital organs. Until Christopher is released, you will deal with me directly. His injuries are severe and documented. So, if you do not comply with my exact demands, I will have you locked up for attempted murder.

He leaned in close to her face and said, 'I'll make sure you never see this baby, young lady.' So you see, it's that simple. I have a marriage certificate, which you willingly signed, and a witness statement from Izzy stating that you admitted to stabbing my son. And that you were on the island on your own accord. So call your mom and tell her to stand down."

"And, before you think ill of Izzy, he saved your life by betraying Christopher. He is the reason I knew how to find you," Mr. Diamond said, scolding Summer as she sat in silence with tears streaming down her face. She had escaped one prison to be forced into another.

"Young lady, do you understand me?" Mr. Diamond asked.

"Yes, sir," she replied.

Their conversation came to a halt when Doctor Brown suddenly walked into the room and said, "Hello, Mrs. Diamond, I'm Doctor Brown."

Mr. Diamond looked confused. "Where is Doctor Santos?" he asked.

"Yes sir, his wife had an emergency today, so I'm completing his rounds," Dr. Brown said as he attempted to shake Mr. Diamond's hand when he refused him.

"Well, Dr. Brown, this is precious cargo, so go ahead and complete your assessment, but my daughter and I would only like Dr. Santos to follow up with her care, and that's not a request."

Doctor Brown nodded in agreement and turned to Summer, awaiting her response.

"Mrs. Diamond, is it okay if I send you for an ultrasound? We need to get images of your bouncing baby boy," he asked.

Summer looked surprised and smiled, rubbing her belly.

"Oh, did I let the cat out of the bag?" Dr. Brown asked.

"That's okay. I've been dying to know."

“Mr. Diamond,” she said softly with a concerned expression. "Would you like me to wait on Christopher for the ultrasound?" She knew how to play their games, and it was evident that at least one of the doctors hadn't been paid off.

Seeing that Summer was in compliance, Mr. Diamond agreed to the ultrasound but left her bedside only after Dr. Brown exited her room. He gave strict orders for the guard to monitor her closely and not to leave her alone with the staff.

Dr. Brown and the nurse returned with a portable ultrasound machine, and the bodyguard followed them back into Summer's hospital room.

"I'm sorry, but she will have to be slightly uncovered for this test. You cannot remain in the room," the nurse said.

The bodyguard stood in the doorway with his foot preventing the door from closing. He took out his cell phone and placed a call while the medical staff continued to explain the procedure to Summer. The nurse leaned in closely and asked softly," Do you need me to call the police?" Summer's eyes widened as she shook her head. No!

The nurse leaned back in again and whispered, "Your mother called back and reported that you were taken and have been missing for six months." Summer didn't know who to trust. This could very well be Mr. Diamond testing her.

Summer gestured for a pen. Dr. Brown blocked the view of the bed, allowing Summer to write on his prescription pad.

"Please tell her to remain calm and assure her that I'm okay." I'll call her later and let her know that I love her. Also, ask her to tell David, "Like father, like son."

Summer knew she couldn't trust anyone, and it was too dangerous not to assume that the doctors and nurses weren't paid off. She hoped that Rose and David would be able to read between the lines and understand that Christopher was indeed his father's son and Mr. Diamond was involved.

Dr. Brown's phone rang, and Dr. Santos was on the other line, requesting an update on his patient. Dr. Brown found himself answering unusual questions as if he needed permission to perform an ultrasound on a patient who was currently on his assigned list to see.

"I have started the procedure. Would you like me to cancel and reorder for tomorrow? he asked. "Yes, sir," he stated before ending the call. Dr. Brown gave the nurse, Stephanie, a strange look.

Minutes later, the bodyguard's phone rang. Seconds after the call, the door closed shut, giving Summer privacy.

"Mrs. Diamond, are you in trouble?" he asked. "We can notify the authorities for you." She immediately thought back to the officer who placed her directly in harm's way from one call made by Christopher. She knew the police couldn't help her. Mr. Diamond's pockets and connections ran deep.

"I promise I will be okay. Thanks for asking," Summer responded.

Dr. Brown started the test with a concerned look on his face. "Do you know how far along you are?" he asked.

She shrugged her shoulders no.

"When was your last cycle?" the doctor inquired.

"I spotted a day or so back in... back in... what month is this?" Summer asked.

"That's okay, Summer; let's just take a look." It was clear she was in some type of danger, but the question was who was involved, and how could he help without causing more harm? He was determined to speak with Rose directly. He scanned her body with his eyes, noting all the bruising.

"Okay, Summer, the gel will be cold. Let's get started." Summer jumped for joy to see her baby boy on the screen.

"Summer, your stomach is quite small; the baby weight measurements are too."

"Did you receive any prenatal care?"

"No. I took prenatal vitamins daily."

"If I were to guess, looking at the length of the baby's bones, he is measuring around 32 weeks. But the weight of the baby and fundus height is putting you around 27-29 weeks. I will order a growth scan for tomorrow. His organs and heart rate look perfect."

'Is there a chance,' she thought to herself. The way her luck was going she didn't want to get excited before knowing. This was good news, if the baby were Stevin's, Mr. Diamond probably would let her be. But on the other hand he would probably still have her arrested.

Summer, I took a look at your chart. You were admitted with a significant head injury, severe bruising, and multiple deep lacerations, along with dehydration. The injuries you suffered do not align with the cause that is being reported. I can only help if you are truthful with me. I will be here for the next hour. If you decide you are ready to talk, have nurse Stephanie page me. Dr. Brown and Stephanic left the room, giving Summer time alone.

"Stephanie, let's involve the patient advocate. We need to see if Susan Benazir can help the patient open up," Dr. Brown requested.

"I tried, Dr. Brown, but she called me back and said that Summer's safety is a top priority, and her Father-in-law sits on the hospital board. She assured me that he would address any concerns I might have," Stephanie replied.

"We must help her," Dr. Brown insisted. "You mentioned that you spoke with her mother. Can I have her contact information, please? And Stephanie, please keep this between you and me."

"Yes, sir, Dr. Brown," Stephanie replied.

The nurse, Stephanie, returned later to inform Summer her shift was ending. She gave report at the bedside with the night nurse holding onto Summer's hand. When the night nurse turned her back to write on Summer's communication board, Stephanie leaned in, squeezing Summer's hand, letting her know she would be back in the morning as she whispered, "I know, I know, and your family knows also. They're fighting to get you home." They know, she mouthed as she exited the room. Summer teared up, feeling hopeful again.

At 2 am, Summer was abruptly awakened by a nurse she didn't recognize and two of Mr. Diamond's hired men.

Confused, she asked, "What's going on?"

The nurse replied, "Dr. Santos has discharged you. Your family is paying for private medical care at home."

Summer objected, "No, I need to stay in the hospital until I am well, and I know my baby is well."

The nurse reassured her, "Dr. Santos wouldn't have signed the discharge orders if you and the baby weren't stable."

Summer inquired, "What does Dr. Brown think? He ordered a test for me tomorrow. I want to talk to him."

"I will page Dr. Santos," the nurse said.

"No, I would like you to page Dr. Brown. It's my right to speak with him."

As Summer waited to speak with Dr. Brown, one of Mr. Diamond's goons handed her his cell phone.

Summer answered, Hello?"

Mr. Diamond asked, "Do we have a problem, young lady?"

Summer replied, "No, the doctor ordered some tests for the baby first thing in the morning. I need to stay for the test."

"Summer, I am only going to say this once. Sign the discharge papers now!" Mr. Diamond demanded.

Feeling intimidated, Summer reluctantly agreed to be discharged. She was wheeled out of the hospital at 3 am. Nothing about this should have been normal to any of the medical staff. Summer couldn't help but wonder what kind of influence Mr. Diamond had to make this happen. It was clear that he was a powerful man.

Summer couldn't help but admit that the smell of the city night air was great, but little did she know what was to come next. After an hour of being on the road, one of the men made a call to Mr. Diamond to inform him that they were just ten minutes away.

Upon arriving at the gate of the large estate, they had to sign in before being granted access to the grounds. Summer's eyes widened as she saw that the mansion's grounds were larger than her first apartment complex, and there was no way for her to escape on foot because she was still fragile and not yet walking on her own.

The men escorted her to a private wing attached to the main house, where Christopher's mother met her; she embraced Summer, rubbed her shoulder, and pushed her around in the wheelchair, dismissing the security. Then, she took Summer for a tour of the mansion.

"Mrs. Diamond, for what it's worth, I didn't try to harm Christopher. I was fighting for my life."

"There, there, my child, no worries, my husband has already sorted everything out," she said while wheeling Summer to the baby nursery located three doors down from the master bedroom. You see, you will have another chance to start fresh. "Christopher is no longer obsessed with you. He just wants his child. You are a healthy young lady and can conceive again. Once our baby is born, you can start over fresh."

Summer felt a lump in her throat and was unable to speak as she choked on her reality. Mrs. Diamond had inadvertently revealed their plan to take her child, and it would be over her dead body. Summer was determined to stop them at all costs. Her tour finally ended with her room being located on the opposite side of the large mansion. It was very obvious that her bedroom was nowhere near the nursery. The Diamonds made it clear that they had no intention of letting her keep her child and planned to rob her of motherhood.

Chapter 45: His Arrival

Summer sat confined within the luxurious walls of the Diamonds Estate, gazing out the window that overlooked the exquisite garden and landscaping that seemed to extend as far as her eyes could see. She was left to her own devices, wheeling herself around in a wheelchair.

She knew she was being monitored, as the security cameras around the mansion were visible. She could only assume that she was not considered a flight risk. Summer felt she was being tested, as she noticed she had access to a phone daily; they were located all over the mansion. She refused to fall for their tricks.

She felt like the only place where she had some privacy was the bathroom located in her bedroom. So, she made frequent trips to the restroom, using the counter to pull herself up, and worked on building her strength. As she started to gain strength in her lower body, she started walking around the bathroom for exercise. There was no way she would let them take her baby without a fight. She had made up her mind and would take her chances and fight Christopher and his family in court.

On her next visit to the hospital, she would make a run for it. If they attempted to stop her, she would cause a big scene and scream bloody murder. She just needed to get in touch with Sofia, and she would have a safe place to hide and have a way home. They would take her son over her dead body!

As the weeks went by, she started having weekly home nursing visits. Summer was shocked when the nurse asked her about her thoughts on having a home birth. They never planned to take her back to the hospital; they would force her to give birth and steal her child out of her child-bearing arms.

Christopher's mother, who was obviously absent from his life both physically and emotionally while he was growing up, seemed to be trying to make decisions for her child as if she weren't a factor. She knew she needed to get away.

While Summer napped in her assigned room, her new prison of luxury, she was suddenly awoken by a tap on the door. She was struggling to turn over and sit up due to her plump, round belly bump, which was sitting low. Unable to turn and face the door, Mr. Diamond walked over to the other side of the room to gain eye contact. He looked down upon her with a condescending expression as if he had to address a peasant.

"My wife and I are going away for two weeks to celebrate our anniversary. During this time, there will be no visitors, including the nurses. I have arranged for Brody to monitor you and oversee your care in my absence. My wife mentioned you seem more comfortable with him, and I want you to feel safe. These arrangements are temporary until you and Christopher can get you guys shit together and do what's best for the baby."

As she thought to herself, the cat was out of the bag, and Mrs. Diamond had already informed her of their plans. It was clear that they only had Christopher's best interest in mind. However, it did provide some relief to know Brody, one of the nicer security guards who was hired to oversee her would be monitoring her.

He was the only security personnel who treated her with respect as if she were a human with a thought process, even taking her on a tour of the grounds as he pushed her around in the wheelchair. Brody's wife was part of the kitchen staff and sometimes joined them on their walks, although she wasn't allowed to answer any questions.

Summer's wheels started to turn. With Mr. and Mrs. Diamond out of the country, she had two weeks to devise an escape plan.

***

Summer was awakened throughout the night by severe cramps. She lay in bed crying, wishing Stevin was by her side to comfort her. She used memories of moments they shared to overshadow the feeling of being scared and lonely. However, at that moment, she was frightened and afraid of the unknown. The fact that she was having labor pains so early made her a nervous wreck. Summer slowly walked out of her room, holding the bottom of her stomach and searched for Brody. She found him in a guest suite down the hall.

"Brody, I need to go to the hospital," she said, feeling an urgency in her voice.

"What's wrong, Mrs. Diamond? I mean, Summer?" he asked, remembering her request not to be addressed by her married name.

"I think I am in premature labor," she replied, struggling to catch her breath. Brody's face turned pale as he realized the gravity of the situation.

"Okay, let me call Mr. Diamond and let him know," he said, as he fumbled for his phone, placing a call to Mr. Diamond, who clearly wasn't too happy from the look and tone Brody assumed seconds after giving him an update.

"Sir, yes sir, yes," Brody said. After a few seconds on the phone, he handed it to Summer. "He would like to speak with you," he said with a discerning expression.

"Hello," Summer said in a shaky voice.

"This is what you pull after one day of us leaving," Mr. Diamond said, as his voice boomed from the other end.

"Sir, this is not a hoax. I've been in pain for four straight hours," Summer replied, her voice quivering.

"Well, tough it out. You will not be going to the hospital tonight," he said, his tone stern and uncompromising.

"Well, can you at least call the doctor to check me? I'm scared, and I don't want anything to happen to the baby," Summer said, her voice filled with fear.

Mr. Diamond could hear the fear in her voice. Recognizing the urgency of the situation, he started to take the call seriously. Okay he said and put Summer on hold before merging her back with Dr Santos on the line.

"Summer, can you tell me what you are feeling?" Dr. Santos asked.

"It feels like bad menstrual cramps in my stomach, Summer replied.

"Where exactly are you feeling the pain, and how long does it last?" Dr. Santos inquired.

"It's at the bottom of my stomach."

"Does the pain radiates to your side or back?" he asked.

"No, it's only at the bottom of my stomach, and it lasts about thirty seconds." Summer replied.

"Okay I see. Summer take a deep breath and just breathe. What you are feeling is normal. It's Braxton Hicks contractions. This is just your body preparing itself for labor. I want you to take a short walk or change position when they occur, " Dr. Santos explained.

After disconnecting the call with Dr. Santos, Mr. Diamond requested Summer place the call on speaker.

"Brody, can you hear me?" he asked.

"Yes, sir," Brody replied.

"The doctor has advised that she needs to relax," Mr. Diamond continued. "Take her out for a drive to help assist her in relaxing." Mrs. Diamond could be heard chiming in the background.

"Tell her a nice massage will help. I will set up a massage therapist who specializes in prenatal massage to come out tomorrow." And with one phone call, she and the baby's health was decided.

Despite enjoying the fresh air and the beautiful scenery of the city lights, the nightmare reality of her situation was becoming increasingly frightening by the minute.

The following morning, the Diamonds delivered on their promise, as she was pampered with massages, five-star restaurant menus, and frequent calls from the villainous duos, The Diamonds. Brody even allowed her to play games on his cell phone as she secretly searched for information about Sofia's salon. Her only remaining concern was making it to the hospital before going into actual labor.

RUN FOR YOUR LIFE

The Diamonds were a week into their vacation when Christopher's therapists started reaching out to inquire about family visitations, as Christopher finally decided to forgive his father for having him committed to the psych ward. He was now willing to participate in private family therapy sessions so he could work on being released. One of the surprising requests made by Christopher was for his wife, Summer, to attend with his parents.

Summer was standing in the kitchen, sipping a cup of hot tea and chatting with Brody's wife and other staff. The same staff who didn't acknowledge her when the Diamonds were present. Their absence brought cheers throughout the large mansion. One thing that was becoming clear was Christopher's childhood stories and why he had distanced himself from this madness; Summer realized that those stories had become a reality for her.

The staff was very friendly and full of jokes, as laughter filled the kitchen. However, their laughter was interrupted when the room fell silent when Summer suddenly screamed out in pain, spilling her tea all over her clothes. She had felt a sudden sharp pain in her back. This pain isn't normal; she thought to herself as she slowly made her way back to the room to change clothes with the assistance of Brody's wife, Carol.

There was a light tap on the door, and it was Brody instructing her to get dressed.

"Mr. Diamond called, and he wants me to drive you to the hospital," Brody said.

"Okay, yes, I need to go. These pains are scaring me, and I am concerned," Summer said.

"No, Summer, he wants you to go visit Christopher."

Summer's eyes widen. "Like hell I am."

"Brody attempted to reason with her. "Please, Summer, don't put me in this position. I really adore you, but this is my job," he said.

Summer immediately started to panic, refusing to get dressed and go. "Brody, please, they are not telling you guys the truth," she pleaded.

He stood in silence, waiting for her to finish her statement. She sat quietly on the bed, knowing she had said too much. Brody left the room, informing her he would inform Mr. Diamond of her decision. A few minutes later, he returned, handing her his cell phone. Summer recognized that it was Mr. Diamond, but she was firm in her decision not to see Christopher. "I don't want to go," she told him.

"Young lady, don't do this," Mr. Diamond replied sternly.

Summer remained resolute. "No, I'm not going. I don't want to see him."

"It's not a damn option," Mr. Diamond retorted. "Who do you think you are? If you thought my son turned your world upside down, try me! Now, not another word. This is his first visit, and we can't attend. He is requesting his wife's presence, and that's you. Now get dressed, and please don't make me repeat myself. Do we have an understanding?"

"Yes," Summer said, her voice cracking and the muscles tightening in her throat. Noticing, Brody had been excused and replaced with another goon who stood over her as if he would dress her himself.

As she walked out the door, she looked back at Brody and noticed him standing in the doorway. He dropped his head, unable to look her in the face. Overwhelmed by anxiety, she felt as if her head was about to explode from the pounding headache. She was being forced to sit and play nice with someone who attempted to kill her and left her for dead. She was ready to risk it all. The moment the car stopped at a busy intersection she was making a run for it.

"Ooh," she screamed out, as the pain in her lower back was excruciating. She kept yelling, "I need a doctor," but the driver didn't respond as he wouldn't acknowledge her plea for help. As her moans became louder, he became nervous and quickly got Mr. Diamond on the line.

"She needs a doctor, sir," said the driver.

Mr. Diamond requested that the phone be placed on speakerphone.

"Summer, this is it. You have tested my patience for the last time. Get her to the appointment for Christopher now!" He demanded.

He suddenly paused in silence as she screamed out, bearing down until she felt a warm sensation, feeling as if she had urinated all over herself. The driver started to freak out when he noticed her water had broken.

"Sir, I need to hang up. I have to call emergency services. Her water just broke.

"You will do no such thing. You drive her to the hospital yourself, and I will call ahead to Dr. Santos," said Mr. Diamond.

"But sir," the driver tried to object.

"Drive her yourself," Mr. Diamond screamed.

The driver frantically drove as he panicked the entire car ride to the Emergency Room, as he watched Summer through the rearview mirror, climbing the seats in agony.

He drove recklessly, running red lights to get there as fast as possible. He pulled into the ER with the car on three wheels. Summer was placed on a stretcher and rushed to the OB Unit.

Upon arriving on the unit she is greeted by Stephanie, who promptly paged for Dr. Brown as Dr. Santos is stuck on the interstate in rush hour traffic. Stephanie returned to Summer's bedside and held her hand as she tried to calm her down with breathing techniques.

"Breathe, Summer. I just paged Dr. Brown. I also called your mother, Rose, and she's catching a flight to be here soon," she whispered.

Dr. Brown entered the room, and the nurses updated him on Summer's condition. She was in so much pain that she couldn't focus. Dr. Brown leaned over and took her hand. "Summer, I can't wait on Dr. Santos. You are 8cm dilated, the baby is breech, and you are suffering from preeclampsia. I need to perform an emergency cesarean now."

Everything was happening so quickly. Summer's room was flooded with staff as they transferred her to the operating room. She could only see bright lights and feel pain before a mask was placed over her face, and everything went black.

His Here

"Summer, Summer, I am so proud of you."

Summer slightly opens one eye as her vision is blurred. Mimi's smile filled the room as she leaned in and kissed her on the forehead.

"Asher is so beautiful, such a handsome boy," Mimi said.

Summer's eyes fluttered as she was confused as she repeated the name, "Asher? Asher?"

"Summer, open your eyes, open your eyes, Summer."

Summer felt someone rubbing her chest and calling her name. Her eyes popped open, and she immediately reached for her stomach.

"My baby, where's my baby?" She asked in a worried voice.

"Your baby is fine, Mrs. Diamond. I will go page Dr. Santos," the nurse said.

"No, please page Dr. Brown," Summer requested.

"Well, your chart says Santos," the nurse stated.

"Please page Dr. Brown," Summer demanded.

"Okay, I will go page Dr. Brown," the nurse said, leaving the room.

As the door closed, it immediately opened back up. Stephanie entered, running to her bedside.

"He's so cute; your little bundle of joy is so stinking cute. I will go to the nursery and get him for you.

"Is he okay?" Summer asked anxiously.

"Summer, he is perfect," Stephanie exclaimed. "He has a head full of curly hair. His father hasn't left the nursery window since they arrived. He's his father's twin," Stephanie added with a wink.

However, Summer's thoughts quickly turned to panic as she realized Christopher was also in the hospital. She knew she had to get out of there.

Just then, Dr. Brown entered the room with a smile. "Well, it was touch and go with you for almost two days," he said. "You lost a lot of blood during the surgery, and you had to receive several units. But other than that, you and your baby are just fine."

Dr. Brown went on to explain that the baby was a bit tiny in size due to Summer's lack of prenatal care, but he had all the external characteristics of a full-term newborn.

Stephanie entered the room, wheeling the glass bassinet cart in. She gently picked up the baby and handed him to Summer. Overwhelmed with emotions, Summer's heart was full as his soft, warm skin embraced hers. Her vision was blurred from the tears that welled up in her eyes as she looked down at him. With a surprising gaze, his widened eyes stared back at her as if he was just as eager to meet her as she was to meet him. He had a head full of curly black hair and Stevin's features. Summer ran her hands through his hair as she whispered his name, Asher.

Stephanie placed her hand on Summer's hand, handing her her cell phone. She looked down at the screen. It was a picture of Rose, David, and baby Asher. Summer dropped the phone as she held her mouth and cried out. Dr. Brown motioned her to be silent as the bodyguard was still stationed outside the door.

"Summer, I don't know what's going on, but do you want our help?" Dr. Brown asked.

"She motioned her head yes."

"Okay, we have to move fast. Your in-laws are traveling back as we speak. Let us figure out the next move," he said.

"Where is Christopher?" Summer asked.

With a confused expression, Dr. Brown said, "I haven't met Christopher, Summer."

"Stephanie, you said Asher's father was here?" Summer asked.

"Correct, Summer, I did say Asher's father was here," Stephanie said with a smile.

***

Summer sat for hours staring at her baby boy. There was no way they would take her baby. She knew Rose was there, and she was determined more than ever to go home. She couldn't shake what Stephanie had said earlier. "His father," did she think David was Asher's father? Or could it be? Did Stevin arrive with Rose and David? That thought came and went. There was no way Stevin would allow the Diamonds to keep her hostage. No bodyguard would keep him from breaking that hospital door down and rescuing her from the pits of hell.

It was time for shift change, and the nurses needed to take the baby back to the nursery for the shift to complete their assessments. As the nurses stood at the bedside to give their shift report. Stephanie introduced Rayla, the night nurse, and Rayla's trainee, Kimberley. Summer jumped as Kimberley raised her head and made eye contact with her. Stephanie gave her a look, nodding her head, motioning for her to remain calm as the three of them exited the room. Summer was confused and ready to kick Kimberley's teeth down her throat. She was ready to run; her first thought was that Kimberley was a spy for Christopher. She needed to get her baby from the nursery and make a run for it. Sister or no sister, she would do whatever it took to save her baby from the hands of the Diamonds and her wicked sister. The big question was where Rose and David were and why she and the baby hadn't been rescued.

Chapter 46: Breaking Free

Kimberley's sudden presence at the hospital freaked Summer out. It was clear what needed to happen. Once baby Asher returned to her room, she needed to find a way to escape tonight.

With a light tap on the door, the baby bassinet was pushed in first, followed by Kimberley. She noticed Summer's concerned expression and thought she might leap out of bed and attack her. She gestured for her to keep quiet.

"Look, Summer, I know you have no reason to trust me, but I lost everything because I betrayed you, leaving you in the home with that manipulative psycho. Unknowingly, I put you and Mom in harm's way. Mom has disowned me and only started talking back to me three days ago because of what I did to you. So please give me a chance to make this right and try to fix what I broke. We don't have much time. I'm not a nurse, and I don't work here. Dr. Brown and Stephanie are risking their jobs to help us get you back home."

Summer's facial expression called bullshit.

"Look, big sis, I only have a few minutes before Rayla comes in. She is standing outside entertaining the bodyguard, so please listen. When Mom cut me off, Dad couldn't even look at me. I needed to leave and grieve the loss of everything I thought I knew. I reached out to Mom's father and told him everything. Summer, he loves Mom and regrets what he and Nana did to you and Mom.

Long story short, he has some property in Minnesota that his parents passed down to him. The property remains in the Richmond name, and Chris-devil-Diamond can't trace it back to us. Grandpa gifted us, well, Mom, the land, home, and business on it. It needed work and still does, but Papa has been a big help in helping to get everything started. One of the things that broke me was when I learned about your character and who you were, Summer. I was devastated when the detective read me some letters from your friends and coworkers. So, I decided to find out the truth for myself, and I got to know you through the people you knew personally. So imagine my surprise when I visited your childhood home.

Well, I had to tell a tiny bit of a lie to Mr. Jeffery's son, she said in a Kimberley fashion. 'But no harm, no foul.' I told him that you and Mom had reunited and that I was gathering keepsakes and memories for her. I also said that I wanted to learn more about you, and that was the honest truth.

However, Levi came out with a big black duffle bag, requesting that I give it to you. And I'm guessing he never looked inside the bag. His exact words were that his dad had instructed him to hold on to your bag and not to open it. And only if you had yet to return to pick it up in a couple of years, he could open the bag and go through it.

After a couple of years went by and the loss of his father, he couldn't bring himself to open your personal bag, and he wanted to honor his father. So, he gave me your bag to give to you.

Well... she said with a mischievous smile. I needed to open the damn bag, so I burst that bag open as soon as I got back to my hotel. "Summer, does that money belong to Christopher?"

"No!" Summer replied in a stern voice. "I have never stolen anything from Christopher except my life back. That was money from my account I saved while I was with him. Christopher took care of everything, and my paychecks were deposited directly into my account. When I tried to escape and run back home, I emptied out my account. I left that money for Mr. Jeffery when Christopher found me at Mimi's home.

Summer shook her head with teary eyes. 'I asked that stubborn old man to use it and start enjoying life,' but he never spent it," she said in disbelief.

"That explains the IOU note I found in the bag," said Kimberley, giggling. "Summer, Mr. Jeffery seemed like a standup guy. The bag has pictures of your dear Mimi and some perfume that has to be hers because it smells like old folks." Summer cut her eyes at Kimberley.

"No shade, sis, no shade. And listen to this," continued Kimberley. "He also left you an IOU note for $175.00 for a door and door framing."

Summer laughed out loud with tears in her eyes as she thought of Mr. Jeffery.

"I have your money, Summer," said Kimberley.

The door opened swiftly as Summer's newly assigned bodyguard scanned the room.

"Kimberley, are you okay," Rayla asked. "Do you need my help with her assessment?"

"No, I'm good, almost finished," replied Kimberley.

The guard left the door open as he turned his attention back to Rayla.

"Summer, be ready to move tomorrow morning. I cannot be seen by the morning staff, so I need you to trust me. Stephanie and I have everything worked out. I just need you to do exactly what I say. Mom is out getting everything arranged with Dad. Tomorrow, you and the baby will be going home with us, so be ready." Kimberley turn to walk away when she suddenly turn and look Summer in the eyes.

"Summer, something has been bothering me since the night of the barbecue. Why weren't you honest when I saw you and Emmanuel together? Excuse me when I saw you and Christopher together." Kimberley asked in a curious tone.

"What do you mean, Kimberley? Honest about what?" Summer replied, in an aggravated tone, trying to understand Kimberley's question.

"I mean, why did you just sit there? Why didn't you ask me to help you?"

"Come on, Kimberley, let's be real. You knew something wasn't right and that I wasn't in his home on my own accord. You chose to believe him because no matter what, that's what you wanted to do."

"Summer, that still doesn't answer my question. Why did you just sit there? Why didn't you try to warn me, are scream for help?"

Summer knew the answer Kimberley was searching for, and although she played a huge role in her current situation, she could not bring herself to hurt her in that manner.

"Did he threaten to harm me, Summer?"

Summer never replied, but her facial gesture was enough for Kimberley as she dropped her head and exited Summer's hospital room.

Summer was eager to know Stevin's whereabouts or to hear his voice, but Christopher now knew who she was with. If it meant saving his life by disappearing again, she would do just that. Taking a big whiff of her baby boy's hair, she held onto him tightly and vowed never to let him go. Although she was still unsure about who his father was, she couldn't help but feel like she was staring at a miniature version of Stevin. But was this just wishful thinking on her part?

Summer was unable to sleep, feeling restless as she sat in bed and held her son. She anxiously awaited Kimberley's return, hoping for answers as her stomach was in knots. She didn't trust Kimberley, and her cluelessness about any plans made matters worse. Summer pondered why neither David nor Rose had come to the room and why they would send Kimberley out of all people. Her actions are the reason she is in this very predicament.

She wondered where Stevin was in all of this. However, she knew she couldn't allow herself to focus on him. She needed to let him go, and besides, she wouldn't ask him to give up everything and go on the run with her. He needed to be able to live his life. Although she felt Asher was a spitting image of him, she needed to be sure. There was no way she could tell him he had a son without being certain she was 100% sure. She couldn't imagine the pain he must have felt upon learning of her pregnancy, assuming David or Rose had updated him.

As she cradled her son in her bosom, Summer found herself drifting off, feeling an indescribable feeling. The warmth and love she felt, she would die for. She had a reason to fight now, and her voice would be heard this time.

The bright sun rays peeked through the blinds, and she was awoken by the wonderful sound of Asher smacking his lips as he turned his little head following the scent of her breast milk. Rayla loudly entered the room, informing her she had her six o'clock morning medication. Brody followed closely behind as he tiptoed into the room, eager to meet Asher. Her heart skipped a beat with excitement. She knew she had a better chance of escaping with Brody on duty. He stood over them, adoring her little buddle of joy.

"Mrs. Diamond, it's almost time for shift change. Since the morning nurse, Stephanie, is familiar with you, I will allow my trainee to do bedside report with her. Do you need anything from me at the moment?"

"No, thank you."

"Okay. I know you requested the baby remain in the room, but he will have to return to the nursery for shift change."

"Okay. He's hungry. Will you allow me to feed him first?"

"Yes, and today, it's vital that we get you up and moving. You had a rough couple of days after your surgery. So, today, the goal is for you to walk and remain up in the recliner. They will be back in to get report and return the baby to the nursery."

Summer was a bundle of nerves. She had no idea if Mr. Diamond's flight landed or if they were already back in town. She just knew it was now or never. As she was thinking of her next move, she overheard Stephanie outside the door, chatting with Brody about how adorable Asher was when Kimberley entered the room.

"Summer, our window is small. The big wigs from administration will be rounding soon, and I have to be off this unit. Dr. Brown and Stephanie risked it all getting me this fake badge; I don't want to implicate them in your disappearance. Here, change Asher into this outfit. I will be right back; I need to grab some items."

Kimberley rushed out of the room and returned quickly with a large nursing bag and clipboard. Stephanie followed behind her, closing the door and informing Brody that she needed to perform a quick examination on Summer.

"We need to move now," Stephanie urged.

Kimberley dug into the oversized bag, pulled out a Mumu gown, and tossed it on the bed, asking Summer to slip it on. She then extracted a lifelike baby from the bag and placed it on the bed. Summer was startled at first glance; she thought Kimberley had placed a deceased baby on her bed. Kimberley chuckled, "It's a reborn baby."

"It's a what?" Summer asked.

"A reborn baby," Kimberley replied.

Summer was amazed at the realistic look of the doll; she picked it up and examined it closely.

"How did you get it to look so much like Asher?" Summer asked curiously.

"Mom used my baby photo and a baby photo of Stevin," Kimberley said with a smile.

Summer's eyes lit up. Stephanie interrupted their brief conversation. "Listen, Summer, I have a mini portable oxygen concentrator in your sister's bag. I'll place the small unit at the bottom of the bag, then a small piece of foam, and cover it with the baby's blanket. Then, we have to place the baby in the bag with the mask covering his face." Summer quickly shook her head no, afraid that the baby could suffocate.

"Summer, we have got to move. He'll only be in the bag for a few minutes," Kimberley urged.

Stephanie took baby Asher from Summer's arm, cutting the security bracelet from his ankle. She attached the bracelet to the reborn baby doll using tape. They dressed the reborn baby in Asher's gown and hat, swaddled it, and placed it in the bassinet.

"Come on, Summer, we must move," Kimberley urged.

"Wait, Kimberley, your sister has had a cesarean, and she has stitches. She hasn't ambulated since giving birth. We must be gentle."

They assisted Summer into the wheelchair. Stephanie gently snuggled Asher into the oversized bag and placed the small mask over his face. They knew they only had seconds to get the baby past Brody, being he wasn't happy having the oxygen mask placed on his face as he thrashed his head side to side, grunting.

"Let's move, Kimberley," Stephanie said.

Kimberley gently placed the oversized bag on her shoulder. Stephanie opened the door and pushed the bassinet with the reborn baby right past Brody. Turning to him, she said, "The baby has to return to the nursery for shift change, and Summer is going down to radiology for a test." Kimberley slowly pushed the wheelchair to the door as Summer's and her hearts raced.

"Brody, when I return, can you take me for a spin outside to get some fresh air?" Summer asked.

"Yes, Mrs. Summer. Would you like me to walk with you now?"

"You will not be able to go down with her for this test, but you can sit in the room and wait for her to return," Stephanie quickly said.

Brody eased back down in the chair, taking a sip of his coffee.

Kimberley pushed Summer halfway down the hall before gently placing the bag in her lap. Summer's heart sank, and a heavy weight of guilt settled in her chest. She knew Brody would pay dearly for allowing her to escape. But this time, she had a baby to fight for, and she had to be selfish at that moment and put herself and Asher first.

As they turned the corner, the elevators were in clear site. Their hearts raced, each second stretching into an eternity as they waited for the elevator door to open.

Both elevators dinged, going down, as Kimberley gently pushed the wheelchair onto the first elevator when the second one opened. Mr. Diamond could be heard speaking on his cell phone. Mrs. Diamond urged him to speed up as she was excited to see her grandchild.

Summer signaled to Kimberley that the voices belonged to Christopher's parents. Kimberley shielded Summer by standing in front of her. She quickly pushed the ground floor button, knowing that there was a possibility they would be caught before they could exit the hospital doors.

Kimberly and Summer were startled as the elevator dinged when it reached the ground floor. Their hearts raced, their minds filled with the fear of the unknown, not knowing if security would be waiting once the elevator doors opened. Kimberley slowly pushed Summer and the baby off the elevators as Asher began to cry. Summer did her best to comfort him as she attempted to gently rock him, afraid his breathing had become compromised. Kimberley began to sing over his soft, tiny cries as she hurriedly pushed the wheelchair to the exit door, urging Summer not to open the bag.

She urgently pushed Summer and the baby out to the parking lot. She began to skip-run through the lot, feeling as if her life depended on getting them to safety. Finally, they reached a large RV. The door popped open, and Stevin and David stepped off to greet them. Summer's heart leaped in her chest, her breath catching in her throat as she covered her mouth and started crying. Her emotions about seeing him were a whirlwind of relief, joy, and shame.

On the one hand, she felt dirty, as if she had betrayed him, knowing Christopher had his way with her. Then, on the other hand, it was the moment she thought would never happen. She was reunited with the love of her life.

Rose immediately exited the RV to remove the baby from the bag. Kimberley quickly handed her the bag to take Asher out. Stevin's legs buckled as he dropped to his knees and hugged Summer. Stevin knew time wasn't on their side, but he couldn't move. He had accepted he would never see her again, so to have her in front of him, touching her and smelling her scent, was overwhelming. He broke down and placed his head on her lap.

"I can't ask you to do this, Stevin. I can't ask you to go on the run with me and give up your life."

"My life is wherever you and my son are," Stevin said confidently. He gently grabbed her face as he passionately kissed her.

David patted him on the back. "Son, we have to move."

Stevin lifted her out of the chair; she wrapped her arms around his neck and closed her eyes, taking in his natural scent. She just needed to be pinched to make sure she wasn't dreaming. He gently sat her down and sat beside her, leaving no arm room. Rose smiled as she placed the baby in Stevin's arm, embracing her daughter with a hug. She, too, struggled with the reality of never seeing her firstborn again. She vowed this time, Christopher would take Summer over her dead body.

Rose looked up, making eye contact with Kimberley. Rose silently mouthed, "Thank you! I love you!"

David and Kimberley smiled from the front seat. They turned and placed their shades on as David drove away, turning onto the freeway. Summer sat crying, taking it all in as she was comforted by Stevin on her right side and Rose on her left. She had no idea what the plans were or what the next step. All she knew was she was free and surrounded by family!

Other Books By Shantanel Payne
Her Lost Words; Her Broken Silence